Celebrate the charm of Christmases past in three new heartwarming holiday tales!

COMFORT AND JOY by Margaret Moore
1860 Llanwyllan, Wales

After a terrible accident, Griffin Branwynne gives up on the joys of Christmas—until the indomitable Gwendolyn Davies arrives on his doorstep and turns his world upside-down. Can the earl resist a woman who won't take no for an answer?

LOVE AT FIRST STEP by Terri Brisbin
1199 England

While visiting friends in England for the holidays, Lord Gavin MacLeod casts his eye upon the mysterious Elizabeth. She is more noble beauty than serving wench, and Gavin vows to uncover her past—at any cost!

A CHRISTMAS SECRET by Gail Ranstrom
1819 Oxfordshire, England

Miss Charity Wardlow expects a marriage proposal from her intended while attending a Christmas wedding. But when Sir Andrew MacGregor arrives at the manor, Charity realises that she prefers this Scotsman with the sensual smile…

On sale 2nd December 2005

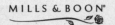

A USEFUL AFFAIR

Stella Cameron

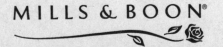

MILLS & BOON®

First published in Great Britain 2005
by Harlequin Mills & Boon Limited,
Eton House, 18-24 Paradise Road, Richmond, Surrey TW9 1SR

© Stella Cameron 2004

ISBN 0 263 84522 2

153-1105

*Printed and bound in Spain
by Litografía Rosés S.A., Barcelona*

A USEFUL AFFAIR

For my friends at www.stellacameron.com

1

Gratitude be damned. When he finally unfolded himself from the inside of this sorry coffin—ouch—when he got out of the hearse driven by his so-called rescuer, his fists would speak for him.

If he got out alive.

Well, if he didn't he'd be in the right place at the right time…

He winced in the blackness, then gritted his teeth as the wheels beneath him left the ground. The rims hit storm-torn ruts again, rattled every board and brace in the hearse—and every bone belonging to John Elliot, properly known as the Marquis of Granville.

Even inside the coffin, the ceaseless beating of rain could be heard. And wind. Wind howled as if through a tunnel and whirled about the Shillibier. Matched black horses pulled the great carriage, and their hoofs clattered and scraped over stone and mud.

The little girl curled against his chest with her hands clapped over her ears didn't ease John's miserable confinement. He must manage to save his young cousin from any injury inside the magnificent but tossing Shillibier with its rushing team. Also, he was desperate to keep her as warm as he could with both of them still wet from their near-drowning in the Channel, and to soothe her without making any noise. And he must pray that Chloe would

not choose a deadly dangerous moment to find her voice
and cry out.

"Chloe," he whispered into her ear. "We shall be
safe." When she addressed him, the child called him
"Uncle John." He'd never considered why, but he supposed she must find it comfortable. "Stay very quiet and
trust Uncle John," he murmured. *Dash it all but he knew
nothing of dealing with children. Would a six-year-old
believe such rubbish? He had no idea if they were safe.*

Cast into the sea by one cutthroat smuggler, John, together with his first cousin once removed, six-year-old
Chloe Worth, had been pulled from the icy, fog-shrouded
English Channel by another lawless sailor. Once ashore,
this one—Albert according to the ruffians he com-
manded—insisted there could be no better chance of escape than by traveling as a dead man.

Tall and thin, Albert had made no sense, muttering all
the time about his damnable conscience and how the Lord
and someone named Snowdrop would reward him for going against the others—and "that evil old sod, Leggit" to
do the right thing. Had he been alone, John would have
fought for his freedom the instant he stepped ashore. As
it was, he'd been unwilling to risk Chloe's safety.

The young smuggler had promised to get them away
and been certain none but his "kin," the oarsmen, knew
John and his charge were still alive. Their secret was safe,
he'd insisted in a huge voice that would have done any
highwayman proud.

A frenzied ride by wagon from the coast to an isolated
inn, and John had been hustled with his charge into the
funeral vehicle driven by Albert. After all, his host said,
no one dared stop the dead on the way to their rest.

This casket didn't fit John at all. True, he was taller
than most and strongly built, but he couldn't imagine any

man of his acquaintance who wouldn't be twisted up in the thing like a bedsheet on wash day, even without a small companion. It had probably been made for a woman, he decided. A rotund woman, for the box was exceedingly deep.

The pace changed. Albert yelled and the horses seemed to dance, rocking the Shillibier in the process. They slowed down.

"'Old! 'Oldisay!"

Another man's bullish and meaningless words bellowed over the roar of hoof and wheel.

So much for the sanctity of the dead.

He'd chosen to accept a promise of help from a smuggler—a criminal who swore his repentance—rather than expose Chloe to the threat of instant death.

Her chances might have been better had John chosen to run with her.

The Shillibier shuddered afresh. Wheels hammered rocks into ground that must be as furrowed as it was muddy. The horses shrieked and John imagined the inky ostrich plumes jostling as they tossed their heads, and yards of black crepe streaming in the shadowy night. Tack jangled, while John felt rolling objects thudding against the coffin—heavy objects. Casks of contraband? Damn Albert and his henchmen, they hadn't been able to resist an opportunity to move some of their spoils out of harm's way. The smugglers' weakness could scuttle what hope there was of escape.

He realized what should have been obvious. The reason the coffin was so deep was that its real purpose was to transport smuggled goods. Little wonder Albert had thought of the ruse for John and Chloe.

John knew the sound of gunshot, even over the night's

cacophony. He hugged Chloe tighter and smoothed her hair.

"I told ye to 'old," the newcomer bellowed again. "Next time I fires, it won't be *past* your 'ead."

"Don't you 'ave no respect for the dead?" Albert roared. "Stand off, there. Stand off, I says."

"Who's in there, then? King bloody George?"

John managed to turn Chloe and settle her face against his neck. "Hush," he told her. "Be very quiet and don't cry." She had not, in fact, made a sound since they'd been brought ashore somewhere on the southern shores of England. He had no idea where that had been, or where they were now.

"You've a perilous bad tongue, sir," Albert told the intruder. "It's a good thing the King—God save 'im—can't 'ear you all the way in his castle. They don't tell me who 'tis gone to their rest. I just drive. The grieving relations is waitin'. They'll send after me if I'm late." Following a pause, the young man continued. "If it'll satisfy you, sir, then be my guest. The box isn't 'ammered down yet. Take a look."

John smiled thinly and held his breath, admiring Albert's daring bluff, but prepared for the sound of doors being opened. He'd lost his pistol in the Channel. The only defense would be to play dead, then to "rise from the dead" with horrible howling if necessary, and hope the shock bought him some advantage.

Chloe's small fingertips opened and closed against John's linen shirtfront. He patted her hair again, awkwardly, and made what he hoped was a calming noise.

Rain pelted the draped windows of the carriage.

Boots hit the ground. "I've thought that over, and I thinks as I'll do what you suggest and pay me respects to the departed." The other man sounded even bolder than

before. "Strangest funeral procession I've seen, I can tell you. No train of coaches and only a young cove still wet behind the ears in charge."

John braced himself and assumed what he prayed was a more corpselike pose. "Don't move at all," he whispered to Chloe. Not that anything would help them if his suspicions were correct and casks of liquor surrounded the coffin.

Heavy footsteps approached the Shillibier.

The handles on the back doors rattled.

It was all up to him then. Force had to be the only course. John, lying on his side, inched up the knee that rested against the bottom of the coffin and blessed God for giving him powerful legs. He'd need them to thrust himself out and overpower whoever was coming for them.

"Al-bert!" A feminine cry carried the name on the wind. "Al-bert! You apology for a man, you. What are you doin'? Allowin' some ruffian to disturb the dead? You'll rot in hell. We all will. And you there, stop that, you raper of corpses, you friend of the devil, you, you—"

"Snowdrop," the hapless Albert called from the driver's seat. "This is no place for you, my flower."

"You keep mum and sit where you are, Albert Parker," Snowdrop shouted. "And *you*, stand back from that carriage and tell me your name? And give it to me honestly, because my father and his men aren't far behind me. They'll cut you to ribbons as soon as look at you. Slasher Pick don't ask questions, 'e just makes up his own mind and he does it quick."

The mystery of Albert's earlier "Snowdrop" mutterings was solved. She must be his wife.

"You've no need to know my name, missus, only that I'm an agent for a ship's master what was attacked by a desperate fugitive from the law. Name of John Elliot. You

might be interested to know there's a pretty price on 'is 'ead and a search is underway all over the countryside.''

The woman didn't answer and John's stomach plummeted. It went lower as the silence stretched without a word from good old Albert, either. John, who had used his family name, Elliot, to travel, was that "fugitive" mentioned, even though he was not guilty of any crime.

Intuition told him Albert and Snowdrop were considering the reward on his head.

A horse whinnied and blew and hoofs beat a dancing tattoo.

"'Old 'im," Albert yelled. "Stop'n or he'll be away."

Scuffling grew louder. The horse's whinny became a shriek and metal jangled madly. The agent hollered, but John couldn't understand a word.

More noise-soaked seconds passed before there came the fierce drumming, clanking and snorting of horseflesh at a full gallop. A full gallop that carried an animal and its rider away from the Shillibier.

A hush descended.

"Snowdrop!" At Albert's roar, John jumped and held Chloe very tightly. "What 'ave you done, then, flower? How did you do it?"

"Ask no questions and you'll 'ear no lies, Albert Parker. Nosey Parker. The gentleman decided 'e had more important people to deal with than us. What's this all about then?"

"Leggit, most likely. Him I told you about before. I've been told he put up the money for that ship I met tonight. Probably pays for other ships and pockets a fortune for his trouble. The captain tonight, captain of the *Windfall,* would be Leggit's man and a frightened man now 'e knows John Elliot isn't dead, drowned like 'e was supposed to be. Leggit's a mean one and powerful to boot.''

"Albert—"

"Tell me what you did." Albert cut his flower off. "You did something to the horse to make it run, Snowdrop?"

"Mayhap I did. Mayhap I didn't. Now drive that thing off the track and hide it in the trees, you oaf, and get to the cottage."

"I've got to make sure they're…" The silence let John know that Albert was indicating his human cargo. "Well, I promised I'd see to it they was safe. How did you know where to find me, anyway?"

"I already got a word or two from one of your ruffians what didn't stop at that inn as how you were coming this way. Shouldn't wonder but the whole world knows where to find you. Hide the carriage in Lock's bower and put the 'orses in the cave."

"Aye," Albert said promptly.

John closed his eyes and prepared for an even more uncomfortable ride once they left the track.

The doors at the back of the carriage opened, slammed wide as they were released into the wind. The coffin lid began to slide and John prepared to leap upon whomever appeared.

"Settle down in there," Snowdrop said. "Keep mum. Do what I tells you and you won't be 'urt."

The lid fell beside the casket and blessedly fresh air rushed in. "Out you get," Snowdrop ordered. "Quick and quiet. There's no time. We've got to be out of the way before someone else comes or that buffoon decides to turn back."

Gingerly, John raised his head and wouldn't have been surprised to lose it to a shot at once.

No pistol fired.

"Out. Quick!"

"Come along, Chloe," he said in as normal a voice as he could muster. "We're to meet some new people who will help us."

With that he moved his cramped limbs and climbed from the casket. Sure enough, brandy casks confirmed his suspicions. They had broken free of the ropes used to secure them. Holding Chloe in his arms, John pushed contraband aside and made his way to the ground outside.

No moon pierced the night, but he made out a winding track into a forest. Dripping trees soared on either side. His boots squelched in mud. Wind whipped rain into his face and all but froze his sodden clothes. Chloe must be made warm.

"Oh, look at the little mite," Snowdrop said, and John saw her for the first time. "Albert Parker, you're 'opeless. Why didn't you say there was a little one in there?"

"At the time, I was trying to 'ide them from an enemy, my flower."

A creature, so diminutive as to resemble one barely out of childhood herself, whirled at John and Chloe, tearing off her cloak as she came. She pulled the little girl from him, wrapped her in the cloak and pushed her back into his arms. "Get on the 'orse. Now!"

"Madam, I cannot take your horse."

This small, pale creature with tossing black hair, gave him a pitying look, put two fingers in her mouth and issued a piercing whistle. Immediately a second, unsaddled, horse clattered from the cover of the trees and Snowdrop hauled herself onto its bare back. "Come on. We're going."

John needed no more coaxing. He mounted the gray Snowdrop had arrived on and followed the woman deeper into the forest, leaving Albert behind to mutter while he got about the orders she'd given him.

2

Surprisingly comfortable, the furnishings in the cottage were bright and clean. "Handsome piece of silk there." John indicated a red rug spread on the stone floor. It amazed John until he recalled the business her father and Albert were in. "Nice brasses, too." Shining pieces lined a rough wooden mantel above the fireplace.

Snowdrop bobbed. "Thank you, sir." She turned away, but looked at him over a shoulder. "It's a big man, you are, and a good-looking one. You look a fine gentleman to me, even if your clothes are soaked."

John arched his brows and she averted her face.

China dishes sat on the table—dishes for two. A single door opened from this main room, revealing a narrow bed in a space not so much bigger than a cupboard. Lively flames in the fireplace heated the whole cottage. The smell of something cooking reminded John that he hadn't eaten in a very long time.

"Take off your clothes," Snowdrop said. "I'll look after the child."

John handed Chloe over but made no attempt to undress himself.

A blanket flew at him and he caught it. "Shy is it, you are? Wrap yourself in that and sit by the fire while I dry your things."

With a little extra heat—from annoyance—in his face, John did as he was told.

Snowdrop had already stripped off Chloe's clothes and swathed her in a soft white quilt. The bundle was plopped on his lap while the woman went about arranging wet garments on a rack close to the fire.

Not another word was said until he held a large measure of what smelled like fine brandy and warm milk had been placed gently in Chloe's hands.

Snowdrop pulled up a stool and sat a little way distant from John. The dark hair he'd noted in the forest was wavy and reached her waist. Her skin was white, her eyes large and brown. A pretty morsel but too slight for his tastes.

He thought about the small bed he'd seen. The right size for her but hardly wide and long enough for Albert, too.

She pointed at him with her right forefinger. In her left hand she held her own mug of brandy. "I'm going to tell you your story," she said, in her anything but slight voice. "If I make a mistake, signal, and I'll let you correct me. We don't have time for a pleasant conversation. Tip the milk to the girl's mouth. She isn't drinking."

John did as he was told and continued to press sips upon Chloe while Snowdrop snapped out her interpretation of what had happened.

"Albert isn't a real smuggler," she said. "Oh, he thinks he is, but he's not at all suited. He's got a good mind and needs to make something of it. When he does, I'll consider marrying him."

John grunted. The brandy felt good inside him. So, Albert hadn't yet picked his Snowdrop.

"I let him take a few runs just to get enough money to set himself up. You were on that ship tonight, the *Windfall*

I think Albert called it. You saw something you shouldn't 'ave and they tried to kill you. I 'spect the little girl's your daughter and you both ended up in the drink. Now they're after you for what you know and you need to escape or you'll be dead anyway.''

"Close," John said. "This is my first cousin once removed. She calls me Uncle and her name is Chloe." Little Chloe, who had yet to speak a word since one of those murderers had thrown her into the water, and whose blue eyes remained round and distant.

"You was coming from France. Where's her—"

John's speedy finger to his mouth silenced Snowdrop. It was too soon to speak of Chloe's parents, John's cousin and his wife. Snowdrop had quick wits. She jumped to a conclusion and sadness replaced the question in her face. For a moment she bowed her head. "Where do you need to go, sir?"

"Where does Leggit live?" John asked without ever having intended to do so.

Snowdrop's eyes widened. "Albert told you about 'im? He must have. Bernard Leggit, Esquire, hifalutin merchant of Bath, and that's where he lives with his beautiful young wife. Not that I've seen 'er, but Albert's told me the stories. Leggit's wife is young enough to be his granddaughter and she's 'is most prized possession. Flaunts her around everywhere, just to prove he's got what it takes— if you know what I mean."

John knew but he didn't say so.

"There's all sorts of stories Albert knows. He's got a friend who's in the know and what tells him about it. Word is that Leggit's wife married him for his money. That Leggit, he's terrified she'll disgrace him in front of his hoity-toity friends. Not that they aren't a bad lot from the sound of it.''

"How would she do that? Disgrace him?"

"Can't say as I know," Snowdrop said. "Albert thinks she's got to make people think she dotes on the old toad or else he'll punish 'er. He forces 'er to do it."

The cottage door opened and Albert entered. A slender man of considerable height, he had a fine-boned, shrewd face. His straight, tow-colored hair stood on end and the spectacles he'd put on tilted askew.

Snowdrop leaped to her feet and ran to tug him close to the fire. "That was your last run," she told him, and held up a hand when he made to argue. "I mean it. You're to find yourself a good job now, Albert, and I think I know where it'll be."

Albert looked at her with interest. So did John.

"Mr.—" She looked at John.

"Elliot. John Elliot," he said.

"Mr. John Elliot is in need of an assistant, a man of letters with a very sharp mind. That's you, Albert. You'll be accompanying him to Bath."

So, she had guessed he intended to go there.

"Mr. Elliot will be setting up a home and he'll be busy so he'll be glad of you. There will be suitable rooms to find, new clothes to be tailored, a nurse to be arranged for little Chloe. And then there'll be a great many other duties for you to perform. Isn't that right, Mr. Elliot?"

He would not suggest that he caught a whiff of blackmail in all this. "Very possibly."

"It was Bath where you intended to go, was it?"

"It certainly was." It was after tonight's events. "Fortunately I have a house in the town, not that I've seen it in a year or more. My two maiden aunts live there."

"Oh." Snowdrop's mouth drooped, no doubt because in her mind, his unexpected household in Bath diminished Albert's opportunities.

"The aunts are elderly," he said, not wanting to dash her hopes. "And so is the staff. I'll need someone I can rely on."

"Snowdrop," Albert said, "I can't leave—"

"You can and will. This is your chance to make up for the ill you've done, and to have a right to ask for my hand in marriage."

"I already did that," Albert said, his light brown eyes puzzled.

Snowdrop sighed loudly. "Yes. Well then, you may earn the right to ask again and I may accept you this time. Now. You're all to be warm and dry. Stores will be packed into that pretty carriage I can't use because it would draw too much question in these parts, and off you'll go. North to Bath. And you'll be away before first light."

Evidently Albert had stopped thinking when Snowdrop mentioned she might agree to marry him. He stood there with glazed eyes and the corners of his mouth turned up. He watched the woman with awe.

"Thank you, Madam—I mean, Miss," John said. "We'll be ready to leave in good time."

Bernard Leggit, merchant of Bath, had brought about the deaths of John's cousin and his wife. And he would give the order for John and Chloe to be murdered as soon as he learned that they had escaped. John was a man of the world who moved in high places and he was no stranger to the depths to which ambition and greed drove men's actions. Yes, he would go to Bath. He wasn't a vengeful man by nature, but justice must be exacted in whatever way proved most hurtful to Leggit.

"I should be most glad of your assistance, Albert," he said. After all, he considered himself a good judge of character and the fellow had yet to betray him, even when

a fat purse was dangled. "Let's hurry, man, and prepare for our journey."

One could only hope that Mrs. Leggit was as comely as her reputation suggested, and that she would be vulnerable to the attentions of a virile, titled man whom some considered good-looking. He narrowed his eyes. Yes, yes, the wife sounded as if she were her husband's Achilles' heel. Perhaps she could help John—unwittingly, of course.

The score would be settled.

3

"Please don't hover, Bea," Hattie Leggit said. "You make me nervous." She made Hattie more annoyed than nervous but Hattie tried not to hurt her maid's feelings.

Bea didn't respond. Neither did she stop hovering and walking circles around Hattie, who sat on a wooden stool with a small easel in front of her, trying to make an acceptable watercolor painting of the busy scene on Bath's Pultney Bridge. The ladies' Grecian-line dresses and sarcenet pelisses, their full ringlets glinting on either side of their faces, their silk straw bonnets decorated with gay feathers and satin ribbons; such a whirl of color and life. And oh, the lace-trimmed pagoda parasols twirling idly in those ladies' gloved hands were all the go.

And all this was to say nothing of the dashing gentlemen, each one dressed to the nines and vying for attention.

"Really, Bea, you keep cutting off my view. How am I supposed to paint a scene to please Mrs. Dobbin if I can't see what I'm doing?" Mrs. Dobbin tutored Hattie in the so-called ladylike pursuits. She also acted as her advisor.

Bea continued, a little more slowly and on tiptoe, to circle Hattie.

"Enough!" Hattie's patience fled. "Kindly sit over there on that wall. Pull your bonnet forward to keep the sun off your face."

"Sorry, Mrs. Leggit." Bea, a robust Dorset girl with the kind of wide, bright blue eyes that suggested a docile nature, planted her sturdy black shoes more widely apart and said, "The master would 'ave me guts for garters if I didn't stay beside you, Mrs. Leggit. It isn't seemly for a lovely lady to be alone in the street."

Hattie breathed slowly in through her nose. On the other side of the narrow, shop-lined road over Pultney Bridge stood Mead, the coachman, a lumpy fellow in an overly large cloak. Mead managed to watch her much of the time without ever actually meeting her eyes.

"I am a married woman," Hattie reminded Bea. "And I'll hardly be alone with you sitting over there and Mead trying to look as if he doesn't know us. And a very bad job he makes of that, too."

"He does his best, Mrs. Leggit. And he's a good person what takes his duties seriously." Bea peered at the sun, then at Hattie. "We've got to be careful of your skin, Mrs. Leggit."

"Thank you." She sat in complete shade. "Now please sit down and let me concentrate."

She supposed she should try to be more reasonable. At least Mr. Leggit allowed her to come and go almost at will as long as Bea or Mrs. Dobbin accompanied her.

"I worry about you getting paint on your pretty white dress," Bea said.

If Mr. Leggit hadn't absolutely refused to allow her to be seen in an apron, anywhere—but least of all in public—Hattie would certainly be wearing one.

Fie, Mr. Leggit must be confronted. The last thing he wanted was for his young wife to seem anything but obedient and adoring. She was to be admired by all of his cronies who would simper to Mr. Leggit that he was the luckiest of men, to be five-and-sixty with a lovely wife of

barely one-and-twenty. He must, they told him, fawning as so many did, be most hearty, and a Corinthian in the bedchamber.

Then they said, with sly glances at one another, glances they made sure Mr. Leggit didn't see, that it would be a day of celebration for all Bath when his son was born. And Hattie would, of course, bear him a son.

She felt her cheeks flush and her body turn cold. She must work harder on her plan to outfox Bernard Leggit and be free of him. A passing cart came too close to the flagway and Hattie flinched.

She stood up and waitcd for Bea to come to a stop in front of her. "Do you find Mead attractive?" she asked, knowing she was naughty.

"Mr. Mead?" Bea looked aghast. "Why, I don't know, Mrs. Leggit."

"He obviously thinks a great deal of you."

Bea lowered her head and attempted a surreptitious glance in Mead's direction.

"See," Hattie said, "he watches you all the time. Here—" She tore a sheet from her sketch pad and scribbled on it. Carefully, she folded the paper and gave it to Bea. "Take this to Mead, please. I must complete the assignment Mrs. Dobbin gave me."

With an expression of uncertainty on her face, Bea looked from Hattie to Mead and back again, as if judging how quickly she could carry out her mistress's instructions. She left at a trot, swiftly skirting traffic on the way.

A dark green town coach approached the bridge, raising chatter among strollers and parting a way through humbler traffic that jostled together on its way to the other side of the bridge. Hattie took notice of the carriage because it was so grand, as grand as Mr. Leggit's, in fact more so since it sported family colors and a coat of arms on its

doors and was pulled by a perfectly matched team of black horses.

She caught sight of a man inside the coach looking in her direction and quickly returned her attention to her paints. Sitting here in the sunshine of a spring day, with lush green hills unrolling toward the River Avon and the glitter-speckled water of that river winding through the town on its way to cross the Cotswolds, could be perfect. The day would be perfect if only she were without her keepers, and if only she didn't have to return to Leggit Hall and her husband afterward.

The green carriage stopped in front of Mead and Bea, cutting Hattie off from their sight. The door closest to her opened onto the busy street and a tall, well-built man in impeccable, rather somber clothing got out without waiting for his coachman to put down the steps.

She should not look at the man, Hattie told herself. He could mistake her curious glance for something more.

Like staring. Staring with interest, and a tipsy little turn of her heart when she saw his thick, curly black hair and lean, tanned face.

Well, she wasn't staring, not really.

He was not the first man she'd seen who had broad shoulders, a chest that filled out his dark green coat and who showed a flat middle when the wind whipped the open coat away from his body.

Hattie studied her painting with determination. A little more gold catching the rooftops of the Marian Chapel would brighten her landscape. She moistened her brush and worked it over the paint.

"Good morning, Mrs. Leggit," a deeply pleasant masculine voice said from behind her. "It is Mrs. Leggit, isn't it?"

It wouldn't do to turn around, but she knew who he

was anyway. There had been quite a flutter about his arrival in Bath a week previous. The Marquis of Granville, young, handsome and a bachelor, had set tongues wagging among mamas with daughters they longed to marry off—well. Considering the marquis a good catch didn't come close to the truth of it. His elevated position would sweep whomever he married into a glittering world.

Still he stood behind her.

She was unchaperoned. He was a stranger unknown to her husband. And she couldn't imagine why he had come to speak to her in so unsuitable a manner.

She should not address him. But she had a theory that women who were confident, but distant of course, were held in higher respect. "Good day to you, er, Lord Granville. At least, from your carriage I assume you to be the Marquis of Granville. Your reputation precedes you. I recommend—with respect of course—that you prepare yourself for a deluge of invitations in Bath."

"You are extraordinary," he said as if he hadn't heard a word she said. "I have never seen hair quite the color of yours. Not red, not brown, not blond. Amazing."

Hattie bent over her paint box. What would such a man see in her? And why would he go out of his way to flatter her when he could have almost any woman he fancied. And he knew she was married! Unless he had an ulterior motive... Surely not.

John crossed his arms and contemplated the top of her pretty straw hat. Turned up around the front and lined with white satin, a shiny green feather curved across the brim. The feather matched her pelisse. Either she had considerable good taste, or excellent advice. He'd removed his hat and a brisk breeze whipped at his hair. The same breeze that tossed Hattie Leggit's hair, which was every bit as lovely as he'd told her. Insincere flirtation didn't sit

well with him, but he must remind himself that this was not, in fact, any lady with gentle feelings to protect. She was an opportunist who had sold a lush body to an old man.

"Green and white suits you," he said. "What color are your eyes?"

Hattie Leggit raised her bottom, a delightfully round bottom, and plopped herself back onto her stool in a position where she could look directly up at him. She frowned. "We have not even been introduced, my lord, but obviously you know something about me."

"Yes," he said, calculating this pigeon. She was no man's fool. "I know you in the manner in which you know me. We are both talked about around Bath. Please forgive my forwardness, but I saw you and was impetuous enough to stop my carriage and introduce myself. I'm ashamed to admit that I wanted to see if you were as beautiful as your reputation suggests. You are more so."

His question about her large, almond-shaped eyes was answered. Deep gray, and her thick eyelashes were black.

He smiled at her and the corners of her pretty mouth almost turned up, but she collected herself in time. "My maid and coachman are my chaperons, my lord."

Those gray eyes of hers held more interest than disdain. He swiveled around, looking in all directions.

"They are on the other side of your carriage," Hattie Leggit said.

"Should you like me to summon them for you?" he said. There was a time to advance and a time to retreat. Clearly she found him interesting. That was a good enough beginning.

"Leave them be," she said. "I just wanted you to know I'm not alone here." Her sudden laughter rang out and whoever trained her in elocution, as someone clearly did,

hadn't succeeded in tempering that full, joyous sound into the expected shrill giggle.

"Observing propriety, hmm?" He bent over her and spoke softly. "You have nothing to fear from me, madam. I am a boring fellow said to be transparent and incapable of flirtation."

Her next laugh was more a snort. He had best be careful. This one was indeed quick-witted and unlikely to slip into his trap too easily...unless she wanted to.

"Laugh away," he told her, and sighed, making sure he appeared downcast. "My fragile self-esteem is accustomed to deadly blows." Inclined toward her as he was, her breasts distracted him. Rarely a day passed when he didn't give thanks for the continuing fondness for revealing a woman's charms. Lud, he was certainly fond of the practice.

Cradled in the scant bodice of a white cambric dress, and with a handsome pearl on a gold chain rolling over their blossoming knolls, her breasts transfixed him. She wore a filmy green pelisse through which her white gown showed. There was much about Mrs. Leggit that beckoned a man to explore closer.

"Forgive me," she said. "Please don't look so, so needy. You may already know that my beginnings are humble. I am not polished and I make mistakes. You have paid me compliments and I thank you."

Needy, she said. He looked needy? Well, he felt needy, damn it all and he'd better excuse himself before he rushed in and said something to shock her. His breeches grew uncomfortable and he longed to find out if she felt as soft and as completely female as he expected.

He held out a hand and waited until she put her fingers in his palm, then he brought his lips lightly to her skin, skin that bore daubs of paint.

He would, John thought, like to paint her. In the nude. And he wouldn't waste such an opportunity on gaudy colors and a canvas. Oh, no, he would spread warm milk laced with honey directly on the skin of each curve and sweep of her body. And he would use a full, not too soft brush, he thought, the better to make her squirm and snatch at him when the bristles aroused her nipples and the swelling place between her thighs. Soon he would abandon the brush and use his hands to lay on the sweet, soft mixture, missing not an inch of her but not lingering either. He wouldn't want to hurry things. But the lingering would wait for his tongue when he licked the nectar from her. He would lap at her breasts until she begged for more. And he'd suck between those rounded thighs until she demanded that he take her.

"My lord?" Her voice startled him, but he covered his reactions quickly enough. She tilted her face sideways to frown up at him. "Are you quite well?"

"Oh, quite." He lied to her and might have chastised himself for the animal that he was, only he'd enjoyed every second of his daydream.

"Mrs. Leggit!" A female screech blasted forth. "Mrs. Leggit, we're coming!"

"Oh dear," Hattie Leggit mouthed.

John straightened. "Please tell your husband we met today and that I look forward to spending time with him. I'm living at Worth House with my young cousin and my mother's two sisters. It's time to give some attention to the property and make sure my relatives are well looked after."

"That would be the child you brought with you." She looked apologetic. "I've already warned you how people are talking."

He smiled and felt the warmth in his own eyes. "Chloe,

yes. I brought her from France so that she could improve her English.'' The child still hadn't spoken a word. ''She will think you lovely when you meet. I'm sure she'll admire your…memorable appearance.''

''You there.'' Mead's voice boomed. ''Not an inch closer, mind you. And don't try to run for it if you knows what's good for you.''

''Here come my coachman and my maid.'' Hattie Leggit stood up and John caught the scent of roses. ''Don't panic, my lord. I'll subdue them.''

Now that really did bring him close to unruly laughter.

Mead tripped over the curb. He staggered, his arms outflung and appearing doomed to crash to the flagway, but he avoided disaster and stood before them, puffing. Bea took up position behind him.

''Not a word,'' Hattie said, standing very straight. ''I shouldn't wish for you to disgrace yourselves.''

''Madam,'' Mead said in his high voice. ''I have a duty to do. Mr. Leggit is my master and he has told me to run off any stranger who dares to talk to you.''

Bea's head appeared around Mead's arm. ''It's true, Mrs. Leggit. That's exactly what Mr. Leggit said.''

John regretted Hattie's discomfort, which he could feel, but this was one charade he must play along with if he hoped to make a friend out of Leggit. This was essential for John if he were to carry out his plan.

''I am mortified, my lord,'' Hattie said, turning so that sunshine and shadow dappled her face and breasts in a most charming manner. She drew herself up and addressed her servants. ''This is the Marquis of Granville. He is in Bath to visit his aunts. Mr. Leggit hopes Lord Granville will be a visitor at Leggit Hall. Now, if you don't want Mr. Leggit to reprimand you—and we do

know how unpleasant that can be—then you had best apologize for your rudeness at once.''

The man, Mead, swallowed several times and muttered, ''Excuse me, my lord,'' without raising his eyes to John's face.

Bea's breathless ''Yes, my lord, please'' was made without her ever leaving the shelter of Mead's body.

''Now,'' Hattie said, fussing with the stand-up collar on her pelisse. ''We must make haste before others are sent out to find us.'' Rather than look at him again, she cast her eyes over tin buckets of flowers for sale in front of a nearby shop.

John caught the attention of a ruddy-faced boy wearing a leather apron and cloth cap who walked in front of the buckets, eyeing their contents critically. He stopped frequently to add water.

Hattie continued to smile at the masses of blooms. He knew what he was about to do would flaunt convention, but he'd do it anyway. He raised a finger to the boy.

John pointed to a bucket filled with yellow roses. The boy started to pull out stems, but John shook his head and indicated that he wanted the lot.

The roses were quickly wrapped and carried to John, who passed them immediately to Hattie while he paid for them.

He wondered if she'd thrust them back at him or simply drop them on the flagway. She did neither.

''You know I must not accept these,'' she said, but hugged them and buried her face in the fragrant blossoms. ''Thank you for the kind thought, but please take them with you.''

''And what should I do with them if I did? I assure you Mr. Leggit won't mind at all.''

She frowned at him and raised her eyes. And while he

watched, the determination slipped from Hattie Leggit's face. She watched something he couldn't see without turning around. If he did so, he might put her in a sticky spot.

Her lips parted and she took shallow breaths.

"Are you well, Mrs. Leggit?" he asked.

She nodded, but he knew she was not all right at all. The two servants angled their heads to see what their mistress looked at and each of them lost the color in their cheeks.

"Mrs. Leggit?" the maid said. "He'll say something, you know he will."

"He will," Mead agreed. "You know how he is."

John wanted to know who "he" was.

"We must leave now, my lord," Hattie said. "I'll be sure to give your regards to Mr. Leggit. I wish you a good day." She set to work packing up her paints and the maid rushed to help.

The coachman just stood there, and muttered, "This won't be pretty. See if I'm not right."

John decided he would not walk away as if dismissed. He swung about, looking for the source of so much distress. Pulled up behind his own carriage, a burgundy equipage idled with good horses standing at the shafts, their tails switching. A hunched coachman in a caped coat of the same burgundy as the coach held the reins loosely between his fingers while he looked down at the cobbles.

A man's pale face showed clearly at the window in the coach door. He leaned forward, watching. The hollow-faced devil watched John with unblinking concentration.

"Who is he?" he murmured to Mrs. Leggit.

"I don't know what you're talking about," she said, no longer glancing at the newly arrived vehicle. "Mead, please pick up the chair and easel. And don't forget my table. I have the paints. I didn't realize how late it was."

"It's barely noon," John pointed out mildly. "And you're afraid of the man in that coach."

"Please." Mrs. Leggit spoke through her teeth. "If you wish me no harm, go away. It may already be too late, but do not make my position worse."

He could not persist in making her panic. "Good day," he said, gesturing with his hat before putting it on again. "I hope you'll look forward to...no, of course, you weren't at home so you don't know. This morning I called on your good husband and he accepted my invitation for the two of you to join me, and my family, for dinner on Saturday."

4

Lionel Smythe arrived at the main entrance to Leggit Hall a few seconds earlier than Hattie. She saw him alight from the coach, his sallow face thrust forward.

"D'you think he'll say anything about, well, you know?" Bea said, seated opposite Hattie in the jewel of a coach Mr. Leggit had presented to her. Gray, trimmed with Mr. Leggit's favorite burgundy color, every head turned when it passed.

Deeply thoughtful, Hattie said, "Mr. Smythe is a problem. He's a sneak and a spy and he thinks he can make sure of Mr. Leggit's gratitude by carrying tales about me."

She would not allow her spirit to be broken by such people. Hattie observed Smythe, who stopped partway up the half-moon-shaped steps to look back at her. Very tall and thin, he had wispy gray hair that flapped beneath the curled brim of the hat he wore pulled firmly down to his ears.

"Oh, Mrs. Leggit," Bea moaned. "You're right about him. He looks ever so mean. He'll go straight to the master, you see if I'm not right. Then there'll be an awful set-to."

Even at a distance Hattie saw Smythe's light eyes narrow. He turned away and carried on into the house. His

skinny legs in unfashionable striped trousers reminded her of a man on stilts at some fair.

"Hush," Hattie told her maid, who must be anticipating punishment for not guarding her mistress well enough. "I shall deal with Mr. Smythe." She only hoped she could.

"You ought to get rid of them roses," Bea said. "Mr. Smythe will tell the master who it was give 'em to you."

"He will indeed." Hattie raised her chin. "And I shall say it's true. Trust me, Bea. I have never been good at telling fibs. In fact I seem to let the truth pop out even when a fib might be much better for everyone."

"I know, Mrs. Leggit," Bea said, sounding glum.

A liveried footman rushed from the house to open the carriage door and hand Hattie down. He wore the worried expression that was part of every Leggit servant's uniform. "Good afternoon, Mrs. Leggit," he said, not meeting her eyes. "I trust your painting went well and the weather remained clement for you."

"It was lovely, thank you," Hattie told him.

She carried her huge bouquet of yellow roses. These she handed to the footman while she tidied her hair, smoothed the feather on her bonnet and straightened her gloves and pelisse. Vast, gray and encrusted with gaping gargoyles, Leggit Hall loomed before her. Just thinking about being swallowed by its dark spaces and oddly hushed atmosphere overwhelmed Hattie.

Only when Mr. Leggit gave one of his excessive gatherings did the house become hot and loud, crowded with often drunken, overdressed people—that was before some became foxed enough to decide they hardly needed clothes at all. Or so she heard from Bea since Mr. Leggit preferred Hattie to stay in her rooms on those occasions.

She heard her carriage move away.

"Come along, Bea," Hattie said, and took the roses back from the footman.

"Mrs. Leggit," Bea said quietly. "Why not let me take the flowers and get rid of them. If I'm asked I'll say some stranger pushed them on us."

"No such thing," Hattie said. "Haven't I just told you how I hate fibs. Besides, since Mr. Leggit will know from Mr. Smythe that I had them, it would look as if I had something guilty to hide."

She followed the footman up the sweep of white marble steps, through brass-studded oak doors and into the cavernous house.

As a girl, even shortly before Mr. Leggit had made the dangerous ultimatum that meant she must marry him or see her parents ruined, Hattie had dreamed of marrying one day and having children. She had visualized a simple man, simple but good and in love with her for who she was rather than what she looked like. Hattie would have loved him so, too, and their home would have been a warm and welcoming place.

The Marquis of Granville's face and smile were easy to recall. She had, of course, never had designs on an elevated marriage and he was far from simple, but the humor and interest in his eyes had stirred the longings she had clung to not so long ago.

The front doors thundered shut behind Hattie and Bea.

"There you are!" Mrs. Sylvia Dobbin, dressed in elegant black, her thick blond hair pulled back from her face and wound into a chignon at the nape, hurried from the darkened reaches of the house with outstretched hands. "So much going on. Such pounding and banging and servants rushing up and down the stairs. A modiste and her assistants are here to see you, and the jeweler has been

sent for. Oh my, such excitement. And Mr. Leggit is calling for you constantly.''

Servants scurried up and down the wide staircase that rose from the center of a great black-columned entry hall. The servants carried bolts of rich cloth, trays loaded with potions and lotions. A footman struggled under the weight of bottles of Mr. Leggit's favorite cognac and plates piled high with the fat ham-stuffed buns in which he indulged daily.

"Come, Bea," Hattie said. "I should like to go to my chambers and rest.''

"Rest?'' Mrs. Dobbin wailed, her large blue eyes moist with concern. "Rest, you say as if this weren't the most important of days. Mr. Leggit calls for you, I say. And you must meet with the modiste.''

Hattie removed her green gloves and patted her hair. "I couldn't possibly meet with anyone until I've had time to rest.'' Time to think was what she really meant.

The butler, Bartholomew, appeared from below stairs. "There you are, Mrs. Leggit. Cook wants you to go over menus if you could spare the time.''

Given that Cook did whatever she pleased and only asked Hattie's opinion to observe custom, Hattie had no intention of venturing into that fierce lady's domain. "Kindly tell Mrs. Sweet I have the utmost confidence in her and since my time is so burdened I shall leave the decisions to her.''

"Concentrate, please,'' Mrs. Dobbin said, drawing up her straight back. "This house is in an uproar. You cannot simply retire to your rooms as if nothing were afoot.'' Suddenly her lovely face showed signs of crumpling in an alarming manner. "Mrs. Leggit, Mr. Leggit told me I should make sure you went to him the moment you arrived home.''

Sylvia Dobbin wasn't a bad sort and it was a shame that she suffered so when Mr. Leggit felt like lashing out. Hattie puffed dramatically and rolled her eyes. "Oh, very well. I shall go to him now. I presume he's in his rooms?"

"Yes," Mrs. Dobbin said, her relief obvious.

Hattie echoed that relief and she felt stronger—for different reasons.

Leggit Hall had many areas in which its master liked to spend his time. Lolling in the vulgar Room of Moon Pools beneath the house itself was his favorite haunt. She had been warned not to speak of the room, or the private chambers surrounding the pools. A spring existed on the estate, its source the same as those at the Roman Baths, and an intricate system brought the water in and out of Mr. Leggit's pools.

Frequently Mr. Leggit tried to entice Hattie into the mysteriously hot, bubbling waters where steam wafted across the surface. She resisted going there.

When he became too insistent and she had to do as he asked, she stayed well away from the pools, where water gushed from the open mouths of strange stone animals, and insisted she feared the water. Sculptures of naked men and women, their bodies writhing together, adorned a platform at the center of the pools.

As much as possible, Hattie avoided thinking about Mr. Leggit's belief that the waters increased his virility.

"Come with me, please, Bea," Hattie said. "You, too, Mrs. Dobbin." She didn't care to go into her husband's presence alone, not that she could always avoid that.

Up the wide stairs she went with Mrs. Dobbin in front and Bea in her wake. There were three flights, each separated from the next by a landing that led in either direction to a black balustraded gallery encircling the entire floor. On looking up, the grand impression made Hattie

feel tiny. Lavish paintings and statues decorated the three galleries. All in all Hattie thought it in really bad taste, not that the daughter of a poor baker and his wife had much experience in such things.

With a sense of foreboding, she climbed two flights keeping her eyes on Mrs. Dobbin's elegantly draped skirts slipping up from step to step. Bea's sensible shoes slapped up behind Hattie.

"Psst," Bea said. "The roses, Mrs. Leggit. *Please* don't let Mr. Leggit see those."

"As I've told you twice, Lionel Smythe will already have mentioned them," Hattie reminded her. "I shall tell my own story and make light of them."

Mrs. Dobbin came to a stop and waited for Hattie. "Forgive me, Mrs. Leggit, but sometimes you are forgetful when you're with Mr. Leggit."

"Yes." How could she deny it when it was true. Her husband often befuddled her.

"Now, *where* is it you've been?" Mrs. Dobbin said. "You know he will ask."

"Water coloring on Pultney Bridge," Hattie said promptly. "You told me I should go there to get some practice." She found that Mrs. Dobbin's instincts were good when it came to Mr. Leggit's moods. Today he must have decided to be petulant and demanding with Hattie. When this happened he usually pretended she had neglected him or left the house without notice.

"What do you think?" Hattie took her painting from Bea and thrust it before Mrs. Dobbin. "It's a beautiful day, full of color and life. Do you think I've captured some of it?"

Mrs. Dobbin studied the painting critically and murmured, "Quite nice. You're coming along." She led the way up the next flight of stairs.

A beautiful woman with a sumptuous figure, her story remained a mystery. All manner of rumors swirled through Leggit Hall suggesting this or that high-flown or outrageous past. Hattie didn't know what to think, but Mrs. Dobbin knew a great deal about a great many things and Hattie was glad she had been retained by Mr. Leggit. Mrs. Dobbin had been charged with "educating" Hattie.

The lady slowed her progress up the stairs until Hattie stood beside her once more. Mrs. Dobbin looked sideways. "I should not tell you this and I may come to regret it, but I've decided I must," she said very softly. "You are not worldly enough to survive here. I fear you may not be safe."

5

Mr. Leggit's expansive rooms occupied almost the whole third floor of the house. Hattie had three rooms there: a boudoir, a dressing room and her bedchamber. Mr. Leggit's own dressing room stood between Hattie's bedchamber and his own, a dressing room which allowed him private access to his wife.

The servants came and went from Mr. Leggit's bedchamber, and Hattie, with a smile firmly turning up her mouth, slipped into the oversize room with Bea at her shoulder.

Mrs. Dobbin had entered first and taken a position beside Lionel Smythe. Her blank expression gave no hint of the warning she'd given a few minutes earlier.

How could she be in danger here, Hattie wondered. And if she knew, would she be able to do anything about it?

Lionel Smythe and Mrs. Dobbin gave their rapt attention to Bernard Leggit, who stood before mirrors suffering the efforts of a tailor and his assistants. He held a large measure of brandy in one hand and a half-eaten ham bun in the other. Several women hovered over lengths of beautiful silks and satins, brocades and lace. Evidently they were the modiste and assistants Dobbin had mentioned.

"Hattie," Mr. Leggit said, catching sight of her in the mirror. "Nobody knew you'd left the house."

She walked toward him, keeping her chin up and a puzzled expression on her face. "They most certainly did, Mr. Leggit. I was sent to paint on Pultney Bridge." She retrieved the paper Mrs. Dobbin still held. "See? What do you think? I think I shall never show any talent, but it is fun. Thank you for my lessons."

Of average height, Bernard Leggit retained a powerful air. He was a little large in girth, but with huge, muscular shoulders and a broad chest. His legs were sturdy.

He glanced at the small, bright but amateurish painting Hattie held in front of him. "Of course you show talent," he said, and swallowed a mouthful of food. "Smythe, make sure this gets framed and hung in my bedchamber."

Smythe took the paper between finger and thumb and tweaked it away from Hattie.

She put both arms around the bouquet of roses. "You're too kind, Mr. Leggit," she said. "I wanted you to see these. A gentleman gave them to me to bring back, together with his regards. He'd called here, so he said. The Marquis of Granville?"

With no change in his nasal voice, Mr. Leggit said, "My wife and I should like to be alone. The rest of you, clear out."

The tailor and his assistants abandoned measure tapes, chalk, books of men's fashion plates and fled. They were beaten to the door by the modiste and her girls and followed by several other servants. Mrs. Dobbin walked out ahead of Lionel Smythe, who held Hattie's painting as if it didn't smell nice.

With a start, Hattie realized Bea hadn't moved. "Thank you, Bea," she said.

The maid's mouth hung slightly open and she didn't seem able to move.

"Out," Mr. Leggit ordered, and this time his voice became louder.

Bea looked at Hattie, who smiled and nodded even though she was frightened of what would happen once she was alone with her husband.

"Yes," Bea whispered, and backed all the way to the door.

"Impudent," Mr. Leggit said when they were finally alone. "Put those things down and take off your clothes." He strode to close and bolt the door then tossed aside the formal blue coat his tailors were constructing. "I'll decide what your gown should be made of."

She trembled and held the roses tighter. "I have so many gowns."

"We are about to move in more exalted circles," he said. "On Saturday I am invited to the marquis's home. Evidently he already likes what he's seen of you. His inappropriate attentions prove that. But when he sees you on my arm at his home, he will be a very jealous man. Your singular attentions to me will madden him. I shall like that. Leave on your chemise."

Each time Mr. Leggit told her to undress, he added that she should keep on her small clothes. For that she was grateful, because she didn't think she could manage to stand naked before him.

He wrenched the flowers from her and buried his nose in the blooms while he studied her. Large and light blue, his eyes protruded beneath heavy gray brows and rested on pouches of discolored wrinkles. Purple veins mottled his cheeks, a testimony to nightly drunken excess.

Hattie reminded herself how kind he'd been about her silly painting.

Immediately thoughts of what he'd done to her parents, and to her, rushed in. He had brought her parents to ruin,

to a point so low they could only stay out of a debtors' prison at his whim. And she, Hattie, was the price of their freedom.

"You are too innocent," Mr. Leggit said, pointing a greasy finger at her. His puffy mouth remained slick from the ham buns. "You *don't* know men's ways. Well, you must learn at least enough to be my helper, the partner I need. Now take off the pelisse first. Then the hat—and very fetching it is, my dear—and your dress. Don't make me have to help you. I'd prefer to sit and watch."

They had been married more than a year. He hadn't started his strange behavior for three months, choosing instead to all but ignore her, but after that he'd found ways to repulse her almost daily. For the past several weeks he had stopped shaming her and Hattie had dared to hope he'd grown bored with his games, but she saw that his need to dominate her had returned.

Best to do as he said quickly so it would be over soon. She took off the green pelisse, her hat and gloves and looked around for somewhere to put them.

"Drop them on the floor. It's past time you knew this room better. Past time for a lot of things."

Hattie dropped the clothes.

She loosened the tapes on her dress and let it fall to her feet.

Mr. Leggit's shiny mouth stretched in a smile. "Good girl."

Hattie closed her eyes—she couldn't help it—and she waited for the fondling to begin.

"The style of the dress is already decided. I have impeccable taste, so you will be delighted. Let's see how this looks."

Rather than his hands, soft fabric slipped across her breasts and she opened her eyes. Mr. Leggit, his head on

one side and the tip of his tongue between his teeth, draped her with black-and-silver brocade. He shook his head and pulled it away. "Too harsh for you. Face the mirror," he told her.

Hattie did so, hating to see herself in the all but transparent lawn chemise that showed her hardened pink nipples and the embarrassing fullness of her breasts. She longed to cover herself but didn't dare.

Humming, Mr. Leggit selected a silk chiffon the color of pale honey. "Perhaps," he murmured.

Showing weakness insured Mr. Leggit's contempt and made him more belligerent. "Why such a fuss?" she asked him, praying he wouldn't notice how hard her heart beat. "One of the gowns I have will be quite good enough."

"The marquis can be a useful man to count as a friend. An introduction into his circles will be invaluable. I may not have the pedigree, but I am a very, very wealthy man. You will help me show him how wealthy. Money has always been able to buy friends in high places."

He wound a length of the honey chiffon into a loose rope and concentrated on sliding it beneath her breasts. "Very nice. Yes, indeed, very nice." What he'd done wouldn't cover her nipples but she didn't speak. Even he wouldn't have her go, half-naked, to another man's house.

"You'll tell the modistes you've chosen this. They'll do the rest." He grabbed the chain around her neck as if he would break it, but dropped it back against her. "No cheap baubles on Saturday. I shall help you dress and make sure you are like a luxurious but understated bird. I want you to give the marquis reason to hope he may have you, but never, ever, let anyone else see you flirt with him. If as much as a whisper reaches me that you show him favor you will regret it. Do you understand?"

"No." He couldn't mean what he seemed to.

Poking the bodice of her chemise beneath the chiffon, he studied the effect.

It was vulgar yet he smiled. "I'll make sure you do understand. I was attended by a sawbones last night. A famous chap from London."

She locked her knees and said, "Are you ill?"

"If disappointment is an illness then I am a sick man. I consulted him about your failings as a wife."

There could be no greater cold than the one she felt now.

"Don't pretend you don't understand, wife. Look at you. Ripe. And you'd be willing with some man somewhere, I'll be bound. Well, that's going to change. At last we will be partners for our mutual good. You will help me get the things I want and I want the connections Granville can get me. I've earned the respect of the highest in the land. And I'm going to get it."

He spun her to face him. "And I want you to bear me a son. You should already have done so. We don't want them to think you're barren."

Hattie looked directly up into his eyes and would not allow herself to flinch. She'd seen tears well in his eyes before. Once she'd forgotten herself and tried to comfort him. Mr. Leggit had sent her away at once.

"Is that all you have to say to me on the subject," he said.

She swallowed. "I say that I am not skilled in things such as flirting. And I will not do it." Surely her reaction would please him.

"I was talking about my son." He smiled, such a strange smile. "You will flirt with the marquis. We can discuss your duties with him first, then return to the other. That man can introduce me to the most influential people

in all England. And if he wants you badly enough he'll do it just to be in your company."

She crossed her arms to contain a shiver. "Why would the marquis have any interest in me? I can't imagine why you would have such notions when the man came with an invitation for you before he saw me at all."

"Very easily, my dear, silly girl. All of Bath speaks of your beauty. Every man who sees you envies me and Granville's type thinks he can have whatever he wants. He's a strapping fellow, wouldn't you say?"

Hattie frowned and her heart beat faster. "He is a large cove."

"Person," Mr. Leggit thundered. "Or man. I've paid well for you to speak like a lady. Another slip like that would be unwise. Sylvia Dobbin shall hear what I think of her efforts."

As strong as she tried to be, Hattie felt perspiration between her shoulder blades. "Lord Granville is a large person," she said, concentrating on her accent.

Mr. Leggit skewered her with his stare. "Handsome, too, hmm?"

She pretended to think back. "Pleasant enough."

He touched her mouth and she did flinch. "Why do you suppose he stopped his fine carriage to speak with you, something no respectful man would do to another man's wife?" Gently he stroked her cheek, and her hair.

"He was only being polite, I'm sure." She wished it were otherwise. Oh, daydreaming about a stranger wouldn't help her.

The bright sheen Hattie dreaded appeared in Mr. Leggit's eyes. He shot out a hand and captured one of her wrists. "The sawbones said the baths are doing me a great amount of good. He noted, er, improvement. But I need

help from you. Enthusiasm, you ungrateful chit. You must be skilled in certain arts.''

With a jerk, he pulled her close until she had to raise her face to see his, and he pushed her hand between his thighs. ''Squeeze. Gently at first...until you feel a response...then more firmly, more insistently. Show me how much you want me.''

The thing he forced her to hold felt limp, just as it always had. He closed her fingers with his own, released the pressure and squeezed again. Sweat popped out on his brow and upper lip.

He breathed loudly and frowned, his grip on her hand convulsive. ''Harder,'' he ordered, and pushed his face against her neck. ''This is your fault. I should have a son by now. You shame me in front of my friends. I know how they whisper.''

Hattie grew still and utterly cold. She couldn't move. He worked with her hand but she felt nothing anymore. Her body became a statue.

''Don't do that,'' Mr. Leggit shouted. ''Don't play your tricks on me. Make me ready, I tell you.''

Hattie looked at her feet.

''Very well.'' He fell back, gasping, his skin gleaming and his face deep red. ''I gave you one more chance to do this easily. Other remedies have been suggested and I shall use them, but not now. On Saturday you will show Granville how you adore me, but you will find private moments to let him know you are a woman of great passion who would welcome a little dalliance also.''

She could barely speak. ''You want me to show fondness for the marquis?''

He raised a hand as if to strike her, but dropped his arm again. ''You will never, ever, betray me, but you will

keep him wanting my company so that he may have yours.''

Now. Now she must push away her fear and remember what she wanted, and soon. ''How much will you pay me if I do this?'' she asked, tossing her head and controlling the shudders that chased down her back. She must never forget the importance of getting him to give her money. Money would set her free.

''You are too stupid to know how close you bring me to hurting you. You are greedy and your little blackmail bores me. What is it you want to buy now?''

She put her hands behind her back and swung back and forth. She forced herself to smile at him. ''I don't know yet.'' She had collected a tidy sum in exchange for doing Mr. Leggit's bidding, but there was nowhere near enough to secure her escape from him yet. He thought she wanted the money to buy expensive fripperies but she carefully bought small, cheap trinkets to cover her deception. She saved almost everything he gave her.

From a drawer in a Chinese apothecary's chest, he pulled two guineas and Hattie struggled not to smile with triumph.

''Come here,'' he told her, ''and bring your beloved roses.''

His tone turned her stomach, but she did as he asked.

Mr. Leggit took the roses and tore off the wrappings around the stems. These he broke in half and threw down, all but one thick and thorny stem.

Her throat dried.

''Hold out your hands.''

She did so, extending them cautiously. Surely he would not really hurt her.

''Take this in your hands and squeeze it tightly.''

''No!'' She made fists.

Mr. Leggit said, "If you know what's good for you, you'll do as I tell you."

She believed he would do something terrible if she refused him again.

Lightly she took the stem from him and the thorns pricked her skin.

"I told you to squeeze it."

She shook her head, no, and he closed one large hand tightly over both of hers.

"Stop," she cried, not daring to try to pull away. She felt her own blood. "Please stop, Mr. Leggit."

He let her go at once, and when she dropped the flower stem he ground one of the guineas into each palm.

Tears slipped from the corners of her eyes but she made no sound.

"There's your bounty," he said. "Pick up your clothes and get out. Go through my dressing room."

She clung to the money but bent to gather her things.

"If anyone asks, you held your bouquet too tightly."

Swallowing her tears, Hattie rushed for the dressing-room door, but her husband cut her off. She looked at the floor, consumed by the pain in her hands.

"Have your maid bathe your hands at once," he said, his voice changed, uneven. "If only you could love me."

He turned from her and rubbed his face. She heard him mutter "Forgive me, Hattie."

6

John allowed his eyes to close for a moment. His head ached. He was in some mad place and it was called Worth House.

"John," Aunt Enid said. Despite the din made by the coming and going of grumbling staff, Aunt Enid's honking voice carried clearly.

"Yes, aunt?" He wandered to the lofty fireplace in the richly appointed salon and leaned on the mantel. The aunts sat, one on either side of the fire, their backs absolutely straight. "You look lovely tonight, Aunt Enid. That shade of pink suits you. And you, Aunt Prunella, are absolutely splendid in purple."

"Rich hyacinth," Aunt Prunella informed him tartly.

Prunella was the taller and broader of the two sisters. Transparent and smooth, the white skin of her face bore a slash of rouge along each cheekbone. Enid, who used a cane but insisted on walking in all winds and weathers, resembled a figure carved from brown cork with a fine blade. Wrinkles on her thin face and neck draped like tea-stained pin-tucks. No paint ever made Aunt Enid's acquaintance, but the exuberance of youth remained in her bright, dark eyes.

She tapped John's arm with her painted fan. "Chloe doesn't say a word. The child's been here going on two

weeks and she has yet to speak to us, isn't that right, sister?''

Prunella nodded. ''Of course, we've never met her mother and who knows what sort of graceless, silent creature she may be.''

''Simonne...is both graceful and charming,'' John said, reminding himself that he should not get angry and that he must watch his words closely.

''We hadn't met Chloe until John brought her here,'' Enid pointed out. ''She is probably shy. After all, everything must be quite different for her. But since your idea is to improve her English, my boy, you'd better do something about loosening her tongue.''

Both ladies stared at Chloe, who sat in a stiff little gilt chair with a cane seat and held a black cat on her lap. John had told a tale about their luggage being stolen and the lack of clothing had quickly been remedied. This evening Chloe wore royal-blue velvet with pink rosettes at the neckline. The velvet matched her eyes. Her auburn hair waved to her shoulders.

Sweet-faced Mrs. Gimblet, the aunts' maid, stood behind Chloe's chair with her plump hands folded in front of her. She would fill in until a suitable nanny could be found. Then would come a governess. John felt the weight of his responsibility to Chloe. He knew nothing about children, but he would learn.

''Look at the child,'' Enid said, her voice softened. ''A gentle, pretty little thing. But Francis is quiet and kind, or he was the last time we saw him. However many years ago that was.''

''Yes,'' John said, glancing sharply at Chloe. She must have heard the reference to her father, but she didn't react. He had tried to talk to her about what had happened and about the importance of not revealing the details of their

ordeal until he told her it was all right to talk about them. Chloe hadn't responded, just dropped her chin to her chest and sighed.

His cousin had been the best of men, too good a man to die for the callous greed of Bernard Leggit. And Simonne...

"Where are those people you invited?" Enid said, her head swiveling on an exceedingly long neck. "We don't like strangers, you know. Anyway, Prunella and I are tired of waiting. We're hungry and we have important things to do."

"Sleep," Prunella said with haste. "We need our sleep."

John had a good idea what his elderly relatives might need to get done. They thought their amusing little secret was theirs alone, but John knew more than they would like him to know. Later, dressed in voluminous night-gowns and robes, their white hair tucked beneath berib-boned sleeping caps, they could likely be present for a most unlikely meeting.

The Leggits were late. Only fifteen minutes late, it was true, but that was enough to throw John's aunts, and the unruly staff into an irritable humor.

A tall, red-faced maid called Dolly flounced into the room carrying two trays of hors d'oeuvres. "Where do you want these, then?" she asked. "I can't 'ang about. Mrs. Whipple's 'aving one of her things."

"It's too soon for those," John told Dolly.

She looked at him with round eyes. "Well, I 'ave to do what Mrs. Whipple says, don't I? She said to bring these 'ere now." With that she plunked one of the trays on a rococo table, causing several Dresden porcelains to teeter dangerously. After staring from place to place

again, she deposited the second tray on the seat of a green and scarlet brocade chaise.

Dolly dusted her palms together. "There. Now then, them people, the upstart ones, when will they be 'ere? Mrs. Whipple's all in a twist because her soup's getting overdone."

"Aunt Prunella," John said, leaning toward her. "This staff—"

"Not in front of the servants." Prunella raised a sharp nose where gold-rimmed pince-nez rested.

"Not in front of the... We'll deal with this in the morning, aunt. You seem to have forgotten who employs whom."

Dolly slipped away with a smirk on her face.

He'd spoken to Aunt Prunella and Aunt Enid about the deplorable attitude of the servants, but they refused to listen to a word against them.

"This is what happens when you mix with riffraff," Aunt Enid announced. "They take advantage. Keep their betters waiting. Pah! Prunella and I arose early from our naps to be ready to receive these people. It's just not good enough."

"They'll be here," John said. He sat down in one of the several red tapestry fauteuils he'd always admired. "And try to remember that Bernard Leggit is one of the wealthiest men in England."

"Money," Prunella said, and sniffed. "I suppose he talks about it. People like him do. Vulgar creatures."

Boggs, the butler, entered and stepped lightly toward John. The man had small, tidy feet in highly polished shoes. His feet were the only small thing about him.

"What is it, Boggs?" John asked with the unhappy thought that his guests might have decided not to come at all.

Boggs leaned forward, his corset creaking, and said in a discreet tone, "We have problems, my lord. Mrs. Whipple is trying to subdue a mutiny in the kitchens."

John stared at the man. "A *mutiny?* By God, it's time this household was sorted out. You may go to Mrs. Whipple and give her this message from me. Her job is to keep harmony in the kitchens and to attend to producing meals bound to delight her employers and her employers' guests. Dinner this evening will be served when I say so and it will be excellent. Now, Boggs, kindly make sure I'm not bothered further with household nonsense."

Boggs's too-small wig had worked its way upward until the top of his sandy hair could be seen. He smacked the thing down, only to have it pop up again.

"His...lordship...not...to...be..." Boggs had produced a pad of paper and a stump of pencil. Between each note he made, and announced out loud, he moistened the tip of the pencil with his tongue.

"No need to do that here, Boggs." John, aware of his aunts' peevish shifting, tried to be calm and, above all, not to let them see how he listened for the doorbell. "Kindly remove the tray of hors d'oeuvres from that chaise, man."

Not two more minutes passed before sounds of a commotion came from the direction of the foyer and front door.

John stood at once. Rather than follow his instincts and go to meet his guests, he pulled a stool beside Chloe and stroked the cat. "What's its name?"

"Raven," Mrs. Gimblet said. "She was brought in as a mouser to keep in the kitchens, just in case, only she had more interest in befriending the occasional mouse than killing it, they say."

An unbelievable vision burst into the room. Snowdrop

Pick had arrived, dressed in demure and good quality black, but with her black hair still curling to her waist. A black taffeta hat with an impossibly tall black feather on one side sat atop her head and she carried a bag that required both of her hands to lift. She lifted it now and dropped it again on the marble floor.

John stood immediately and looked down at Chloe. The child had seen Snowdrop come in but was already engrossed in the cat again.

"There you are, Mr. John Elliot," Snowdrop announced. "A fine time I've just had getting in here. If your brother hadn't come along, I'd probably be on my bottom in the street."

"My salts, Gimblet," Enid cried, bringing forth the ancient ladies' maid who had served the sisters for fifty years. "*Mr. John Elliot?* Such impudent familiarity. I feel quite faint. John, *do* something!"

"Snowdrop—" John began.

Snowdrop interrupted him. "Gawd, what a fuss. I came because you said I should, Mr. Elliot." She winked so broadly he almost laughed. "You know, to 'elp with Chloe?"

Mrs. Gimblet, who didn't appear to notice anything unusual about Snowdrop, said, "She's a good little girl, but too quiet for a young one."

Snowdrop came closer and dropped a curtsy. "I know, Mr. Elliot said as much. But I'm good with nippers, isn't that so, Mr. Elliot?"

John cleared his throat. "Quite so," and felt bound to add, "Snowdrop is from the southern counties where I believe they call children, er, *nippers?*" Albert had already gone to his room for the night, not that uniting him with Snowdrop would help this situation. "I should prob-

ably explain all this… My *brother,* did you say? Which brother? What can you mean?''

''Name of Nathan. You can see he's related to you. A handsome one as well. He said to tell you he's going to his rooms to get settled but he'll join everyone for dinner.''

''Nathan!'' the aunts cried. ''How delightful. He's such an uncomplicated boy.'' They aimed a joint glare at John.

''That would be the Earl of Blackburn, Lord Blackburn to you, young woman,'' Aunt Prunella informed Snowdrop.

Nathan? The finishing touch to a ghastly situation. ''Boggs, kindly take Miss Pick with you and have Albert help her get settled in the nurseries. He wrote the letters regarding her employment and he'll know what to do. Tell him that, will you? He'll know what to do. And kindly carry the lady's bag, Boggs. Good night, Miss Pick. We shall discuss things in the morning.''

Grumbling under his breath, Boggs tried to lift the bag in one hand and hold it at a distance. Too heavy for that to work, the bag slapped against his knees and he barely kept his balance. Snowdrop giggled and Boggs stalked from the room, leaving her to follow.

Regardless of the obstacles thrown in his way, he would, John decided with some force, push this mess into acceptable order and carry his plan to its successful conclusion.

The main thing was to keep a cool head in all things.

But *Nathan.* ''Does Nathan visit you often, aunts?'' he asked.

Both ladies shook their heads. ''Almost never,'' Enid said. ''We sent word that you were here and hoped he would come. And you see, our prayers are answered. Your

brothers, including young Dominic, don't spend nearly enough time together.''

Keeping the truth of Francis and Simonne's deaths from Nathan for more than a short time would be out of the question. All he could do, John decided, was to persuade the middle Elliot brother to support the plan.

Dolly, the maid, entered the room with Bernard Leggit, and Hattie immediately behind him. Dolly held her head high and said, ''Mr. Boggs is otherwise engaged so I'm the butler for the moment. The upstart guests have arrived.'' She peered closely at a card. ''Mr. Bernard Leggit and his missus.''

7

The beautiful room grew instantly still.

Hattie didn't care about the rude introduction; after all, they were upstarts in these circles. She suspected Mr. Leggit had the truth of it and that the marquis was bored in Bath and looking for a diversion. Apparently he was considering Hattie for the position. How could Mr. Leggit imagine she would be able to encourage a worldly man such as the Marquis of Granville.

She felt others present but saw only the marquis. He looked back at her, the slightest smile turning up the corners of his mouth. Hattie looked at the carpet.

"My dear Lord Granville," Mr. Leggit said, leaving Hattie's side. "You do me such honor. Lovely little house you have here. A jewel—" he guffawed "—or should I say a *bijou?*" He bowed and spoke in conspiratorial tones meant for his host alone, patted the head of the sweet-faced but silent child seated in a chair beside his lordship, and even scratched a black cat on the girl's lap. The cat raised its head and showed lips pulled back from sharp teeth. Mr. Leggit quickly removed his fingers.

Mr. Leggit bent over the marquis's hand again. His lordship looked beyond her husband's back at Hattie. His lips parted a little and his nostrils flared.

She caught her breath and dropped her gaze again. He

was sophisticated, intimidating—exciting, and from another world.

Mr. Leggit straightened and one of the ladies by the fire tapped the arm of her chair with a fan. She was a small woman but sat very straight and said, "Kindly come here, sir, and introduce yourself to my sister and me."

When Mr. Leggit drew closer to them, she added, "Worth House is not *little*. It is large and certainly beautiful. It is a house to be appreciated by those who recognize the finer things."

Hattie's face turned hot. She and her husband were out of place here and, although she hadn't spoken a word, Mr. Leggit's obsequious bluster shamed her. Mr. Leggit had misjudged badly; this was not a circle which could be bought.

"It is my honor and pleasure to be here, dear ladies," he said, bowing.

Hattie stopped listening to them. She fiddled with the gold strings of her reticule and her attention returned to his lordship. He continued to look at her, to study her from head to foot, as if they were the only people in the room. He beckoned to her.

She glanced at Mr. Leggit. The marquis couldn't be beckoning her. Not so openly and with her husband present. She was imagining things.

When she returned her gaze to his face, his eyes were on hers and they didn't waver. He definitely smiled this time, and urged her toward him again.

Hattie breathed through her mouth and pretended she hadn't noticed his gesture.

"Mrs. Leggit," he said. "We should also become acquainted, don't you think?"

He came toward her and she hastily offered a smile of her own. "Good evening, my lord," she said, and felt her

lungs fill properly for the first time since she'd entered this house. She dropped a curtsy she hoped would make Mrs. Dobbin proud.

The marquis extended a hand and, before she could make sure of her balance and place her gloved fingers in his, he enfolded her hand in a warm, firm grip and bent to place his lips there with much more pressure than was suitable.

Hattie hoped the attention had not been noticed.

She opened her mouth to breathe. His thick, dark hair shone and she liked the way it curled to his collar. He wore all black with bright, white linen and when he raised his face to look at her—so close she felt his breath on her face—her heart pounded in her ears.

"Do stand up," he said softly, smiling and urging her to her feet. "Remember how I told you your hair was extraordinary, not brown, or red or blond? Tonight it shows all those colors. And the gown—" his slow downward look caused Hattie to blush wildly this time "—well, I do believe I should call it a blond color, and what lovely things it does for your skin."

Before her stood a practiced flatterer, probably a practiced seducer, and he was so handsome, so masculine that she reacted to him despite her reservations. In fact, if it were not inappropriate, she would be perfectly happy to have him continue with his flattery.

Something needed to be said. "It's a pleasant evening, if a little chilly. Mr. Leggit and I enjoyed the drive from Leggit Hall."

"Did you?" He didn't blink. "How nice. I'm glad you could join me."

Not join us but join me. And his welcome didn't include Mr. Leggit. His lordship's dark blue eyes were...hot? Yes,

hot. He studied her as if he were hungry and he'd decided she could satisfy that hunger.

"This must be your little cousin," she said, turning to the child beside him. "I'm Mrs. Hattie Leggit. What's your name?"

The only sign that the child had heard Hattie was the slightest of pauses in her rhythmic stroking of the black cat on her lap.

"Chloe," the marquis said. "She is very shy and probably overwhelmed by the company but I wanted her—" he dropped his voice barely above a whisper "—I wanted her to meet you."

"I see." Hattie bent over Chloe and stroked the cat who immediately broke into a loud, rough purr and licked her hand.

She smiled up at the marquis, who made no attempt to hide how he took advantage of her position to look inside her bodice. He touched the tip of his tongue to the edges of his upper teeth and her belly tightened. The private place between her legs also tightened, and stung…which felt quite delightful. *My goodness.*

"Our cook promises to feed us well," he said, startling Hattie.

"I'm sure she will," Hattie said. The child watched her but ignored the hand Hattie offered. "His lordship speaks very highly of you, Chloe, and I can see why."

No flicker of reaction entered the little girl's eyes.

Granville continued to stare at Hattie. "I'm sure Mr. Leggit won't mind my saying that you look fetching. Your modiste is a skilled designer."

Mr. Leggit faced them and held a hand out to Hattie. "I am the designer," he said, his eyes fixed on her overly exposed breasts. "First I choose the material, then I drape it on Hattie until I'm satisfied. When I'm certain she is

shown off to her best advantage—'' he snickered and gave their host a man-to-man look ''—well, then it's time for the seamstresses to do their jobs. Every one of Hattie's gowns is an original.''

Muscles tensed in the Marquis of Granville's lean face. ''Any gown would be an original on your wife simply because she wore it,'' he said, recklessly, Hattie thought.

She knew what she had to do. Mr. Leggit had told her to flirt, which she'd been unable to do, not that the marquis had needed her help. She moved too quickly in her haste to wrap her hands around one of Mr. Leggit's arms and look up into his face. She inclined her head to smile at him and made certain she appeared adoring enough. Mr. Leggit breathed heavily and kissed her cheek. ''Good girl,'' he murmured, ''but don't forget my warnings.''

''Mr. Leggit?'' Miss Enid Worth cried in her nasal voice. ''What can you be thinking of. We want to meet that beautiful wife of yours.''

Hattie actually moved a foot in the direction of the door before she gathered her wits and smiled at the ladies.

Mr. Leggit walked her forward. From the corner of his mouth he whispered, ''Don't make a mess of this or Mrs. Dobbin will suffer.''

Her stomach rolled horribly.

''Ladies,'' he said when he stood before them, ''this is my wife, Mrs. Hattie Leggit.''

She held her ground and kept her chin up while Miss Prunella fixed her pince-nez more firmly on her nose and studied her from head to foot while Miss Enid made ''Mmm'' sounds.

''I'm pleased to make your acquaintance,'' Hattie said. That must be close enough to the little speech Dobbin had taught her. Nothing about the ladies' expressions reas-

sured her. "We think Worth House is ever so grand, don't we, Mr. Leggit?"

"We do indeed." He lowered his voice. "That's enough groveling." His meaty fingers dug into her arm.

John strode to twitch an ornate, tasseled bellpull, signaling the kitchens that it was time for dinner.

"I hope we're all hungry," he said. The force of his hatred for Leggit shook him. He loathed the man and wished him dead, but reminded himself that sticking to his plan was the thing to do and that killing the lascivious bounder would be too kind.

The woman, who wasn't much more than a ripe girl, unsettled him. He had no need to pretend an interest in her. He had already plotted ways to get her alone, just for the shortest time on this first occasion. He must not move too fast, but could he be blamed for wanting to kiss her? Kiss her and fondle her, slip his hands over her breasts, throw her down and bury himself deep inside her.

He ran a thumb along his brow and felt sweat. His body quickened, grew hot and heavy and he glanced away. He had a reputation for his control and this wasn't the time to lose it.

Aunt Prunella piped up unexpectedly. "Congratulations on having such a sweet girl agree to be your wife, Mr. Leggit," she said. "Charming, isn't she, Enid?"

"And refreshing," Enid said, adding her seal of approval.

John gave each of his aunts a kiss on the cheek. Difficult they might be on occasion, but he'd always found them good judges of character and champions of the underdog.

Boggs opened the door. "Dinner is served, my lord, not that Mrs. Whipple isn't having to pick burned bits out of the lobster soup."

John fixed the man with a glare. ''We'll go in, then.'' He offered his arms to his aunts while the Leggits leaned close together as they walked. At the door he turned back to Chloe and Mrs. Gimblet, who had dined earlier. ''If you would like something more brought up, please let Boggs know. And you might ask if Miss Pick has eaten.''

''I shall see to it,'' Mrs. Gimblet said.

Walking behind the Leggits into the foyer and beside the staircase to the dining room, John found it impossible to watch anything but the provocative sway of Hattie Leggit's hips.

8

John noted with annoyance that the flunkies on either side of the dining room doors wore soiled livery and untidy wigs lacking in fresh powder. And they giggled from time to time. He rolled his eyes and said nothing to his aunts. But tomorrow, ah yes, tomorrow…

"Oh, dear," Aunt Enid said. "Prunella, we should have suggested the little dining room. We are few and this is too large. What are we going to do?"

"We are going," John said, eyeing the immense length of the dining table where six places were set with what seemed like yards between them, "We are going to have the table rearranged."

"We can't do that," Aunt Prunella said, gripping John's arm tightly. "Boggs wouldn't be at all pleased. Don't ask, John, for our sakes."

He opened his mouth to say what he thought about allowing servants to run the house, but closed it with a snap.

The under butler held a chair for Hattie. If he were in good voice, John supposed he could occasionally shout a comment to her from his own place at the head of the table.

Seated opposite Hattie, Leggit's closest neighbor to his left was Aunt Enid. Prunella took the seat to Hattie's right and at least a few feet closer to John. He squinted down

the length of table to the empty chair and place setting at the other end.

"For Lord Blackburn," Boggs said, catching John's eye.

He seethed. Things were out of control in this house. Seasoned at his work, Boggs knew well how to arrange any table to suit the number of guests in the most agreeable manner.

Then there was the matter of Nathan. When he learned of Francis's murder he would be hard to restrain. All three Elliot brothers, including Dominic, who was the youngest, had been cursed with tempers that made them fearless— and dangerous. John had learned control. He knew Nathan had matured but could still be rashly aroused. And Dominic, ah, yes, there was Dominic, the unreadable one, who preferred to battle with his brain rather than his brawn.

"Boggs," John began. "This isn't at all—"

"Lovely table," Aunt Enid said rapidly. "I've always liked the Sevres, such a beautiful blue. And the silver—"

"Is the everyday," John finished for her. At least he didn't have to worry that their guests could overhear every word, although Hattie's head turned in his direction. He bowed his head to her and smiled. Lovely, lovely creature. Why had she married such a blackguard?—not that he wasn't glad she had, given the part he intended to play with her.

"The best silver needs a polish," Boggs said.

John spoke through barely moving lips, "Then get it polished and keep it polished. I intend to spend a good deal more time in Bath now and things are going to change in this house."

Boggs slapped at the top of his wig, and he *had* bothered to powder it. John sneezed.

A maid staggered in with a silver tureen. She set it

down so hard that the crystal chandeliers rattled. "Soup," she announced. "This is heavy. Pass your plates."

"Boggs?" John said.

The butler came forward, gave the maid's bottom a pinch and set about serving the soup appropriately. When John looked into his own helping he could, indeed, see small flecks of black floating there. The soup smelled burned.

"Delicious," Aunt Enid pronounced, touching her lips to the edge of her spoon. "Don't you think so, Prunella?"

"Wonderful, sister." When candlelight caught the lenses of Aunt Prunella's pince-nez, bright prisms shot in all directions.

"It certainly is wonderful," Hattie said, smiling at the aunts who seemed taken with her, or could that be fascinated curiosity he saw in their sharp eyes?

"Jolly good soup," Leggit boomed. "My compliments to the cook. I've heard good things about you, Granville."

Leggit wasn't familiar enough with John to call him Granville. He was, in fact, still at the Lord Granville stage, where John intended to keep him, but he wouldn't embarrass Hattie by putting her husband in his place.

Leggit didn't allow John's failure to respond to dampen his enthusiasm. "Trusted in very high places, that's what I've been told about you, and you're the man who gets called upon for dangerous missions."

God only knows how Leggit had discovered so much. "We mustn't bore the ladies with such matters," he said. "Mrs. Leggit, I was impressed with your painting the other day."

She looked at her frightful soup. "Thank you."

"My mother does a bit of daubing," John said. "Very private woman so we never get to see her work." He loved and respected his eccentric parent.

"Henrietta is so talented," Prunella said. "What a pity she's become so reclusive since your father's death. We've asked her to come here and live with us many times, but she pretends she doesn't understand what we mean."

His mother, John thought, was a clever woman. "I wish she were less solitary," he said. "But you know, as soon as father died she moved to the dower house at Heatherly and she's made a life there now. She has announced that she doesn't intend to travel again."

"Heatherly's in London," Prunella remarked. "Or almost in London. Can't imagine why our sister would prefer to live there rather than here. Everything is so much nicer here."

"And *we* are here," Enid said.

"I expect you spend a good deal of time traveling," Leggit shouted at John. "All over the Continent, I've heard. And the occasional trip to South America, Africa and other parts."

Just looking at Leggit made John's gorge rise. "You seem to know a good deal about me," he said.

"O'course. All over Bath, it is. They all talk about you. You'll be the toast of the town, m'boy."

John gritted his teeth at that bit of cheek.

"Hattie and I are having a gala next week, aren't we, Hattie? Or so we call it. Few people know I've got hot pools beneath the house. Found a Roman spring everyone else had missed. Quite the experience, I can tell you." He guffawed. "There aren't many houses that provide indoor swimming parties. We really think of these marvelous events as pool galas."

Hattie Leggit looked at her hands in her lap. She had lost all vestige of color and, when she looked up, her eyes shone like dark coals.

Indoor swimming parties? The mind boggled.

"We do hope you'll join us," Leggit said to John. "We have a bit of fun as you can imagine." Leggit winked.

"What would one wear to a swimming party, John?" Aunt Enid asked, her brilliant eyes sharp with interest.

"What would one *do* there?" Aunt Prunella said. "Surely it wouldn't be like those nasty sulphur baths everyone comes here to take. Have you seen the canvas monstrosities those poor people wear just so they can pop around in that foul-smelling water? With sick *pigs* and dogs paddling among them? And riffraff leaning over the walls to watch and jeer and *throw* things, no less!"

John shared Prunella's opinion of the famed baths and their famed physic properties. Just the thought of all those ailing souls being rolled forth in their bath chairs and tipped into water where God knows what lurked beneath the surface sickened him.

Bernard Leggit laughed as if the aunts had told a hugely funny joke. He slapped his sides and coughed, and downed a large glass of hock.

Tears squeezed from the corners of his eyes. "Oh, you dear old things," he said to the aunts. Even the staff stood still and sucked in loud breaths at that impudence. "Nothing like that goes on at my house, I assure you. Nothing at all. It's all very elegant with tasteful music playing and guests dipping their toes into warm water if they so choose. I call them my Moon Pools because if the moon shines just so, its light comes through stained-glass plates and makes the water look all colors."

Aunt Enid pointedly ignored Leggit. She wrinkled her nose and said, "Moon Pools?" to Aunt Prunella.

"Dipping one's toes?" Aunt Prunella responded in an outraged tone.

The soup was removed and replaced by tiny portions of lemon ice.

"Evening all!"

John swiveled enough to see his brother, Nathan, scuff into the stone-floored dining room. "Hello, Nathan. So the aunts coerced you into coming down." John got up to shake his brother's hand and slap his considerable back.

Ignoring John's hand, Nathan took him in a bear hug and laughed aloud as they thumped each other the way they always had. "No coercion needed," he said. "I like to lay eyes on you every few years and this seemed the perfect opportunity. I understand you've got young Chloe with you. Can't imagine why Francis and Simonne would trust their little angel to you."

"We have guests," John said in Nathan's ear and, because it would be impossible to exclude his probing brother from what was going on, added, "I'm not here for the pleasure of it. There's something very serious afoot. I'll tell you later."

"Ah." Without changing his delighted expression, Nathan addressed the table. "'Evenin' all. Enid and Pru."

Aunt Prunella turned bright pink and simpered over her melting ice.

Nathan, his dark blue coat flapping behind him, marched to Leggit. "Lord Blackburn, sir. Pleased to make your acquaintance." There was a good deal of the poetic air about Nathan, who had never written a line of anything other than business correspondence in his life. His carelessly tied neck cloth had never seen starch and flopped in a lopsided bow. As he walked, overlong hair aglint with red among dark waves swept away from his flamboyantly handsome face.

"Bernard Leggit." Leggit burped and got to his feet. "The lady is my wife." He shook Nathan's hand, only

Nathan quickly forgot him in favor of Hattie. John couldn't suppress a grin. There was little wrong with his brother's instincts when it came to women. Leaving Leggit with his right hand still in the air, Nathan strode around the table to bend over Hattie. Whatever he murmured to her resulted in her bowed head and hunched shoulders—and a smile she couldn't quite hide.

Damn the man for the rake he is.

John stood up. "Boggs. Enough of this. We have charming company and we'd like to enjoy it. Now, do as I say if you please, and do it quickly. Move Aunt Enid closer to Mr. Leggit, with Nathan on her other side. I will sit on the opposite side of the table with Aunt Prunella at my right and Mrs. Leggit at my left. Hurry man."

He doubted the staff at Worth House had ever moved so fast. Chairs and place settings were shifted at great speed and everyone seated again with a minimum of fuss. John caught Nathan's eye and gave him an angelic smile in response to a narrow-eyed glare.

Hattie glanced cautiously at Lord Granville and Lord Blackburn.

They were, she thought, overwhelmingly…*male.*

Mr. Leggit kept his bulbous eyes on her as if daring her to look at their host and his brother. She smiled at him, blew him a kiss across the table and saw with relief that he relaxed a little. How she was supposed to flirt with Lord Granville if she wasn't allowed to look at him she had no idea. She took it that Mr. Leggit had changed his mind and felt relieved.

The marquis was close enough for her to feel him, at least she imagined she could. If she touched him his flesh would be hard. There was a wildness in him. In his dashing brother the daring nature was obvious, but in Lord Granville maturity had brought—and added—a subtle

edge of danger. Her skin prickled and parts of her tightened. She hitched at the scanty bodice of her gown. What could have come over her?

Those blessed moments of relief disappeared.

Lord Granville looked sideways at her, his head tilted, his thick black lashes lowered a fraction over those very dark blue eyes. His Aunt Enid spoke to him and he started to turn away, but paused, staring at the table in front of her. Hattie looked, too, and realized her wounded hands had caught his attention. Quickly she put them in her lap. When she'd told Mrs. Dobbin she intended to keep her gloves on all evening, including during dinner, that lady had all but swooned. Hattie must, Dobbin told her, remove her gloves at table and simply be careful not to show her palms. Dobbin, who had surprised Hattie with the depth of her distress, told her she could even manage to rest a hand on the table if she did so carefully.

A veal and vegetable pie tasted good, as did the curry of rabbits and muffin pudding that followed. They might have tasted even better if Hattie hadn't been constantly aware of Lord Granville's dark attention. Lord Blackburn smiled at her with open interest, but she didn't feel threatened by him.

Once more she glanced at Lord Granville. There was nothing open in the way he looked back at her. That was it, the difference between the two brothers. She'd met many men who played the accepted game of looking for entertainment among married women. They were obvious. If Lord Granville wanted something from her, it wasn't the dalliance Mr. Leggit hinted at.

"Aren't you in the foreign service, Blackburn?" Mr. Leggit said.

Lord Blackburn looked around as if to make sure Mr.

Leggit spoke to him and said, "Actually, no. I am in an occupation one doesn't talk about in polite circles."

Mr. Leggit guffawed some more, shooting muffin crumbs from his mouth, and said, "Something to do with ladies, is it?"

Hattie shrank back in her chair, ashamed that these people must think she was like her husband.

Lord Blackburn said with complete seriousness, "Oh, I should be glad to talk about it if I were so fortunate as that. No, my occupation concerns trouble and money."

Hattie paused in the act of putting a piece of rabbit in her mouth.

"You mustn't mind my brother," Lord Granville said. "What he means is that he gets into trouble and it costs money to get him out of it."

Lord Blackburn's grin suggested he enjoyed his reputation.

"I'm in shipping myself," Mr. Leggit said. "Importing and exporting. Very lucrative, I can tell you." He fixed his eyes on Lord Granville. "Many a man has made his fortune with me. I'm a generous fellow. Nothing I like better than to know I've changed a man's fortunes, or made them many times better than they were. For myself, everything I touch turns to money, which is just as well since I have an expensive habit."

He got up from the table and walked around to stand behind Hattie. From his pockets he withdrew a handful of glimmering sovereigns. "My lovely wife likes her frills and furbelows, don't you, sweetest? And whatever Hattie wants, she must have." With that he dropped the money down the front of her dress, ran them like a river of gold between her breasts. "I call her my little magpie, y'know. She loves shiny things, especially money."

Mortified, Hattie tried to catch all the sovereigns against her middle and sat very still.

"Aren't you going to thank me?" Leggit said.

She didn't answer. She might be in his debt and under his power, but she would suffer whatever indignity he heaped upon her at home rather than let these people see her grovel.

"Well," Mr. Leggit said. "In that case perhaps I should take them back."

Hattie clutched the front of her dress to her.

"Disgraceful," Aunt Enid muttered. "So common."

"I don't advise you to try it," Lord Granville said, getting to his feet. Mr. Leggit wasn't a short man, but his lordship made his guest appear soft and pathetic.

"Telling me what to do with my own wife? I say, that's rich. Like me!" He found himself so funny he had to stumble back and flop into his chair. His expression cleared and he looked up and around the table. He wiped his mouth. "Good heavens. What can have come over me? I've been pressed by a great many responsibilities lately. Forgive my regrettable behavior. Most sorry, most sorry," he finished in a mutter.

Lord Blackburn pushed his chair back and crossed his legs. For once he didn't look amused.

"It's your wife to whom you should apologize, sir," Lord Granville said. "You are a fortunate man to be married to one so demure and considerate of her husband."

"Can't think what came over me," Mr. Leggit muttered again.

All Hattie could think of was the sovereigns she must somehow remove from inside her clothes without making a cake of herself.

Boggs, standing at one end of a great ebony sideboard, inclined his head to hear what a maid had to tell him. He

then left the room, to return very quickly and go to Mr. Leggit. He spoke low and Hattie couldn't hear.

Mr. Leggit shot to his feet. "Oh, my, this is a disaster. Oh, my dear people, I must throw myself on your mercy and ask you to help me. Something has come up which needs my immediate attention. I must leave at once."

Hattie made to push her chair back, but Lord Granville stopped her with a hand on the back of hers.

"I'm hopeful this will not take long," Mr. Leggit said. "But my coachman will not have time to drop Mrs. Leggit at home before driving on to my destination. I must ask if it might be possible for Mrs. Leggit to remain here until I can return for her."

Hattie stood up straight and the coins cascaded to the floor. Again Lord Granville stopped her from following instinct. He restrained her from bending to pick up the money and did so himself. This he put on the table in front of her.

She felt him staring at her and glanced his way again. His lordship's close attention was on her left hand where the palm showed again, together with deep puncture wounds still ugly and scabbed. Hattie turned her hand over.

"That nice Albert Parker who drives you now, John," Enid said. "Surely he would take Mrs. Leggit home."

"Kind of you to offer," Mr. Leggit said. "But I really would prefer her to wait for me here, where I know she will be safe."

Lord Granville waved Mr. Leggit on. "Please go about your business. We men know how it is when duty calls. Fear not, we shall take care of Mrs. Leggit."

What Hattie felt defied description. She believed this had been her husband's plan all along, to deliberately leave her at Worth House where he expected her to be-

guile the marquis and keep him seeking out the Leggits' company.

"Mrs. Leggit," her husband said, already leaving the dining room. "I am leaving you in Granville's care. Be certain you do nothing to displease him."

9

As John had expected, shortly after he and Nathan accompanied the ladies to a parlor at the foot of the staircase, the aunts excused themselves and went to their rooms. They said they were tired but seemed in a state of high excitement.

Left alone with two men she hardly knew, Hattie Leggit wouldn't sit. "Please just go about your business. You must have catching up to do. If you don't immediately need this room, I'll wait here for Mr. Leggit."

John had the thought that Leggit was even more of a bounder than expected. What possible reason could there be for the man to insist his wife remain among strangers until his return?

"I would gladly drive you home, Mrs. Leggit," Nathan said, and John believed his brother only intended to be helpful.

A film of dewy moisture shone on Hattie's skin and she trembled visibly. "You are kind. But Mr. Leggit prefers me to follow his instructions. I wouldn't want to displease him. Unless it is too inconvenient for me to stay."

John felt like asking what Leggit would do if she did displease him. "You are entirely welcome and we'd like you to sit down over there." He indicated a comfortable, overstuffed chintz chair pulled close to the fire. "No matter how pleasant the days, this old house has thick walls

and doesn't warm easily. We need our fires in the evening. Isn't that true, Nathan?''

"True." Nathan frowned at John. "Should you like a cup of chocolate, Mrs. Leggit? John and I are experts and make a fine pot.''

Hattie Leggit shook her head. But she sat in the chair John had suggested. "I could wait in the foyer," she said. "I saw a chair there and I am horrified to take up your time this way.''

"You will not sit in the foyer," John announced. "Nathan, do you think the ballroom would interest Mrs. Leggit? I could show it to her to pass the time, and the aunts' miniature collection perhaps, and their shells. I could show her the house, or as much of it as there's time for before Mr. Leggit returns.''

Nathan stood behind Hattie's chair. His brows shot up almost to his hairline. "I should think that might be entertaining," he said. "I have reading to do and I can bring it down here. When your husband comes, Mrs. Leggit, I shall tell him where you are." The look he gave John was far too knowing. If he did know what John intended, he might try to stop him.

"Should you like that, Mrs. Leggit?" John said, his heart beating a little faster in anticipation of her refusal.

She regarded him speculatively before standing up with her hands too tightly entwined in the strings of her reticule. "Why not? If you're sure you have the time I should love to see Worth House.''

Nathan studied the ceiling.

John offered Hattie Leggit his arm. Wearing gloves once more, she slipped a hand on his wrist and they left the parlor.

He paused in the foyer. "Chloe's in the nurseries and probably asleep or I would show you the doll house that

was made for my mother and her sisters. It's perfect in every way. But I know what we'll do. There is something more interesting to show you. My grandfather, my mother's father, was a secretive man. He liked to come and go as he wished without anyone being certain if he was here. Let me show you one of the hidden entrances to his rooms. Or are you afraid of a little gloom?'' He smiled down at her.

"I'm afraid of very little," she said and he heard, as he had on one or two other occasions, a hint of cockney in her accent. He found it charming.

"Very well, off we go."

He returned to the salon and took Hattie through a door that led to the adjoining library, his favorite room in the house. In a corner, where inner and outer walls met and heavy green draperies provided a screen, John reached beneath a shelf and pressed an indentation there. An entire bookcase slid straight back, just enough to allow a man to enter. He ushered Hattie ahead of him and, when they were inside, sent the bookcase sliding forward and into place once more.

"Oh," was all she said.

John lit one of the candles left there for the purpose and pocketed a second one. This was no moldy, earthen tunnel. The walls were paneled and jewel-toned mosaics covered the floors. He walked ahead of her until the passageway began to narrow and their shadows flickered to meet overhead.

"It seems silly," she said in a small voice. "Everyone must know about that entrance."

"I assure you everyone doesn't. But that's only one way in. There's one from the uppermost hallway in the house. That's the entrance everyone knows about. On another occasion I'll show you how to enter from the outside

without being seen. You have to be more cautious with that one.''

''Perhaps we should go back.''

''We have to go on. That bookcase doesn't open from this side.''

He measured her reaction and heard her swallow. He offered her his hand and she took it. They climbed one flight of stairs, and another, and another. He made her stand still and catch her breath.

Before arriving in Bath, he'd assumed he had plenty of time to exact the price he needed from Bernard Leggit. Now he felt a sense of haste. There was more to Leggit than met the eye. Why would he leave his wife here, knowing she could be alone in the company of men? Certainly she was a married woman, but if Leggit was as possessive as he seemed to be, what could he have in mind?

Hattie continued up the stairs and John admired her courage. She could not have anticipated this situation and he'd felt her anxiety, but she put up a brave front.

''That,'' he told Hattie, pointing into a shadowy alcove, ''leads to a flight of steps down to a door at the side of the house.''

''And all of this is just to be mysterious about a suite of rooms? How strange.''

Strange, yes, and it could become very useful in the days to come. All he needed to do was win the lady's affections and plan the perfect time to lie with her. He would not waste tonight's opportunity to get closer to his goal.

''This is where we enter.'' He took a key from his pocket to unlock the door they'd reached. It slid open and he guided Hattie into what had been a beautiful ballroom, and could still be beautiful if there were ever any need to make it so.

"I thought you said you'd changed your mind and we weren't coming to the ballroom." Hattie removed her hand from his.

"I didn't make myself clear. I meant we would come here by a different way."

"And your grandfather's rooms? Where are they?"

John gestured vaguely. "On this same floor."

She gave him an uncertain look. "How odd. And a ballroom at the very top of the house seems unusual. Why does it feel so abandoned?"

"Because it is." He went about lighting a few of the wall sconces and gradually the room came to life. Striding around, John tugged sheets away from royal-blue velvet chairs and couches and threw them aside. Dust-covered wall mirrors reflected a ghostly scene. "That's where the orchestra played," he said, pointing to a low gallery with gold balustrades at one end of the room. "You see the dance floor? Very grand. I saw it as a child when my parents visited and there were still balls here. The mirrors would reflect the scene, the whirling of the gowns and the fine dress of gentlemen, many of them military. The aunts have no reason to keep it up, of course. Do you know how to waltz?"

She shook her head fiercely. "Of course not. Whatever next?"

"I wager you'd learn easily."

"The waltz isn't considered appropriate."

"The Prince Regent dances it all the time and so do a great many people. I'm very fond of it myself, not that I often have time for such things. Never mind. I'll teach you another time, perhaps."

He returned to her side. Waltzing with Hattie Leggit? Now there was a thought. "Can't you imagine what all this used to be like?"

"Oh, yes. I can see it clearly."

Her soft smile didn't help his self-control. "Come along then. I'll show you what else is up here."

"Why would your grandfather have a secret door to a ballroom?"

"I told you he loved mystery. Perhaps he also enjoyed impressing the occasional visitor. I admit I hoped to intrigue you by bringing you this way."

He led her into a room beneath the floor of the musicians' gallery. A pile of dusty chairs and some music stands looked forlorn there. "Now, you may be certain that this is absolutely secret. Passed on from grandfather to son-in-law. My mother's parents had no sons and this sort of thing was hardly appropriate to reveal to ladies."

What a damnably stupid thing to say.

"I mean—"

"I know what you mean," Hattie said with a thin smile. "I've met a few ladies who really were ladies. Then I've met more than a few who were called ladies." She stood her ground and looked him straight in the eye. "What a shame that the privileged are often quite false."

"I assure you, Mrs. Leggit, that I was thinking about my sheltered spinster aunts and my unworldly mother."

"Yes, I know. You weren't talking about common women. Thank you for bringing me to see all this. I find it an engaging distraction."

There were sensible instructions on what to do about impossible situations. John decided he'd follow the most obvious one and stop trying to dig himself out of his own faux pas.

A faint smile looked pretty on Hattie's mouth, but there was steel in her gray eyes.

He decided to press on. "My father told me about the hidden way. No one else knows, except my brothers."

"Then why are you showing me?" she asked.

Prepared for her to slap him, he put his lips to her ear and whispered, "Because I want to impress you. And because you will not betray me since that would only tell the world you were here with me and compromise your reputation."

She didn't slap him.

Lord Granville thought she was like many married women in his own set, pretending to be faithful wives while they entertained other men. And he felt even bolder with her than he might with another because he didn't consider her a lady at all. He'd told her so.

"Mrs. Leggit?" His lordship appeared amused by her silence. "I should love to know what you're thinking."

Hattie swung her gold reticule and peered around the dismal room. "I must say I'm disappointed. After all you said, I expected much more than a dirty ballroom and this storage hole."

He turned from her abruptly, but not before she saw his jaw stiffen with irritation. "We have just begun, madam. We'll see how long you remain unimpressed."

Another door, as clearly visible as the one they'd just used, led to a musty space filled with some sort of props, obviously for plays. A rack of costumes, dingy but covered with decorations that sparkled in the candlelight, took up a good deal of room. His lordship closed them in again and went to a large mirror on one wall.

Coming here with him had been foolish, dangerous.

"See this," he told her, and gave the mirror a push.

Hattie heard a click and watched a black space appear where the mirror had been. "In we go," Lord Granville said curtly. His manner was completely changed.

She gritted her teeth and followed him again.

The mirror slid back into place, Lord Granville held his

candle aloft and pressed yet another spot in another wall to reveal another opening. This time he bowed and waved her ahead of him.

Hattie thought of the fearsome events she'd lived through and walked on. She'd survived ugly things before and if this was to be ugly, well, she'd survive again. The place she stepped into was barely wide enough for one person.

"Go to your left and out," Lord Granville said.

Taunting him about the silliness of his secret had not been wise. Hattie turned left and walked between a wall papered deep green and one that was of smooth ebony. At the end of the narrow passageway, she pushed aside a heavy green drapery edged with gold tassels and stepped into flickering candlelight.

Lord Granville followed her and she had to move or have him collide with her.

Slowly Hattie advanced into a room where many candles sent lights leaping over a fresco painted on the lofty ceiling. Ladies with exposed breasts and very round tummies lounged beneath blue skies.

A fire burned brightly in a white marble fireplace.

Hattie swung around and saw where the little passage was located: behind a huge, elaborately carved ebony bed.

"What do you think?" Lord Granville asked. He stood with his hands on his hips, his long, strong legs braced apart, and a satisfied grin on his face.

"I think I should go back to the parlor. Mr. Leggit will be looking for me."

"If he were, my brother would have come to find you."

"Yes, but I'd like to go now."

"You haven't seen everything, yet," Lord Granville said. "And you haven't told me what you think of this room."

"Overwhelming." She had been such a ninny, so gul-

lible. Mr. Leggit had played right into this man's hands and no good would come of it. The marquis had only been looking for a means to get her away, alone. "Overwhelming in a grand way, of course. Your grandfather's bedchamber, and the servants light candles and keep a fire burning. How charming. He must have been loved a lot."

"He was. He was indeed." Lord Granville's chuckle didn't warm Hattie's heart. "My man Parker sees to the candles and so on these days. Now that this is my bedchamber."

Did he think she hadn't guessed this was where he slept? His condescending behavior infuriated her. "It is?" she said with wide eyes, and surprise in her voice. "Oh, my." She drew her shoulders up and giggled.

Apart from her dad she'd never met a man who didn't want something from her. She attempted a coquettish glance at Lord Granville and, from the flaring of his nostrils, decided she'd done quite well. She would learn to flirt yet and, as long as she kept her wits about her, come to no serious harm.

"I like this place," she told him, swaying a little and smoothing her gown over her hips. "Let's see what's in here."

She trotted through an archway into a very manly room lined with books and furnished with brown leather furniture worn shiny by age. A large desk took up a good deal of space.

At last she had a plan, a daring plan. It had come to her so quickly, her mind tumbled and more pieces fell into place by the second.

She knew what Mr. Leggit wanted. And what he didn't want.

She knew what Lord Granville did want. And what was the last thing he'd ever want.

She knew what she needed.

10

"**I** would like to make you a proposition."

That, John thought, was not what he'd expected Hattie Leggit to say next. There were times when it was best to be silent. This was one of them.

She fidgeted with the reticule, which must be heavy, given the number of sovereigns it contained. Rather than appearing out of place among his grandfather's big leather furniture, she became the perfect ornamental addition. A pretty picture she made in her soft, revealing gown.

"You're staring at me."

He shrugged faintly, and smiled at her. "Yes, I am."

Hattie Leggit turned her back on him but not before he saw the start of her own smile. "Why are you staring?" she said.

"You really don't know?"

"Perhaps I do." She reached back to check the hair at her nape.

Mmm. He was not himself with this one. The things he noticed and dwelled upon unsettled him. Her pale, uplifted arm, the angle of her slim neck, the way the arm, when her short sleeve fell back, showed shallow tracings of feminine muscle and swept into the soft, exposed side of a breast.

"Oh—" she swung around "—oh, *dingdong bell.*" She blushed brilliantly.

"Dingdong bell?" John said, puzzled.

"Forgive me," Hattie said. "I'm beside myself with all this and it just, sort of, came out of my mouth. Look, there's something I'd like to discuss with you."

That would be her *proposition*. A man could hope she might mean the kind of thing he'd mean if he said that word to a woman in certain circumstances. "First, my curiosity forces me to ask what the, er, other meant? Just so that I may know how to react if you should say it again."

"I won't. Now—"

"You might if you became beside yourself again."

"Oh, *hell*. That's what it means. There, now are you satisfied?"

John remembered to close his mouth.

"You have already reminded me I'm no lady. I don't suppose you thought I could be a cockney though, did you? We rhyme things, that's all and I haven't done it for ever so long. It's because you've agitated me."

"Me?" He flattened a hand over his heart. "I have tried only to entertain you."

"That's not true. You have some other motive for trying to shock me. I don't know what it could be unless you're nothing more than a bounder looking to take advantage of me, or a cruel one who likes to frighten women."

"You judge me harshly, madam."

Hattie Leggit tapped the toe of a silk shoe. "At any moment Mr. Leggit is certain to return so I must *throw* myself on your mercy. And quickly."

He was tempted to tell her she might throw herself on any part of him she chose. "I'm listening."

"First, do you intend me any harm, my lord, or is it just natural for you to toy with women?"

"No, to both." That wasn't a complete lie.

"Very well. I shall believe you because I have no choice."

"Kind of you."

"Yes," she said. "Well, I've always been considered kind and I usually am—unless I'm pushed, and I'm being pushed. But what I'm going to ask you isn't easy for me. You will refuse if you don't want to do it, won't you?"

He would wring her lovely neck if she didn't get to the point. "I would suggest further discussion if I felt your aim unwise."

"Yes—well, it's not. There are things I cannot tell you, at least not yet. You do understand?"

"Why would you be able to tell me things later if you can't tell them to me now?"

"I don't know you well enough yet."

The suggestion being that they might come to know each other a great deal better? They would if he had his way. He only wished his reasons were different, but Francis and Simonne must be avenged. He would not be with this woman otherwise. "I will be patient," he said. A lie of the highest order this time, but a necessary one for now.

"I am in the most terrible pickle," Hattie Leggit said, and the cut of her chin lost its saucy thrust.

One surprise after another. "Don't say so. You couldn't be in a pickle if you tried."

Her somber expression warned him not to make too light of her words.

"This is horrible." She frowned and he saw her swallow—but she didn't resort to the tears so many women used to gain sympathy. "I can't say too much, I really can't, but if I'm not nice to you, Mr. Leggit will be angry with me."

"I beg your pardon?"

"I have to be nice to you and make you want to... to...be nice to Mr. Leggit."

John put his hands in his trouser pockets and rolled from heel to toe. "You should probably explain that more clearly." He concentrated on her changing expressions.

"Mr. Leggit wants you to like him." Her frown deepened. "I have a complicated life, my lord."

More complicated than he could ever have guessed apparently. He would soothe her and get to the bottom of this. "Dear Mrs. Leggit, I don't usually share so many secrets with others, in fact I never do. I should say you're the first person I've felt I wanted to know any of the things I've held to myself. Formerly, that is."

Hell's teeth, he sounded like a blithering idiot. "You see the brass box by the door? That door leads to the hallway inside the house, by the way, so you have no reason to think yourself lost and alone with a stranger."

"Oh, I don't! Not at all. My dad taught me what to do...that's not important. Thank you for reassuring me. You were talking about the brass box, the one with the numbers and little things on it."

"Yes, well, those are nothing more complicated than a similar contraption one sees in kitchens." When she least expected it, he would revisit whatever her parent had taught her. "If I want it to, this one alerts me to certain things. For instance, when someone comes to the front door. My grandfather, as you have already discovered, loved secrets. He also loved to make sure others didn't have any he might enjoy—or need to know about."

"I'm not sure I would have liked him much," Hattie said.

John opened a grill on the side of the box. "Be grateful to him now, because we shall know when someone comes

to the house, and the only likely candidate this evening is your husband.''

She didn't look convinced, but her shoulders did fall almost to their normal position.

''So perhaps you could finish proposing.... Tell me what's troubling you. In detail.''

She surprised him by backing into one of the chairs and flopping down. ''Please may I behave in a flirtatious manner with you? Whenever there's no one else to see it? Other than the two of us, or Mr. Leggit, of course.''

Leggit must be more twisted than even John had imagined. He paced the width of the room while he considered how to use this turn of events to his advantage.

He paused, then advanced until the toes of his boots were only inches from Hattie's silk shoes. ''And you ask this because your husband wants me to like him?''

''Yes,'' she muttered.

''Why?''

''Connections.''

He shook his head.

''I have not handled this well. I wasn't supposed to reveal my husband's motives, but how else can I accomplish what doesn't come naturally? I hope you will guard my indiscretions.''

''What exactly is it that doesn't come naturally?'' John asked.

Hattie's face tightened. ''Don't pretend you don't know. I have no experience in encouraging men's attentions. Mr. Leggit wants you to include him in your circle because he thinks it would be advantageous to him. In business. And because it would make him feel even more important.''

He would, John thought, make sure Leggit became the center of attention, but not in the manner he sought. John

said, "You said *other than the two of us,* or Mr. Leggit?
Your mission is to use your charms to ensnare my attention?"

"That's true."

"And I am to allow myself to be manipulated, and to
welcome being made to look the fool in front of your
husband?"

"Yes—" Her discomfort didn't bring him any pleasure. "No. I don't think he wants you to look foolish. He
just wants what he wants."

But Leggit didn't want anyone else to know about it.
In other words, John thought, his original plan only got
better. Leggit's ego was his most vulnerable point. He
longed for recognition, evidently among the ton, and to
use those associations if he got them. The possibility for
this man's total public destruction grew more real.

"Do you love your husband?"

She raised misery-laden eyes. "Those intimate things
shouldn't be discussed."

"They shouldn't, but you owe me something in return
for my cooperation."

"I have little to offer."

So she thought! "Answer the question."

"I'll not beg you to spare me these indignities. The
answer is, no, I do not love him, but it isn't the way you
think. I did not marry Mr. Leggit because I wanted his
fortune. I had to marry him."

"Why?" If he could achieve his ends without damag-
ing her too much, he would—if her story proved true.
Regardless of her protests, she had married the man and
accepted a life of comfort in return. A fresh idea took him
by surprise. "How long have you been married?"

"Just more than a year."

"How old is your child?"

Hattie stared at him. "I have no children." She moistened her lips and spread a hand over her flushed décolletage. "I have never mentioned any and neither has Mr. Leggit. Why should you asked such a thing?"

"I was looking for a reason why you might have had to marry the man."

She stood up and put her hands on her hips. "You think because my beginnings were humble, I'm a trollop? You're despicable."

"But you want to entrap me anyway. You are not a trollop, you say, yet you would play the inviting lovebird with me while you are married to someone else. Didn't I hear you judge women who do such things?"

"I've just thought of something," Hattie said. "We need not have anything at all to do with each other except in Mr. Leggit's presence. And you could perfectly well rebuff me. After all, that wouldn't be *my* fault, would it?"

It wouldn't be her fault, but neither would it happen. The idea of Leggit helping make a complete fool of himself was almost too good to be true. "Forgive me for being harsh with you," John said. "I had to make sure there didn't seem to be a more devious reason for this outlandish suggestion."

She tossed her head and stared at him sideways. "You have been quick enough to make advances to me."

"I haven't touched you. And if you want me to help you, I suggest you manage more respect. I also expect your advances to be convincing."

"*My* advances? You will be doing the advancing. Do it tonight as soon as Mr. Leggit comes and let's have the whole thing over…oh, no, I have it all wrong, don't I? This is terrible. *I* must advance on you, mustn't I? So you can rebuff me and be done with it."

A bell tinkled.

"Mr. Leggit!" Hattie's stricken face stopped John from teasing her for the moment. "What shall I do? How shall I do it?"

"It's not the front door." John decided the lady toyed with him, at least to some degree. He was certain he had caught her looking at him with interest, and not, he thought, because she was impressed by the cut of his clothes.

To demonstrate that he told the truth about the bell they'd heard, the door to the study opened, inch by inch, spreading a pale wedge of light from the hallway.

The first part of the intruder to appear was a small foot beneath the hem of a white nightgown. Chloe's auburn hair, loose and mussed from her pillow, came next, followed by the rest of her face.

John hurried to her and caught her up into his arms. The tears that poured silently from her eyes soaked his collar. "Chloe, it's all right, my pet. I'm sure you've had a bad dream, but Uncle John has you now." He held her tight and rocked her from side to side. "You are very brave, you know, finding your way all the way from the nurseries to my rooms."

Chloe's English was not good. If she answered it would as likely be in French and he doubted Hattie would understand more than the odd word. He glanced at her past Chloe's cheek and saw how worried she seemed. The woman was intelligent. No doubt she would learn anything she chose to learn with little difficulty.

"What shall I do with you?" he said to Chloe. "Take you back to your bed, I suppose. Not that I don't like it when you hug me so."

She did indeed hug him so. Her thin arms were surprisingly strong. His heart turned with wanting to take away her pain. He had insisted on leaving France aboard

that damnable boat just to save himself the inconvenience of dealing with an opportunistic woman who considered herself scorned. And with that, he'd cost the lives of his cousin and his wife and ruined this little one's childhood.

"Hush, hush," he crooned to her. "I shall always look after you." Of that there would never be any doubt. Regardless of what turns his own life took, Chloe would be provided for and given every comfort. He would find a way to help heal her broken heart and take away the fear that kept her silent.

Where, Hattie wondered, were Chloe's parents? And why should the marquis be the one responsible for her. She watched him with the child and her heart softened toward him. As he was now, she saw not only his exterior, the handsome, confident man he was for all the world to see, but the gentleness inside him. Chloe's heaving back shuddered and gradually calmed, but she didn't let go of her uncle John.

Another jangle from one of the bells and a tap at the door gave a moment's warning of a new visitor, this one a diminutive woman wearing one of the ugliest night rails and robes Hattie had ever seen.

Made of brown flannel splotched with badly embroidered turquoise flowers, the garments completely hid the woman's form, if not her profusion of black hair. If the garments were meant to disguise how lovely she was—in a wild way—they failed.

Shining dark eyes flickered from the marquis to Hattie, but although the woman would be drawing her own conclusions, she didn't cast any knowing glances.

She nodded to Hattie and said, "Mr. Elliot, I mean, *my lord*. Fancy you leading me on like that, pretendin' you was ordinary like Albert and me. I should 'ave followed

me instincts. When you took your clothes off and I 'ad a good look at 'em I could tell they was quality.''

Hattie enjoyed the uncomfortable puckering of the marquis's forehead. ''You asked my name and I gave it. John Elliot is my name. I saw no point in mentioning the other. What are you doing here, Snowdrop?''

Snowdrop? So this was the way his lordship treated women he no longer desired. Hattie doubted the Marquis of Granville had been so brusque when he was undressing in front of dramatic-looking *Snowdrop.*

Rubbing Chloe's back, the new arrival spoke firmly. ''I had to come and make sure my Albert was settled in and giving his best to this fine opportunity. I thank you for that. And I thank you for agreeing to let me help Mrs. Gimblet with this young maid.''

''I didn't agree.''

Snowdrop laughed. ''I don't suppose you'd want to say that to all the fancy people what you told how Albert wrote letters to offer me employment.''

''I haven't the time to discuss this now. As I told you earlier, we'll speak in the morning. Did you find Albert?''

Her nose scrunched up with scorn. ''What do you think? Mr. Boggs—he's got quick 'ands, that one—he took me to Albert straight away. That's how I knew where your rooms were, with Albert just down the 'all from you. Not that I saw inside 'ere till Miss Chloe decided to pop out of bed and take a walk. Come along, sweet thing, Snowdrop will take you back to the nursery.''

Hattie felt like an intruder.

''Where has Albert put you for the night?'' the marquis asked, and his face was the autocratic, rather frightening one Hattie had already seen a number of times.

''What do you think? In his room? Well, you're wrong. We aren't married. We aren't even officially engaged al-

though that might happen now. I'm in the nurseries with Chloe, just the way you said I should be, and I like it there. Mrs. Gimblet and I will take the best care of her.''

With that, Snowdrop, who was surprisingly strong, pried Chloe loose from his lordship and carried her. ''I'm going to get you some warm milk, little one. Snowdrop's warm milk is famous for relaxing upset little people. Then I'm going to climb in bed with you and tell you a story until you go to sleep.''

''A good idea,'' the marquis said. ''Much as I enjoy Chloe's company.''

Hattie met Snowdrop's eyes and received a large wink before she slipped out with Chloe.

As soon as they were gone, the marquis locked the door. ''Kindly don't look as if I am about to ravish you. We may not have much more time and should complete our business rapidly. Do as I say. Stand beside me as if we were about to descend the stairs into the foyer. Put your hand on the back of my wrist as if we're on very formal terms.''

''We are,'' Hattie said darkly.

John thought her priceless. ''Indeed. Now tilt your head away from me a little—no, too *much*. Concentrate. I said, *a little*. That's right. Now bow your head slightly. Good. Look sideways and up at me. And lower your lashes while you smile just the smallest smile.''

She tried to follow instructions but with ridiculous results. ''No, Mrs. Leggit. *No*. Keep breathing, and move your face. You are trying to entice me, not dying of a broken neck.''

''I can't—''

''Do it now.''

Hattie straightened up, took in a deep breath, blew it out and tried again.

John relaxed. "You've got it. Perfect! That's all you have to do. Mr. Leggit will be watching us and I assure you he will be pleased."

"Oh, thank you, thank you. How can I ever repay you?"

Shall I tell you the ways? "I do believe I'll give you another simple lesson in these things, just in case you ever need it."

Her trusting attention should shame him. It didn't.

John took hold of her arm. While she struggled against him, he unbuttoned her long glove and worked it off carefully. "Please don't resist, Hattie. May I call you Hattie?"

"Mr. Leggit wouldn't like it."

"As long as Mr. Leggit isn't with us?"

She still tried to withdraw her wrist from his grasp. "We aren't likely to be alone again."

John uncurled her fingers from her palm and took a good look at the wounds he'd already noticed. "These were deep," he said.

"They're nothing. I was careless with something."

"Something like a bouquet of roses, perhaps?"

She stopped struggling but wouldn't meet his eyes.

"Yellow roses given to you by a man who should know better than to send a married woman home with a token of his esteem."

"You were being kind. I held them too tightly, nothing more. And my skin is healing."

"Bastard," he said, not as much under his breath as he'd intended. "Your husband did this, didn't he? He was angry about the roses so he somehow made you squeeze the stems until you were hurt. Not difficult for someone bigger and stronger than his victim."

"You are wrong," she said staunchly.

He was right. Of that he had no doubt.

"Look at me, Hattie," he coaxed her. "I enjoy seeing your face, particularly so close." Leggit's manhandling of his wife was an added incentive to make the man suffer.

She did look at him and his chest tightened. He ran his gaze from her soft eyes to her moist mouth, to the quick rise and fall of her bosom, and downward. The result was that a great deal more than his chest tightened.

"You said you would like to do something for me." He couldn't smile at her, or do anything to stop the sexual rush he got.

"I did." Her lips parted and the tip of her tongue traced the tender flesh that met her teeth.

He released her arm and put a hand on her shoulder, between the flimsy cap sleeve of her dress and the diamond necklace she wore. And he waited for her to protest. Not only didn't she protest, but she stood as if both rooted and mesmerized.

With both hands holding her head, he brought his mouth to hers, settled it there and shared her breath while the air around him took on its own faint sounds. John opened his mouth, but she turned her head at once and he brushed his lips across her cheek instead. He felt the stiffness in her body. She held back parts of herself but, nevertheless, she didn't move away from him.

John raised his head and waited for her to look at him again. When she did, fear hovered in her eyes, but she raised her hands to his shoulders and would have rested her face on his chest if he hadn't stopped her. She wanted him to comfort her, to turn the moment into something innocent.

He urged her chin up and played a thumb over her mouth.

Hattie looked at him with a troubled expression but, as if experimenting, she touched her tongue to his thumb.

This time it was he who trembled. He wanted her. Not just her kisses, but all of her. Evidence of his arousal grew. He pulled her closer and held her against the ridge in his trousers.

The chiffon dress was no shield. If he'd doubted she felt the power of his reaction to her, the heightened color in her cheeks, the catch in her breath, proved him wrong.

If he didn't stop, he would take her now, here on the carpet and, from the excitement that made her tremble, he could only imagine the wild passion of their lovemaking.

He couldn't give in to his own weakness, or hers. Not yet.

Easing himself to stand straight, he looked into her eyes. The black pupils had dilated to obscure the gray. Very deliberately, John decided to take one more pleasure for himself. Softly he caressed the fullness of her breasts above the neckline of her gown. Hattie gasped and closed her eyes.

When he spread his fingers, her flesh filled his hands.

One more small liberty.

He bent to run his tongue over the top of each breast and his knees weakened. Hattie clutched at his coat and held on tightly. He felt shudders chase through her body.

Somehow her nipples were exposed and stiffly budded. How could he deny them the pleasure of taking them, one then the other, into his mouth and playing his tongue over the tips, sucking her in deeper, replacing his mouth with tugging fingertips and watching her cry out and sag against him.

The damnable bell rang again.

Hattie's expression cleared slowly, then turned to panic.

"That will be Mr. Leggit," John told her. "Do you remember exactly what I told you to do?"

She leaned against him and he stroked her back and

shoulders. For a moment he gave himself permission to put an arm around her and hold her close, his hand cupped beneath a breast.

She seemed unusually passive. "Hattie, do you remember?"

"Yes," she whispered. "I remember everything."

He didn't analyze what she might mean by that. After straightening his jacket and adjusting his neckcloth, he gave her a critical look and decided there was no sign of what had just transpired between them.

She glanced down and pulled the bodice of her gown a little higher.

John threw open the door and offered her his arm.

Boggs met them on their way downstairs and announced Mr. Leggit. Boggs didn't attempt to hide his avid curiosity.

"Thank you," John told the man, and carried on down with Hattie. The several flights took a few minutes, but when they reached the top of the stairs that led to the foyer, he paused with Hattie at his side.

Leggit stood at the bottom looking remarkably unruffled and relaxed for a man who had rushed off to deal with desperate matters.

"I hope all went well for you, Leggit," John said.

"Very well, thank you, Granville. Very well indeed."

"Things have gone very well here, too. I shall return your charming wife to your protection."

"Now," he instructed Hattie quietly.

She inclined and ducked her head, peeked up at him from beneath lowered lids as if she had flirted with many gentlemen in just that way. For all he knew, she had. That was not the point now.

This was his moment to rebuff her.

With a smile that suggested he'd forgotten there was anyone else in the world but Hattie Leggit and himself, he raised her gloved hand, bent over it and settled a long, long kiss there.

11

The sound of whistling annoyed John. Always had... hadn't it?

Albert Parker whistled. Usually when he felt particularly cheerful, which seemed to be the case this morning.

"I have a headache," John informed him.

"That's a terrible thing, me lord," Albert said in that loud voice of his, and whistled afresh.

"You do know you were wrong to write to Snowdrop and offer her employment here, don't you?"

Albert paused in the act of brushing the coat John intended to wear and raised his eyebrows. He pushed his spectacles firmly up the narrow bridge of his nose and cleared his throat. "Not to argue with you, m'lord, but I didn't write to Snowdrop and offer employment. You only said I did because you needed to explain her unexpected arrival without letting on that you're up to other things."

"Thank you, Albert," John snapped. "How nice of you to remind me. The perfect gentleman's gentleman—and man of letters, although it's unusual to mix the two—but someone practiced in your position would willingly accept responsibility for anything that annoyed his employer."

"Fancy that," Albert said. "I'll write that down somewhere and look at it when I'm practiced, then." He returned to whistling and brushing John's black coat. Black fitted his mood today.

"Dash it all," John said in a low voice, "of course I made up that poppycock about you sending a letter to Snowdrop about employment here. There, I've said it and it's forgotten."

"As you wish, m'lord," Albert said, amazingly without a hint of derision in his tone or any amusement on his face.

"Do you know who Beau Brummel is?" John asked, standing before a mirror atop the washstand in his dressing room. He took Albert's silence to mean that the man didn't know. "Well, I don't have time to tell you his whole life story. A complete dandy. One of the bow window set at White's. That's a gentlemen's club in London. I have a membership there, myself. Rarely have cause to use it."

"Ah." Albert's sage but completely disinterested response stirred John's innards even more.

"Yes, well, anyway, the man managed to convince society that he was of the first stare when it came to fashion. The Prince Regent fawned on him. The haut ton still does. And all because he began this damnable habit of starching neckcloths until they crease the moment you touch them, and tying the things with as much attention as a government pays to a war. And I don't give a farthing for all the folderol."

"And what's 'appened to Mr. Brummel now? Still tying 'is fancy neckcloths, is he?" Albert's own simple neckcloth looked smart, dash it all. Nosey Parker learned from example and learned quickly.

"So I understand," John told him, "although he managed to fall from grace with the Regent in '13. Called him Alvanly's fat friend. Big mistake."

"Is there a point to all this, me lord, or should I perhaps pour you a tonic for your nerves?"

Dressed in his shirt, trousers and waistcoat, John rested his fists on his hips. "There is absolutely nothing wrong with my nerves, do you hear me? I'm perfectly calm and in control of myself. And the point is that I am not a man who cares to primp. I detest fiddling with neckcloths, and I don't like being fussed over. You, Albert, have a tendency to fuss. Change that."

"As you say, me lord. Where would you like me to throw this coat?"

John rubbed his face. "No respect," he muttered. "You're supposed to be terrified for your post, but no, you give me lip instead."

"Sorry, m'lord. There's something I have to talk to you about."

Instantly John recalled Hattie Leggit saying, "I want to make you a proposition," in her sweet voice. He glanced at Albert, "Very well, I have a few minutes now. Let me finish here."

A long mirror stood beside a chest of drawers. On top of the chest, a dated white wig still adorned a wooden form. The wig had belonged to John's grandfather, and John kept it because it reminded him of the old man. He glanced at the wig now and wondered how that gentleman would have dealt with Albert.

"Look at me," he said to Albert. "Ten o'clock and I'm still not ready for the day. I am not a man who believes in loafing around."

Since his fingers wouldn't cooperate, John tired of trying to tie his neckcloth. He pulled it off, tossed it aside then left his dressing room for the bedchamber.

Everything that crossed his mind angered him, reminded him that time was his enemy, or dealt him a fierce blow that made him sweat. He could not contend with a

continual flood of reminders about Hattie Leggit. She was a pawn, nothing more. "A *pawn*."

"Beg pardon, me lord," Albert said, emerging from the dressing room. "You were saying?"

"You're a ruffian at heart," John told him, and actually looked with some longing at the great, green-draped bed. It was comfortable and he slept well there. And when he slept he forgot. And if he were there with Hattie Leggit he wouldn't need to forget.

Hell and damnation!

He concentrated on Albert again. "You know you're a ruffian at heart, don't you? You may have fallen into soft digs, but I remember how we met."

"If you say so, m'lord." With a thoughtful expression in his eyes, Albert rolled his sleeves down and fastened the cuffs. He reached for his own coat and shrugged it on.

John waited, fuming without knowing exactly why he clung to his foul mood.

Albert's brushed fair hair, his spectacles and studious air ruffled John. But he didn't know why that was, either. In a few weeks, the man had turned from the roughly dressed leader of a smuggling band into an almost perfectly understated valet. And he wrote an excellent letter, could keep good books, kept John organized, and continued to absorb the niceties of polite society so rapidly he seemed like an ambitious chameleon.

And now there was Snowdrop, that acid-tongued harridan intent on making sure *her* Albert became indispensable while she slipped into Worth House so naturally that everyone would think she'd always been there.

Manipulation.

Interference.

Women!

Which brought him back to Hattie Leggit, only he re-

fused to allow himself to become diverted by that lady again, at least not so soon again.

"How settled are our plans, m'lord?" Albert asked.

"So they're *our* plans now, are they?"

"You'll be glad enough to have me with you, and not just because I can deal with matters you'd rather avoid. Sooner or later you'll want evidence on Leggit and I can round up plenty of people to help us get it. We may have to pay them a shillin' or two for their trouble, but there's plenty as bears that man a grudge."

"If that don't take all," John said. Keeping his voice down took too much effort.

"I'm glad you're pleased," Albert said. "But what I really wanted to talk to you about was the progress I've made putting together, well, I could call it an army. Not a big one, mind you, but a good twenty strong and every one with a score to settle with Leggit. A more blood-thirsty, violent lot you'll never meet. We'll have to study the lay of the land for a bit, but then all you'll have to do is give the word and the enemy disappears—for good."

John propped himself against a bedpost and crossed one booted foot over the other. After a couple of deep breaths, he said, "Before I go completely mad, explain yourself. What on God's earth made you think I wanted you interfering in my plans? An army? *An army?* This is to be a covert action. This is going to be subtle, Albert, an insidious and devilishly designed plan to keep a smile on the enemy's pompous face until he turns around one day and discovers everything he values has crumbled."

"Ah."

Abandoning the bedpost, John paced while Albert's sincere brown eyes regarded him through his shiny lenses.

"No paying people to tell tales about Leggit. I know

all about him. *And no bloody army.* Not a soul, do you understand? You don't tell a single soul.''

''My Snowdrop knows. The others aren't what you'd call society types so they won't be hobnobbing with the snobs.''

The fringed velvet drapes at the windows had been pulled aside and Albert had opened the casements a crack. John went to stand there, looking down over the town spread before him. Even at a distance and through leaded panes that distorted the view, he could see the parade of bath chairs on roads approaching the baths.

''I think you've got company,'' Albert said. ''I don't suppose you heard the bell.''

''No bell rang,'' John said, swinging away from the windows.

''It did, m'lord, but you was shouting at the time.''

''I've got to finish dressing,'' John said. ''Obviously whoever came went away again. Good riddance.''

Albert cleared his throat and jerked his head toward the alcove in the study.

With a sense of doom, John took a look and saw Chloe, looking decidedly primped in pink with a profusion of pink rosettes among freshly made ringlets. Her brow puckered and she blinked as if trying to decide if he had turned into something fearsome.

''Good morning, miss,'' he said, smiling at her.

She didn't smile back, but her features relaxed and she walked hesitantly toward him in her pink satin slippers. A few feet distant, she stopped and looked back. Snowdrop's voice followed a tap. ''Are you decent?''

For Chloe's sake John kept on smiling. ''Do come in, Snowdrop. Everyone else does.''

Snowdrop appeared, miraculously decked out in a gray nanny's uniform with starched white apron and a saucy

white lace concoction on her head. Nothing about her re-assured him.

"Albert Parker," she said, "you shock me. I thought you more a man than to put up with nastiness but, as usual, I'll have to deal with what needs to be dealt with. Now, take Miss Chloe to the desk and draw something for her. She likes that."

Albert's moonling expression suggested he hadn't re-ally heard a word. He stared at his beloved with adoration.

"Albert! Do as I tell you."

"Yes, my love. I will. What was it?"

"I have business with the marquis. Draw something for Chloe. Use the desk."

"Of course, my flower." He bowed to Chloe and ush-ered her toward the desk. When he passed Snowdrop, he said, "Draw? I can't draw."

"You, Albert, can do *anything*. I'm sure there's lovely paper there and I know Chloe loves cats most of all. Draw a picture of Raven."

"I will, me love." He looked back to discover Chloe hadn't moved.

John went to one knee in front of the child and kissed her cheek. He wasn't surprised when her small arms went around his neck and held on tightly.

"Be a good girl, poppet," he told her in French. "Al-bert will draw a picture for you, of your black cat." He dropped his voice to a whisper. "I'm glad you rescued her from the kitchens. Her sensibilities are too tender for such a lowly station."

Chloe patted his face softly, then turned to Albert.

Snowdrop walked about the bedroom for all the world as if it were the most usual thing for her to do. John was close behind and she confronted him, or confronted his shirt buttons. Up she looked, all the way up to his face.

"Sit down," she whispered. "I'm not ruining my neck for you."

"You are above yourself," he told her. "But until I discover I'm wrong in trusting you, I'll humor you—and I'll insist on more appropriate manners in future."

He sat in a chair from India. It had no arms and was covered with heavy brown and gold stuff that resembled carpet.

Snowdrop stood beside him immediately and leaned close to his ear. He did note again, as he had in her cottage, how clean and sweet she smelled. "You are disgraceful," she said. "Without my Albert you'd be dead at the bottom of the sea and so would that dear little girl." At that thought, tears welled in her eyes.

"Please don't cry," he hissed at her. "I will not deal with crying females."

"You will not deal with a woman being a woman, you mean. This is what I have to say to you. I was glad we could help you when you was in a bad way. You could even be a good man and I hope you are. You've done a good thing, bringing Albert to such a fine place and giving him a chance, but that doesn't mean you can speak to him the way I heard you when I come here this morning. You was yellin' so loud you didn't even hear Chloe and me. And don't think it doesn't frighten a little bit of a thing like Chloe when she hears such things."

She paused for breath.

John gave her a moment or two before inquiring, "Finished, are we?"

"You might be. I'm not. I wasn't goin' to mention it but I've decided it's me duty. Mrs. Leggit. I know it was her you had here in your rooms last night. Just the two of you. All on your own. Alone and—"

"You're right. That was Mrs. Leggit and while she was

here in my rooms there was no one else with us. Kindly send Chloe to me and wait for her in the hall.''

"I know a good woman when I sees one. That Mrs. Leggit is a good woman and she isn't an 'appy one. If you hurt that woman on account of you hate her husband, I shall…I shall think of a way to make you wish you 'ad drowned in the Channel.''

Only a few inches separated Snowdrop's face from John's ear. He turned and looked into her black eyes. He stared. He flared his nostrils and turned the corners of his mouth down. And he raised one eyebrow.

Rather than back off, she moved in even closer to say, "Slasher Pick's daughter knows a thing or two, like how to deal with big bullies." She turned on her heel and flounced from the room calling, "Come and see your nice Uncle John, Chloe. You, Albert, out in the 'all if you please.''

Chloe entered the bedroom.

The blasted bell rang.

John heard Nathan speak with Albert and Snowdrop as they were leaving, then he arrived before John wearing a black silk robe that reached his feet—which were bare.

"What the blazes are you doing dressed like that at this time of day?" John said.

Nathan pointed to Chloe and put a finger to his lips. Next he made expansive motions as if he were pushing down air on either side of him, or imitating bat flight.

John narrowed his eyes. "Right," he said in a low voice. "Understood. Nothing else to worry about. Now sit over there and don't say a word. I must speak with Chloe and *you*, Nathan, will say nothing. You'll get your turn later—unless you say something out of turn, in which

case you will be dead and unable to say anything else at all.''

Rolling his green eyes, Nathan leaped on the bed and settled on his stomach, his jaw propped on his hands, facing John and Chloe.

''Comfortable?'' John said.

''I could use a cognac.''

John ignored him and spoke in French again. ''Chloe, are you ready to talk to me now?''

Her silence was broken by Nathan saying, ''Don't blame you for not talking to him, Chloe. I don't if I can help it.''

''Please be quiet,'' John said, gritting his teeth. ''This is important, Nathan, and not a bit funny. Sad and serious would be closer.''

His brother stopped grinning and gave a brief nod.

''You're not ready to talk yet,'' John said to Chloe. ''I understand. But now I'd like you to listen to me carefully. A terrible thing happened to your mama and papa and you are very unhappy. I'm very unhappy and so is Uncle Nathan. I have begun to deal with the bad man who brought this thing about.''

Nathan swung long, strong legs from the bed and hopped to the floor. He walked around John and Chloe, keeping his eyes on John's face. His own was pale and rigid. At last he sat down.

''I want, more than anything else, for you to stay with me now,'' John told Chloe. ''And I want you to be happy again and to hear you chatter. These things will come. But first I need your help. I mentioned it before, but please don't say anything about the ship or how we came here, not in front of anyone else. This will help me, Chloe. Soon these days will be over and we'll—'' He stopped. How

could he try to tell a child she'd get over the loss of her parents?

He met Nathan's eyes over her head. Never, ever, had he seen his brother so stricken, other than when their father had died.

John rocked Chloe. "Can you let me know if you understand?"

She leaned against him, settled the side of her face against his chest and ran the forefinger of her right hand over the soft palm of her left, tracing the lines there. Chloe sighed and grew still. She didn't answer him.

Whatever was about to happen, would happen. He rubbed his jaw on top of her springy curls and held her close for a long time.

"Francis and Simonne are dead?" Nathan said as soon as John had taken Chloe to Snowdrop and closed the study door. "Our cousin and that sweet, patient woman...my God!"

"Don't, don't," John said, shaking his head again and again. "I need you and I need you with a calm mind."

Nathan's mouth was open.

"I can do this alone, but it would be good to know you were there if I needed you."

"What...in God's name, what has happened? Tell me. Tell me all of it. And why doesn't Chloe speak? She doesn't, does she?"

John shook his head, no. He went to the trolley, poured a hefty measure of cognac and gave it to Nathan. "Now you need this," he said. "Drink. I'll start by telling you the part Albert and Snowdrop play in this." His brother had been known to rush and take matters into his own hands, with disastrous results. "They are good friends to Chloe and to me. Albert will help with whatever I ask

him. Snowdrop is a shrew but a good woman. Now listen—and drink.''

"I can't believe this," Nathan murmured.

John shook his head slowly. "I feel it's my fault even if it isn't. We were set to leave France a day later than we did, but someone told me about the *Windfall* departing a day earlier and Francis agreed we might as well get started.

"I confess that a certain lovely lady had been a willing participant in a little dillydallying with me. She'd assured me she was single, but then she produced a husband bent on blackmail—or worse."

"That's why you were in such a hurry to get away," Nathan said. "I'd have done the same thing."

Sympathy didn't help John. "We traveled on the *Windfall* and it turned out her captain was a smuggler in the employ of an inhuman Englishman. The captain's share of the bounty wasn't enough for him, so he took the four of us aboard—for a pretty price."

They both fell silent. Neither of them touched their brandy.

"He never intended for us to reach England. When he stopped to offload his cargo of contraband, he ordered a group of his men to get rid of us. We had no warning until we all felt the ship heave to and went topside to see what was happening. They...they...'' The pictures were too vivid.

Nathan went to him and put an arm around his shoulders. "Take your time, brother. You have suffered a great deal."

"So has Chloe and now you're suffering, too. They shot Francis in front of Simonne and Chloe and threw him overboard, then turned a gun on Simonne. I ran to try to stop it, but Simonne started toward me. She all but

threw Chloe into my arms. The last words Simonne said to me were 'Save Chloe,' then she was sent to join Francis. I jumped overboard with Chloe in my arms at the same time and watched Simonne hit the water. There was blood everywhere.''

"My God, my God," Nathan moaned, hanging his head forward.

"I was going to tell you all about Albert and Snowdrop. Albert led a band aboard one of the boats that came to pick up the smuggled goods. Once they had what they wanted, he took off with all the other boats and the *Windfall* pulled away as fog rolled in. I thought we were done for, but Albert Parker turned back and picked us up. He and Snowdrop got us away to safety.''

John finished his tale with the explanation of Leggit's involvement as the power behind the scurrilous affair.

"I'll kill him!"

Predictable, John thought.

Nathan downed all of his cognac and poured as much again. "You had him at your table last night." He set his glass down and came at John in a rush. "You allowed me to eat with my cousin's murderer. I'm going to thrash you. Then I shall deal with him."

John had no time to get rid of his glass before Nathan slammed into him. Glass shattered, cognac flew, and Nathan took John by the throat.

In a single motion, John brought his arms up beneath Nathan's to smash them apart, landed a punch to his chin and caught him before he could fall backward.

"Control yourself." He cursed the slippery stuff of the black robe. "I'm taking care of Leggit in my own way. Last night was part of that. Francis and Simonne had no immediate family left. Chloe is mine and I have to make

sure I don't do something stupid and leave her alone again.''

Gasping, holding his jaw, Nathan staggered away. He breathed loudly and cursed every time he exhaled.

"Sometimes the mercenary can inflict more damage than the cavalry," John said. "Kill Leggit and it's over. He dies once. Francis and Simonne deserve to be better avenged than that. And for Chloe, I'll make sure that man suffers until he *wishes he were dead.* For you and me, this is a test of our strength, our real strength. Are you with me?"

Nathan's eyes misted, on account of the strong drink numbing his control, John thought.

"I've got to think." Beneath the robe, Nathan was naked and resembled a desert warrior. "Leggit's wife is his prize. Even though he humiliates her."

John took more brandy down his own parched throat. "At his age and with a young and beautiful wife to do with as he pleases, he feels a bigger, stronger man. He feels indomitable. And flaunting her as his doting, faithful wife puffs him up like a pigeon."

"So instead of killing the man, you intend to do as you please with her and spread the news throughout Leggit's friends. Am I right? You will suffer the distasteful task of cuckolding Leggit. Is that your plan?"

John recognized, with sudden and maddening clarity, that he might have done well to toss his scruples to the wind and deal with that little matter the previous evening. By now he would be setting about spreading a storm of gossip throughout Bath and London, and Leggit would be a laughingstock.

"Speak up," Nathan demanded. "You'll sacrifice yourself to lie with that woman, then call it done. Not enough, brother, not nearly enough."

"No," John agreed. "Not nearly enough."

Nathan regarded him sharply and John turned away. He hadn't intended to suggest he would enjoy lying with Hattie many times. "What I meant was that what I intend will be worse than a slow death for Leggit." He would like to sleep with Hattie Leggit, in fact he was going to sleep with her and should it happen on more than one occasion, well then, he felt sure he'd enjoy her company.

"You are the head of the family," Nathan said. "I shall follow your instructions, although I don't see what part you intend me to play."

"You will help me *court* Leggit. We will suck him in until he is giddy with his newfound position in society."

"And all the while you'll be—"

"I will make Mrs. Leggit my mistress."

He didn't tell Nathan what Hattie had confided about her marriage, and he wasn't sure why.

12

Her money, Hattie thought, was not safe at Leggit Hall. Mr. Leggit could be perverse enough to have her rooms searched, particularly now that he had spent many hours in a rage just because she'd done exactly what he'd told her to do at Worth House. She would find a new hiding place for the treasure she would need to help her parents when she found a way to flee from her husband.

"You're not yourself this morning, Mrs. Leggit," Bea said. "I've spoken to Merna and she'll be bringing up a tray for you. Mr. Leggit's been in a fair state because you wouldn't go down to breakfast."

"Look at me, Bea," Hattie said to her maid. "Thank you. I don't often tell you how much I appreciate your kindness and loyalty to me, but I'm telling you now."

"Oh, no." Bea shook her head and pieces of her thick, shiny brown hair began to slide free of her white cap. "Any girl would be happy to be your maid. And grateful. It's you who are good to me." Regardless of how she tried, Bea never quite accomplished a tidy appearance.

Hattie, still wearing a beautiful embroidered white robe and night rail, sat on the dusky-pink velvet chaise she thought of as her refuge.

"Mrs. Leggit," Bea said, her round face flushing. "If there's ever anything I can do for you, *anything,* you've only got to ask. And I'm a person who keeps my word."

She puffed at the fallen strands of hair. "I hope I'm not being too disrespectful when I say that although it's Mr. Leggit what pays my wages, I work for you. I care about you, Mrs. Leggit. You're the bravest lady I've ever met."

At one-and-twenty, Hattie doubted she was older than Bea, except in certain experiences, experiences Hattie hoped Bea would never suffer.

Impulsively Hattie held out her arms to Bea, who hesitated before returning her mistress's hug with a great deal of enthusiasm.

A single hard knock and Merna entered carrying a breakfast tray. Annoyance with her task showed on her pretty face. "Here you are then," she said, and made to set the tray on the end of Hattie's bed.

"Over here, if you please," Bea said. "I'll take it from you." She smiled but got a look of dislike from Merna.

The door from Mr. Leggit's dressing room into Hattie's bedchamber opened and Mr. Leggit entered. His evil humor crowded in with him. "You," he said, pointing to Bea. "Out. Now."

Bea, holding the breakfast tray, seemed uncertain what to do.

"Give it to Merna," Mr. Leggit said. "And hurry up about it."

With lowered eyes and not daring to glance directly at Hattie, Bea did as she was told and slipped quietly away.

Hattie looked into her husband's bloodshot eyes and puffy face and she smiled at him.

He frowned. "Merna, put the tray where Mrs. Leggit can eat her breakfast."

The maid behaved as if the order he'd given was beneath her and flounced to place the tray across Hattie's lap.

"I'm glad you're here, Merna," Mr. Leggit said. "I

want you to take note of some instructions. And they have never been more important." His thick voice rose.

Hattie had discovered that Mr. Leggit gave final approval on the hiring of most staff. With some exceptions, the men were youthful, sturdy specimens and the women had things in common: pretty, often petulant faces, large round breasts and round bottoms. Voluptuous, Hattie would have called them. Most of them fawned on Mr. Leggit and treated Hattie with forced deference.

Once the tray rested across Hattie's lap, Merna stood and smiled at her employer.

"We're having a pool gala," he told her. "A very *special* pool gala." He made no attempt to hide a wink.

"I understand, Mr. Leggit. You can be sure we'll all do our part. I'll go to Crispin and Bartholomew at once. I'm sure they'll report to Mr. Smythe smartly. Is there a date, sir?"

"The coming Saturday."

Merna frowned, "But that's only—"

"A few days. Far too late for invitations to go out in the accepted manner of course. But the people I want here will come, even if they have to beg off from some other affair. Now you will all have to work extra hard, especially since this event will be talked about forever in certain circles. No chatter about this, you understand?"

"Oh, no, sir. You can rely on me." Merna bobbed and went away quickly.

Hattie looked at the food before her with little interest. She selected a roll sprinkled with sugar and took a bite.

"I hope you appreciate the consideration I showed you last night," her husband said. "I knew you were tired, so I saved this conversation for this morning when you were rested."

He may have been silent, but his malevolent stares

when they were in the coach, and the way he stalked away when they arrived home, had let her know how angry he was.

And she was not rested. Between drifting asleep and waking again, she had spent the night considering every detail of what had happened with the Marquis of Granville. Hattie had pondered every word he had spoken, and every word of her own, including the information she'd given about Mr. Leggit's scheme. But most of all she had continued to turn over the marquis's actions and, while she tossed in her sheets, a marvelous plan had occurred to her.

"I spoke to you, Mrs. Leggit."

"Yes. Thank you."

Mr. Leggit pulled a chair beside her and sat so close she smelled the perfumes he often used in place of a needed bathe. He did not believe in too much washing. Bad for the skin, he had told her.

Rather than comfort her, his smile alerted her to be prepared for something she wouldn't like.

"Marmalade," he said, examining the contents of her tray. "I know how much you love that." He spooned the sweet stuff onto her plate, took a triangle of toast from the rack and spread it thickly. He held it to Hattie's mouth. "We have been at odds for too long, Hattie. Let me change that. Take a bite, my love."

What plan did he have? What would follow this repulsive show of attentiveness. She bit into the toast. The marmalade tasted like brine in her mouth and she chewed, wondering if she could force the food down her throat.

"I have been thinking about you, dear one, and about the opportunity we have for great happiness."

She managed to swallow only to have the toast pushed against her lips again. Obediently she bit and chewed.

Mr. Leggit surveyed her bedchamber. "Do your rooms please you? The colors? They can be changed, you know. If there's one thing I've got plenty of it's blunt. You can have anything you want. All you have to do is ask."

The instant her mouth was empty, and before he could push more food upon her, Hattie said, "This is the most beautiful room I've ever seen and my boudoir makes me so happy that I laugh whenever I go into it."

"Like a satisfied child," he said, showing his teeth. "A charming child. But that's what you are and that's why I had to have you."

"These shades of pink and pale green go so perfectly together," Hattie said in haste. "What woman wouldn't be thrilled with such lovely things around her?"

In fact the rooms were pretty. Green and pink satin ropes tied the bed draperies back at all four posts. Overhead the fabric swept up to an embroidered coronet at the center.

An exquisite daybed Mr. Leggit had obtained from a French palace dominated the boudoir next door. In that room even the fireplace tiles had been made to match a blue-and-silver cherub design on the upholstery.

Mr. Leggit watched her so closely her forehead grew damp. "Thank you for all you've done for me and my parents," she said.

Hattie wasn't surprised when his eyes shifted from her face. Any mention of Tom and Alice Wall reminded him that he had bought his bride with a cruel and cunning plot. She didn't intend to let him think she had forgotten.

He cleared his throat and reached into one of the large, sagging pockets of the poppy-colored coat he wore over an embroidered green waistcoat and striped trousers. "This is for you," he said, pulling out a large velvet box.

"I had been saving it for just the right moment and I know this is the time."

He looked for Hattie's reaction and she pressed her hands together in mock anticipation. If only it didn't take so long to collect enough money to pay her parents' debts. But it did and that's where the overly amorous marquis came in.

Mr. Leggit held the box to her ear and shook it. "What do you think it is?" he asked, bringing his face closer to hers. "Guess."

"Oh, I can't."

"Never mind. I want us to become much, much closer, dear. I know I was the one who insisted we address one another formally, but I'd like you to call me Bernard now—when we're alone. And I shall call you Hattie."

She'd proved herself brave, but on this occasion he was truly frightening her. "Yes…Bernard," she said.

"Good." The man's wet mouth descended on hers and she suffered the bruising force and absence of finesse. He raised his face and said, "Now tell me if the marquis kissed you like that?"

Leggit's stale taste clung to the inside of her mouth, but she collected herself and made certain she seemed appalled at what he'd said. "The marquis?" His lordship might be guilty of many things, but kissing like Mr. Leggit wasn't one of them. "That's a cruel joke, Mr.…. Bernard. Why would you be so nice, then suggest a thing like that? As if a man in his position would force his attentions on another man's wife. Besides, he could have any eligible woman he wanted."

"Hattie, dear, men in his position are forever forcing their attentions on other men's wives. Such things are all the go with his set. In fact a great many so-called aristocratic women look forward to marriage in part because

it offers them more freedom to spread their legs with any man they fancy.''

His crude language disgusted her, not that she didn't know a thing or two about the ways of society. At first she'd thought the marquis's behavior toward her outrageous, but then, when she'd been awake in the night, she had recalled exactly the so-called sexual conventions Mr. Leggit had just spoken of.

''And another point, Hattie. Do you think a man of my standing would choose a wife who was not the most alluring creature he'd ever seen?''

Smiling as if he pleased her was one of the hardest things she had to do, but she smiled at him now. And she thought about the way this man had gained her hand in marriage. He had threatened to call in the loans he'd all but forced on Hattie's parents if she didn't accept him. They had no way to repay him and she'd gone against their wishes by agreeing to be his wife.

''Are you saying Granville didn't kiss you last night?'' Mr. Leggit asked.

''I cannot bear that you think so poorly of me.''

''Hmm. I suppose I could be wrong. But he wants to, you can be sure of that.'' His smile turned smug and calculating. ''He wants to do a lot of things with my wife. I saw it by the way he hung over you last night.''

''Oh, dear.'' Hattie contrived to appear distressed. ''And it upset you a great deal, so I must not go near him at all.'' She held her breath for fear he would agree.

''Now, let's not be hasty. You're mine and I'm a jealous man is all. We're going to continue as planned, but I wanted to be sure of your loyalty, and I am.''

''Thank you.'' In time she would give him reason to rue his words.

''I haven't been as patient as I should have been with

you. You're young and innocent and, unlike most society ladies, you weren't taught about the womanly ways of exciting a man. That's the only reason I…er…we haven't, you know. But you'll learn. My sawbones is a sensible man and he'll assist me in making sure you carry out your duties properly.''

''Properly?'' She hadn't intended to respond at all.

''Poor little thing.'' He undid the top of her robe and pushed a hand inside. ''Coming from nothing the way you did. No idea of how to encourage and inflame a gentleman.'' He cupped a breast and lifted it into view above her neckline, then opened the gown all the way to her waist and spread it apart. ''There's many a man who envies me these fine bubbies. Including Granville. You may have to suffer some pawing from that one, but it's all in a good cause—our fortune—and as long as you think of me while he's touching you, you won't be committing any sins. You'll be obeying your husband.''

Hattie squirmed under his avid stare, but still irreverence overtook her. She wanted, more than anything, to laugh at the thought of even remembering Mr. Leggit existed if the marquis had his hands on her body. She covered her face. In her position, only a wicked woman would be excited by the thought.

''Now, now,'' Mr. Leggit said. ''Don't worry your head about any of it. Everything will be all right now and we're going to get exactly what I want out of Granville. Also, before you know it, you'll be increasing with my son.'' He held up a hand. ''But I'll not rush you. There's plenty of time.''

''Whatever you say, Bernard.''

''I made the right choice when I married you. You've got the makings of a useful mate. And you'll soon enough become practiced at correcting the hesitancy you've

brought about here.'' He patted himself between his legs and hitched his trousers around his crotch.

Hattie blushed and looked away.

''So ingenuous,'' Mr. Leggit said. ''You'll come to the pool gala next Saturday. It will be instructional for you.''

''I cannot,'' she blurted out before she could remember to hold her tongue. ''I mean, you never wanted me there before and I am afraid when everyone is so loud. On other occasions I've heard them all the way in my rooms.''

''Never mind any of them,'' he said, still looking pleased with himself. ''Unless I misjudge the man, Granville will be there, and only because he will be looking to spend more time with you.''

''Oh, dear,'' Hattie said, and this time suffered no shame about the thrill she felt.

''All you have to remember is that when the two of you are alone together, it must not be where anyone else may happen upon you. Already I have the perfect plan for accomplishing that.''

All she dared say was ''Yes, Bernard.''

''I'm sure I don't need to warn you not to allow him to do anything he shouldn't do.''

Hattie wished she could cover herself. ''You told me I should allow him to touch me, and if he does I'm to think of you.''

He reddened. ''Quite so. I refer to the other, that which you will eventually submit to with me, and only with me.''

He referred to that which he had, on a number of occasions attempted to force upon her after creeping into this bedchamber at night. She lowered her eyes. ''Of course, Bernard.'' He would have done the awful thing if something about her hadn't caused his thing to flop. At least she could be grateful that he'd only come to her in

darkness and she'd never actually had the misfortune to *see* his misfortune.

He rewarded her with another long kiss, after which he opened the velvet box with a flourish. "For you, dear wife. A little advance gift for becoming the mother of my sons." He frowned. "And perhaps even a daughter."

The glitter of stones inside the box dazzled Hattie. "A diamond necklace," she said, after almost calling the fabulous thing *another* diamond necklace.

Mr. Leggit actually laughed. "Not a necklace at all." He lifted the glittering piece and placed it on her head, arranged the circlet carefully, allowing a single large diamond to dangle at the center of her forehead. "Irresistible, but then, you would make anything irresistible."

Moment by moment fear gathered in the pit of her stomach. Men of his age didn't change their natures. Everything he said was part of a ploy to achieve his own ends.

He got up and brought a mirror from her dressing table. "What do you think?"

"It's lovely," she told him truthfully. "Thank you."

"Yes.. Very good. You will wear it at the gala. There will be those who curse me for giving new and expensive ideas to their wives." He sat again and clasped his hands over his belly. "Or their ladybirds."

"Thank you," Hattie repeated, wondering if there might be a way to turn the valuable bauble into some of the money she needed.

"This has been a charming encounter," Mr. Leggit said, getting up once more. "I look forward to many more." He bent over to lick the tips of her exposed breasts and she barely stopped herself from pushing him away.

When he straightened again, Mr. Leggit felt himself in

that place Hattie didn't want to think about. He felt this way and that, rolled and poked the thing.

He looked pleased. "Clever man, that sawbones. If I don't feel some improvement, then I'm not the best man in Bath. To hell with Bath—in all England!"

13

John lowered his head to shield his eyes from bright sunlight and a sharp wind. He peered ahead from the shelter of his hat brim. The horse he rode, an able fellow, took John's sudden change of direction toward Barton Fields without complaint.

In returning home now, he took a risk. Since early light he'd hidden in a thick stand of trees to keep covert watch over any comings and goings at Leggit Hall. Somehow he must get to Hattie Leggit. She should not have too much time to build any resistance to him. He knew full well that by showing his interest in her in front of Leggit, he'd gone against the lady's wishes and, quite possibly, endangered his effort to gain her trust.

Not long since, a carriage carrying Hattie and a woman who could be some sort of companion had started from Leggit Hall and made for the center of Bath. John had bided just enough time to allow the carriage to leave the estate before following as close as he dared.

He was probably a fool to hope he had made the right assumption in thinking Hattie was headed for Worth House, or that such a visit could be a good thing for him. The carriage definitely went that way and, for the rest, he had decided to trust.

Reaching the house before the carriage arrived—if it arrived—was essential. That was his reason for cutting

across Barton Fields, to save time. He intended to greet Hattie before she went to the door and make an excuse to show her some particularly wonderful bloom in the gardens. He had no idea what bloom that might be, but he knew where it had better be.

His mount exchanged the solid thud of hoofs on grass and dirt for a deafening clatter over rough paved road. John leaned over the animal's neck and urged him on, at the same time looking in the direction from which the carriage would come. No sign of the unmistakably expensive vehicle as yet.

When he reached the lane leading to stables behind the house, he wondered if his fair prey might already be trying on hats at some millinery establishment, or picking out little cakes in a tea shop.

A groom ran to take the reins. John nodded to the boy and strode along the side of Worth House, working his gloves off as he went. *Damn it.* He didn't want to appear before her looking as if he'd been taking a stroll to smell the bloody flowers.

Making a quick sprint for the potting shed, he was relieved to find no one working there. He threw his gloves down on a bench, took off his coat, rolled it and dropped it on top. Leaving his hat behind and rolling up his sleeves as he went, he returned to the path and continued on toward the front of the house.

No carriage stood before the entrance.

With swift tugs, he pulled his neckcloth loose and let it hang. Too damned hot for the thing anyway.

He heard the door open and in moments Nathan strolled to meet him. John looked beneath leaves on a hydrangea bush.

"Taken up gardening, have we?" Nathan said. This

morning he sported a blue coat with gold buttons and tight buff trousers tucked into top boots.

John smiled and raised his face to the sky as if enjoying the sweet scents of late spring. "I've become quite fond of natural things, in fact. As I see you have, or should I say have remained. You continue to favor the naked look, brother." He glanced pointedly at his brother's trousers.

"Not many men should wear these things." Nathan laughed. "They're fashionable among those of us who do them justice. You've been known to make a lady or two look faint when you wear them yourself."

John chuckled and checked the driveway again.

"Waiting for someone?" Nathan said.

"As a matter of fact, I am. And you could help me if they come. I'd like to separate Hattie Leggit from the lady she travels with. I shall ask to show her something in the garden. Would you behave as if my notion is nothing remarkable and take her companion inside?"

"I forgot to ask how far the romp went last night?" Nathan asked. "All the way to heaven, I take it."

John quelled a ridiculous and unaccountable urge to punch his brother's straight nose. "No, that did not happen," he said, but after all, that was his eventual goal.

He was given a view of Nathan's handsome profile.

"You know I'm not for this plan of yours. Not really. The issue should be dealt with swiftly and that means we get rid of Leggit," Nathan said.

"Living with the shame of being cuckolded will be worse than death for that arrogant bastard," John said. "He considers a beautiful young wife, trained to show him adoration, a boon to his reputation. It's said around the town that he must be an accomplished lover to keep such a woman hanging on his arm and gazing at him the way Hattie does. The pumped-up toad lives for that."

"Have you considered that she may love the man? Stranger things occur."

"I think it more likely that she fears him and does what she must to please him."

Nathan shrugged and picked an orange rosebud for his lapel. "In that case we'd be doing her a favor by making her a rich widow."

"Not good enough for me," John told him. He ran his hands through his hair and blessed the breezes that cooled him. Since the night Francis and Simonne died, he hadn't known peace and his seething drive to find vengeance often overheated his blood.

"Our mother should—"

"I know," John said, cutting Nathan off. "She should know, as should the aunts. And I need to give all my attention to helping Chloe. I think what happened did her mind an injury. You've already seen how she doesn't speak."

"Poor child," Nathan said. "Did I hear you correctly? *You* are going to give the child all your attention? You have never shown particular interest in children before."

"There has never been a child for whom I felt responsible before. She is alone. There is no one on her mother's side to care for her and of this family, who is better qualified than I am? Mother may be glad to have Chloe for short periods, or even the aunts on occasion, but Chloe needs someone she can trust will be there for her—always."

Nathan narrowed his eyes and pursed his lips. He thought for a moment or so. "A tall order, but now I think of it I should have expected you to take responsibility for her. Under all that rapier-tongued toughness there is a good man. Have you considered what might happen to Hattie once you achieve your goal. You don't think Leggit

will allow the two of you to parade your situation around Bath, do you?''

John had thought about it, continued to think about it day after day. ''I shall make sure she is safe.''

''She'll have no future except as some man's mistress and probably poverty in her old age,'' Nathan pointed out.

''I told you I'll make sure she's safe. She doesn't share Leggit's guilt. This is a subject for another day. Now, if Hattie comes, *will* you help me?''

''I think the splendid gray carriage turning at the driveway may be your pigeon,'' Nathan said.

John looked over his shoulder and, sure enough, Hattie's carriage approached. ''Took them long enough to get here,'' he muttered.

''Mmm. In a hurry to see the lady, are we?'' Nathan said, barely moving his lips. ''Have a care, brother dear. Leggit is no gentleman and that way disaster may await you.'' He slapped a hand on John's shoulder to stop his protests. ''I shall do as you ask. You know I am bound to you by respect as well as blood.''

John had no time to respond before the coach drew to a stop only yards from them, but he caught Nathan by the arm and looked him hard in the eye, showing as best he could how he cared for him.

The coachman climbed down and handed a blond woman in black, to the ground. She straightened her bonnet, preparing to approach the house.

''Good morning to you,'' John hailed. ''Can we be of some assistance?''

The woman turned and he saw a quietly elegant face. ''My name is Mrs. Dobbin. I'm with my mistress, Mrs. Leggit. She is hoping to call upon the Misses Worth.''

Really, John thought. ''My aunts will be delighted to see her,'' he said. ''And you, of course. I'm the Marquis

of Granville and this is my brother, the Earl of Blackburn. Allow us to escort you inside.'' Under his breath, he added, ''Come along, Nathan. We can do this.''

Hattie left the coach and did not immediately see John.

She stood quite motionless, the soft colored stripes of her matching pelisse and gown shimmering in the sunlight. Her bonnet, decorated with flowers to complement her dress, shielded all of her face except her firm chin. Her light brown ringlets, streaked with blond and red, skimmed her neck.

Her small stature took nothing away from a straight-backed stance. John allowed himself the luxury of a quick study of her figure. Breathtaking.

''For God's sake, John,'' Nathan muttered. ''Wake up and stop staring at her.''

''Yes,'' he said, remembering to breathe, and reminded himself of his real business with this woman. ''Good day to you, Mrs. Leggit. How nice of you to visit us.''

She spun toward him and color rose in her cheeks. He didn't think he would ever, no matter how long or short his life might be, forget her fathomless gray eyes. ''I came to call on your aunts,'' she said with a sweet smile that turned his heart. ''I have several missions really, but I wanted to thank you and your family for your generosity toward my husband and myself last night. I have brought a note.'' Hattie carried a basket to which mauve silk rosettes had been tied and from this she took an envelope.

''You are too kind,'' he told her. ''And the pleasure was all ours, hmm, Nathan?''

In his best courtly manner, Nathan bowed. ''This old house isn't graced by a beautiful lady often enough,'' he said.

''Steady on,'' John muttered. He raised his voice and said, ''Mrs. Leggit! I have something I'd really like to

show you. Knowing your fondness for flowers, I know you will want to see it.''

The lady in black returned at once to her mistress's side where she stood sentry duty.

''Come, Mrs. Dobbin.'' Nathan offered an arm to the lady, who took it with some hesitation. ''My aunts get very lonely. They will be ecstatic to have company.''

Hattie's indecision ruckled the smooth skin between her brows but John stuck his hands in his trouser pockets and smiled so amiably she relaxed visibly. ''A moment,'' she said, removing another envelope from the basket, which she gave to her companion. ''Now Mrs. Dobbin, please go in and make my apologies for being diverted by Lord Granville. I shall be along shortly and I'd rather you didn't offer my little tribute until I'm there.''

Mrs. Dobbin didn't look happy but she went with Nathan.

Clutching her envelopes, Hattie trod slowly toward the marquis and her heart beat harder with each step. His ruffled state of semi-dress disconcerted her. The dark gray waistcoat he wore fitted his chest very closely, and rolled-back shirtsleeves showed heavily muscled forearms where a sprinkling of dark hair showed.

''I really am pleased to see you,'' he told her. ''More pleased than you can know.''

His lean, flamboyantly handsome face and very blue eyes welcomed her. He *looked* glad to have her there. But then, this was what she wanted, wasn't it? To discover that his ardor hadn't faded. After all, she knew he had made an excuse to get her alone, just as she knew she was wrong to allow it. How long, she wondered, should she encourage him, and when would the time come to tell Mr. Leggit she would reveal to his world that she had a lover—and threaten to hint at her husband's failure to

make her truly his wife. She might not know every detail involved in that piece of business, but she did know enough to be certain it had not happened. Praise be!

"Hello, sunshine girl," the marquis said, his smile softening. "I should like to hold your hand, but I know I must not."

Her heart thundered now. "You said you had something to show me."

"Indeed." When she reached him, he looked into her face for far too long and she thought him reckless. "Since last night I haven't stopped thinking about you. I didn't sleep all night."

"Neither did I." Hattie closed her eyes and bowed her head. What had come over her to be so careless with her tongue.

"Thank you," he told her quietly. "Please, please don't be embarrassed at your honesty. You have given me a gift and I thank you. Now follow me, if you will."

She opened her eyes to find he had turned from her to walk along a stone path leading to the side of the house. Hattie followed, unable to look away from his broad back and narrow hips. The sun had browned the back of his neck and his unruly shirt collar showed very white. The marquis had a purposeful walk and she noted again how the muscles in his strong legs flexed.

He looked at her over his shoulder and this time there was no smile, just a slight lowering of his eyelids over eyes heavy with some emotion.

"Here we are," he said, walking backward now. "Tell me if these aren't the most vivid things you've ever seen."

Hattie joined him in a place where the wall of the house jogged in and potted plants crowded a tiny courtyard. "See these," he said.

What he showed her were bloodred Tudor roses with specks of yellow at their hearts. "What a shame to hide them here," she said without considering that she might be rude. "I mean—"

"You're right. Almost no one sees them here." He was well aware of the courtyard but hadn't exactly noticed the plantings before. A row of large tubs, each one containing a mature holly tree, lined one wall almost to the corner. He did hold out his hand to her and she looked around, wondering if anyone saw them.

"We're alone," he said quietly. "We don't have long, of course, because of the aunts and your keeper, but you could spare me a little time to show you what I promised you'd see last night."

He took keys from one of his pockets, waited until she put her hand in his, and led her to the corner and around the last holly tree there.

"This isn't a good idea, my lord," she told him. "Surely you could show me these things without risking…well, it is dangerous."

"No, it's not dangerous. I should not allow it if it were."

A weathered wooden door, tucked away behind the holly, opened when he used one of the keys. He pulled her inside and she saw a flight of stairs, then a landing where another flight turned to the left. She tugged against him and said, "I want to go back."

His swift kiss, planted on the corner of her mouth and a second on the tip of her nose set her nerves to throbbing beneath her skin and she went with him, flying up several flights of stairs to a landing she recognized.

"Do you know where you are?" he asked, lighting a candle in a wall sconce.

"Outside the secret door to the ballroom—and to your own suite of rooms."

"Correct." He took out two more keys and pressed them into her hand. "One is for the outside door, the other for this one. You know how to find me from here. If you are ever in need, any need at all, come to me at once."

She spread a hand above her breasts. "Why should I ever need to do such a thing?"

"I don't know, but what can it harm to know you have a friend who will protect you under any circumstances?"

Hattie thought about it. "None, I suppose."

"And if I may be so bold," the marquis said, "there could be other reasons for you to come here. If the mood moved you, or whatever."

Again she reminded herself that he offered exactly what she wanted. The difficulty might be to keep him satisfied with playful encounters that didn't include the other. Whatever happened, she did not intend to do what her husband apparently couldn't—particularly when she wasn't sure she would like it at all. She nodded at the marquis. "Yes. Thank you, my lord, you are generous to offer me your friendship. This is an uncertain world and life is not always easy." Dangers lay ahead. She could well need a refuge from Mr. Leggit. If she did, matters would have come to a dangerous pass.

He stroked the back of a finger across her cheek, settled a thumb on her bottom lip. "Why not tell me exactly what you mean by that?"

She shook her head emphatically. "Nothing at all. I was just rambling. I do that sometimes. I've been told I tend to be overly dramatic."

"I don't think so," he told her, sliding an arm around her waist and pulling her against him. "You are a sensible woman, Hattie, but I don't think all is well with you.

That's why you are to keep the key—just in case you need my help. And if I should not be here when you come, wait for me.''

When she dared look up into his face, he raised her to her toes and brought his mouth crushing down on hers. He breathed heavily and a sound, half moan, half groan came from deep in his throat.

Hattie didn't want to think anymore. After her inept, discouraging responses to him last night, she was intrigued that he could continue to pursue her as if he'd been encouraged. She rubbed his chest and returned the kiss with all the strength she had, gasping when he opened her mouth and moved her head wildly from side to side. His hands came to rest with his fingers around her ribs and his thumbs beneath her breasts.

"You know how much I am attracted to you," he breathed against her mouth.

"You shouldn't be."

John raised his face and looked down at her. "You mean you aren't attracted to me?"

"Not at all."

He laughed and she punched him lightly.

"Do you love your husband?"

"You asked that last night and I told you. Please don't ask me such questions again."

"You alluded to having no choice but to marry him," he told her, and settled his lips on her forehead. "You said something about your parents. Why exactly did you marry him?"

"I've said enough on that subject."

"Very well. I won't press you, but at least you have agreed we can be friends. You meant that, didn't you?"

"Oh, yes," she told him, and he kissed her again.

He stopped as suddenly as he'd begun and leaned his

forehead on hers. "You are no fool, Hattie. I won't lie about my desires, but I shall not rush you."

Reluctantly she stepped away from him, but she did incline her head and rest a hand along his jaw. "You are a passionate man, my lord, but you are, first and foremost, a good man. I think perhaps we should never be ashamed of honest emotion. Please, we must go at once." She made sure he saw her put the keys into her reticule.

"Of course. Are those letters for me? Perhaps I should have them before they are too wrinkled to read."

She made a poor attempt to smooth out the envelopes, and gave them to him.

"I'll read them outside, where we can be seen in all our innocence from any window in the house."

"We are not innocent," she murmured.

His lordship paused as he was about to blow out his candle. "You may have to learn that in certain circles people may see what they want to see. That can lead to thinking what they want to think."

Once in the gardens again, the marquis picked one of the flat red roses and carefully removed all thorns from its stem. "Here," he said. "Perhaps the other ladies would like to see it." They strolled around to the front of the house and stood in front of the salon windows with a suitable distance between them.

John's erection had subsided somewhat but continued to pulse. This girl, for that's what she was, had power over his control. He glanced at her, at her lips, and opened the first envelope. It contained a folded sheet of paper on which Hattie had written thanks on behalf of herself and her husband for last night's dinner.

"I am more glad you came than you will ever know," he told her, noticing the hand she placed over her heart. He envied her hand.

"And what is this?" The second envelope was fancier, made of heavy gray parchment outlined in burgundy. His name was written on it and so was Nathan's. He pulled a thick card from inside and read what had been formally penned there.

"Mr. Leggit made a special request for me to deliver his invitation to you personally."

He kept his eyes on the card. "A pool gala. Exotic, I should think. But this Saturday is rather soon."

"Yes," she said in a small voice. "Mr. Leggit has these whims. He does love to host parties. If you can't come I'm sure he will understand."

Her tone suggested she would not enjoy carrying John's regrets to her husband. "Will you be there?" he said.

She swallowed loudly enough for him to hear. "Yes. Mr. Leggit wants me to go this time."

"This time? I take he's had other, similar events but you haven't been present?"

Hattie shook her head, no. "I'm afraid I'm not particularly good at parties. Not much experience, you see. Anyway, my husband hasn't insisted that I attend—until now."

"Well then," he said, offering her his arm and walking toward the front doors. "In that case I shall have to come."

14

"Where are you from?" Miss Enid Worth asked Hattie.

"London," she said. The ladies had sent Mrs. Dobbin to the nursery to take tea with Snowdrop. "And you?" Hattie added politely.

Apparently Snowdrop had taken over from Mrs. Gimblet in the nurseries, leaving that lady free to return all her attention to the aunts.

Miss Enid and Miss Prunella looked at each other. "*Where* are *we* from?" Miss Prunella said. "Why, Bath, of course. We were born in this house."

"Yes," Miss Enid agreed. "Bath, of course. Where else? I should hate to have been born in London. Such a dirty, loud place."

Lord Granville lounged on a red-and-green sofa while Hattie sat on a small, green chair close to the Misses Worth. Those ladies looked as if they hadn't moved from their places since Hattie arrived the previous evening. She knew they'd been to dinner and undoubtedly to bed but still they seemed rooted there.

"How old are you?" Miss Prunella asked.

"I don't think—"

"Well I do," Miss Prunella snapped, cutting off the marquis's mild rebuke. "When you get to be our age, my

boy, you may ask whatever question comes to mind and be grateful you still think at all. How old, Mrs. Leggit?''

''One-and-twenty,'' she said, smiling despite her discomfort.

''Married how long?'' Miss Enid asked, fiddling with her cane.

''A year,'' the marquis said on Hattie's behalf.

Both women glared at their nephew. ''Children?'' Miss Enid said.

''No.'' Hattie spread her fingers and played with the rings she didn't like.

''Can we expect that to change in the near future? Or even the distant future?''

''Aunt Prunella, that was unforgivable.'' The marquis sounded fierce, but Hattie noted the amusement in his eyes.

''I know,'' Miss Prunella said. ''What do you say, Mrs. Leggit?''

''That I agree it was unforgivable,'' Hattie told the old lady.

The marquis laughed at once. The ladies looked archly at Hattie, then gave self-satisfied little smiles.

''Your husband is said to be one of the wealthiest men in England,'' Miss Prunella said. ''Wealthy but not well-bred.''

''What makes a person well-bred?'' Hattie asked. ''Who they know? Or perhaps it's whether or not they were on the right side in a war?''

''Blood, my girl,'' Miss Enid said in resounding tones. ''Who your people are and were, and your people's people. And you're right to suggest it's important to know the right people. But it certainly has nothing to do with money. Not directly.''

Hattie considered these things absurd. ''Perhaps I'm

well-bred. After all, I was born poor and would still be poor if it hadn't been for my marriage.'' She snapped her mouth shut and wished she could disappear. Mr. Leggit would be furious if he found out she'd said such things to the Misses Worth, *and* to Lord Granville—on more than one occasion. *The genteel orphan of military parents.* Why couldn't she remember to say what she'd been told to say?

It was a lie.

The Misses Worth cleared their throats and made twittering sounds.

She felt the Marquis of Granville staring at her. When she caught his eye he shook his head slightly. ''Would you like me to summon your carriage?'' he said. She couldn't tell if the conversation amused or bored him.

''Don't you have business to attend to, John?'' Miss Enid said. ''Prunella and I should like to get to know Mrs. Leggit—''

''I've taken enough of your time,'' Hattie said, horrified at the idea of being left alone with the marquis's aunts. ''I'll give you my little gifts and go home.''

Miss Enid frowned at her. ''We didn't say anything about having to be poor to have breeding, you know,'' she said. ''The Worths were not poor. This house has a distinguished history, even if our nephew, being an Elliot, is not impressed.''

''Run along, John,'' Miss Prunella said. ''Tell that Albert of yours he's not to give orders to Boggs and he's not to hang around in the kitchens, either. Boggs says he's making the staff nervous.''

Something shiny caught Hattie's eye. Miss Prunella had taken a lace-edged handkerchief from the sleeve of her mauve gown. When she did so, a deep red stone fell from the handkerchief to the carpet at the lady's feet.

Hattie glanced at the marquis, who had risen from his couch. Smiling faintly, he showed no sign of seeing anything unusual. Hattie looked back at Miss Prunella just in time to catch her using a foot to scoop the gem beneath the hem of her skirts.

"Albert and I have business to attend to," the marquis said, and gave Hattie a speculative stare. "Nice to see you again, Mrs. Leggit. Do have a care. It's so easy for the openhearted to be used by the cunning."

"Yes," Hattie said, not understanding him at all.

"What can you be thinking, John," Miss Enid said, "walking around talking nonsense, and dressed like that? Or should I say, undressed?"

"I've been gardening," he said, strolling toward the foyer. "I find it peaceful. I'm considering going into propagation, you know, seeds and whatnot."

"I'm sure I don't know," Miss Enid said, but the marquis walked purposefully from the room.

"Good," said Miss Prunella, shifting to the front of her chair. Light shone on the lenses of her pince-nez, obscuring her eyes. "Now we can talk. Oh, this is exciting, isn't it, Enid?"

"One hopes so," Enid said, looking hard at Hattie. "I think it will be as long as we have not misjudged this girl, and as long as Boggs doesn't find out what we're up to and make a fuss."

To make a comment, any comment at all, would be pointless, or so Hattie decided.

Using a cane, Miss Enid got up, took a delicate china bell from the table beside her chair and walked slowly to the door. With surprising agility, she bent over and placed the bell on the floor, right where the door met the jamb. "There," she said, standing straight again and flourishing

her cane. "Let someone try to get past that without being heard."

"There," Miss Prunella echoed. The rouge on her cheeks was as bright as ever, but agitation added a shade of pink all over her face. "There is the keyhole…"

"The *keyhole*," Miss Enid said. "But Boggs could just as well listen with his ear to a panel, sister. We must speak quietly, whisper in fact."

"Now, Mrs. Leggit," Miss Prunella said. "We will explain ourselves, of course. But the first lesson you must learn is never to say a word in front of Boggs. Can you remember that?"

The lady jutted her chin as if she were talking to child, or someone of questionable intelligence.

"I think that's clear," Hattie said. She felt chilled and vaguely overwhelmed by the scent of lavender her hostesses wore. The fire hadn't been lit today and, as Lord Granville had mentioned, the thick walls of the house kept out the warmth of the day.

Miss Prunella nodded. "You see, Boggs has been with us a long time and, although he can be annoying, we shouldn't like to hurt his feelings, even though it's his fault we're forced to throw ourselves on your mercy. He's being silly, you see."

Bewildered, Hattie smiled and hoped that was the right thing to do.

She noticed that Miss Prunella had dropped her handkerchief, and retrieved it for her. Before she could straighten up, Miss Prunella said, "There's a ruby under my skirt. Would you mind…"

Using the flat of her hand, Hattie patted the carpet until she found the stone. "This would be the one," she said, holding it aloft between finger and thumb.

"Don't do that!" Miss Enid surveyed the empty room

and searched the windows for anyone who might be looking in. "Someone will see it. Put it down at once. Not back on the floor, silly. My sister will take it."

"Don't mind Enid," Miss Prunella said, extending a palm and watching Hattie place the gem there. "She worries too much."

Hattie longed to see Dobbin's familiar face. She picked up the basket she'd brought. "These are for you," she said, placing her gift on a table beside Miss Enid. "Homemade blackberry jam and a loaf of fresh bread. Simple but good with a nice cuppa. They're not as good as my mum and dad's, but the cook at Leggit Hall does quite nicely."

"I told you, sister!" Miss Enid's smile turned her brown wrinkles into miniature replicas of Austrian blinds and she pointed at Miss Prunella. "I just knew I was right about her. Sit down again, Hattie. May we call you Hattie?"

Miss Prunella didn't wait for Hattie's answer. "You said you had been poor," she said, while she wrapped the ruby in her handkerchief once more. "Your mother made her own jams and bread?"

Bewildered, Hattie said, "My mum makes jam. My dad makes bread. He's a baker."

"And bread and jam's good with a *cuppa*," Miss Enid said, chuckling. "Just like that. You tell the world you're a nobody without as much as trying to hide the fact. Your husband wouldn't like that, I imagine, not when he's trying so hard to be a gentleman. But never fear, he won't learn your indiscretions from us."

"Oh, please, no," she said. "I mean, I'm not supposed to talk about my family. Oh, dear."

"We think it sounds interesting, don't we, Prunella?" Miss Enid said.

Miss Prunella nodded and said, "I expect you've known all manner of questionable characters."

She had been too distracted to concentrate, Hattie thought, and now she had ruined everything. These ladies could not be trusted to keep her secret. They would forget their promise and let the truth about her be known. She wouldn't be welcome here again. Lord Granville would ignore her. What he knew in private was one thing. Having the whole world know about her, quite another. He'd change his mind about the gala, and Mr. Leggit...oh, dear, Mr. Leggit could do almost anything.

And she'd be back to saving, guinea by guinea toward paying off her parents' debts and finding a way to make a life for herself alone. That could take *forever*.

"My dear Hattie," Miss Enid said. "Your eyes are filled with tears. Oh, no, no, that will not do. Did you say we might call you Hattie? After all, you're only a very young thing. And don't you worry. Your secret is safe with us. In fact, we've already forgotten you grew up poor in London and your mother makes jam and your father makes bread."

She sniffed. Crying? She never cried. Her mother and father were better people than any others she'd met. "I feel well, thank you. Call me Hattie, if you like. May I send for Dobbin?"

"Oh, don't be so quick to leave us," Miss Enid said.

Miss Prunella and Miss Enid smiled at each other again. "Isn't she the sweetest girl," Miss Enid said. "I just knew something would come along in time."

Hattie assumed they were saying she was the "something" that had come along just in time and all she wanted to do was get out of the house.

"Bring your chair closer," Miss Prunella said. "And keep your voice down."

"Now," Miss Enid said. "What exactly did we decide we needed to ask, sister?"

Miss Prunella shook her head and sighed. "We talked all night, you know," she said to Hattie in hushed tones. "We often do when we're really excited. Then we're sometimes too tired to remember what we said."

The three of them gradually leaned closer until only inches separated their heads. "You mean you didn't go to bed last night?" Hattie asked.

"Life is short," Miss Prunella said. "Sleep wastes too much time when you have so much to do."

"We prefer naps in the afternoon," Miss Enid added. "Most of the really interesting things happen at night. Now concentrate. We have a problem and we hope you may be able to help us. First we must make sure we are not mistaken in our assessment of you. Are you honest?"

Hattie's palms grew hot and sticky. "Yes."

"Godfearing?"

"Oh, yes."

"If you cheated someone, would you expect to burn in hell?" This was Miss Prunella and when she was so close, her pale blue eyes were as large as her lenses.

"Cheating is wrong," Hattie said. "People who cheat don't win in the end."

Miss Enid reached into a bowl on her table and selected a large chocolate. She popped it into her mouth and chewed with energy. She mumbled something to Miss Prunella.

"Quite right. You are exactly the kind of person we're looking for. We have to know if you're interested in a project that does a great deal of good for some very good people."

"What people?" Hattie asked.

"Us."

"And you," Miss Enid added. "It would do you good, too. You don't like Mr. Leggit, do you?"

Hattie was, she decided, abandoned in a place where mad people were sent. "Mr. Leggit is my husband."

"What does that have to do with anything?" Miss Prunella said. "We have to hurry along with this, Hattie, don't we, sister."

Miss Enid agreed, "Yes, or that nephew of ours will be back sniffing around you again. Best watch out for that one. Apparently women find him irresistible. He wants you, and if you don't want him you'd best keep your bodice up and your skirts down."

"Thank you for the advice." Hattie bit her bottom lip. This was the most extraordinary conversation she'd ever had.

"But of course, you do want him," Miss Prunella said. "We know the two of you were alone in his rooms last night, you know."

Hattie put a hand to her throat. "You couldn't have known that. You'd gone to bed."

"Aha," Miss Enid said, sounding triumphant. "We didn't know for sure, but we do now. Not that we have any plans to speak of it to anyone else. Although your husband does seem a jealous sort of person. I don't suppose he'd mind if John showed you the house, but taking you to his rooms would probably be another thing, entirely."

Hattie felt so hot. *She had trapped herself.*

"You need money, don't you?" Miss Enid whispered to Hattie. "I saw the way you looked at the guineas your disgusting husband—*gave* you last night. If you could have, you would have said what you thought of him, but you wanted the money more. You *needed* it."

When Hattie didn't say anything, the two ladies moved

in so close their heads all but touched Hattie's. "We understand what it's like to need money of one's own," Miss Enid said. "Money so that one need not *beg* for a few pennies. And we found a way to make sure we have plenty. Unfortunately Mr. Boggs, who has been invaluable to us, has decided that he cannot play his part while John is in residence. Too dangerous, he thinks. Pah. That's where you come in. We need you to take his place until he comes to his senses."

"Stop!" Miss Prunella poked her sister's leg. "We must not overwhelm the girl."

"Oh, no," Miss Enid agreed.

"Or be presumptuous."

"Absolutely not," Miss Enid said.

"Not overly presumptuous anyway," Miss Prunella said. "You will benefit from the venture, too. All for money and money for all. We would work out what your share would be. The point is, Enid and I consider ourselves fine judges of character and we judge you to be lacking...finer feelings...or squeamishness perhaps?"

"Quite," Miss Enid said. "My sister is not always subtle. She means you won't faint at the thought of taking a thing or two to a receiver."

They had decided, Hattie thought, that they could blackmail her into doing what they wanted. "I'm an honest woman from honest parents. I have never had anything to do with stealing."

"We aren't talking about stealing anything," Miss Prunella said. "Er...*finding* it is the thing. What we have was found by someone, two someones, and given to us. The rightful owners were never known."

"I don't know what you mean."

"Oh, dear," Miss Enid said, and lay back in her chair with her arms trailing over the sides. "She's going to be

more difficult than I thought. There is a most moving explanation for our situation.'' She sniffed and touched the corner of an eye. ''One day we may be able to tell it to you, when there's time. Let's leave it that two wonderful people did their best to make sure Prunella and I would never want for anything. Thanks to them, we haven't, and we don't intend to start now. So, do you or do you not know of a good, trustworthy receiver.''

''That's the question,'' Miss Prunella said, her own eyes moist.

Hattie gulped. If Mr. Leggit heard gossip about her and Lord Granville, she'd have nothing to blackmail him with. And the blackmail she planned was nothing like the blackmail the sisters were using. Hattie's was for an honorable cause.

Dingdong bell, she had become wound in an ugly web.

''Receivers aren't trustworthy and I don't know any of them. There must be another way to solve your problems. Surely your nephew—''

''No, we've already said he must never know any of this,'' Miss Enid said. ''We already have someone to meet our needs. If we could go to him ourselves we would, but it's out of the question. All you would have to do is find an address we'd give you and exchange goods for money. Only very occasionally, of course. Perhaps just this once. Your challenge would be to make sure you're paid a fair price. We'll share the money with you. We had hoped you'd know of a rival fellow, though. You know, competition to drive the prices up, that sort of thing?'' She sighed. ''Never mind.''

Hattie found her composure and her common sense. ''Even if you think you know something that could hurt me, what would possibly make you decide to approach

me, a complete stranger, and ask if I'll be your accomplice?''

Miss Prunella giggled first. She held a hand in front of her mouth and her shoulders rose. The sound Miss Enid made was more a titter and they waved their hands at each other as if they had never heard anything funnier 'than what Hattie had said.

''You tell her,'' Miss Prunella said.

Miss Enid pressed her cheeks and said, ''I shall. Since John's unexpected arrival, we've been in a state. He has upset our plans, you see. We'd been trying to decide what to do—things are getting desperate—and when we met you last night we saw the perfect answer. Potentially. If things fell into place, which they did.''

Miss Prunella broke in. ''You're married to a nasty man you don't like. You need money. We don't know exactly why but we don't have to. And you are no stranger to the lower classes—being that you're one of them. Then we saw the way our nephew watched you at dinner, and the way you responded to him. Yes, yes, we could tell you were very attracted to one another.''

''So, my dear,'' Miss Enid took over again, ''you have a reason to help us, and we will help you, and not just with money. But you absolutely must promise that you'll never tell John what we've talked about? He would not approve and he would certainly not give us more money. He thinks we get plenty, but he doesn't know of our, er, *charities* and so forth. We couldn't risk his trying to put a stop to those.''

The opulent room with its high ceilings and open spaces seemed to shrink before Hattie's eyes. She felt faint, both with excitement and fear. What choice did she have? ''I'll do as you ask.''

''Oh, good girl.'' Miss Prunella glowed. ''Because you

have no money of your own, you must do what that cox-
comb Leggit says. Am I correct so far?''

Hattie kept her eyes lowered.

''You'll do very well,'' Miss Enid said. ''Our nephew
is an unusual man. Strong, self-assured and in command
of his feelings—usually. But he is not in command of his
feelings with you. We have known him all his life and
this is the first time we've seen him as he is now.''

Such matter-of-fact remarks distressed Hattie. She
turned aside in her chair.

''Don't be a ninny,'' Miss Enid said. ''We may be old
but we're not dead, and we haven't forgotten certain *in-
clinations*. Work with us. Sell what we give you and we'll
help you get what you want. Everything you want.''

''Do you think Mr. Leggit would object if we took you
under our wings and had you visit us regularly?''

''No,'' Hattie said. Now she might manage to turn this
situation to her benefit after all.

''Perfect. If he should have any reservations, remind
him that we could elevate your social standing. His own
entrée into the ton would be guaranteed.''

''Yes,'' Hattie said. How vulgar and obvious she and
Mr. Leggit must be. Circles within circles. Hattie sighed
at the irony of her situation.

''This is absolutely perfect.'' Miss Prunella stood and
held her arms out to Hattie. ''We shall just have to start
having people in again, sister. Now Hattie, let's send you
on your first mission. You must arrange your own trans-
portation, but you are resourceful, we're certain of that.
And we insist you be very careful. We couldn't bear it if
anything happened to you.''

*And they would have to look for another victim to do
their bidding.* Hattie stood but said, ''I haven't agreed to
anything.''

"Are you oppressed at Leggit Hall?" Miss Enid asked.

"Yes, I am."

"Would you like to spend time in a marvelous pursuit that would make your heart pound with joy?"

Hattie thought sneaking along alleys to sell items that came from goodness knows where would be guaranteed to make her heart pound, but not from joy.

"I see we are agreed," Miss Prunella said, and embraced Hattie. "Everyone will get what they want most. Now join hands while we make a vow."

With a sense of having passed into another world, Hattie allowed the two ladies to hold her hands while the three of them stood in a tight circle. "We will use what others no longer want," Miss Enid chanted. "For the sake of doing the needy good." She and Miss Prunella raised and lowered their arms sharply, taking Hattie's with them.

With ceremony, Miss Prunella unfolded her handkerchief to reveal the large ruby. She covered it again and gave it to Hattie. "Take it to Porky," she said. "You'll find him at ten Farthing Lane."

15

"You're leaving us, I see, Mrs. Leggit."

Hattie whirled around. She'd just escaped from the salon and her mind tumbled. The sight of Lord Granville standing in the foyer, arresting as he was, didn't do a thing to calm her down.

He had changed into a dark green jacket, buff trousers, and his neckcloth was perfectly tied. He managed to make Hattie want to do nothing but stare at him.

"How did you enjoy the aunts? Did they wear you out?" He clasped his hands beneath the tails of his coat and watched her speculatively as if gauging her reactions.

Now that she thought about it, his unexpectedly reserved demeanor made her wonder if all the flirtatious charm he'd shown her so far could be an act. Perhaps the real Lord Granville was this serious-faced man with the slight, enigmatic smile. After all, he wouldn't be the first man to use flattery and gaiety to lure a lady to do his will. Only she hadn't done his will yet, so unless he had decided her lack of pedigree was a reason to give up the quest, he'd best look to his manner.

Hattie wasn't beyond creating some mystery herself. She had been called "quite the little actress" on occasion.

"Miss Prunella and Miss Enid are dear ladies," she said, knowing such enthusiasm over his crusty relatives would confound him. "It's little wonder you like to come

and spend time with them. Oh, yes, they are wonderful and they insist they want to take me under their wings.'' She laughed. ''Imagine such generosity.''

She swung her reticule by its strings and smiled at him. What would he say if he knew she had a ruby the size of a wren's egg wrapped in Prunella's handkerchief and resting at the bottom of that reticule? And how would he take the news that she would be venturing into Bath that very evening to sell the stone?

Once, when her mother was in one of her girlish moods, she'd told Hattie that the best way to keep a man interested in a woman was for her to shock him...often. How unfortunate that his lordship could never know about her visit to *Porky!*

Lord Granville sauntered closer until he stood over her. She had noted that when men were with women, particularly tall, confident men, they had a way of drawing attention to their superior size. ''What exactly do the aunts mean about taking you under their wings?'' he asked.

She raised her shoulders and blinked more times than was necessary. ''Just what they say. We get along so famously we're going to visit often. They say they'll start having people in again and I think that's a good thing, don't you? They will stay young if they have things to plan for.''

The marquis looked from her face into the middle distance. He seemed about to comment, but stopped with his lips parted.

''I must not take up more of your time,'' Hattie said. ''Dobbin is still upstairs with that nice Snowdrop.''

''Yes,'' he said slowly, his eyes coming into focus and narrowing on her face. ''Come along and I'll show you where they are. I expect you'd enjoy seeing the nurseries. The dollhouse I mentioned is there.''

Hattie went to the stairs and Lord Granville joined her. "Don't forget the keys, will you?" he said quietly. "Remember. I am at your service at any time, day or night."

He stood too close. Hattie sensed tension in his body. They both knew why he wanted her to go to him. Together they were like dry tinder waiting for a spark. She felt fluttery and foolish because of her reaction.

When she'd been speaking with the aunts, she'd been cross with his lordship for not making certain their allowance was adequate. The day might come when she would discuss that with him, but for now she had other things on her mind. Such things as finding her way in and out of Leggit Hall and back and forth between the house and Bath without giving herself away. The thought of secret night journeys to meet with Porky might be a little daunting but it also thrilled her. Hattie did not care for a boring life.

With Lord Granville at her shoulder, Hattie climbed the stairs to the first landing.

At that point, he took her by the elbow and steered her into a corridor where they would be out of sight of prying eyes. He faced her and said, "I apologize if I embarrassed you in front of your husband last night."

Hattie didn't believe he was at all sorry but she said, "Thank you. Your apology is accepted."

"You are generous," he said, but he managed to make every word sound like an invitation to other things.

"Do you ever wish you could see the future?" Hattie shook her head. "Don't mind me. I've been told I should think more and speak less."

"I see no reason for you to speak less," he said. Not a trace of a smile remained on Lord Granville's mouth. "I am mesmerized by you. I find you more engaging than

I've ever found any woman. I would like to know where all this will take us. Does that answer your question?''

Revealing her entire hand could be disastrous. ''That wasn't what I meant to ask—exactly.'' These were deep waters for a girl with so little experience in social games. ''Please don't make such rash comments. Gallantry is charming, but unnecessary. I am a married woman, remember.''

''Oh, I remember,'' he said, and the bitterness in his voice astonished her. ''I wasn't joking just now, Hattie. I want you.''

Flustered, she bowed her head. ''You can't say things like that.''

''I just did, and I'll say them again. And whether or not you intend to do so—and I think you do—you encourage my interest in you. And you succeed. I want you and I intend to pursue you until I make you mine. You're a woman of the world. Such arrangements are no mystery to you.''

Such arrangements?

''Do you already have a lover?''

Silly thing that she was, she felt hurt that he should even think such a thing. This was not a matter of the heart, even if she wished it were. He had a goal in mind. Fair enough. So did she. ''There is no lover,'' she said.

He inclined his head. The reserve she'd noted became even more closed. He was, she decided, a man of little patience. He had decided what he wanted and, after the minimum of pretty words, he was ready to get things done.

If he thought these silences disquieted her he was mistaken. Each step she took must be careful, and time to think could only work to her benefit. Hattie glanced from his face to his feet, missing nothing in between. The tight

buff-colored trousers showed off a fine form and she should be ashamed of the way she took stock of him, but wasn't. In fact, she had only one regret as far as his lordship was concerned, that she'd responded to him at all during their first times alone. She had read enough to know the chase was the thing.

John didn't miss Hattie's glances or where her eyes lingered, and he enjoyed the ripple of heat in his loins. He would lay odds she was a steamy little piece between the sheets. A good thing since that was where he intended to get her.

"Are we likely to be overheard here?" she asked him.

He shook his head. "No."

"It has been openly suggested that you intend to seduce me."

He managed, with considerable difficulty, to meet her eyes in a leisurely manner, and to smile inquiringly. "Really? Whoever would dare to say such a thing to you?" The chit thought she could match wits with him.

"You've admitted it's true so it doesn't matter who said it to me. It does matter that no one else draws the same conclusion."

"I can't believe someone said any such thing to you," he said, moving closer. "The question is, what do you want? After all, it would be a shame to deprive ourselves of pleasure if we're both ready to proceed."

Hattie slid sideways and ducked from his reach. "Come now, we wouldn't want to miss the fun of the pursuit. We hardly know one another yet."

Irritation, the slightest tightening around his mouth, came and went so rapidly she might have thought she imagined it, only she hadn't. The smile returned and with it the dimples beneath his cheekbones and the flash in his eyes.

She made her best attempt at a coquettish dip of the head. "I do think you should try not to kiss me whenever you get an opportunity."

John tapped his chin. "Why ever not? You kiss me back."

"I kissed you back today." She gave him a cross look. "I would never have done such a thing if you hadn't incited me—and caught me off guard. I assure you that in future I shall follow your aunts' instructions. They are wise women."

He sank his hands into his pockets and looked away while he collected himself. "You discussed…you talked about me, and you, to the aunts?"

She looked at him very directly. "In fact, they talked to me about us, my lord. They are the ones who believe you have designs on me."

"What were their *instructions?*"

"To keep my bodice up and my skirts down. Whenever we encounter one another, if we should." If she laughed, he might be offended, and offended males could be such boors.

"What?" The word exploded from him. "They told you to do *what?*"

"Yes, well, I took notice."

To *hell* with his aunts. "Come, Hattie, you and I need no advice from others. I have to know when I'll see you again—alone."

"I don't know. I've been here too long today. Mr. Leggit will be looking for me."

Heavy footsteps sounded on the stairs and John drew her deeper into the corridor. A maid passed without looking their way and carried on toward the top of the house.

"Just answer my question," he told her. "I can't wait until Saturday."

"You may have to," Hattie said. "If and when we are together again, I hope you will remember that you promised, passionately promised, to be my friend. Friends do not put one another in dangerous situations."

The tone in her voice, the breathlessness, moved him, damn it. She had the power to touch him, perhaps to touch him deeply if he didn't keep a firm hold on his emotions.

Emotions? Ha, it was said he didn't have any. "I will not let anything happen to you." And he meant it, *double damn*. The added complication of discovering he liked the girl was a nuisance.

"Thank you," she said. "I was indiscreet enough to tell you my husband wanted me to give you a reason to be nice to him, and I also said he wanted me to make certain no one else saw us together."

"You did say that," he said.

"Yes, but what I didn't say earlier, and should have, was that he absolutely did not and does not want me to, to...to..." Her sideways glance quickly lowered. "My husband is a proud man. What others think of him matters to him almost more than anything else. He...having a young wife seems to raise his reputation as a *man?* A faithful, fulfilled young wife, that is."

John watched her struggle with interest. This was a warning, but not, unless he was mistaken, one she wanted to give. "Really? He wants you to lead me on, to use my associations, but not to allow me to bed you?"

"Absolutely not," Hattie said.

He cupped her chin and turned her face up to his. "And you? Are you telling me you don't want me to bed you either?"

And this, Hattie thought, was the rub. She might well enjoy lying in the marquis's arms, in the dark, kissing him, even doing what Mr. Leggit could not do, thank

goodness, but surely that could not be. On the other hand, if she said, right now, that she didn't want it he might decide to turn his attentions elsewhere.

She didn't want that, and not only because it would ruin her plans for a faster escape from Mr. Leggit.

"My lord," she said, and had to swallow because her throat hurt, "I'd like it very much if we could have the friendship you spoke of. For the rest, I cannot say."

"But whatever happens must be on your terms?" he said.

He would turn from her now, she was sure of it. She nodded yes.

She didn't expect his faint smile, or the thoughtful expression in his eyes.

"So be it," he said. "We'll see what we see, hmm?"

Hattie hadn't expected that response, either.

16

Chloe looked up at John the moment he entered the schoolroom. She sat at a small desk drawing while Snowdrop and Mrs. Dobbin, their heads close together, chatted and laughed over their tea at a table on the opposite side of the room.

The child slid from her place and rushed to John. For an instant he thought she might speak. She didn't, but she did hug his legs and hold on tightly.

He lifted her into his arms. "Good morning, young Chloe. I brought Mrs. Leggit to see you. You met her last evening, remember? You're having a busy day with so many visitors."

"Hello, Chloe," Hattie said. "I see you've been drawing. I like to draw, and paint a bit. Mrs. Dobbin gives me lessons." She indicated her companion.

"Mrs. Leggit!" Mrs. Dobbin saw Hattie and stood. "Have I kept you waiting?"

"Oh, no, I've been busy," Hattie said, and John met her glance but managed to keep his expression neutral. She would never know how he seethed, deep in his gut, because his plan for a speedy resolution to the Leggit issue had been thwarted.

"Mrs. Dobbin knows everything, my lord," Snowdrop said to him. She had mastered the correct form of address but still treated him like John Elliot naked in a blanket

before her cottage fire. "You should remember to ask her if there's something you need to know. I've learned all about the royalty, and a slimy lot they are, too."

Snowdrop's demeanor turned wistful. "I must say, I'd like to see that Brighton Pavilion one day."

Mrs. Dobbin didn't quite hide a smile and John looked at her with fresh interest. In fact, she was graceful with a beautiful, intelligent face.

"Slimy royalty, eh?" he said.

"Not exactly my description," she said, "but close enough. I did not, of course, refer to *all* members of the Royal Family."

He found her comments oddly bold. "Quite."

"Dobbin is funny when she wants to be," Hattie said. "Or when she needs to be, I should say. She can make me laugh."

And, John wondered, how often did Hattie Leggit need someone to make her laugh in that great, oppressive house where she lived with a criminal, lecherous husband old enough to be her grandfather.

"Finish your tea, ladies," he said. "Take your time. I'm sure Mrs. Leggit would like to see the rest of the nurseries before she leaves."

Mrs. Leggit said, "Yes, of course," but he doubted she was interested in the nurseries.

"First the dollhouse," he said, and set Chloe on her feet again. "It's next door in the actual nursery. This is the schoolroom. And on the other side of the nursery are the nanny's quarters."

"Lovely they are, too," Snowdrop said. She returned to the table and refilled cups for herself and Mrs. Dobbin.

John entered the nursery with a sense of déjà vu. He and his brothers had slept there when, as young children, they'd come to visit their grandparents. Little had

changed. Four wooden beds marched in a row along one wall, and a baby cot stood near a window facing a court-yard at the back of the house. The door to the nanny's quarters stood open with pleasantly warm light showing a comfortable sitting room.

The black cat, Raven, whisked past them and leaped onto the first bed, where she turned around and around before settling down. Her yellow eyes remained open and fixed on John and his companions.

"I expect that's your bed, Chloe," Hattie said. "I see you've tucked your doll in there."

Chloe looked at the floor.

Hattie referred to the peg doll John had bought. Thinking of her as "Hattie" had become natural, perhaps too natural. It wouldn't do to speak her first name aloud in public.

"There's the dollhouse," John said. "Believe it or not, Grandfather Worth actually made it himself—with the help of a gardener, I was told. My aunts treasure the thing. I've suggested they should have it in their own rooms, but they insist it belongs here, where it's always been."

"It's a lot like Worth House," Hattie said.

In fact, John's grandfather had made a perfect replica of his home. This stood on a cabinet with cupboards beneath. "It is a copy of the house," he said. "As you see, the place is fully furnished, but in the cupboards there are all manner of extra pieces. I think it should be under glass and the cupboards locked. One day it will be worth a great deal as a historical memento of the times."

"Oh, not locked up." Hattie walked around all four sides. "Your grandfather made this for his daughters and they obviously understand it is for children. I made my own dollhouse when I was a child."

He almost said he found that hard to believe. "Really?"

"Yes." She smiled as if remembering. "My father gave me a wooden medicine chest he'd found on the docks. A small one. It was old and damaged by water. Chinese, we decided. But when I took out the drawers I pretended the spaces inside were rooms and made furniture with whatever I could find. I played for hours." She looked at Chloe. "When you don't have brothers and sisters, you learn to make up your own games."

Chloe glanced at Hattie. John hoped just being here in Bath, with people who accepted and loved her, would help the child heal.

The walls of the dollhouse, complete with windows and doors, were hinged. Hattie said, "Is it all right if I look inside properly?" and John nodded yes. She slipped up a tiny hook fastening and opened a world in perfect miniature.

With finger and thumb, she lifted the tiny carved figure of a child standing in the basement kitchens. "I'd like a piece of cherry pie, please, Cook," she said, only her voice seemed completely changed. A cook held a wooden spoon aloft before a cauldron suspended in a fireplace. Hattie turned this figure to face the boy. "You be away upstairs where ye belong, wee one, or I'll be tellin' nanny ye're down here beggin' again."

John held his waist and laughed. "You're a marvel. How do you do that?"

Her blush charmed him. "I forgot myself. As I said to Chloe, when you don't have other children at home, you learn to invent things. I invented people who had adventures and they came from different places so they spoke in different ways. Where I grew up I heard all sorts of people."

Yes, John thought, he was sure she had.

Chloe hadn't looked away from Hattie, who went back, somewhat more self-consciously, to talking for the figures in the dollhouse.

Hattie pulled a chair close to the cabinet and lifted Chloe to stand where she could see better. She seemed comfortable with children, another sign of her original station in life. Most ladies of his acquaintance had little to do with their offspring other than to show them off when they were clean, primped and fed.

"Let's have the boy go upstairs," Hattie said, bouncing the figure lightly from step to step, through a hole between floors and into a sitting room.

Hattie stood close to Chloe and the child leaned against the woman, engrossed.

"Here's a little girl who looks like you." Hattie pointed to a girl with painted copper hair who sat reading on the floor. "And this must be her mother." Hattie's voice changed to another quite unlike her own. "Chloe. Here's your cousin come to join us. Find a book for him to read."

Chloe stared at the side of Hattie's face, then reached to pick up the mother figure.

John stiffened. *"Attendez!"* he said. *"Faites attention!"*

He clamped his mouth shut too late to stop the damage. Chloe put the play figure down and scrambled from the chair. Pale, her mouth pinched shut, she huddled against the cupboards.

"What did you say to her?" Hattie asked, and although she kept her voice even, her eyes flashed fury.

John took a calming breath and smiled at both Chloe and Hattie. He had feared Chloe might actually talk and say something about the way her mother had died. "I told her to be careful," he said. "After all, as I told you, the

house is to be looked at not played with. Come, Chloe, show us what you were drawing.''

The child walked away, but to her bed rather than back to the schoolroom. She climbed up and lay beside the cat who curled contentedly against her chest.

Without a word, Hattie left the nursery and didn't stop moving until she'd put a flight of stairs behind her.

John caught up. ''Chloe didn't mean to be rude,'' he said. ''She has had some difficulties recently.''

Hattie raised a forefinger in the air, looked at it and dropped her hand again. ''She doesn't speak, does she?''

He should have rehearsed these answers. ''Her English isn't the best. She has spoken mostly French.''

''She doesn't speak that, either. What's wrong with her?''

Saying it was none of Hattie's business would be a convenient way to end the conversation, but he didn't fool himself he wouldn't suffer more later. ''I told you she's had some…unfortunate things to deal with. I'd appreciate it if you wouldn't discuss any of this elsewhere.''

The finger reappeared and this time she poked him solidly in the chest. ''You don't have to worry about me being a gossip. Before my marriage, I was too busy to have time for such nonsense, even though it does seem very popular in my current circles. I don't think gossip is clever, I think it's cruel. I also believe it to be nothing more than a pastime for idle minds.''

''Well, yes. I agree with you. Thank you. Since your companion seems occupied, perhaps—''

''Perhaps what?'' She lowered her voice. ''Perhaps you could take me somewhere to show me something— alone?''

''You are presumptuous.'' The teetering balance of power between them was dashed inconvenient.

"I am honest and I understand far more than you think I do. Chloe didn't do anything rude. You frightened her and she went in search of comfort. The cat asks nothing but that she love her, so she went to the cat."

"I think you have said enough."

She squared her shoulders. "Why? Because I make you think? Or just because you don't believe women should talk at all unless they're saying silly things while you make love to them?"

"Hattie."

"Mrs. Leggit, please. The little girl is unhappy. For a few moments she began to be a child again, but you were so concerned with *things* and their value, you forgot that people matter most of all." She didn't flinch. "It takes time and work to understand a person. What you see on the surface is what they choose to let you see. If you want more, if you want to go deeper, it takes patience. Of course, you have to really want to make more of a relationship with someone, but if you do, first you have to make them trust you."

He wasn't amused by her tone, or the fact that she chastised him. He also didn't remember being as impressed by the wisdom of one so young, certainly not a female.

Her words didn't have to refer only to Chloe. Hattie had shaken him.

A great deal hung in the balance, that he knew. A bad misstep now and he could face a complete change of plan.

Sadness filled her eyes and her lovely mouth trembled. "I have no right to tell you how to deal with your cousin, but I think you're a fair man so you won't punish her for my audacity. Carelessness, a few hasty words, a cross look or forgetting to let a person know they're more important to you than a *thing*—or getting your own way—

can cost you love, sometimes forever. I think you want Chloe to love you.''

He didn't trust himself to speak.

Hattie had managed to crowd his brain in a way that made concentration on anything else damnably difficult. But he had a debt of honor to settle. He knew if he didn't accomplish it in the way he'd chosen, Nathan would push for Leggit's death. There had already been too much dying and John would rather avoid that solution.

''What are you thinking?''

''Thinking?'' He tilted his head. She never looked away from his eyes for an instant. ''I regret being sharp with Chloe. I've never been a parent and I make mistakes. From now on I'll try to do better.''

Hattie's eyes did flicker then. She nodded and glanced at his hair, then his mouth.

John passed his tongue along his teeth.

Her lips parted and she moistened them.

His jaw caught her interest and he barely stopped himself from making sure he'd shaved recently enough.

Hattie's dark lashes curled at the ends. When she lowered them, those tips were a lighter shade.

He had satisfied her that he would be more careful with Chloe. That had been enough to settle her entire attention on him.

Hattie. An honest woman without pretensions. An intelligent woman who didn't doubt her own reasoning. A woman meant for love, for passion of the wild kind and the sweet, subtle, languorous kind.

With each breath she expelled, he was sure he felt its warmth brush his mouth. Her breasts rose and fell softly, as if she'd slipped into a place where she felt quiet and safe.

He could stay there with her, and say nothing, forever.

Her attention reached the level of his waistcoat, then slid away, up, settled where she looked beyond his shoulder. What she saw he couldn't guess, but what she felt was him—of that much he was certain.

And he felt her as surely as if he held her.

He must, and he would, do what he had set out to do. A different kind of woman would make the seduction easier to justify. But with Hattie, the promise of ecstasy waited, and the whispered warning that even sweet revenge could leave a bitter taste.

Their eyes met again. This time he was the first to look away. He took her hand and kissed it, gently and with a sensation that he was touching her, really touching her for the first time. She didn't pull away and he felt her watching what he did.

Briefly he rested his cheek where his mouth had been.

The fingers of her other hand, lightly touching his hair, moved him. But then she made a sound, like a small cry, and withdrew from him.

She fled downstairs.

17

Mr. Leggit had a preoccupation with grandeur and no inhibitions about mixing periods and styles in his quest to show off his wealth. Hattie detested the oppressive walls, the shape of Leggit Hall. Gothic, Dobbin called it, and the pavilion atop a flat knoll where they sat looking down on the house, Greek. "The Greeks built temples to their gods that looked like this," she told Hattie. "I'll show you some pictures in the library."

Hattie peered between the pillars that supported the domed roof of the white stone open-sided building. She and Dobbin seemed quite alone. Forest swept away to the north. On two sides sheep grazed on meadowland and Hattie could see a dog, as small as a black speck, working back and forth between animals in the distance. "I suppose this place is all right in its way," she said. "I just don't know why he built it here."

"Because he could," Dobbin said flatly. "Money does that. If you have it, you can do as you please. If you have none, you must do as others please." She colored and tightened the ribbons on her bonnet.

"I know what you mean all too well," Hattie said with feeling. "For now I'm just glad we could use this place, because I think we'd know if someone tried to get close enough to hear."

Dobbin gave her a curious look. "It may not be a good

idea for us to linger here too long,'' she said, peeling a windblown blond lock away from her face. ''We could certainly be seen if anyone were to look hard enough.''

That was true. Only Hattie couldn't imagine that even Mr. Leggit would care about her being up here with Dobbin. Anyway, he and Smythe were locked away with their preparations for the gala on Saturday night. She frowned down upon the ornamental gardens surrounding the house and couldn't help but think about having to be present in the nasty Moon Pools room.

Then she thought about Mr. Leggit's plan for her to spend time alone with Lord Granville at the party and her skin tightened all over. Their earlier encounter still bemused and intrigued her.

How long had they stood, only inches apart with so much feeling between them? She tutted. *She* had felt so much. And when his lordship had kissed her hand... Hattie brushed her fingers over the place and felt his lips again, so real she trembled.

''You're troubled,'' Dobbin said. ''I shouldn't mention it, but I was disquieted when Lord Granville came and told me you were leaving Worth House. You were upset and you remain upset. He was not himself.''

Without understanding his extraordinary change toward her, she had still thought him deeply moved. Some struggle had overcome him and she was sure she shouldn't try to decide what that might be. She tried anyway.

''Mrs. Leggit?''

''I was aware that I must hurry back here, that's all.'' Hattie lied and couldn't look at Dobbin. ''The other day you told me I shouldn't be here at Leggit Hall,'' Hattie said. ''You said I wasn't safe. What did you mean?''

Dobbin left one of the stone benches that lined the pavilion and walked slowly from pillar to pillar. ''I

shouldn't have said it. It was wrong of me.'' She turned to Hattie. ''But I'll say this, too, and be finished with it. You are spirited, brave, but you have too little experience of life to deal with certain...practices.''

That had been true before she came here, Hattie thought, but it wasn't now. ''Don't worry about me. I know a good deal more than you realize, even if I despise most of it. And you have helped me become less ignorant.''

Dobbin shook her head once. ''Things go on here that shouldn't.''

''I know that.''

''Of course you do.'' Dobbin's sudden smile transformed her. ''I suppose, and forgive me for saying so, but I suppose you seem like a young sister to me and I feel protective.''

''Thank you,'' Hattie said. She would like to take Dobbin completely into her confidence and might have to eventually, but she wasn't secure enough yet. However, a test of Dobbin's loyalty had presented itself. A test for Dobbin, and a necessity for Hattie, who had no idea how to proceed with Prunella and Enid Worth's request.

''Enough of all that,'' Hattie said, praying Dobbin wouldn't refuse to as much as hear her out. ''Wasn't it nice of Snowdrop to ask you back for tea again? You must go—if you would like to.''

''I would. She is entertaining. One wishes she didn't have that silly name.''

''Dobbin, dear...''

She got the woman's full, questioning attention. Dobbin said, ''What is it this time? Am I to take another excuse to Mr. Leggit because you don't feel *well* enough to join him for dinner?''

Hattie wrinkled her nose. ''No, I shall take dinner with

him, of course. It's not my fault if my stomach doesn't like it when I smell so much food.''

''Of course not. And dinner goes on so long, doesn't it?''

Dobbin was making fun and it suited Hattie to enter the game. ''It really does. I should be forgiven for eating in my rooms sometimes. And who can blame me if I occasionally fall asleep when I join Mr. Leggit?''

''And snore,'' Dobbin said. ''Or so I've heard said.''

Hattie didn't protest. Her gentle snores at the table only started when Mr. Leggit was finally unconscious from drink and she needed an excuse to ''awake'' with a start and say she must go to bed.

Mr. Leggit knew all about the custom of ladies withdrawing after dinner, but when he had company to impress, he liked to keep Hattie with him at table. This meant all the other ladies stayed and most of the gentlemen's companions were as loud and excessive as their escorts. Hattie invariably slept on those occasions.

''I need a way to go into Bath at night,'' Hattie said quickly, before she could change her mind. ''Tonight, in fact. It must be absolutely secret and absolutely certain not to become known to Mr. Leggit. That means I can't take my own coach.''

Since, after a number of moments, Dobbin didn't say anything, Hattie pressed on. ''I've decided how I will get out of the house and walk as far as the road without being seen. But I can't walk to Bath and back without being missed. It would take too long.''

''You cannot mean this. Say you are bamming me.''

''I'm serious. And I ask you to trust me and not ask a lot of questions. Later I may be able to tell you more. Is there a way, do you think?''

Dobbin propped a fist beneath her chin and paced until Hattie thought she might pop from nervousness.

"There isn't a way, is there?" she said.

"Yes, there is." Dobbin lifted the front of her skirts and made for the steps to the ground. "I was told something that surprised me a little. I never thought I'd give it another thought, but now I have and I know how this journey of yours can be made—I hope." She halted. "But Mr. Leggit. How can you be sure he won't discover your absence and start a search?"

"I shall not leave until after he thinks I've gone to bed. After he's already drunk himself into a stupor, that is."

"Very well," Dobbin said. "I'll have to be quick. Let me explain what I'm going to do. Of course, I shall accompany you."

"No," Hattie said. "You will not and that is the end of that discussion."

Enveloped in a dark cloak, Hattie let herself out of Leggit Hall through a door from the conservatory. The key was kept in the lock and she had only to use it.

Slim and pale, the moon barely shone through skeins of wispy clouds. She was grateful for the darkness and sped away, her heart thudding too quickly. Even through her half boots, damp grass soaked her feet almost at once, but all she cared about was keeping her footing and getting to the road outside the estate.

First she negotiated the rose gardens to return to the front of the house. Once she reached the driveway, she slipped into the shadows of trees that lined both sides. She was far more likely to escape injury this way than if she tried to go through forested land in the dark.

Keeping her mind on what she must do in Bath helped lessen the fear that made her legs weak. How a girl who

had grown up in London's small, treacherous streets could be afraid out here in the fresh air, she wasn't sure, except that she'd lived most of her life in London.

Small animals darted in shrubs and dashed up tree trunks. The farther she ran, the louder the wildlife sounds seemed. How different things were when a person was alone. If someone had been with her, she would have enjoyed the noises. If she'd walked this way with Lord Granville, in the dark, she was sure…she was sure she'd barely hear them at all.

A final turn and the great stone entrance came into sight. An arch topped with the sculpture of a bat joined the soaring posts. Mr. Leggit insisted the creature was a hawk. The too-small body convinced Hattie that her husband had been duped by the stone mason into taking a bat with its wings spread instead. She hated the thing.

Hattie heard hoofbeats and the grinding of wheels and paused. Perhaps she'd been too hasty in attempting this mission.

She had made a promise to the old ladies, though.

Running faster, attempting to let the chatter of her teeth drown out her doubts, she reached a stone post and edged past—without allowing herself to look up at the dreaded bat.

Hedges, high and lining the wall that surrounded the estate, still gave her cover and she used it to creep forward.

Hattie jumped and clutched a hand over her heart. Two horses drew to a snorting stop right in front of her. Cautiously peeking around the hedge, she got another surprise. The horses pulled a coach, yellow, she thought and with an almost-round shape. The lamps were turned well down, but a trim of painted flowers was still discernable. When Dobbin had told her who would drive the coach,

Hattie had almost refused but had finally been persuaded by the other woman's sincere conviction that it would be safe.

The person who all but leaped from the box wore a top hat and many caped cloaks. Hattie's pale face must have been visible in the darkness and boots ground gravel in a direct path toward her.

"There you are, Mrs. Leggit," Snowdrop said, assuming a quite manly stance despite her minute size. "I don't know what you've got yourself into, but I'll do anything I can to help." She had drawn her hair back and tied it behind her neck. Unfortunately, one with such a mass of curls had a hard time restraining them and a great many had popped free.

Hattie smiled despite herself and said, "Thank you, Snowdrop. Dobbin is a good judge of character and she was right to think you'd be a good person to help me. I do worry I might draw you into some sort of trouble, though."

Snowdrop laughed, and promptly slapped a hand over her mouth until she controlled herself. "Mrs. Leggit," she said. "You don't know so much about me, but I can take care of myself. And you, if I have to. You just come along and get in the coach."

Meekly Hattie followed and smiled when Snowdrop actually handed her up and inside a plump leather interior of a rich red color. Shades pulled down over the windows had lace edging and embroidered flowers. Dobbin had said nothing about all this, merely that Snowdrop had a carriage of her own. Later, Hattie would have to know more about it.

"There you are, then," Snowdrop said. "Where to?"

"Ten Farthing Lane," Hattie said, feeling foolish. "It's

not far from Bath Abbey, and the Baths. Get that far and I'll explain the rest.''

Hattie thought Snowdrop drove too fast, particularly since her little coach was both light and sprung high, but they flew along without one instant when it seemed possible they would come to grief.

They traveled to Great Pultney Street, and the bridge, in smart time. Once Hattie could peek out and see the abbey, she opened the trap and called more directions to Snowdrop.

The carriage slowed, the horses clopping along at a measured pace. A sharp turn onto North Parade and Hattie was certain she had seen the area before, if only in passing through.

Her throat dried so badly she had to cough again and again. She'd discarded the reticule in favor of placing the handkerchief-wrapped ruby securely into an old pocket she'd hung around her waist. With shaky fingers, she checked to make sure the stone was still safe.

Another turn, this time onto a narrow passageway, and another, and Snowdrop drew the horses to a complete stop. The springs hardly moved when she got down and opened the door for Hattie.

''This would be it,'' Snowdrop said, pointing up at a soot-covered sign announcing Farthing Lane. ''Not much more than an alley, really. The houses are so crowded I doubt a body could say a word that isn't heard by the neighbors.''

''It's well enough built,'' Hattie said. ''But I don't like the feel of it. Too many nooks and crannies where someone could hide.''

''Hide?'' Snowdrop sounded surprised. ''Why would anyone do that?''

Hattie remembered something Dobbin had told her

about Snowdrop and said, "Of course, you come from the country, where very little happens. Even if you do have some criminal elements there, it could never be like London, or even here, I should imagine."

This time Snowdrop clamped her hands over her mouth in time to stop herself from laughing aloud, although Hattie couldn't think what she'd said that might be funny. "I expect you're right," Snowdrop said when she had stopped chuckling. "The closeness of everything here makes me think there's no place to hide, I suppose. Where I come from there's all sorts of places. Woods, holes in the ground, rocks and hills—even in a good fog."

Hattie said, "Hmm. I see nine and eleven. Where can ten be?"

Snowdrop peered into a shadowy entryway between 9 and 11 Farthing Lane and said, "It's here. Back a bit and up some stairs. Built over the entryway."

They left the carriage and trod softly into the mean space. Not a speck of light reached the ground, or the sides of 9 and 11. "I don't know how you saw the place," Hattie said.

"If it wasn't up off the ground where there's a bit of moon shining—and if the ten wasn't so big—I wouldn't have."

Hattie stopped again, pulling Snowdrop with her. "I want you to go back and wait in the carriage," she said. "I'll be faster on my own."

"No," Snowdrop said.

"But—"

"No, Mrs. Leggit. I couldn't live with myself if I didn't stay with you. Let's just hurry up."

Flummoxed, Hattie said, "What I'm doing is secret. It has to be. Even Dobbin doesn't know about it."

"Well, you can take it that I don't know, either."

Hattie knew when to give up the fight. "Very well. Thank you."

They hurried. Uneven steps built into the side of 11 Farthing Lane rose to number ten, a house supported by its neighbors. Snowdrop ran straight up, but Hattie still dawdled a little. She knew all about the hidden dangers in such places.

She couldn't stay here. She put a foot on the first step and a hand snaked around her head to cover her mouth and nose. Hattie kicked and tried to squeal, but whoever had her was much bigger and stronger—and he reeked of all manner of foul things.

He didn't say a word, only bundled her beneath the flight of stone steps and pushed her down, this time on her back but with her mouth still covered. Plucking at his hand, she fought to drag in a full breath.

"Mrs. Leggit?"

Snowdrop's whisper reached her, but there was no way to answer.

The man crammed his mouth against Hattie's ear and whispered, "You were goin' to see 'imself. You got somethin' to sell. Or is it the other one what's carrying it?"

Unable to answer even if she wanted to, Hattie's mind raced. This was her fault. She would not allow Snowdrop to suffer.

She tapped the man's hand.

"You goin' to shout?" he said.

She shook her head.

"Right. Is it you or 'er?"

He released the pressure over her mouth just enough for her to whisper, "Me."

"Well, well, well," he said into her ear. "That was stupid. Now it's you I'm goin' to have to deal with. What

you got and where is it?'' He started to paw at her and Hattie tried to squirm away.

"'Old still. Don't tell me this is the first time you've been in an alley with a man. You wouldn't be walkin' in here like this if it was. I've got a knife, me darlin', so just give me what I wants.''

Hattie heard two things: the clatter of hoofs along Farthing Lane, and Snowdrop raising her voice to call out more loudly. The cry wasn't very far away, which meant Snowdrop was coming down the steps again.

The hoofs suggested the horses had bolted with the carriage.

Boots, Snowdrop's, landed none too quietly on the entryway cobbles. "Where are you?''

An instant later, Hattie's captor let out a muffled oath and shook some part of himself, a leg, she thought.

"Let her go at once,'' Snowdrop said on a hiss. "Right now or you'll wish your scurvy self had never been born.''

The man said, "Ouch,'' and slapped behind him. He moved violently and his hold on Hattie slackened. Instantly she rolled away and threw herself back from the steps.

Snowdrop had her teeth sunk in the fellow's leg.

Hattie saw a flash and remembered the knife. She flung herself at the villain's arm, got her hands around his wrist and hung on—until he threw her to the ground.

"He's got a knife,'' Hattie told Snowdrop in a desperate little voice she hardly recognized as her own. "Get away from him.''

Another body, piling on top of all three of them, arrived without a sound that Hattie had heard.

"That's it for you, mister,'' a new male voice announced. "I'll just take the knife if you don't mind.''

Snowdrop was already on her feet and Hattie soon joined her. They stood close together. "That's my Albert," Snowdrop said. "The cabbage head must have followed me. When's he going to learn I can look after myself?"

In the gloom, Hattie smiled. Snowdrop had a fiery temper.

A fierce scuffle followed, but suddenly the robber grew still. He lay on his face and muttered, "Ow, ow, ow. I'm sorry, guv'ner. I'll never do the likes of this again. Just let me go and I'll change me life."

"He will not," Snowdrop said.

"No, he won't," Hattie agreed.

Albert said, "Get up," and the man did so, still making sounds of pain. "I've got your knife and I've seen your ugly face. And I've smelled you, gawd help me. Now I want your name."

"Fred Smith," came the too-immediate reply.

"Of course it is," Albert said. "And I'm your brother, Tom. Well, I've got to have some way of picking you out of a crowd."

To Hattie's dismay, Albert opened a slit above the man's eye and stood, stoically holding him until he stopped prancing about.

"Go," Albert said. "Before I change my mind. And remember, there are three people here who know how to pick you out. When we leave I'm going to warn everyone hereabouts to be on the watch for you, and that's only the start. I'll spread the advice all over Bath. Are you leaving?"

Without another word, the creature pressed the place above his eye where his blood ran freely and hurried away, limping.

"I did his leg," Snowdrop said, not without pride. "Bit

him, I did. And I'd do it again. And Hattie did her best to get the knife away, but he was too strong."

Apparently Albert wasn't in a talkative mood.

"Who said you could follow me anyway?" Snowdrop said. "And if you were going to do it, how come it took you so long to find me? Got too far behind, did you?"

Hattie cleared her throat. "Well, you two stand guard down here while I run up and do a little business."

"Foolhardy behavior," Albert said in clear tones but not in any accent Hattie had heard before. "If you don't mind, I want to get my fiancée back where she belongs and I'll be taking you home first."

Very tall and rather thin, Albert wore glasses. She could see their wire frames and the slenderness of his face. But he had broad shoulders and an air of confidence about him. She was sure he could look after himself.

"It was Albert who got me my job," Snowdrop said, looking up at him. "He's Lord Granville's man of affairs."

"I'm his valet and I take care of some personal paperwork," Albert said.

Hattie couldn't decide what to say first. Now she realized she'd seen this man at Worth House. Lord Granville retained him! "I must ask you to indulge me for a few more minutes, Albert," she said. "When I can, I'll tell you exactly why. Please trust me for now and let me finish what I came to do."

He drew Snowdrop against him and she whispered something.

"All right, then," he said. "But we'll have to come with you."

She didn't try to stop them, and she continued her desperate search for a clever way to make sure Albert didn't say a word about tonight to Lord Granville. If that man

were more concerned for his aunts' comfort, this evening's events would never have come to such a pass anyway.

At the top of the stairs she was able to read in faded gold letters the word "Apothecary" over a window crowded with bottles and jars. Faint light, very faint, showed from somewhere inside.

She turned back, raised her chin and said to Albert, "Please don't say anything to the marquis about what's happened. I'm doing this more for others than me, but I don't want him to know I was here."

When Albert didn't answer at once, Snowdrop said, "You can rely on Albert, can't she, *Albert?*"

He sighed and raised his face to the sky. "Yes, of course. But I will have to insist you don't take such risks again."

"She won't," Snowdrop said, sounding as if she had her own private joke. "Will you, Mrs. Leggit?"

"Um, no, of course not." What else could she say? And, after all, the Misses Worth had said these events were rare. She might not still be acquainted with them when the need to come here arose again. "Don't worry, Albert. Now, let's see how I manage to speak to the person who lives here."

Hattie stepped into a recess in front of the shop door. Albert and Snowdrop crowded in behind her and there wasn't enough space, but she hadn't the heart to complain.

She raised her hand to ring the bell at one side of the door, but stopped herself.

"What is it now?" Albert said.

"Um, um." Unable to form better words, she pointed.

Written on a piece of stiff paper and jammed beneath the bell, a brief note read, "DRUNK AND VIOLENT TONIGHT. COME BACK TOMORROW."

18

"Stop wearing out my carpets and sit down," John said to Nathan. "I invited you here for a drink before we leave, but I can uninvite you. You're infuriating me."

"Why do you always have to decide what shall be done?" Nathan said. "About anything and everything? I've got a mind of my own, too, y'know."

John swirled his brandy and watched it coat the glass. Nathan had a tendency to state the obvious.

"Look, I'm not putting up with this. Francis was my cousin, too, and I loved Simonne like a sister."

"And I don't care as much about their deaths as you do?" John looked up sharply. "Some things take time and this is one of them. If I move too fast, I could ruin everything." Not that he could choose to move fast now that Hattie had decided to be a problem. Possibly decided to be a problem. He hadn't imagined her response to his restrained advances the last time he'd seen her.

"If you haven't had enough experience at seducing a woman, let me do it for you."

"Don't be bloody rude," John told him.

That made Nathan smile. He liked to arouse John's temper. "Dominic is going to have something to say about all this," he said.

"No!" John held his head in his hands. "Dominic is *not* coming here. Tell me now that he's not."

"He is. He's being very un-Dominic at the moment. He's in trouble with Mama so I suggested the aunts would love to see him."

John threw up an arm. "That does it. He'll be reasoning me to death—" Dominic preferred to battle with his brain than with his brawn and he had plenty of both "—and you'll nag me to death. The only satisfied people around here will be the aunts."

Nathan gestured. "I meant to say that Dominic wants to surprise them so keep mum. He's due here in about three days." His voice rose again. "It'll be two against one and we won't put up with your lolloping about when there's something to be done. *Now.*"

Nathan finished with his mouth open and it stayed that way while he watched Albert, who had knocked once and entered the study—after the bell had rung—without Nathan hearing a thing. Not a thing but his own raised voice, that was.

"You've less than an hour before you leave, my lord," Albert said, giving one of John's coat sleeves a tweak. "I'll have the coach outside in good time."

Animated again, marching back and forth, Nathan's very shoulders seemed to drive forth his rage. "A valet. Or is that a coachman? Or a man of letters? Coming into your rooms without as much as a by-your-leave, and you don't say a word. You carry on as if he had every right to be here while we're having a private discussion."

John smiled. "Albert is all those things here. If you hadn't been shouting, you'd have heard the bell, and his knock before he came in. And if it weren't for Albert, I wouldn't be here and neither would Chloe. He hides nothing from me and I hide nothing from him." *Unless it is private.*

Rather than appear humbly grateful for John's kind

words, Albert busied himself straightening books, a job that belonged to another servant.

"Well." Nathan's explosive tone prepared John for the worst. "I *still* don't bloody know why we have to go to that scoundrel's *gala* or whatever he calls it, tonight unless we plan to kill him." In his ire, he had obviously forgotten Albert's presence again, but now he remembered and looked horrified.

"Death's too good for some," Albert said in a monotone.

Nathan stared at the man as if a look could make him disappear.

"Should make mention of a note Mrs. Dobbin delivered to your aunts, my lord," Albert said, with no apparent discomfort at switching subjects. "This afternoon when she came for tea with Snowdrop."

"What would that be about?" Nathan asked.

"Damn it all, how should I know?" John said. "And why should I care, or you?" But he did care because the note had to be from Hattie and he didn't dare interfere. He would keep a closer watch over the aunts.

Nathan poured himself another drink but didn't attempt to touch it. He looked hard at John. "What I was saying when we were interrupted," he said, "was that I think we should put an end to the thing, tonight."

"You seem to have forgotten my plan," John said, growing weary of the argument.

"You're the one who seems to have forgotten it," Nathan said. "You haven't done a thing about it as far as I can see."

"In that case," John said, "Perhaps you could borrow Albert's spectacles."

Leggit Hall was a cold place. Sitting before her dressing table in her chemise, with Bea hovering behind her, Hattie

rubbed her arms and shivered. Goose bumps covered every inch of her skin.

"Are you catching cold, Mrs. Leggit?" Bea asked. "If you are, you shouldn't be going down to that nasty damp place tonight—even if it is a *hot* damp."

"Bad for the lungs," Dobbin said while she spread Hattie's willow-green gown on top of the bed.

Her failure to complete the aunts' mission weighed heavily on Hattie. She turned over possible ways of making good on her promise. Dobbin had delivered a message to Miss Prunella and Miss Enid, who had kindly written back to say they could manage a day or two more, but Hattie wished she knew exactly when she could make another night getaway from Leggit Hall.

Bea handed her a soft lavender-scented handkerchief and Hattie touched it to her nose. Perhaps she was getting a cold and had an excuse not to go to the gala, Hattie thought. "Dobbin, do you think you could—"

"Give your regrets to your husband for not attending his party tonight?" With her chin on her chest, Dobbin gave Hattie a look in the mirror.

"No, I suppose not," Hattie said. In truth, the goose bumps were as much from excitement as from being cold.

"Mr. Leggit mentioned that you should wear the circlet he gave you for your hair," Dobbin said. "And this is his gift to you for the evening's performance."

"What?" Hattie turned on her stool. "For the evening's performance? What can it be?"

"He said you should open it when you're alone." Dobbin said, and she bent to pull a shallow white box from beneath the bed. "With all this fuss, I almost forgot."

Why, Hattie wondered, would Dobbin put a gift from

Mr. Leggit under the bed. She took the box and almost dropped it. She hadn't been prepared for its weight.

"I already know what's in it," Dobbin said. "That's why I didn't leave it in the open. The noise it makes gives it away."

Hattie lifted one end of the lid and looked into the rich glow of at least fifty guineas. Her heart beat a little faster.

"After all," Dobbin said. "It isn't as if I haven't seen him give you those before."

Hattie closed the box. She didn't know what to make of Dobbin's cross tone or choice of words. "You have seen him, haven't you?"

"The staff knows," Bea said. "There's always gossip. I don't know where you keep so much money, but I hope you're careful. There could be someone here who would try to take it."

"Bea," Dobbin said shortly. "Who would do such a thing? I doubt there's a soul in the house who doesn't feel badly that Mrs. Leggit has to put on such an act or face Mr. Leggit's temper. It's known that public affection doesn't come easily to you, Mrs. Leggit."

"And that Mr. Leggit pays me for it?" Hattie whispered. He had never given her so much money before and she should be glad that he'd made a significant contribution to her escape fund. The idea that other people knew about it shamed her.

Nevertheless, she would take Bea's advice and find a safer place than her dressing room to hide her treasure. "Dobbin, dear," she said. "Would you slide this under the bed again for now, please? And, both of you, I will be grateful if you help stop any silly notions about the reasons for my husband's generosity."

An uncomfortable pause followed before Bea said,

"Let me finish your hair. I want to put on that circlet. It must be ever so lovely."

Hattie opened a drawer in her dressing table and pulled out the velvet box. She knew this should also be locked away, but she hadn't found the enthusiasm, or time, to do it.

Bea had done a particularly good job on Hattie's hair this evening. Sleek and shiny, it swept a little back from its center part and her ringlets were large and loose, all but touching her shoulders. She looked a little closer in the mirror. Bea was also magical with paint. She used very little on Hattie, but the hint of pink in her cheeks and some color on her lips were perfect.

"Let's put on your gown before the circlet and ear-bobs," Dobbin suggested.

Obediently Hattie rose and went to stand before Dobbin.

"Step into it."

Hattie carefully threaded a toe into the pale green dress of lustrous glacé silk Dobbin had pooled on the floor, then she placed the other toe and she fidgeted while Dobbin drew the dress up and helped her slip into short, puffed sleeves. The tapes were drawn tight and the wide velvet ribbon of a much darker green cinched in close beneath her bosom.

Hattie faced the mirror again and thought about a shawl or even a spencer. Her breasts were too large and too exposed. Mr. Leggit might take pride in that fact, but it embarrassed Hattie.

A box of money to look like this and hang on Mr. Leggit's arm, to gaze into his face as if she adored him? She shook her head. Then another, even more disturbing thought came: Was part of the money to pay Hattie to be very nice to Lord Granville? Of course it was. Very nice

but not *too* nice. Allow him to do whatever it took to procure important invitations to Society events for Mr. Leggit. Lead his lordship on until he tried to do much more than kiss and fondle her, then pat him away with one of the much-touted coquettish looks and string him along until the next time they met.

"Please, Mrs. Leggit," Bea said, waiting with the diamond circlet in her hands.

With a heavy heart, Hattie sat on her stool once more and Bea carefully placed the circlet over her hair.

Dobbin clapped her hands together and smiled, showing her pretty teeth. "You are a beauty," she said. "You had best hang on very tight to your husband tonight. He'll need to protect you from some of the lechers he invites here."

Hattie said, "Thank you, Dobbin." She detested thinking about the descriptions Dobbin had given her of sweating bodies and the liberties taken as much by women as men. "I think I'm ready."

"Too bad Smarmy Smythe is escorting you down," Bea remarked.

John and Nathan were fawned over from the moment of their arrival. They stepped through the impressive front doors at Leggit Hall to be greeted by a double row of trumpeters in burgundy and gray uniforms trimmed with gold braid. A gold *L* shone on each chest.

Nathan leaned close to John and murmured, "The man's a bit above himself, isn't he? Gaudy exhibition, if you ask me."

At the sound of the music, two women came forward to escort the newly arrived guests. The women's gowns were apparently nothing more substantial than heavily pleated lengths of imperial muslin draped about their bod-

ies. With each move they made, the wide weave of the muslin showed skin.

Nathan looked at John over the women's heads and raised his eyebrows. John longed to make some comment about the fall of Rome but held his tongue.

An upward glance swept most of the way to the top of three broad flights of stairs. If John had built the house, which he most certainly would not have, but if he had, the marble wouldn't have been black but probably a subtle green. Better yet, there would be none of the grotesque pillars.

The house stirred premonitions of barely hidden debauchery and he wondered if they were about to be called upon to sample some of what Leggit obviously considered the very thing in daring entertainment.

The ladies took them along a corridor beside the staircase and down a wide expanse of marble steps, white this time. The trumpeters had stopped playing and the sounds of harp and fiddle music reached them from below.

"Bit of a cliché, wouldn't you say?" Nathan asked in a low voice.

"So far," John told him. "But perhaps we're in for a big surprise." He put his mouth to his handsome brother's ear. "My advice to you is to sample anything appealing but to keep your trousers buttoned."

Nathan cast John an amused look and they followed the women into an extraordinary place where rays of light—blue, red, green and yellow—shot across the scene at random intervals.

John hadn't been mistaken about the music. Men and women, all scantily clad, played fiddles and harps along a ledge some feet above water that bubbled and steamed. Stone steps led down to the pools which fanned out from a central sculpture of larger-than-life males and females

intertwined in a mad sexual orgy. Guests lounged on the many steps leading to the pool and a few swam through the wraiths of vapor that veiled all but their heads and languorously moving arms.

He caught sight of two large leaded-glass disks. They capped two circular openings at one edge of the ceiling. It was through them that the moon shone when clouds shifted to reveal its face.

"Look over there." Nathan tapped John's arm and pointed with his own head. A voluptuous woman stood naked while two men smeared oils on her body. Her firm, thrusting flesh shone and she shook her black hair back. One of the men sat down, caught her by the waist and pulled her into his lap. Facing him, her body fused to his, she wrapped her legs around his waist.

Supported on their arms, they ground together, giving up shrill cries. The second man pulled their arms from beneath them and they fell back but still strained toward each other, even when he set them rocking like a thrashing boat made of jerking, pumping flesh.

John said, "Perhaps we're supposed to throw coins and applaud."

Nathan said, "You can't say they aren't making an effort."

"My lords!" Leggit strode toward John and Nathan with arms outstretched. His reddened face shone with delight, and the effects of drink. His brawny body and sturdy legs moved with vigor while his jaw lunged forward with each step he took. When he drew close he spread his arms and made a leg, resulting in the appearance of a bloated ballerina taking a bow.

"Good evening," John said.

"You honor my humble home," Leggit boomed and

hurriedly continued, "not that there aren't many people of note present."

"I noticed as much," Nathan told him. "Most notable people, I must say."

Leggit raised an arm and snapped his fingers, all the while displaying an alarming set of big teeth in a smile that didn't charm John.

Two more voluptuous, muslin-clad females trotted forth and knelt before John and Nathan, offering up gold goblets filled with what appeared to be pale golden wine.

Nathan took his, murmuring very softly, "Two by two." He sniffed the contents and John pretended not to notice.

"Cognac," Leggit said, laughing. "French brandy, French wine, French delicacies of every kind—including some of the women."

Contraband, the same kind that had packed the ship and helped cost Francis and Simonne their lives. John accepted his own goblet and took a gulp. The brandy was fine indeed, yet he didn't enjoy its fire.

A couple approached, leaning on each other. "Welcome to Leggit's club," the man, an average-enough-looking fellow, said. "I'm Paul Afters and this is my...fiancée, Polly."

Lush and brown haired, Polly squealed and said, "Ooh."

"This is the Marquis of Granville," Leggit announced, loudly enough for most of the room to hear. "And this is his brother, the Earl of Blackburn."

Afters made a civil enough nod of the head and shook hands.

Polly the fiancée said, "Ooh," again.

"Paul's well-known in these parts," Leggit said. "A man of considerable means."

Afters waved a dismissive hand but grinned nevertheless.

"He's filthy, stinkin' rich," Polly said, giggling when her swain pinched her bottom. She cupped his private parts. "And he is the *biggest* man in these parts. Afters for After. Do you see? He's Bath's most sought after undertaker."

As Polly and Afters' sounds of merriment rose, other guests drifted toward them.

Leggit clapped his hands and the kneeling women rose. One took Nathan's arm, the other, John's, and both led the men away, in opposite directions.

John's last backward glance at Nathan left him with the impression that the Earl of Blackburn wasn't entirely unhappy with the latest turn of events. He was known to have a fondness for pretty blondes.

The woman who steered John beneath festive banners looped between pillars had blue-black hair and olive skin. Her full mouth formed a perpetual moue and her opaque blue eyes laughed up at him. "I'm to show your lordship a special place," she said, her voice low and full. "I'm told you have a serious life and need to be relaxed. I'm very good at relaxing serious men."

John wouldn't question that she spoke the truth.

On the side of the room farthest from the entrance, the woman approached a door set into the marble wall, one of several doors spaced widely apart, and he saw why Leggit referred to his pool as being in more than one room. He was soon closed inside an intimate chamber with its own pool, an extension of the main area and fed from there through pipes, he was certain.

"Sit down and be comfortable," the woman said, indicating a low cane divan strewn with plump silk pillows in brilliant shades.

This was the only furnishing in the room, apart from a marble table heaped with food and drink.

"I'm Lucia." She touched his elbow and, when he looked at her, unwound her muslin drape and stood naked before him. A tiny waist made even more of round breasts and hips. She stroked herself and moved close to him, wetting her lips with a curled tongue. "Ah," she said, caressing his chest beneath his coat and making a move to loosen his neckcloth. "Please, lie down and let me make you happy."

"Thank you, but I'd rather stand."

"You do not like me." She dropped her hands at once. "I'll leave by another way so I'm not seen. But please, wait awhile before you go out again or I shall be punished for failing with you."

John nodded and watched her sweep up the drape and hurry around the water to a second door. Of course, there would be a discreet way to depart the place if necessary. Lucia looked at him over her shoulder and smiled. "Thank you for doing as I ask. I'm grateful."

She left but the door never quite closed; in fact, it opened almost at once and Hattie stepped inside.

19

Pieces of gold. For pieces of gold I am to trick this man into doing what my husband wants. Hattie used the moments she spent closing the door to compose herself.

"Hello, Hattie," John said. A punch to his belly couldn't have made him more short of breath. "Beautiful lady in green."

"Hello." She had been in one of these chambers on a single other occasion—when Mr. Leggit had decided to seduce her there. He would have done it—she could not have stopped him—but other factors conspired against him.

"I take it this meeting wasn't your idea." John knew it must be true but wished she would argue with him.

She didn't. "No, it wasn't. I am embarrassed, my lord. Please forgive me."

If he was embarrassed, she saw none of it. His face was pale and taut but his eyes welcomed her with pleasure, and with intense desire. "That woman was part of the plan," he said. "Her part was to get me here."

"I assumed as much. I saw her leave."

John flinched at the thought that Hattie had witnessed a naked woman leaving his company. "There was nothing—"

"Hush," Hattie said. "I know there wasn't. You are a better man than that."

She trusted him, thought him honorable and above taking advantage of deliberately arranged trysts. By God, he trod a path of deceit. John tried not to dwell on the thought, but it wouldn't leave him. "Will you sit down and let me get you something to drink? Have you eaten yet?"

He spoke so politely, Hattie thought, as if she were a guest in his home rather than a woman in her own home sent to imply a willingness to be seduced by someone other than her husband. "I'm not hungry," she told John. "But I'll have a little wine." The warmth of it would be welcome.

Perhaps Nathan was right, John thought, and Leggit should meet his maker tonight. The man deserved to die for his part in the deaths of Chloe's parents, and for his treatment of this gentle girl.

Glancing at her repeatedly, he poured wine into two glasses. The gown wouldn't be lovely if she didn't wear it, and the elegant diamonds surrounding her head could not possibly glitter and shine unless they were drawing attention to her beautiful face.

He all but dropped the bottle, but set it down firmly and carried the glasses to the divan. "Sit with me," he said. "Even if someone were to come, we could not be blamed for sharing this thing when there's nothing else to use."

Hattie thought to refuse, but she didn't want to. All she really wanted was to be here with him, to look at him and hear his voice, to watch his strong hands and the movement of his clothes over his fine body.

"Don't refuse me," he said quietly. "I think we have a good deal to talk about."

When she walked, the pale green silk gown rustled, a muted rustle since the silk was so thin. Her limbs showed

in outline and he had to force himself not to stare at them. In her gray eyes he saw something that made him stronger, made him want to laugh yet caused weakness in his legs and sharp contraction in his gut. His buttocks drew tight and his male parts hardened. Hattie looked at him like a wondering, inexperienced girl who longed to have him take her.

Clearly infatuation must have befuddled him. She had been married a year or more to a sex-obsessed man who must lie with her frequently. John envisioned the gross and bowing Leggit sweating over Hattie. Unspeakable.

Craving muddled his reasons for being here. His supposed reasons. Despite knowing she had come to him on her husband's orders, he glanced at the divan and thought of her stretched there, bare-skinned and waiting for him.

She must control her mind and heart, Hattie thought, and her body. What she knew of lovemaking between a man and a woman she'd learned from Dobbin, who had spoken in matter-of-fact sentences, pausing between but never quite giving enough time for questions. She had, however, said things that suggested there could be a sweet, perhaps an irresistible joining between a man and a woman rather than Mr. Leggit's frightening, often bruising attempts. Hattie thought of Dobbin as a friend and admired her courage in speaking of such matters although she couldn't understand how the other woman managed.

John went to Hattie, gave her a glass and took her by the hand. "Come along," he told her, grateful she didn't resist. "Sit and talk with a friend. You have nothing to fear from me."

She did as he asked, sitting very straight at the edge of the divan. "I feel a fool." A sip of wine did warm her veins a little. "What must you think of me? First I go

with you to your rooms when we've barely met. Then I surrender to your touches, encourage them even.''

"You have never behaved as less than a lady, a real lady." He sat beside her. "You didn't know I was taking you to my rooms."

"I would probably have gone anyway." She felt touched by his compliments but still heat blossomed in her face. "I thought you dashing and still do. I thought you everything I could want a man to be. There must be something wanton in me.... I shouldn't say such things."

He put a hand on top of one of hers and felt a deep chill on her skin. "Honesty isn't a sin. Why shouldn't you say I appealed to you? You shook me, Hattie. Since I saw you that first time, when you were painting near the bridge, you have never been far from my mind."

She bowed her head, not before he saw the glisten of tears, and said, "I am a married woman."

"And I hate it that you are. Why did you do it? Why did you agree to marry him? You have been vague and I should like a full explanation."

Hattie looked at him. "You could never understand and I won't talk about it." Never, never, because a powerful man like his lordship would have little patience with her tawdry story. "I had a life before Mr. Leggit became obsessed with me, a simple life but a good one. I didn't want to leave it. That's all I can say."

"Very well. Tell me what your husband expects you to accomplish tonight?"

She could weep from humiliation.

"Hattie," he murmured, rubbing the back of a forefinger up and down her neck. "Sweet girl, please don't feel awkward with me. Never. If you do you will destroy me." She might destroy him anyway. Every moment he spent

with her made it more difficult to focus on the reason he had come to Leggit Hall tonight.

"I'm ashamed," she said, resting her cheek on his hand. "No woman with any self-respect could bear being in my position. You asked me what I am supposed to accomplish this evening. I shall tell you."

He could scarcely bear the way she closed her eyes so tightly, squeezing out moisture that shone on her lashes. "It's all right," he said. "There is nothing you cannot ask of me." He set down his glass, and hers, and guided her head to his shoulder. "Get it over with."

Staying where she was, never moving from the safe hollow of his shoulder, would be heaven. He settled a hand on top of her bare shoulder and nuzzled her head with his chin.

"I am never going to be ready to let you go again," he said. "Allow me to make your life easier." Where was the cold fellow others thought him to be? He'd best recover that man and fast.

"There's something you can do," Hattie said.

She turned toward him, kissed his neck above his neckcloth and his blood heated. How much more could a man be expected to take? This had become about much more than cuckolding a vicious, arrogant man who should be made to choke on his empty pride. This was not so simple anymore. Now John had a dual purpose, to seduce the girl for sure, but also to save her from Leggit's wrath afterward.

"If you *could* arrange for Mr. Leggit to attend a grand affair or two, and secure some invitations for him to intimate gatherings of people in high places…"

"Why does he want this so, I wonder?" John said. He chafed Hattie's chilled arms then released her while he shrugged out of his coat. "Don't protest or I shall get

angry with you,'' he said, wrapping her in the coat, pulling it around her, holding her still with his thumbs on her full breasts, barely above a neckline that scarcely covered her nipples.

And she looked into his face every second of the time.

"My lord," she said.

"No," he told her. "When we are alone, you are to call me John. That is my name and you, of all people, should use it."

"John," she said softly and for the first time. "Mr. Leggit wants to meet all these people because he expects to start moving within their circles and to form lucrative alliances with his new acquaintances."

He could not imagine Leggit circulating among members of the ton. Many of these people he secretly disliked himself, but he understood them and they were quick to sniff out an interloper. Still, something could be arranged if it would make Hattie's life more pleasant, at least until he'd completed his mission.

"What are you thinking?" Hattie asked.

"That you are a very brave girl who could be forgiven for running away from all this."

"*No.*" Hattie held on to his waistcoat tightly. "I cannot run away. Not until I have done what I must."

"And that is?" Could it be that money and position meant so much?

"All I can tell you is that I cannot think only of myself, but I am determined to protect…" She raised her face to look at him. "There are people in my life who have suffered too much, in part because of me. I cannot abandon them."

"But you could abandon me?" he said, feeling no shame at his manipulation.

"No," she said slowly. "No, I could not abandon you

if there was any other way. But we cannot go on like this.''

John's breaths grew shorter. She had already told him that Leggit expected her to tantalize but never to satisfy him. "You're right," he told her. "But neither can we deny ourselves a little pleasure."

Hattie trembled. She placed her hands over his and held them tightly against her. "There is no reason for you to put yourself out for me. If you go your way and never have anything to do with Mr. Leggit again, I shall do well enough. I have been... I know about your needs. You cannot be expected to play with a woman as if you and she were barely grown and experimenting with new feelings. Encounters like this can only leave you feeling...pain, I suppose. And a certain inflammation of the mind.''

Inflammation of the mind. Now there was an interesting term for being so frustrated and aroused that the only help to be found, other than with another woman, was in mounting his horse and riding until he became exhausted.

What made Leggit so certain his wife would not succumb to another man—or be overcome by him? He glanced at the door and knew the answer. Some sounds couldn't be avoided and he presumed someone was listening and ready to break in.

But he was, after all, just a man.

His senses pooled where she held his hands to her breasts, and in his longing to taste her, and to make love to her until they slept. That would be a more pleasant way to exhaust himself than riding a horse.

But even while he held her she was out of his reach.

Hattie couldn't fathom his expressions. They changed but were all fierce. He had trapped her fingertips between

his while he stroked her breasts, and he never took his eyes from hers. His intensity frightened and thrilled her.

"I must hold you," he said, gathering her into his arms, tucking her face into his neck. His hands on her back, stroking, smoothing, holding her so tightly, felt like armor against the world. He kissed her neck, her shoulders, and she clung to him with her eyes closed.

"Hattie," he murmured into her ear.

She didn't want to open her eyes and see her surroundings—and feel the magical sensations slip away. She didn't want to face the reality that these might well be their last moments of intimacy.

John kissed Hattie's chin. She wouldn't look at him, but he felt desperation in her. This was his fault entirely. Before setting out on his hastily conceived quest to use Leggit's wife against the man, he should have taken measure of the woman. Vengeance he would have, but what else? A life haunted by Hattie's face?

"Are you listening to me?" he murmured.

She nodded yes.

"I should like to kiss your mouth."

"Would it make any of this easier?"

"I think so." And he lied.

With her hands at his waist, Hattie settled her mouth on his jaw and trailed her tongue as far as his ear. She continued toward his temple, but he was too tall for her to reach it. The flimsy dress rustled afresh and before he guessed her intent, she knelt on the divan beside him with her elbows on his shoulders and his head caught between her forearms and hands. He had only to move inches to bury his face in her breasts—and risk ending the moment.

His hair felt crisp between her fingers. His brows flared above those very blue eyes. She wanted to take her time exploring him and sat sideways on his lap to touch her

mouth to the skin between his brows, to the corners of his eyes, to his nose, and the grooves that slashed downward from cheekbone to jaw.

Getting close enough seemed impossible. Wriggling, she raised one knee to bring her where she could push up his chin and kiss him there.

A man was only a man, John thought once more, even at best. Hattie's kisses and embraces had made his blood pound. The urgent rubbing of her bottom over his already unruly manhood could hardly be tolerated at all. It couldn't be tolerated, damn it!

His hands flailed in the air and he was grateful her eyes were shut.

No more.

"My turn," he said, and kissed her lips with twice the force he'd intended. He parted her lips—she wouldn't have been able to stop him this time—and plunged his tongue deep inside.

And the lady rocked on top of his penis. The blood that had thundered throughout his body made a rush for a single part, or so it felt. He was light-headed, wasn't he? Or could he be in shock?

Try as he might, and the effort was pathetic, he couldn't hold back the need to thrust past her lips, again and again. He prayed the parody of penetrating her body would lessen the urge that raised his hips toward her each time she shifted.

Their wild tousle inflamed Hattie. She had never experienced such a thing before. Dobbin had spoken of times such as this and now Hattie believed her.

So abruptly that Hattie forgot to breathe, John swept her up and stood, holding her in his arms with her feet a long way from the ground. She kissed him again and he kissed her back. They were like animals devouring each

other. His strength, the ease with which he carried her, turned her bones to jelly and if she could, she would have disappeared into him forever.

"Hattie?" Not a whisper or a shout but a broken plea. "Nothing has changed for me since I met you, except that I grow more desperate to have you. There's no point in being subtle. You don't love your husband. You are almost his captive slave and he doesn't prize you. I worship you, my love. Please, will you allow me to find ways for us to be together?"

"Together how?" She knew what he meant but must gather herself enough to make wise decisions.

"As if we were man and wife." How could he be more explicit. He was sure she had not had an affair before and he wanted her to understand exactly what he was asking. "I could ask you to be my mistress, but that is not the way I want to think of you."

"I *would* be your mistress," she said, surprising him with her bluntness.

Pretense would get her nowhere. Putting off sleeping with him would drag out her unhappiness and rob her of whatever brief moments of ecstasy she could grab. And although he couldn't guess as much, their times together would give her a way to free herself from Mr. Leggit with enough money to rescue her parents and provide for the lonely life that waited for her.

In that life she would be always a wife, for she held no hope of a divorce, but never a lover, not again. A man like John might enjoy an affair with a woman who pleased him, but in time he must marry and have children and the affair must stop. Hattie wouldn't consider any other course after his marriage and anyway, he wouldn't want her once she revealed how she had used him.

"Answer me, Hattie," he begged. "Will you have me?

Will you grant me the responsibility for your safety, because you will need it when you become mine?"

"Put me down," Hattie said, gathering her courage.

John did as she asked at once. He hoped he still appeared in command of himself and capable of taking care of her no matter what came their way.

She shook out her skirts and smoothed her hair. The circlet had shifted so she placed it squarely on her head once more.

"I am sure it is past time for me to be back in my rooms. Mr. Leggit will be waiting to see how successful I've been with you."

"Don't go yet."

While she backed away from him, Hattie looked at the floor. "You must be the one to lead the way."

He frowned at the top of her head. "Lead the way?"

"I have never been a mistress before."

20

Four days, well three and a half anyway, and not a word from John. Lord Granville. Hattie corrected herself at once although, as far as she knew, no one could hear her thoughts. Three and a half days if she didn't count the bit of Saturday that had remained after she left him by the pool in that room, that's how long it was since she'd heard a word from the man who had insisted he intended to protect her—and make her his mistress.

Les Mead had protested that the rain would be unhealthy for them, but leaving the coachman and the carriage near the Baths, and with Dobbin on her right and Bea on her left, Hattie walked downhill on popular North Parade Passage to buy Sally Lunn tea cakes at number four. She swung the paper and string-wrapped copy of Jane Austen's *Mansfield Park* she'd finally managed to obtain from a tiny bookshop Miss Austen was rumored to have visited herself. Mr. Leggit didn't hold with her reading. He had also been rude enough to suggest she only pretended to read because she couldn't possibly know enough about it when Dobbin had only started tutoring her the previous year.

Hattie's mother had taught her to read as a small child and somehow the Walls had managed to supply themselves and their daughter with books, even if there were times when Hattie longed for more.

Knowing how close she would be to 10 Farthing Lane and Porky's Apothecary Shop, Hattie had wisely left the aunts' ruby at Leggit Hall. She knew she would have been tempted to ''lose'' her companions, for at least long enough to sneak away and make the transaction she knew must be dealt with, and soon. The result might have been disastrous.

But she had made up her mind to come back here this evening. Before returning to Leggit Hall, she was to drop Dobbin and Bea at Worth House to visit Snowdrop. Dobbin had promised to find a way to speak with Snowdrop alone and arrange transport for tonight if possible.

The three of them swerved to allow a puffing coster-monger, yelling out that he had meat pies for sale, to pass. The pies, flat, overly brown things, gave off steam that smelled of something, but not meat. Then the three of them swung wide in the opposite direction so that a strapping fellow could push a bath chair, occupied by a nodding old gentleman with a red nose, uphill to the Baths.

The shop's fragrant scent of fresh-baked goods wafted out before it was reached. ''Stay where you are at your peril,'' a rotund boy with blond curls and pink cheeks cried. He whipped a hoop along with a stick. ''Out of the way, ladies, or you shall surely fall when my hoop tosses up your feet.''

Hattie smiled and pulled her companions against the wall to let the cheeky, satin-dressed boy go by. He showed no regard for raindrop splotches on his rich clothes. A black-clad nanny, hands behind her back, plodded uphill in her charge's wake—she called out a gruff ''Have a care, Master Toby,'' from time to time—wearing a deeply irritated frown on her face.

Lined up once more, the three ladies continued toward

their tea cakes, and almost collided with Lord Granville and Chloe.

With one hand he held Chloe's while he tucked the other behind his back. Quickly he doffed his hat and bowed. With his black hair and dark gray caped overcoat, relieved by the merest hint of white at his neck, he appeared an elegant but grim-faced fellow with the weight of the world on his shoulders.

"Good afternoon, my lord," Hattie said, her stomach jumping in a most unpleasant manner. "I'm glad we're not the only ones who enjoy walking in the rain." She closed her mouth and swallowed several times.

Lord Granville drew Chloe against him and she looked out from the hood of a pretty red mantle. "Sometimes one walks in the rain because one has no choice," he said, his voice deep and gruff. At last he caught Hattie's eye and she feared he intended to treat her like a stranger.

He smiled, and was definitely the John she knew. As quickly as he'd softened toward her, he replaced his hat and seemed ready to continue on.

Chloe raised a gloved hand toward Hattie. Three figures from the dollhouse—the mother, the copper-haired girl and her cousin—were clutched there.

"Good Lord," John muttered, and Hattie wondered if this was the child's first attempt to communicate with another since…since whenever it was she last spoke.

Hattie felt emboldened. "Dobbin and Bea. Please go and buy the tea cakes. Get some for Chloe to take home for everyone, too." She reached into her reticule for money, but John's fingers, curling around hers, put a stop to that.

"Please, allow me," he said, and gave money to Dobbin, who backed slowly away with Bea. They both showed reluctance at leaving the spectacle of handsome

Lord Granville and Mrs. Leggit exchanging pleasantries on the pavement.

"After all," he said softly. "We both know you have another purpose for your money."

She blushed and hunkered down beside Chloe. "I see your cousin has decided you should play with the dollhouse people. He's a kind man." She glanced up at him and all but fell sideways. The gruff, serious marquis had transformed into an irresistible man who looked at her with his heart in his eyes.

"You were right," he said. "Such things are meant for children. Chloe takes those everywhere now."

Hattie took the mother figure from Chloe and walked it along her own knee. "Hello, Chloe," she said in the voice she'd invented for the character. "I'm so glad to see you. Mothers don't like to be parted from their little girls."

To her alarm, Chloe sniffed and her lower lip trembled.

John said, "How is that badly behaved cousin of yours?" in a squeaky voice and in such a rush that Hattie stood again and looked at him. He shook his head slightly and murmured, "Too soon. Leave it for now." And in the same tone he added, "We will be together soon. Trust me and be ready when the time comes."

The best she could do was nod. She handed the figure back to Chloe, who seemed still, and heard Dobbin and Bea laughing together at the same time.

"Here we are, then," Bea said, her cheeks red from exertion and the snap in the weather. "These cakes would be yours, Miss Chloe." She held a box out to the child but John took it.

"I hear you're going to visit with Snowdrop shortly," he said, not looking at Hattie. "Why not let us take you

back in our carriage, as long as Mrs. Leggit has no objection. It would save you another journey.''

''I don't mind,'' Hattie said, although she wished, with an ache in her throat, that she might also go with him. ''Mead will get me back safely.''

After the shortest possible hesitation, both Dobbin and Bea agreed that the idea was perfect and started back up the hill.

''May I offer you my arm,'' John said, and his lips curved when she slipped her hand beneath his elbow. Chloe trotted along holding his other hand. ''We could be mistaken for a family,'' he said, peering at the sky from beneath his hat brim.

She glanced at the side of his face. The corner of his mouth turned down now and there was a bitterness about him.

They gained the road in front of the Baths and Hattie saw John's splendid green coach waiting only yards from her own conveyance. Albert had just finished spreading blankets over the horses, but he removed them at once when he saw John. Snowdrop's bespectacled fiancé showed little expression while he helped Chloe, Dobbin and Bea into the coach but then, and to Hattie's amused consternation, he winked at her.

She attempted to wink back, but both eyes closed at once.

John led Hattie to her own coach and helped her inside. He took a throw and arranged it over her knees. ''A surprisingly cool day,'' he remarked. And again he looked directly into her face. ''Tomorrow afternoon Leggit has an invitation to a gathering of gentlemen. They are all in high places. There will be talk of world affairs, followed by dinner, followed by gambling. He is unlikely to return home before morning. Remember the keys?''

She nodded.

"Can you ride?"

"Not well, but yes."

"Do you have a horse of your own?"

She shook so that her teeth chattered. "A pony."

"The tyrant will be gone. Find a way to take the pony and come to me just before dusk. Wait in the lane beside Worth House until it grows darker. Tie your pony there, just inside the hedge. Use the keys and put everything else in my hands."

21

"**J**ust call me Porky. Everyone else does."

The journey to Farthing Lane had worked as planned, only this time, Snowdrop and Hattie had taken the coach lamps and held them aloft to make sure no oaf lay in wait for them. After that, Snowdrop returned to her coach to keep watch in case an odd ruffian or two did show up while Hattie was inside the apothecary shop.

"Thank you," Hattie said. "That's what I shall call you, too, then. Porky. I'm pleased to meet you."

She shook hands with a smooth-faced fellow who must be at least eighty, probably more. The skin that stretched tight over a round face fell in folds beneath his chin, and provided but a thin cover for ropes of purple veins on his hands.

He said, "Hmm, hmm, hmm," and bounced on his toes behind a shop counter crowded with bottles and jars, tins and wooden boxes, mortars and pestles, a bulbous bowl balanced over a candle flame. Blue-green fluid bubbled in the bowl and thin snakes of steam climbed into the air spreading a scent like cooking rhubarb.

"It was suggested I should come and see you," Hattie said. "I came the other night, but you were drunk and violent." She closed her eyes and shook her head. "Forgive me, I am too blunt."

"I should say you are, young lady." Porky spoke like

a gentleman. "Never touch a drop of anything but tea. How about some tea? River root tea—from roots harvested in the bed of the River Avon, of course—is very good for females. Helps with hysteria, vapors and the like. Yes, I see you need root tea."

If she didn't need it now, she soon would. "Mr. Porky, I didn't come about potions. I thought you conducted another business here."

"Don't get excited!" The bobbing became hops. "Keep your bonnet on. Root tea coming right up. Back here with you and sit down. And it's Porky, not *Mr. Porky.*"

He hurried from behind the counter to take hold of her arm in surprisingly strong fingers and pull her past the counter. The silver tassel on the round, orange silk hat he wore atop white curls swung back and forth in front of his black eyes.

"Sit *there.*" In a room behind the shop, he plunked her into a large, soft chair. "And *calm* down."

"I am calm, Porky."

"You are?" He took a kettle from the hearth and poured boiling water into a teapot. "It has to steep," he said. "So, if you're not agitated or hysterical and you don't have the vapors, why are you here?"

Hattie took a settling breath. "I told you, because I understood you were in another business." She waved a hand toward the shop. "Another business other than that."

He frowned. "Hmm, hmm, hmm." Pallid tea streamed into pink china cups and he gave one to Hattie. "Drink up," he said.

Sensible people didn't drink anything supposedly made from roots harvested from the bed of the River Avon.

Porky drained his cup, smacked his lips and poured some more.

Hattie sipped her tea.

"Good, isn't it?" Porky said.

"Wonderful. It tastes like—"

"Lavender," Porky said. "I do have another business. Or I can if I want to. Did Prunella and Enid send you?"

When the shock wore off, Hattie reached to the bottom of the pocket she wore tied around her waist again and pulled out the ruby wrapped in Miss Prunella Worth's handkerchief. "They did," she said. "I feel so badly for them that things have come to such a pass."

Porky's bright black eyes bored into hers. "You're kind. They would know that. Intuition. It's a female thing."

"I understand you can buy something from me then sell it again."

"Absolutely true. What is it this time?"

He didn't know her, yet he didn't attempt to find out if she might have come to expose his wrongdoings. "It's a ruby," she said, opening the handkerchief.

"Why didn't Boggs come?"

Hattie cleared her throat. The tiny room, separated from the shop by a bamboo screen, hemmed her in. Large pieces of furniture crowded together and the fire put out blasts of heat.

"Hmm, hmm, hmm. Boggs?"

"The marquis is in residence at Worth House and Boggs wouldn't come in case he got found out and lost his place."

"Marquis? That would be Henrietta's boy. The oldest one. Don't blame Boggs. Can't take chances at his advanced stage of life. Know all about taking ruinous chances." Porky, who was really quite thin, took the ruby

between finger and thumb and lifted it before his eyes. So quickly Hattie wondered if she'd imagined it, he also snatched the handkerchief and stuffed it up the sleeve of his dark green velvet coat.

Hattie didn't suppose she should mention the handkerchief.

"Nice, very nice," Porky said. He'd produced a glass to look more closely at the jewel. "Here you go then." From a crockery pot with a cork stopper he counted out fifteen sovereigns.

When they were in her hands, Hattie examined them. They certainly didn't seem much in exchange for a big ruby. "Porky, just the other day the Misses Worth were explaining to me how difficult it is for them to manage. I got the impression that since things have become so dear, and you continue to give them what you've given for years, they are not quite as flush as they once were."

"Naughty," he said, and smiled like a pleased boy. "Their spirit doesn't fail. Now you run along and give the blunt to them but don't say you've mentioned needing more money. They know our little rules."

"Porky?" A big voice boomed from another room. "Who are you talking to? It's not—"

"No," Porky called back. "Just a customer. Leaving now. Leaving, leaving," he said, waving Hattie to her feet and taking the cup away at the same time. "Out you go, whoever you are. Out you go."

Hattie all but ran from the shop and dashed down the stone stairs, peering hard into the darkness as she went. Her head spun at the strangeness of what she'd just experienced.

The money made the pocket heavy. It clinked as she hurried along.

She called, "I've done it," to Snowdrop and opened the door of the coach.

"You most certainly have done it, you silly woman."

The voice belonged to John, as did the coach. She had been in such a flurry that she had been about to climb into the green coach without as much as a thought.

She turned around to be confronted by a solid chest and two strong arms that lifted her into the coach. Without ceremony, John sat her down hard on a seat.

"Snowdrop," she said in a croak. "Snowdrop's expecting me."

"She is sitting inside that dreadful conveyance of hers and Albert is at the reins. Fortunately for all of us I saw him dashing toward the stables and followed. Being the honest man he is, he told me everything. Why we honest men must be cursed by you dishonest women I cannot imagine." He waved a hand high. "On you go, Albert. I'll deal with this one."

The yellow coach moved off and John climbed in to sit opposite Hattie.

"Since you've interfered with the way I was getting home," she said, "I think the least you can do is drive me there yourself. All you have to do is drop me on the road that passes the estate. I can go alone from there."

"Oh, my—" John swept off his hat and tossed it into a corner of the coach. "You *are* mad. Are you *trying* to fall foul of some villain?"

He slammed the door and pulled down the shades.

"I can take care of myself," she said, feeling every bit as silly as he suggested. "I grew up in London and learned all about avoiding things that were dangerous."

"So what went wrong? How is it that you know about avoiding dangerous things, but you came here tonight and went into that, that…what is it?"

At least she didn't need to talk about the real reason she'd come. "It's an apothecary shop," she said.

John looked at her in the dim light. Disbelief gleamed in his eyes, and real anger, the kind she hadn't seen in him before. "I don't believe you."

Albert could have told him about the other evening and the fight. Hattie had bruises on her back from that. "Let me take you up there," she said, knowing she was bold. "I'll introduce you to the man who runs the shop."

The rain had stopped in the late afternoon, but she heard it against the windows now, and a gust of wind buffeted the coach.

"I need to go home," she said, keeping her face down and her hands tightly together in her lap.

"You like living at Leggit Hall?"

She hadn't thought he could be cruel. "You know I don't."

"Then why are you in such a hurry to get back there?"

Hattie thought he knew the answer and didn't repeat it for him.

"Is something wrong with you, Hattie?" The change in the way he spoke to her made her look at him. He searched her face as if he'd find his answer there. "Are you ill?"

"No, of course not."

"I think you are. I think that's why you went to that shop. You don't have anyone to depend on in that desolate house you live in."

Hattie inclined her head. She could tell Albert hadn't said a word about the other night. Of course, he would protect Snowdrop.

"Tell me," John said softly, scooting across the narrow confines of the coach to bracket her legs with his own.

"Please. You wouldn't do such a dangerous thing if the stakes weren't high enough to make it your only choice."

He was worried about her. He cared. She inclined her head, blinked, willed the tears that started to stop. John didn't look away from her, and now he must see the tears that stood in her eyes.

Shifting until his knees pressed the seat on either side of her, he held her shoulders and kissed her forehead. "Whatever it is, I'll help you. I'll take you away now and make sure you get the best care."

No, she couldn't let him imagine terrible things for a moment longer. "Root tea," she said, wishing she had a supply of it in her pocket. "I heard it's good for…female problems. For those times when a woman feels sad or angry and can't set those feelings aside."

He blinked.

It was true enough that she suffered during her times of the month. She'd never expected to discuss such matters with any man. "And pain," she said in a tiny voice. "Roots from the bed of the River Avon. The tea tastes like lavender and makes a woman feel stronger." She did feel stronger! "I heard this was the best place to come for it."

"I don't like to think of you suffering," he told her and he shifted, uncomfortably, she thought. "You should be in bed. You need to be kept warm and have plenty to eat and drink."

She was barely in time to suck her lips in and avoid laughing. The sincere air about him was too much and she was a wicked, wicked thing. "I don't need to do that. Honestly, I was just experimenting for when I might have to. I think I'll arrange to have a supply of root tea delivered to Leggit Hall."

John looked even more closely at her. "You're sure? You aren't, er—you know?"

Thank goodness for the gloom. "No, I'm not. In fact the tea I sampled was so good I feel twice the woman I really am."

The great sigh John let out sharpened Hattie's guilt. He leaned forward to rest his brow on hers. "You frightened me," he said. "I've heard of these things being so bad they are dangerous."

"Not the case with me."

He smiled and kissed the tip of her nose. "Good. I couldn't bear it if you were ill. You funny girl. You really are brave, aren't you?"

"About some things." She'd had to be. "I'm not fond of rats."

He drew back. "Why would you say a thing like that?"

"They came into the… I saw them sometimes when I lived in London." He didn't need to know that dealing with rats coming for the flour and other baking needs had been part of her life. Sally, the big orange cat who lived in the bakery, was in the habit of presenting her nightly kill on the hearth in the morning. Hattie shuddered.

"One day I hope you'll tell me all about your life." He chuckled. "And perhaps I'll tell you all about mine, although I daresay it won't be as interesting."

They grew quiet and looked at each other until their smiles went away. John took Hattie's face in his hands and kissed her with so much tenderness she heard a moan come from her. Again he kissed her, and again, and she felt his restraint.

Next he concentrated on her fingers, not missing a tip or a space between, and finished with deep kisses on her palms.

The way he made her tingle felt strange. Strange but

wonderful. Her breasts seemed to swell, her nipples to harden and make her want him to touch them. But most concerning of all, she became moist between her legs. Moist and urgent and unable to keep her hips still.

The kissing grew more fierce.

John undid her cloak and pushed it from her shoulders. He spread his legs wider and pulled her to sit on one of his thighs.

"I've stayed awake at night thinking about this—with you." The sound of their breathing filled the space. "I've got to have you."

With her arms around his neck, Hattie allowed him to run his fingers up and down her neck, gradually going lower until he spread his hands over the tops of her breasts.

Under her bottom she felt that Part of him grow larger and harder. That was what Mr. Leggit couldn't make his body do. She didn't want to think about that. John grew harder still and she felt a pulse through her clothes.

He fastened his lips and teeth over one of her nipples and she couldn't keep still. She rose up and bared her breasts for him, moved them back and forth, intoxicated by the sensation he made when he pulled on them with his mouth.

"Hattie," he murmured. "You are so beautiful. Let me in."

She ducked her head to kiss his lips with her open mouth and copied what he did when he put his tongue in and out of hers.

Laughter, a rumbling in his throat came unexpectedly. She must be making him very happy. She grew wild at the thought and kissed him with desperation.

Finally she fell to sit on his thigh again and found that he had slid a hand beneath her skirts. He smoothed the

insides of her legs all the way to the top. He hooked his hand, all but the thumb, beneath her. With his thumb, he probed past the hair that covered *that* and found a piece of flesh she hadn't known could send such sharp sensations into her.

Hattie raised her breasts to him again and he nibbled at them. He nibbled there and rubbed his thumb over the other thing.

"Oh," she cried. "Oh, John. Oh, oh." She bobbed up and down then plopped to sit and pushed back and forth against him.

"Oh!"

Her body convulsed and she snapped forward, clung to his other thigh. One after another she absorbed the most extraordinary burning, throbbing, wonderful sensations.

"Oh!" At last she was still and quiet.

The uproar that had shaken her, the clamoring, settled down and she was left limp. "John," she murmured. "That was wonderful. Thank you."

"You were wonderful," he told her, but his words ran together and he continued to breathe in great gulps of air. He pushed her skirts up to her hips and kissed her...*there*. She liked it, but they were in a coach and someone could come at any time. What was she thinking of?

Hattie slumped against him. She was thinking of him. Only of him.

He touched her again.

"John," she said quietly. "It's too soon. I want to do that a lot more but not exactly now."

"Not exactly now?" His smile was pure wickedness. "This is exactly the right time, my love." With one hand he began loosening his trousers, all the while kissing her in places she would never touch again without thinking of his lips being there.

"You are so sweet to me," she whispered. "It makes you tired. That feeling. Have you noticed that?"

"Mmm, yes. Eventually. I'm going to make love to you now, Hattie. Stand up and sit astride my hips. Oh, Hattie, I've waited for this. You are my dream."

Hattie watched John unloose his trousers and reveal himself. The sight of his straining flesh shot heat over her skin. She burned as if she would never be cool again.

"Come on," he urged. "Stand up and come to me."

The coach shook and she heard the wind howling up the narrow street.

And she looked down at him again.

"Hattie?"

Very carefully she touched him, stroked him, rested her hand where she could feel an answering jerk in his flesh.

She wanted him.

But not here. Not in a coach on a mean road with the wind tossing them and the rain hammering the windows.

Hattie couldn't do it. "Tomorrow I am to come to Worth House," she said. "Remember? I have the keys."

"No."

"You don't want me to come anymore. I don't understand."

"No, you don't understand, do you. The devil take it. Ah!" He sucked air through his teeth. "You know better than this, madam. To take your pleasure and leave me in such a way."

"You wanted to make love to me," she said, inching her skirts down. She tried to help him do up his trousers but he pushed her hands away. "I'm sorry. It's just that I feel vulnerable out here like this."

"You didn't feel vulnerable until I'd finished—until I'd finished."

"Well, I couldn't think then. And I didn't expect to

lose my mind like that. I didn't lose my mind, but it felt like it while you…''

"Yes." He had straightened his clothes and he leaned to retrieve his hat. "I understand perfectly. I believe there are certain favors you want me to perform for you—re-garding Mr. Leggit."

Hattie held her breath.

"I see you haven't forgotten. I shall drive you home and find a way to see you safely inside."

"Thank you but that's not nec—"

"Enough! Not another word. Make sure you aren't late arriving at Worth House tomorrow."

She bowed her head. "I'm not coming."

He laughed and that laugh froze her heart. "I think you are. I understand your faithfulness to your husband. Admirable. There are other ways for you to pleasure me—as I'm sure you know. *Don't* keep me waiting tomorrow."

22

Whatever she had done, she had done it wrong. Whatever it might be. What was it that she was supposed to do in response to what John had done, so magnificently, to her? Well, perhaps she wasn't being quite honest with herself. She knew what he had wanted, at least the last bit, because Dobbin had told her about it and Mr. Leggit had tried to do it to her.

"Mrs. Leggit? Are you awake now?" Dobbin had come into Hattie's bedchamber several times to ask the same question and, as before, Hattie remained, facedown, on her bed with the bedsheets over her head.

"Oh my, oh dear," Dobbin said. "What have you done?"

Hattie held quite still. Dobbin had not asked *that* before.

"Is it true? Mr. Leggit told me he will come to see you after he goes to his solicitor this morning, and now he has left. Staff in the breakfast room heard him and some of them smiled at one another. As if they had expected whatever it is Mr. Leggit is about. With the solicitor. And with you."

Hattie rolled onto her back but kept the sheets over her face.

"Mr. Leggit sees his solicitor regularly," she muttered. "There's nothing unusual about that."

"He looked angry."

"He always looks angry in the morning and we both know why."

The draperies swished open, sending bright light into the room. Hattie peeked over the sheets and squinted. "I don't want it to be morning," she said. "Not this morning or any morning."

"Let me get you a nice cup of tea," Dobbin said. Anxiety pushed her brows up in the middle and she was quite white.

"Is there any with roots in it?" Perhaps Porky's tea was well-known and she hadn't heard of it before because she wasn't from these parts.

Dobbin stared down at her. "Are you talking about poisoning yourself? Oh, please don't say it's true. There is nothing bad enough for that. I will help you. Whatever happens, I'll be with you."

Hattie snapped the sheets down and hauled herself up to sit against her pillows. She hadn't bothered with a nightcap and her hair tumbled into her face. "What can you mean, Dobbin, dear?"

"They all talked together about what they think Mr. Leggit intends to do to you when he comes back."

Hattie smoothed her hair back and narrowed her eyes. "What exactly did they talk about?"

"Mr. Leggit being angry with you."

"Dobbin!" Hattie had a sudden thought. "I do not always *think*. Sometimes I just don't think at all. If he could—why didn't *I* think of riding into Bath?"

"Please concentrate on our present problems." Dobbin looked at the ceiling and sighed. "You didn't think about riding to Bath on Jolly because you're not allowed to, that's why. Mr. Leggit would never countenance such a thing."

"How would he have known? I'd have done just what I did before, only taken Jolly instead of Snowdrop's coach."

"Shh!" Dobbin stood close to Hattie and whispered, "We'd better be careful. Someone found out about that. That means they've been listening and following, and sneaking about. Don't you even *think* of riding that pony in the dark. You'd be bound to take a fall—or worse."

It was Hattie's turn to stare. "Mr. Leggit knows about my trips to Bath?"

"I don't know. But the staff does. Some of them. And Smythe looked pleased, which isn't like him. He had his head at that funny angle—sideways. And he smiled. I think Mr. Leggit knows what you've done."

"If he does, I've spoiled everything." Trembling, Hattie scrambled from the bed and slipped her arms into the robe Dobbin held.

Mr. Leggit knew what she'd done?

She felt sick and clammy and desperate. Bad enough— terrible enough that she must think about the things John had said to her, what he had suggested, after giving her such delight. To consider that Mr. Leggit could be aware that she'd been in that coach with John, and that he'd...done what he'd done was impossible.

She'd loved every moment of it.

But for Mr. Leggit to know?

"Horrible."

"There, there," Dobbin said, stroking Hattie's back. "Can it be so terrible that you went to a little shop?"

Hattie whirled toward her. "You do know," she whispered, and her scalp tightened. "You know where I went." Snowdrop must have told her.

"I didn't till after Mr. Leggit left the house this morn-

ing and I heard two of the maids whispering about it. So it's true then. That's where you went, to a shop?''

''Yes,'' Hattie said shortly. ''I must have been followed. But how could that happen when I told no one?''

Without warning, Dobbin broke into sobs. ''You—know—you—told—me.''

Hattie considered. ''Hush. I must think.''

''You think I told Mr. Leggit,'' Dobbin wailed. ''I suppose I must have, only I didn't.''

''Pull yourself together.'' Frightened she might be, but she couldn't afford panic, her own or anyone else's. ''Did you tell Mr. Leggit?''

Dobbin shook her head, no, over and over again. ''I did not. I promise you, Mrs. Leggit, I would not.''

''Then you did not. I have little doubt where we should look to find the weasel who prattle-prattled.''

''Mr. Smythe?''

Hattie nodded, yes. ''The same.''

''But he wouldn't do that if Mr. Leggit didn't tell him to.''

''Yes, he would. He doesn't like me. Never has. And he'd do anything to get rid of me. I think he believes I'm in his way when he wants to be the closest person to Mr. Leggit.''

Dobbin shuddered. ''He could have that honor.'' Her mouth fell open, then she swallowed. ''Oh, Mrs. Leggit, what have I said? I didn't mean—''

''Yes, you did. I have other things to think about.'' Like a broken heart, almost broken. It would be broken if she were not so furious with John. He'd behaved as if she'd made him do *it* when she had not even known *it* existed. After all, the only other man who had been near her was Mr. Leggit and he absolutely had *not* done that first bit.

"Men can be so unreasonable, Dobbin."

"Indeed, they can, Mrs. Leggit," Dobbin sniffled.

Hattie knew that John had wanted to get to the last part of everything and she had let him know, very reasonably she thought, that she wanted it too—under the appropriate circumstances. She stirred. Not just in her womanly places, although they pinched together as if trying to close around something.

Yet she was wrong to plan what she planned at all.

Marriage to Mr. Leggit had been right for the right reasons, but surely she had paid enough now and could be forgiven for wanting freedom and a taste, if only for a little while, of bliss.

Like winds coming from many corners and throwing themselves together in a swirling assault, she felt tossed, spun. Ooh, what a lovely feeling.

Hattie Leggit: the wicked one.

Dobbin coughed and waited to get Hattie's attention. "There is no doubt that your husband is maddened by some dangerous emotion. I fear for you. Please let me help you run away."

Her heart softened and tears burned her eyes. Hattie reached for Dobbin. "You mean it, don't you? You would risk everything to run away and try to help me."

Dobbin nodded vehemently. "I would and be glad of it."

"And then you would never have another place. Who would retain you after Mr. Leggit gave you bad references? You would stay with me, of course, and I should try to care for both of us, but we would have near nothing."

Dobbin's chin rose high. "I don't care. This is a bad place."

Hattie agreed with that and was touched by Dobbin.

"Well, it may not always be easy here, but take as much pleasure as you can in a secure place."

Now she sounded the resigned wife bound to make the best of any insult to her person. "I believe things will become happier." Perhaps, when Mr. Leggit became too old to pester her anymore. She literally shook herself. "I should dress. The jonquil taffeta would be perfect for today and Mr. Leggit likes the color on me."

"Oh, Mrs. Leggit." Dobbin trotted to the wardrobe, sniffling as she went. "You're so good and brave."

Bea knocked on the door and popped inside with a breakfast tray. She smiled at Hattie and Dobbin. "I don't suppose I should even tell you what Cook said when I asked for this." She giggled. "But it was so funny, I will. She said it will be time for dinner soon enough and it's a shame your head isn't a clock because then it could be sent out for mending."

Hattie smiled.

Bea slapped her knees. "Isn't she cheeky? She's also spreading a rumor you might want to put a stop to. Unless it's true."

"Oh, no," Dobbin said, her hand pressed over her heart.

Hattie didn't feel patient but she waited anyway.

Bea turned a shade of red that ought, Hattie thought, to hurt her skin. She muttered something and giggled into her hand.

"Speak up," Hattie said, more kindly than she would have thought possible.

"Oh." Bea swung her skirts and let out many sighs. "All right then. She said she thinks you're increasin' and that's why you stick to your bed so much. She said…she said there's going to be a little Leggit and unless it's going to look like you, it had better be a boy."

Hattie digested Bea's extraordinary statement.

Dobbin chuckled. She flapped a hand as if at imaginary flies.

"It would be fun though," Bea said. "I do love babies. Perhaps you'd let me be nanny. I've had a lot of experience, being the second of twelve."

"Twelve?" Hattie, who had been poor but always with her own space and her parents' attention, could not fathom having so many souls in one place.

"It's lovely with lots of brothers and sisters, Mrs. Leggit," Bea said. "We're all so close, or we are when we see each other."

"Er, yes. Unfortunately there is no babe expected." Her reaction was one of relief. A sad thing when she wanted so badly to have children. She just knew they shouldn't be Mr. Leggit's if she could help it, that's all. Of course, if he was able to, well, make his part hop to the way John's had done last night and they did have a baby, she had little doubt that Mr. Leggit would stop pestering.

It wouldn't be like that because it couldn't be. For a large man, and from what she'd been forced to feel, Mr. Leggit had rather a small quantity…she should be more generous. If he couldn't become swollen, and that is what happened because she'd watched how John got bigger, but if Mr. Leggit couldn't do that then it wasn't his fault, was it? And it surely wasn't *her* fault, either, much as he tried to blame his dilemma on her.

Could it be her fault? So many questions.

"The yellow dress," she reminded Dobbin, who had retreated into a world where she nodded and shook her head and scurried back and forth but accomplished very little.

Bea, expressing her disappointment that there was to be no baby, helped Dobbin get Hattie into the dress.

"It's lovely," Bea said. "Just like the day. Why, you'll match the daffodils outside."

Hattie adjusted her bodice. "Perhaps a fichu? There is one made of Devonshire lace and embroidered with tiny yellow flowers."

"If you put it on, Mr. Leggit will take it off," Dobbin said matter-of-factly. "He did it the last time and you cried after he left."

Hattie didn't say that she frequently cried after seeing Mr. Leggit regardless of what he did or didn't do.

She caught sight of Bea's face in the mirror. The maid had her back to Hattie and must have forgotten the mirror. Surreptitiously she wiped tears from the corners of her eyes and she repeatedly dabbed at her brow with a handkerchief.

"What is it, Bea?" Hattie said, gripped by a bad premonition. "What is making you unhappy?"

The door flew open and in marched Mr. Leggit in a yellow-and-white striped coat, richly embroidered silver waistcoat scattered with mother-of-pearl buttons shaped like flowers, and the nude trousers that caressed every dimple and bulge in the flesh they covered. Hattie suspected Mr. Leggit might be using a little padding today. She wasn't impressed.

"Out," he said to the air, and with a wave of a hand. He walked with a prance to his step and trailed a large, lace handkerchief from his fingers. Dobbin and Bea didn't move fast enough for him. "Get your deplorable persons out of my wife's chambers." As Bea sped past, he tweaked her ear. He looked at departing Dobbin with dislike.

"Now," he said. "You and I have a great deal to talk

about. My dear, you haven't dressed your hair. Come, sit in front of your mirror and let me brush it for you.''

Hattie's stomach behaved as if she'd swallowed tadpoles, but she sat at the stool in front of her dressing table and he let her hair down completely.

''So pretty.'' He sighed. ''The best decision I ever made was to marry you.''

A trick. He intended to lull her into relaxing, then shock her by berating her.

Leggit lifted her hair away from her neck and kissed her there. She made herself touch his hand on her shoulder and he positively puffed up with pleasure.

He brushed her hair firmly but gently. The long strokes dispatched what was left of the ringlets Bea had fashioned the previous day and she was left with waves that reached beyond her shoulder blades. ''Mmm.'' Mr. Leggit pushed his face into her hair and sounded ecstatic.

''You, Hattie, have been a bad girl, haven't you?''

Light-headed, she held the edge of the dressing table.

''I know all about it, you know. How could you think you'd hide it from me?''

Mr. Leggit pulled her head against his round stomach and rubbed his big fingers over her neck. He shook his head and spread his hands to hold her breasts beneath her gown. He laughed and said, ''First things first.'' His tongue snaked around his lips. ''You've done beautifully with Granville.''

Her lungs wouldn't inflate again. He was playing a horrible game with her.

''Absolutely marvelous. I'm going to a gathering of gentlemen this afternoon. Gentlemen who are all members of the ton. What do you say to that?''

Telling him she already knew just wouldn't do. ''That's wonderful.''

"Granville came to me positively drooling after you'd finished with him. I could tell it. He fawned on me." Leggit turned his face sideways, raised his soft chin and studied his profile in the mirror. "Bernard Leggit, fawned upon by the nobility. And so I should think. I could buy and sell the fribble."

"I expect so," Hattie said, still waiting for Mr. Leggit's wrath.

He turned his head to view his profile from the other side. "Important discussions about England's affairs this afternoon, then dinner at Gaythorpe—in the Circle. Belongs to a Sir Percival something."

"Why, that's wonderful...Bernard." How dreadful it would be if someone came to tell Mr. Leggit he was no longer invited. It seemed unlike John to be so mean, but he did hint at something like that last night.

She frowned. He would not manipulate her, and she wanted her chance to tell him what she thought of a man who frightened women. But not tonight. No, tonight she would not go to him, because he had ordered her to do so.

"After dinner there will be more discussion," Mr. Leggit said. "Don't worry about me, my dear, but I don't expect to return until very late. Possibly morning."

"Be careful," she said, and her tongue felt thick.

"Thank you, my dear. It will be your turn to shine again one week from Friday when we attend a ball held by the Honorable Simmington Partridge and his wife. Didn't catch her name. The invitations are already here. Fancy that."

"Fancy that," Hattie said. She grew desperate for this interview to be over.

"And Granville talked about having us to a house party. He's got a place near Oxford. Big holding from

what I've been able to learn from my solicitor. That wouldn't be until July or so. You've done it, my lovely one, my peach. You've got us going where the real money is. The really old money.''

He grinned at her but immediately sobered and turned the corners of his plump mouth down. ''But still you've been naughty and it won't do.''

Hattie didn't look at him.

''Why did you visit the apothecary shop?''

What could she say? She held her tongue.

''You are the dearest of girls, the sweetest of wives and I thank you for what you tried to do.''

Hattie kept her forehead lowered but looked up at him.

''You could have been hurt, dear one. Some ruffian might have attacked you and robbed you—or worse. But you have made me think.''

If she didn't say anything, she couldn't give him information he didn't already have.

''I know how badly you want to give me my son. Smythe thinks otherwise, but that's Smythe. He only wants to protect me from disappointment. You went to that place to ask for help. Come now. Admit it. You asked for help in fulfilling your duties to me.'' He looked at her. ''I don't want you taking any potions made by some madman, is that clear? You're likely to be poisoned and die. No, you are to leave these matters in my hands.''

He opened his coat and panted while he pulled up his waistcoat to reveal a heavy band fastened around his middle. This he removed and Hattie heard the unmistakable cascade of clinking coins. ''I've considered this carefully. You've been poor. Once you've been poor you never want to be like that again. Ask me about the feeling. I know.''

Hattie couldn't even manage a nod.

''I'm a self-made man. You found ways to get money

out of me because you wanted to be sure you'd always have money. And I should think so. I know now that you would have shown me wifely respect regardless, but I want you to have peace in your mind. There are two hundred sovereigns here and it's not a penny too much. Put them with the rest of your little nest egg. I want you as calm and happy as you can be.'' He placed the money belt at her feet.

She breathed again, drew in air to fill the places she'd emptied. ''Thank you.'' Nerves jumped around her eyes and beside her mouth.

He smiled and draped her hair over one shoulder. ''Lovely,'' he said. ''Hattie, you are desperate to have my son and the longing drove you to the brink of disaster. My fault. Please forgive me. I've spoken to people who have explained what can happen in these cases when a wife's fears make her unreceptive.''

''Yes, of course.'' Yes, of course he'd found more and more people to blame her for his own failings. Now it was her fear that made his little worm want to crawl away. Hattie kept on smiling. She would not care if he blamed her as long as he stopped doing all those dreadful things to her.

''There will be no need for some brew to do what nature must do,'' he said. ''Trust me in that.''

He'd been advised on some new form of torture to visit on her.

''I have discovered a way to remedy things. Now I want you to get used to this and I want you to be brave. I'll give you a little time. I have to proceed carefully anyway. And remember that no one else will ever know. I shall find a virile man, a stranger to these parts. He will be offered enough money to make certain his finer feelings don't deter him from enjoying you—until he's no longer needed.''

23

Nathan had seen his brother upset, angry, murderous even, but he didn't recall seeing him quite as he appeared this evening.

And he had not explained himself as yet.

Guilt? Over something simple even? Could that be the reason for this foul mood? "You didn't forget what I told you and let it slip to the aunts that Dominic's coming, did you?" Nathan said.

"No."

"Good."

John had come to him after he'd gone to sleep, routed him out and insisted this was the perfect time for a brotherly chat.

Brotherly chat, be damned. The rattle had the other thing on his mind and hadn't a clue how to deal with the way he felt.

"Interesting woman, that," Nathan said, knowing full well that he played with fire. The mighty venting of temper could come at any moment.

John ignored him, damn his cold hide. He ignored him and continued to stare through Nathan's second-floor windows at what faint flickers of light showed in Bath below. "I need someone in that house," he said. "It's not acceptable for her to be there without a friend—a friend capable of dealing with anyone who threatens her."

Nathan scrubbed at his hair. Naked but for his robe, he yawned and turned sideways in his chair. He tried to pull up his legs, but they were too long and his heels shot off the seat.

"For God's sake, wake up, man," John said. "Throw cold water on your face if you have to. This is serious."

Stabbing a forefinger in John's direction focused Nathan and gathered his sagging energy—and wits. "You are the one who should leap into cold water, my friend. You have dragged me from my bed to rave about protecting the woman you swear you will use to settle our scores with Leggit."

"The man is a fiend," John said. "He is gladly using her to gain entrance to polite society."

"Hmm." Nathan stretched out his legs and regarded his rather elegant feet. Big feet, it was true but without unsightly lumps or bumps.

"Nathan."

"Aren't you bent on gladly using her for something or other?"

"Hell and damnation."

"You curse too much, brother."

"Do you want to live until morning?" John said, and Nathan didn't like the deadly gleam in his eye.

"Since I'm not foxed, I plan to be clearheaded and charming in the morning," Nathan said. He bent forward and let his head hang down. "Oh, all right. What do you want? Get it over with."

"I bloody want someone I can trust at Leggit Hall."

Drowsiness swept over Nathan.

"Someone I need have no reservations about. The only reason she isn't here tonight has...to be..."

Nathan kept his hands clasped together between his knees but raised his head to look at John. *"Yes?"*

"Put your mind to the problem, Nathan."

"*She* would be Mrs. Leggit? You expected her *here* this evening? You dog you." He chortled. "And she never arrived? Probably came to her senses and realized she wanted me, not you."

"She would have come if she could. You may be sure that foul husband of hers found some way to make a prisoner of her before leaving for the jolly afternoon and evening—and night—I arranged for him."

"Mmm. Are you certain of that?"

John's stare reminded Nathan that less could be more when speaking to a frustrated, evidently besotted man of great strength. "Who could we possibly get into Leggit Hall?" he said, and flashed a smile. "Forgive me if I have sounded, mmm, *disinterested,* but the late hour fuddles me." He had a horrible thought. "You're not suggesting that *I* infiltrate the place?"

"You, sir, are a blithering idiot," John said.

"I regret your need to say that."

"What earthly good could you be at Leggit Hall? And how would you insinuate yourself there, and…"

Nathan coughed and pounded his chest. "I wouldn't be any good at all and there's no way for me to infiltrate the place. Ignore me. I'm really asleep, talking, but asleep. Look, old chap, Leggit is off somewhere making more of his dreadful bows to God knows who and your Hattie is at home alone—except for a dozen or so nubile women dressed in gauze bedsheets. And a few overly endowed men who are probably with the nubile women. Don't you think she would be here if she wanted to…be?" His voice faded away.

Now Nathan saw everything clearly. "Mrs. Leggit is supposed to be here doing whatever with you. I see. How in the blazes would a young woman like that get here and

into this house, alone, without *everyone* knowing about it?''

''I had that worked out,'' John said.

Nathan noticed how his brother's throat jerked and he colored a little.

''What did you have worked out?''

''None of your damned… She was to ride her pony over at dusk, wait for nightfall, then come into the house by a route I had devised.''

''Wonderful.'' Nathan slapped his own cheeks, which brought two perfectly good results. He felt wide-awake, and he hid his laughter. ''Well, there are choices here. She changed her mind and didn't come. She came then changed her mind and went back. She came and fell asleep wherever she was supposed to wait until—''

''I've checked—several times—and she's not there.''

''That brings us to the last possibility. She came. Some-one robbed, ravished and murdered her and made off with the corpse and the pony.''

John reached Nathan in one stride, pulled him from his chair by the collar of his robe, and brought them nose to nose.

Nathan smiled.

John threw him back into the chair and laughed. He bent from the waist and chuckled until he was spent. ''You're a bastard, Nathan.''

''Our mother will be pleased to know you think so.''

''Pax!'' John staggered into a chair himself and spread his feet. ''She didn't come, did she? Even though I ordered her to.''

That was it. Nathan convulsed and made a dramatic fall from his chair to the floor where he rolled around and let out great howls of merriment.

Not a sound came from John.

The effort was too much. "You *ordered* her to come?" Nathan said. "And you're angry she didn't? I have seen precious little of the lady, but she isn't your wife and I doubt she took kindly to your orders."

Still nothing from John.

Nathan sat up cross-legged and arranged the robe to make himself decent. "None of my business how you deal with women," he said. "This behavior of mine is your fault for waking me from a sound sleep. I'll return to your original subject. What am I supposed to say when you talk about installing a guard at Leggit Hall for La Leggit herself?"

"That Dominic is the perfect candidate."

"Dominic?"

"Dominic." John pushed out his lips in a soundless whistle.

"You consider that a less stupid idea than attempting to send me in?"

"It is not a stupid idea at all," John said. "This cannot be allowed to take much longer. I mean that Leggit's comeuppance has been due for too long already."

Was that, Nathan wondered, still John's first concern, or had Hattie Leggit become his only obsession?

"What?" John said. "Why the pitying look?"

Nathan rearranged his face. "You're imagining things."

"I am not in the mood for your foolishness," John said. "What must be done, *will* be done in short order. That means the man who finds a way into Leggit Hall will not remain there long. Leggit doesn't know Dominic and there's no reason for him to find out who he is if we manage well enough."

"You need sleep. You're deranged. Someone who does know him will tell Leggit and the game will be up. Our

one advantage is that Leggit doesn't know what we're about. Anything could happen if we lose that.''

John stood and Nathan wished he'd bothered to pull himself from the floor. "I haven't changed, brother," John said. "I am the same man as ever. You need not tell me the obvious. Now, enough talk. We have to intercept Dominic before he gets to Bath. Then you can both hear what is to be done at the same time.''

"You will tell me now or I'll have nothing to do with it. And since you don't know Dominic's plans, you will have no way of finding him.'' He dragged the robe together and sprang to his feet. "I'm wide-awake now, m'lord.''

"Very well.'' John had achieved his purpose and a smug tinge to his voice proved it. "Dominic has some resemblance to you and me, but he's the most different of us. Put him in servant's clothing and the connection won't be made.''

"I don't agree.'' He'd be damned if he'd go along with an idea that might be dangerous for Dominic.

"Is his hair still long? I know the answer will be yes. He'll tie it back, wear cheap but respectable clothes, and become Walter Stack, formerly in the employ of a squire in the north. He'll arrive at Leggit Hall, insist he's been sent to give Mr. Leggit a message and can't speak to anyone else. Leggit is told about the mysterious visitor and, because he can't resist finding out what this is about, has Walter searched for weapons before seeing him. Walter admits he's audacious but he's looking for a position and from what he's heard of Mr. Leggit, he thinks that he'll see Walter's potential and hire him.''

John paused, frowning, and Nathan congratulated himself on not commenting.

"Walter says he was an under butler, very talented, rose

fast, but he'll do anything. Leggit asks if the squire will speak for him? Walter begs indulgence but he won't be getting any recommendations from his former employer because the gentleman's daughter tried to seduce Walter and the gentleman blames Walter for it. Imagine that.''

''Even Leggit wouldn't fall for that one,'' Nathan said. Two of his candles guttered and the room grew dimmer.

''No, he wouldn't,'' John said, spacing out his words as if Nathan might not understand them otherwise. ''But he'll take one look at that handsome little brother of ours—''

''Dominic is not little.''

''*Don't* state the obvious. Leggit will retain him, mark my words. He'll love the cheeky approach, the flat lies they both know he'll see through, and the idea that *Walter* is a bounder at heart, just as Leggit is. And to get back where I was before you cut me off, he'll see the possibilities. How easy can it be to find enough of what you call *overly endowed* men? Not easy, I'll wager. I'm sure the ladies present the other evening would have enjoyed a few less women and a lot more men for their entertainment.''

''Gawd!''

''When do we leave to meet Dominic?''

''What if Leggit kicks Dominic out?'' Or, worse yet, puts him straight to work below stairs, below, below stairs, that was?

''He won't kick him out, but if he did, we'd have to find someone else and quickly. Albert might get away with it, but—''

''You don't know if he's up to it,'' Nathan finished for him and laughed. ''I've met Snowdrop, remember. My advice is to drop the thought altogether. She would kill him—after she had done away with you.''

''Do we leave now?'' John said.

"It will not work. And I'm going back to bed."

"Did you tell our mother anything about your latest…adventure? The full extent of your losses. Sorry, I meant accomplishments."

"I'm a reformed man, damn you, John. I've seen my faults."

John crossed his arms and waited.

"Oh, very well then. Dominic is making a stop to visit friends—the Trambys. If we leave at nine in the morning we'll be sure to meet up with him there."

24

John didn't intend to sleep. He didn't intend to try because it would not work.

He folded a letter from the Customs Service, placed it in the false back behind a desk drawer and locked that drawer. So far he had withheld Leggit's name, but he had warned Customs that they should be ready to make an important arrest. When John had finished with the man, let them deal with him.

Finding clothes for Dominic to wear tomorrow would be simple. Albert would see to it. They would also need to pack a valise. There would be no need to beg the youngest Elliot brother to do as John asked. He'd want to go to Leggit Hall. It could be necessary to get his word that he wouldn't kill Leggit on sight.

John got up and walked slowly into his bedchamber. He paused, legs braced apart, and looked at the empty bed. His plans for tonight had been for Hattie to lie there with him. He rolled his shoulders back and arched his neck. Why did his muscles plague him when he'd done nothing but pace around for hours?

If she'd come and not wanted to let him make love to her, he'd have settled for holding her, perhaps kissing her if she was as willing as she had been last night.

She had been so willing.

Hell and damnation. He would settle for *holding* her?

No, he would not. He was known as a man who always finished what he started and the deed must be completed.

If only the woman would make up her mind and do what she obviously wanted to do!

His feet took him to the green draperies extending from the bed to cover the narrow space that led to the rooms beneath the musicians' gallery, and to the ballroom.

What else was there to do but walk around until sleep or morning came? He all but sidestepped to the first entry, pressed the release and passed through into the boxlike place behind the mirror.

Sounds reached him. John put his ear to the back of the mirror and listened. Scrabbling. Some might walk away muttering about mice but not he, not when these would have to be people-size mice that moved solid things, scraped them along and bumped them.

Swiftly retracing his steps, he took a pistol from a drawer in his bedchamber and moved rapidly back until he stood behind the mirror once more.

He smiled and felt the fool. If only he could be sure this was Hattie, but he couldn't. It could as well be Leggit. Should the man have heard a rumor and then forced Hattie to tell him about tonight's arrangements, well then, he could have come with a plan to attack John in his bed. Hattie might well have misled Leggit about how he could enter the rest of the house, and he was still searching for a door. Which would account for the noise.

With his pistol hand relaxed, the weapon pointed at the ceiling, he shifted the mirror with the slightest pressure possible. Since Leggit still didn't know he had a sinister connection to John, he would assume that while the situation with Hattie had gone a little further than planned, John would have no interest in making that fact known.

No doubt many more favors would be demanded in exchange for Leggit making light of the whole thing.

Candlelight flickered in the room where costumes were stored.

No one rushed at him.

The hard sounds had stopped and the rustling was no more than a softer swishing now. Using care, John leaned forward enough to look right, in the direction of the hanging costumes, the only possible source of swishing he could think of.

Hattie faced the gaudy clothing. She held on to a sleeve and rested her forehead on the backs of her hands.

John hesitated. If he spoke she might collapse. If he didn't speak she might turn...and collapse.

"You are there, aren't you?" she said, and it was John who jumped, John whose heart raced. "I feel you. Please say something," she said.

He slumped against the wall. "It's me." He needed to collect himself before he tried to sound more intelligent. *She felt him?* "What do you mean, you *feel* me?"

"What I say." She pulled her shoulders up. "A current of air meant you were coming, then I felt you here."

Best not pursue the subject, he thought. "You are hours late."

"I wasn't going to come at all."

"You rode the pony in the dark?"

"I knew of no other way to get here."

She was impetuous. Such a woman would be difficult to control, not that he need concern himself with such things.

"I'm glad you changed your mind. You were coming to me after all."

At last she looked at him.

"You've been crying, Hattie. Oh, my dear." He held

out his arms but rather than run to him she pulled back, her eyes open too wide.

"Damn it," he said, remembering the pistol. He set it down. "I wasn't sure the noises I heard in here were you, so I came armed. Forgive me. Come to me and let me hold you. I'll take you where you'll be comfortable, and pour you a little brandy."

"I cried because I got frightened when I rode through the trees and it was so dark. Silly of me." Her dark blue riding habit became her.

"Of course you got frightened. When you return to Leggit Hall, I shall ride with you. Fear not, I'll make sure I'm not seen."

Hattie took a step forward. "Thank you, but that would be impossible. I'll go now."

"Go?" Did she think he'd allow her to change her mind again? "You came because you wanted to be with me. I'm so glad, Hattie, and I cannot let you leave me again so soon."

"I didn't come to see you."

"But…" *Say nothing without thinking first.* "You're here, sweet one. That's all that matters." He smiled at her.

Hattie didn't smile back. "This room has been cleaned, and that one." She nodded toward the musicians' storage space. "All the drapes have been taken from the furniture in the ballroom, too."

"I wanted you to see it all more clearly. And I wanted your path to me to be a pleasant one."

"I didn't come to see you."

"So you have said." Only with difficulty did he keep his voice even. "Nonsense, every word of it. Here I am and here you are."

"I thought you would be sleeping by now."

"When I was waiting for you and wanting you more…" *Enough said.* "Why are you here, then?"

Hattie pursed her lips and crossed her arms tightly. "I'm here because I couldn't think of another place to go."

She tapped a toe. "All right. You have heard Mr. Leggit talk about my frequent requests for money. You saw him give me some—in an embarrassing way. When he said I asked for money, that was truthful. But it has never been to buy *fripperies.* I have something important to take care of. What I collected isn't near enough, but I must have a safe place to keep it. If it got stolen, I don't know what I should do."

Before he could react, she swept aside lace and velvet and satin, sequins and bright stones, and crawled between the costumes on her hands and knees.

Her muffled voice emerged. "I had to get it out of Leggit Hall, so I brought it here."

John watched her wiggling derriere with interest. Could she really have brought her money here? "Did you plan to use my keys and this room as you pleased? Were you expecting to come and go from here but never to have anything more to do with me?"

More wiggling was the only response, then thumps and metallic sounds and Hattie dragged a wooden box into view. Her small bonnet hung from the back of her neck by its ribbons and her cheeks were flushed. Strands of hair trailed free.

With effort she pulled two bags from the box. These were tied together, presumably because she'd hung them across her pony, and the clink of coins spoke for itself.

"Before you say a word," she said, setting the bags down. "Hear me out. I am not a bad woman, but I am a desperate one. I have nothing to bargain with, but I will

appeal to you, John. Would you allow me to keep this here? It may be stolen here anyway, but it's the best thing I can think of."

"Of course," he said, vexed at sounding stilted. "And your money will be safe."

"Thank you." She smiled and almost moved toward him again. Almost.

"You really didn't want to see me this evening?"

Hattie looked at him directly. "I wanted to see you. I can't imagine there will ever be a moment when I won't want to see you. If you hadn't been angry with me last night…and threatened me, then I would have come to you. As long as you didn't say I had to."

How Nathan would chortle at this. "I didn't threaten you."

She raised her eyebrows. "Yes, you did. You suggested that you wouldn't keep your promise to indulge Mr. Leggit so that he wouldn't punish me."

John pushed the bags out of the way with a shoe, caught Hattie by the arm and pulled her close. "Explain what you mean by *punish*. How would that man punish you? He has punished you before? Of course he has and that's why you are afraid all the time. Tell me what he does to you? In addition to wounding you with rose thorns."

"There's nothing to tell. I didn't mean that. I…please, don't give it another thought."

She did mean it, John knew. He'd seen the shadows in her eyes and the trembling downturn of her mouth.

"I'm ashamed," he told her and meant it. "I did hint at what you suggest, but I would never have done it. I was a little, well, not quite myself." *Ha.* "I spoke out of turn. It's unthinkable that I should go back on my word to you, no matter if you don't—"

"I do. I've said so. To be with you is amazing. Just to

look at you gives me sensations I never had before we met. I have never loved, but if I had I think it might feel like this.'' She stopped, a horrified expression on her face. ''I mean that if, when I was a girl, I had experienced such feelings toward a man it could have been like this.''

John felt a fullness in his heart, and fear at the same time. To be torn so was a curse.

''I'm not saying I love you, John.'' The words tumbled out and her shining eyes belied them. ''I'm married, after all. But I like you immensely. Very, very much... immensely...''

''Thank you.'' A wise man allowed a woman to extricate herself from a difficult position, or to allow her to think she had. ''I think a great deal of you, too.''

She bowed her head and made to replace the bags of coins. John took them from her and put them back in the box. Rather than return them beneath the costumes again, he went to his knees and removed two short floorboards. Beneath, in the gap between the joists, lay a jumble of lumpy things wrapped in paper or cloth and a collection of small boxes. He wedged Hattie's treasure on top and replaced the boards.

''Only you and I know of this place.'' He thought a moment before saying, ''And my brothers, if they even remember. We used to hide things here.''

''Thank you,'' Hattie said. ''Leggit Hall isn't safe anymore.''

Her lashes were wet and, rather than his usual feeling of panic at the possibility of tears, John enjoyed sensing the emotion he'd brought about by a simple kindness that cost him nothing.

''Why do you need to gather this money?'' he asked. ''You protect it so desperately. It's important to you. You

say you don't know what you would do if you lost it. What is it for, Hattie?''

The tears did well along her lower lids then. ''I could never tell you.''

''Why?''

She parted her lips as if intending to tell him after all but shook her head. ''If I can ever explain, I will.''

He knew better than to press her further now. ''I had intended to ask you about a note Albert saw Mrs. Dobbin give to my aunts. Is there something else I should know about? Another problem?''

''No. I like Miss Prunella and Miss Enid, so I sent them a note.''

Ah, once again he'd best not ask more questions—for now.

''If this is a weakness, so be it, but I longed to see you this evening, Hattie. I don't recall ever wanting to be with a woman as I want to be with you.'' The damnable thing was that it was true, but he must not be too careless with his tongue.

''I am married,'' she murmured, but he sensed she said it from habit and because she believed she must.

''Yes. Would you come with me, please. I cannot bear to let you go just yet.''

''I would be wrong to say yes.''

By the law, perhaps. ''Just to be with you awhile. In the same space. To breathe the same air, would be enough. I ask for nothing more.''

Madness.

She gave the loose coat of her habit a few tweaks and straightened the wide sleeves. But she didn't seem to notice the trailing bonnet or disarranged hair.

''Hattie.'' He held her hands before she could evade him. ''Is that so much to ask for?''

"No." She looked everywhere but at him. Her pretty bosom rose with the huge, sighing breath she took. "But I will not go to your rooms. I would remain with you here. Just for a little while."

John thought to argue. But the better part could often be to accept what was offered rather than have nothing at all. He swung their joined hands, then released her. He gathered several armloads of costumes and heaped them on the floor. Albert had made a good job of airing the place out and getting rid of dust, including from this pile of rich fabrics.

"A place for you to sit, dear lady." He made a formal bow and swept wide an arm.

What was a man to do? She looked closer than ever to tears. But Hattie did come forward, spread the skirt of her habit and sat down with more grace than most would have managed.

She looked up at him with a soft smile that did nothing to calm him. "May I join you, Hattie?" he said.

"Yes, John. Please do."

He lowered himself beside her, unfortunately without her grace. His weight made their grand divan sag and they landed, arm to arm, in the middle.

Hattie covered her mouth.

"Don't you dare laugh," he told her. "For your information, I find this comfortable."

"So do I." She kept her hand over her mouth.

For several moments he was satisfied to watch her, and to push aside thoughts of why he was supposed to be with her. "Has Mr. Leggit ever hurt you?" He hadn't intended to say it.

Hattie looked away.

So he had, the bastard. He would suffer extra for that. "Last night you said there was a way for me to do

something for you," she said, looking at him again. "You said I would know what it was, but I don't. I would like to do anything I can to make you happy."

"Don't give it another thought." *Please don't. Not now.*

"I must. I keep my word."

"You didn't give me your word to do anything and you owe me nothing." Least of all the kind of sexual favor he had clumsily suggested.

"Please, John. You are so good to me and I have nothing to give you." Even in the poor light he saw her blush. "You...what you did...to me. For me. It was wonderful and completely unexpected. I had no idea, well, I had never felt anything quite like it before."

She had no idea? That could only mean that Leggit's one interest was in taking his own pleasure with no concern about returning the favor. Foolish man without finesse. Apparently he didn't know the potential heights of ecstasy a woman could bring to him if he excited her enough first.

"It is all right for me to speak of this?" she said.

"All right, but not necessary."

"I want to. And now I demand that you tell me what I can do for you. I'll do exactly what you had in mind last night."

Her sincerity shamed him and started a wild clamoring in him.

"It was I who did something wrong," Hattie continued. "I spoiled everything."

His back grew damp between his shoulder blades. "You don't know how to pleasure a man?" He stripped off his coat.

Her puzzled expression made her even more endearing.

"You have never brought Mr. Leggit—to the brink as

it were, and over the brink, without—the other? Without his lying with you. Or—with him lying with you but not performing—marital duties?'' Dash it all, he sounded idiotic.

Hattie's big eyes grew even bigger. ''No,'' she whispered. ''How would I do that?''

You cad you, Granville. ''One day I hope I can explain, but not this evening. It is intimate, Hattie, but I think you know that.''

She nodded yes.

John reached for her and lifted her. He stretched her out then lay himself full length on their makeshift couch, divan, bed, whatever it was. Face-to-face, they were only inches apart. Hattie sucked her bottom lip between her teeth. Had she no idea how such little things could tighten a man inside his trousers and slam his belly into his backbone? Or so it felt. She rested a hand on his cheek and he closed his eyes. It would happen. Possibly tonight. He felt her bending to him. More patience and he might wear down the last of her defenses.

He looked at her again and found she had let her eyes close. Having her beside him, her face vulnerable and so lovely, drove him to desperate longing. And why shouldn't he long for her? Once her husband was ruined in every way, someone would have to take care of her. Why not John Elliot?

''Hattie,'' he said, and rolled her to her back. He put a leg over hers, expecting her to protest, but she didn't. ''We can have so much. I asked you to let me—to be my lover. If you thought nothing of me, you wouldn't be here at all. You have said you do. Please, be mine. You will have nothing to fear. I shall always watch over you.''

Her eyes opened, and gradually closed again when she slipped a hand behind his neck and brought his mouth to

hers. They kissed with all the pent-up passion he held within him, and Hattie's reaching tongue, the way she nibbled his lower lip and shifted her face beneath his, left no doubt that she wanted everything he wanted.

Her body sent heat through her clothes. "Take this off," he said. "You are too warm. You will catch a chill when we go out if we aren't careful."

She let him help her out of the loose-fitting coat and he took the opportunity to undo the ribbons and set the bonnet aside.

John pressed her down again and propped his head on a hand so that he could look at her. He placed frequent, firm kisses on her lips, and with each one she tried to capture and keep him longer.

Breathless, she turned her face aside and he felt the spirit go out of her.

"What is it, Hattie?"

"This is hopeless," she said. "I cannot make you happy."

Rubbing his fingers back and forth on her jaw, he said, "If being with me is too painful, I understand. I will let you go, but not graciously, I fear."

What was he thinking, what was he saying?

Oh, God, had he fallen in love with Hattie Leggit? He'd just told her the truth—he would let her go if he would only bring more unhappiness into her life.

He rolled away from her and sat up, buried his face in his hands. Whatever she wanted, he would give her—except a reprieve for Bernard Leggit. That he could not do. If the scheme must be changed, so be it.

Hattie cried so softly he barely heard her. John let his head hang back and he made a silent plea for inspiration. He could not bear the sound of her sadness.

"John." She slithered across the slippery stuff of the

costumes and crowded against him with her knees pulled up. She slipped a hand past his hip and ran her fingers up and down the inside of his thigh.

He felt her breasts pressed to his back and he gritted his teeth.

"Don't cry," he said. Muscles in his jaw locked. She told him he could not have her, but used her body to show that she did want him. Which should he believe?

"I cannot go on as I am," Hattie said. "You deserve to know what I intended to do. I wanted to use an affair with you to help me get the money I need more quickly." She made to withdraw her hand, but he held it where it was. "You are too generous, John. You have thought me better than I am. I need the money so that I can pay off a debt for my parents. Then I mean to leave Mr. Leggit. Getting money from him in small amounts has taken so long. I had come to think that if I could taunt him with my betrayal, threaten to let all of his cronies know I had been unfaithful, he would pay me handsomely to hold my tongue."

John couldn't move or speak. *She* had intended to use *him?* That was rich. It was ironic, comical even, but he didn't feel like laughing.

"You are angry," she said. "Of course you are. But I didn't get the idea until after you had shown interest in me."

"I see." Perhaps he did. "Blackmail. Your silence in exchange for money."

"Yes, I've warned you how I asked for money."

She had, and he had no right to feel chagrined. They had both been about the same business but for different reasons.

"But you've changed your mind," he said. "Even though there is something distasteful about Mr. Leggit,

something you never quite reveal, you have decided he deserves your loyalty.''

''I have decided it would be wrong to use you to get what I need. My husband is powerful and if I revealed that I'd been intimate with you—if I had, that is—to get what I want from him, in all likelihood he would try to punish you. He would have you…hurt and I should never forgive myself.''

Once more she attempted to pull her hand away and once more John stopped her. The idea that she considered Leggit a more dangerous enemy than he was, rankled. She would refuse him in order to protect him, *damn it.*

''You need not worry about…me.'' He caught his breath. She had spread her hand beneath his and squeezed his leg with her fingertips. Only her thumb curled over. He couldn't make himself move her away. He also couldn't stand what she did to him. ''I am a strong, capable man with enough power of my own. In fact, I order you not to waste your…sympathy on me.''

''I feel full,'' Hattie said.

She felt full? He *was* full and perilously close to losing his composure.

''You don't want to listen to my troubles, or my feelings. I know we have no future, but when I am with you my heart is full and I feel extraordinary.''

''Let me help you.''

''If only you could. I did come tonight to hide my money, and I told myself there was no other reason. But I wished I could come to you, because I'm frightened.''

John stiffened. Against his body's wishes, he swiveled sideways and looked down at Hattie. ''Explain at once.''

She appeared almost ill. ''There's nothing you can do about it. Mr. Leggit wants a son. He is tired of waiting for me to produce one.''

''I don't understand.''

"He believes that it is my fault because I...don't... can't do with him what a woman is supposed to do with her husband."

"What is that?" He held his breath, turned over the possibilities in his mind.

"I have not conceived because I have not performed my wifely duties properly."

"Hattie, sometimes these things don't happen immediately, or even very soon." Landing his fist in Leggit's mouth would feel good, but not nearly good enough.

"Mr. Leggit and his doctor are convinced I am responsible."

Poor girl. He had a wild notion to keep her with him, to get away from Bath with her and keep on going until they were lost to this place. "I will help you deal with this," he told her. "Don't argue, because it will do no good."

Hattie scooted to sit up, then to kneel. She rested her hands on his shoulders. "I am from a different world than you, but I wish it were not so. There, I've said it and I mean it. I wish we had been able to know each other before—before Mr. Leggit came into my life."

Careful, careful. "That would have been nice. You can still trust me."

"Very well." She held his face as if to make him concentrate more. "I need you. I'm terrified of what Mr. Leggit has in mind. He has made a decision. He wants a boy he can call his son. That means I have to increase."

John looked back into her luminous eyes and he felt a sudden, deep shock. It couldn't—yes, it could be. "He wants you to get with child by another man if necessary," *with John, in fact,* "and pretend the child is his?"

"Yes," she whispered. "He's looking for someone, a stranger, to sleep with me at Leggit Hall. I am to allow this until what he requires is accomplished."

25

"*As arranged?*" Hattie had rushed into her boudoir and now closed the door firmly. "What do you mean, you came *as arranged?* Mrs. Dobbin told me that was the message you gave her for me after you arrived. And she had nothing to add when I questioned her, except that she must dash away to take your place with Chloe. I'm delighted you're here, but I don't understand why you are."

Snowdrop, dressed in a lovely peach walking dress with three flounces on the skirt, looked directly at Hattie. "Perhaps we should keep our voices down just in case. We could sit on the window seat."

The window seat was about as far from the door as any point in the boudoir. "Very well. Your dress is gorgeous, Snowdrop. And your bonnet. They look lovely on you."

"A present from my Albert," Snowdrop said, and for an instant her look became faraway. "He'd have me wear fancy clothes all the time. That's not appropriate, but for when we go out walking, he makes sure I do him justice. Silly thing."

"Quite natural, I should think."

Since the previous night, and the hours Hattie had spent wrapped against John's solid, reassuring body, she had made herself believe he would allow no harm to come to her. But try as she might, she couldn't stop slivers of doubt from wedging themselves around her hopes.

"I came in one of Lord Granville's lovely carriages," Snowdrop said. She bubbled more than simply spoke. "My Albert drove me and he'll wait for me until I'm ready to leave. They're all agreed that Mr. Leggit isn't going to notice much about who drives the carriage, and Albert should be just a man without a face to these people 'ere. I don't like to think of it, mind you. My Albert's a good-looking man and he's intelligent to boot. He shouldn't be invisible to them that thinks they're better than everyone."

"The preoccupations of the rich are sometimes unfortunate," Hattie said, but her nerves jumped and she hoped she could stop herself from pushing Snowdrop for an explanation before she was ready to give one.

"It was Lord Granville what sent me 'ere." The more excited Snowdrop became, the more unpredictable her speech. "He's a lovely man, Mrs. Leggit. I never saw a more handsome one, except for my Albert, but he can be frightening when he loses his temper."

Hattie kept her responses to nods, afraid that if she spoke and gave Snowdrop more to think about, the things she was waiting to hear might be even slower in coming.

"I don't know what got into the marquis today, but he was in such a black mood. Everyone scurried around and talked in whispers. When he called for me I expected the worst, I can tell you. Snowdrop, I said to myself, he's going to let you go. He's not happy with the job you're doing. Then I got a bit cross myself, since I do a wonderful job with Miss Chloe."

Hattie thought she might pop at any moment.

"It turns out Lord Granville is more than pleased with the way I look after Chloe. I should think so, too. He says she looks ever so much more relaxed and more like a little girl since she's been with me."

"Of course he says that. I've seen for myself how Chloe loves you."

Snowdrop shrugged. A deep crease settled between her eyebrows. "If she'd talk again I'd think I'd done her some real good."

Hattie said, "Hmm," and studied the mulberry slippers that matched her French spotted silk dress. Should she give Snowdrop a little nudge toward her reason for coming?

"Lord Granville asked me to come and visit you," Snowdrop said, and she stopped wiggling and swinging her legs, which were too short to reach the floor. She frowned again. "He told me to say that everything will be all right and you're not to worry."

Snowdrop swung her feet again, and Hattie could almost hear her puzzling about something.

"That's all he said?" Hattie couldn't be patient any longer.

"No."

For what felt like hours, Snowdrop's eyes roamed over the blue furnishings in the room.

"Snowdrop—"

"I don't know what it means, but I expect you do," the girl said. "You are no longer alone there. That's what he said I was to tell you. You are no longer alone there. The problem will be taken care of. He said you knew where to go if you needed, or wanted to. I've got a good memory and those were his exact works. What does it all mean, Mrs. L.?"

"Please call me Hattie."

"What does it mean, Hattie?"

Shaking her head, she held Snowdrop's hand and shook it gently. "When I can, I'll explain. For now I must thank

you for being so kind to me and for coming here like this when you must have been scared."

"Scared?" Snowdrop laughed with gusto. "Me? Slasher Pick would have a good chuckle over that one."

Hattie gave her an interested look.

"Me dad," Snowdrop said, "Slasher Pick. He didn't have a son. He had me, only he didn't seem to notice I wasn't a boy. The world's waiting for fools, he used to say. Then it does 'em in. You ain't no fool, Snowdrop. You're as tough as the toughest."

Fascination got the better of Hattie. "But he gave you a, er, soft name."

"No." Snowdrop looked at Hattie and didn't seem so tough. "Me mum wanted me called that and me dad would have done anything she wanted, so I'm told. That's how I got my name."

"I think it suits you," Hattie said. "And Albert goes all soppy every time he says it."

"Look," Snowdrop said, and scrambled to kneel on the window seat. "There's my Albert and that fancy carriage. I'm so lucky. Never thought I'd have experiences like this. And I used to take Albert for granted 'cause he was just there and one of us. Now I look at other men—there's lots of top-lofty ones in Bath—and not one of them is as much of a man as my Albert."

Hattie's eyes burned and she blinked fast. The carriage below was green, just like the one John used, but it didn't have the coat of arms on the doors.

"I think it's the aunts' carriage, not that I've ever seen them use it," Snowdrop said.

The aunts. "You remind me that I'd like to ask a favor of you, another favor. Would you take something to the aunts for me? I should have got it there a day or more ago."

"Gladly," Snowdrop said. "Aren't they a pair? A lot goes on under that white hair, I can tell you. They're mad at Boggs now. They sniff and put their noses in the air every time he gets near them." Her wide smile showed pretty teeth. "That is, if he doesn't get 'is nose up first."

Hattie chuckled at the picture she imagined. "Spirited, all of them." And unfortunately she knew the reason for the feud. "Let me give you this. Then I'll show you how I got in and out of the house when you were kind enough to drive me."

The fifteen sovereigns, wrapped so tightly they couldn't make a sound, were in her reticule. She'd carried them with her ever since her visit to Porky's. She took them out and gave them to Snowdrop. "Put it away carefully and go straight to the aunts when you get back."

"I will." Snowdrop gave the packet a long, curious look before she dropped it into her reticule.

"Shall I send for refreshments?"

"No, thank you. I'd best be getting back. Don't like to leave little Chloe for long. Show me your secret coming and going place and I'll run along."

On their way to the conservatory, Snowdrop caught sight of the coach and Albert through a different window and her hand went to her breast. "See how he keeps looking at the house. He's waiting for me to come because he doesn't like it if he's not sure where I am." Partway down the middle flight of stairs, she stood on tiptoe for the best possible view of Albert.

"Sounds like love to me," Hattie said. And she envied Snowdrop her certainty that the man in her life was hers for the asking. There was no reason she couldn't be with Albert.

Snowdrop sighed loudly. "He is a silly, you know. But

I suppose I'll have to marry him and put him out of his misery.''

Hattie gave Snowdrop's hair a small yank and said into her ear, ''You are bad. Perhaps too bad for a good man like Albert. Better snap him up before he changes his mind.''

Skipping from stair to stair, Snowdrop carried on and down the last flight of stairs to the main floor. She glanced back and laughed at Hattie, then looked up the many stairs they had just descended. ''Why would someone with lots of money make it so hard to get from one place to another in his own house? With all the land he's got, your husband could have built the whole place on one huge floor. Now that would be really different.''

It was Hattie's turn to say, ''Perhaps we should keep our voices down.''

''Oh, dear,'' Snowdrop said. ''You're right. Do you know how much Dobbin loves to be with Chloe?''

''Yes.'' Hattie laughed, recalling Mrs. Dobbin's endless rhapsodizing about the child. ''She tells me about it frequently.''

''Now that miserable Dolly goes up there—if Dobbin comes—and she follows her around. I think she's trying to learns how Dobbin behaves because it's so pretty, the way she talks and moves.''

''Dolly's an intelligent person,'' Hattie said. ''She knows when she's around a good example.''

They hurried through several rooms to reach the conservatory, where Hattie went to the door with a key in its lock. ''This is it,'' she said and quickly added, ''Would you come for me again if I needed you?''

''Of course, I would,'' Snowdrop said. The rubber trees, banana and royal palms inside the conservatory kept her staring from place to place and leaning back to see

how the leaves of the tallest trees brushed the glass ceiling. "Look at that. Those leaves look like they're painted on the sky."

Heavy footsteps approached and Hattie made sure she was nowhere near the door.

"Why there you are, Hattie dear," Mr. Leggit said, stepping into the conservatory. Sequins on his waistcoat caught the sunlight. "I've been looking for you. I know you've wanted to be more involved in running the house so I'm going to start including you in my decisions." He seemed to notice for the first time that Hattie wasn't alone. "Who is this person."

"Miss Snowdrop Pike," Hattie said before her companion could ruin everything with too much honesty. "We met in Bath and I invited her to visit me." That wasn't a real fib.

"Hmm." Mr. Leggit lost interest at once. "Mr. Stack, come forward if you please." He swung around with his right arm extended as if he'd asked a lady at a ball to dance.

A man who had apparently been hanging back, stepped forward and stood beside Mr. Leggit, who said, "This, Hattie, is Walter Stack. Some might consider it odd for me to retain him when I haven't been looking for servants lately. But anyone who made that remark would prove they don't have any flair when it comes to seizing a fine opportunity."

Snowdrop made a faint noise.

Hattie tried not to stare at Walter Stack. His thick black hair must reach well past his shoulders, only he wore it tied back with a length of black ribbon. His clothes fit him well and although they were not of high quality, the man himself made them look splendid.

"Walter worked on a fine estate in the north. You

might say he's a jack-of-all-trades. Well, not *all* trades, but a number of tasks requiring a superior sort of servant. He's a man after my own heart and he'll go far.''

''Yes, so it would appear.'' Hattie nodded. ''How do you do, Walter?''

''Well,'' the man said, disquieting her by studying every inch of her person with his startling blue-green eyes. Tall, much taller than Mr. Leggit, he held himself erect but not stiff. His broad shoulders couldn't be straighter, yet Hattie felt as if he were like a powerful animal, relaxed on its haunches but ready to spring at any instant.

She realized Mr. Leggit stared at her, too. ''So you approve of my decision, dear Hattie?''

''Oh, yes, of course.''

Something about the man disturbed her. His eyes were kind enough, but there was a piercing intelligence there that made a person wonder what he was really thinking.

''If you want something of a special nature, something not just any servant could perform, call for Walter,'' Mr. Leggit said. ''I would say he's a chap who could satisfy you in whatever you ask.''

Hattie said, ''Thank you,'' as Mr. Leggit departed the conservatory with Walter Stack behind him.

Walter looked back once and the curious expression on his handsome face shook Hattie. He looked straight at her and only at her before disappearing with his new employer.

Snowdrop's mouth was open. She stared after Mr. Leggit and Walter Stack and her mouth remained open.

''What is it?'' Hattie asked.

Snowdrop remembered to bring her lips together. She swallowed with difficulty as if her throat had dried out. ''What a beautiful man,'' she said, and winked at Hattie. ''Perhaps you'll have to think up lots of special needs.

Needs of a special nature, like Mr. Leggit said.'' She winked again.

Hattie searched her mind for the key to whatever code Snowdrop used. "What sort of special needs?" she said.

Snowdrop swung her reticule and said in a breezy voice, "Ooh, I should think you could come up with some."

26

To Snowdrop, her life near the coast seemed far away and long ago.

Here in Bath every day became an adventure and there were so many secret things going on she had to stop herself from hopping and skipping with excitement.

"Good afternoon, Boggs," she said, sweeping through the front doors at Worth House. "A very fine afternoon it is, too, don't you think?"

Boggs muttered and looked past her as if she wasn't there.

"Excuse me, Mr. Boggs, but I didn't quite hear what you said."

"I said," he told her in a raised voice, "that servants don't use the family entrance in this house. You're above yourself, you are. Like some other people around here who forget some of us know too much about them— enough to get them in hot water."

Snowdrop gave him an innocent look. "You're a powerful one, Mr. Boggs. And quite right, if I may say so, after you've been here *so* many years."

The haughty look slipped away behind Boggs's pride. "I'm glad you see that. Mrs. Dobbin is with Chloe." He smacked his wig down on top of his head.

"Thank you very much," Snowdrop said. She hiked up

the front of her skirts to run upstairs but remembered Boggs would be watching and climbed sedately instead.

Albert had insisted he drive her to the front of the house because, he said, she was too good for any servants' entrance and he wouldn't stand for her not being respected. Silly man. She smiled as she climbed. Albert had become quite the gentleman. Even the way he talked was more like Lord Granville than the Albert of old.

What a day. Stairs, stairs and more stairs. Snowdrop arrived at the nurseries and approached the open schoolroom door. Mrs. Dobbin's voice, soft and persuasive, came from inside.

"That's a lovely painting, Chloe. I shall have to make sure your cousin hears about your talent. Would you like me to come and teach you sometimes?"

Snowdrop held her breath, waiting for Chloe to say something. If she did it would be wonderful, but it could also be dangerous because this wouldn't be the best time for the little one to talk about what had happened on her way from France to England.

Chloe didn't answer Dobbin.

"I think she's naughty." This was Dolly, and Snowdrop couldn't believe what she'd said. "Only naughty girls don't do what their elders tell them to."

"Dolly," Mrs. Dobbin said, sounding as shocked as Snowdrop felt. "Please don't say such things. They aren't true and you'll hurt Chloe's feelings. Chloe, do tell me what's upsetting you. I know all about being upset, so I could help you. Just tell me what it is."

Silence followed until Dolly said, "There could be something wrong with her, you know. Lord Granville and her parents could be pretending she's just shy when she's really a bit off in the head."

Mrs. Dobbin took her time to say, "That's unkind and

untrue. Look at her paintings if you don't believe me. She's better than certain adults.''

Snowdrop smiled. Dolly shouldn't annoy Mrs. Dobbin unless she wanted to feel the sharp edge of that lady's tongue.

''So we're to expect Mrs. Leggit, are we?'' Dolly said. ''If she accepts the old ladies' invitation?''

Stomping her feet down hard so they wouldn't think she'd been eavesdropping, Snowdrop showed herself at the schoolroom door. ''Hello, Mrs. Dobbin. Hello, Dolly.'' In she went and started pulling off her gloves at once. ''Having a lovely time, are you? Hello, Chloe. Mrs. Leggit said to tell you she loves you.''

''She doesn't know her,'' Dolly said, her tone cross. Spite glittered in her eyes. ''These rich women can be so stupid.'' The maid's color was as high as ever and she sat with her long, large-boned body hunched over the table where she took tea with Mrs. Dobbin.

Snowdrop looked at Chloe and all but fainted away. True, it lasted only a moment, but Chloe had smiled a little.

''How did you find Mrs. Leggit?'' Mrs. Dobbin asked. ''Did you think she seemed quite like herself?''

The idea of discussing Hattie, with anyone, didn't feel right to Snowdrop. ''At her best,'' she said, still keeping an eye on Chloe's face. ''What a dear person Mrs. Leggit is. May I see Chloe's painting?''

Since there weren't any objections voiced, Snowdrop went to the desk where Chloe sat and stood behind the child to look over her head. ''My, that is a good painting, Chloe.'' Keeping her voice steady didn't come easily.

''Tell Snowdrop about your visit with the aunts,'' Dolly said.

Snowdrop couldn't look away from the watercolor painting.

"Nothing to tell, really," Mrs. Dobbin said. "They're lonely so they do what they can to find someone to talk to, apart from one another."

Snowdrop didn't think the aunts were as lonely as people suggested. Mostly they were happy to be together and only sought out company when they wanted something done.

If only she could find a way to get rid of Chloe's painting. A number of what were obviously small boats, filled with men, pointed toward the heads of people who were in the dark water. One, two, three, four heads. And red streaks on the water near two of the heads weren't supposed to be reflections of a setting sun. There was no sun.

Mrs. Dobbin and Dolly had no way of knowing the painting depicted something that had happened to Lord Granville and Chloe—and her parents. She must not over-react, Snowdrop reminded herself. But she couldn't help seeing how Chloe concentrated on what she'd done and fearing that at any moment she'd describe it all aloud. She'd probably speak in French, which Snowdrop didn't understand, but Mrs. Dobbin did and when Dolly asked—and she definitely would—what Chloe had said, Mrs. Dobbin was likely to repeat it. Then just see how quickly Dolly spread the information to everyone and started the tongues wagging.

She reached for Chloe's unresisting hand and urged the little girl to stand up. "You'd best be getting back to Mrs. Leggit," she said to Mrs. Dobbin. "We've already stolen enough of your time, but I am glad you like to come. Will you come again soon?"

Mrs. Dobbin tied on her black bonnet and gathered her

reticule and gloves. "When Mrs. Leggit can spare me, I will," she said.

"We'll see you out," Snowdrop said, casually gathering up the painting before following Mrs. Dobbin downstairs.

Chloe ran to hold her hand and Dolly came, too. Snowdrop smiled at her. "Thank you for keeping Mrs. Dobbin and Chloe company."

"What are you doing, thanking me? You're just a servant like me." Dolly flounced away toward the back of the house.

Mrs. Dobbin didn't comment on Dolly's rudeness and neither did Snowdrop. She glanced at Chloe. Had she really felt thin little fingers squeeze her hand?

"There you are, Chloe," Lord Granville said from behind his desk and his smile was genuinely pleased. "Aunt Prunella and Aunt Enid have been asking about you. They expected you to come and sit with them this afternoon."

Snowdrop gave Chloe enough time to answer the comment before saying, "Mrs. Dobbin came over from Leggit Hall to visit Chloe," as if Lord Granville didn't already know as much.

"Chloe painted this, my lord. Mrs. Dobbin and Dolly thought it was wonderful and so do I."

Lord Granville took the piece of paper and studied it closely. If Snowdrop had doubted her own conclusions about the painting, the expression on the marquis's face confirmed she'd been right in her assumptions.

Lord Granville looked at her and nodded a little. He set his mouth in a straight line and a cheek twitched.

Chloe pulled herself into a big leather chair and stared at him. She leaned forward as if about to say something.

Snowdrop saw Lord Granville lean forward, too, and

hold his breath. Gradually tears formed in Chloe's eyes and slid down her cheeks.

Before Snowdrop could react, Lord Granville strode from behind his desk and swept Chloe into his arms. He held her as if she were breakable and guided her face into the crook between his neck and shoulder. He whispered to her, very low, and Snowdrop couldn't hear what he said. When he sang, just as low, she didn't need to hear any words. The way he closed his eyes while he swayed with Chloe didn't need an explanation. He loved the child and wasn't afraid to show he did.

"Chloe's tired," he said, and the child's drooping eyelids suggested he was right. "I'm going to tuck her into my bed."

Snowdrop followed him as far as the alcove into the bedroom but went no farther. She liked watching the man and the child together.

"I'd have asked you to do this for me," Lord Granville said, and chuckled. "Somehow I doubt the top of your head would reach the mattress, even if you stood on the steps."

She had lived too long with jokes about her size to be offended. "I'm sure you're right, John Elliot."

He set Chloe down in the very middle of the great bed and gave Snowdrop a cool stare before popping his cousin beneath both coverlet and sheets.

That look had been intended as a reprimand because she'd used his given name, but she hadn't forgotten when he'd come into her cottage and dripped all over the pretty silk rug her dad had given her. He'd been John Elliot then, all right. So there.

She approved of the way he pulled a sheet tight over Chloe and tucked it under the mattress. For a man he had

some common sense and thought to make sure the child couldn't easily roll out of bed.

"Sleep a little," he said, and kissed Chloe's cheek. "I will be in my study. Call out if you need me."

He trod lightly to join Snowdrop and indicated he wanted her to join him in the study.

Automatically she sat in the chair Chloe had used, then remembered herself and jumped up again while Lord Granville resumed his place at the desk. He glanced at her, and said, "Sit close. We don't want to be overheard." He pulled the chair beside the desk and gave her a completely unlordly grin. "Come, let me lift you in."

Snowdrop grinned back. "What a gentleman you are, my lord. Fortunately I don't need any help." She hurried around him and sat down again, keeping her grin in place as she worked herself far enough back in the seat to be comfortable.

Lord Granville sat in his chair, facing her and only inches away. "First, thank you for bringing Chloe's work. We have, or rather, I have a problem."

"We have a problem," Snowdrop corrected him. "You, Albert and me have plenty to lose if Chloe starts telling everyone what happened. It would be bad if Mr. Leggit caught wind of it."

Lord Granville gazed into the distance and said, "I must make certain that doesn't happen. Now, tell me about the other."

He didn't need to explain that he wanted to know what had happened at Leggit Hall. "I told her exactly what you said," Snowdrop told him.

"And what did she say?"

"Well, she really likes this new dress my Albert bought for me."

"It's a delightful dress. What else did she say?"

Snowdrop looked into his face. It didn't take a genius to see he wanted her to tell him something, something he expected, and he was only stopping himself from snapping at her because he didn't want her frightened. Or, more likely, distracted from the one thing that interested him...Mrs. Hattie Leggit. Snowdrop felt a delicious shiver. Just what was going to happen there, she wondered.

"Snowdrop?"

"Um, she thanked me when I told her you said she wasn't to worry."

"Then?" He had such a way of going paler when he was cross and trying not to show he was.

"We talked about my Albert and me. And Hattie said— she told me to call her Hattie—she asked what else you'd told me to say to her."

Oh, thank gawd. Some color came back into his face and he smiled a little bit.

"I said what you said, about her not being alone. And I told her you said she knew where to come if she needed to. Or if she just wanted to come."

The marquis breathed out for a long time. "What else?"

Phew, nothing would be enough for him. "I asked her what it all meant and she said she'd tell me one day, if she could. You'd think I couldn't figure out you meant that she could come to *you* whenever she wanted. And you're soppy over her, just like she is over you, not that I approve even if her husband is a nasty man who says nasty things to her."

For all the world his lordship looked like he had a big pain somewhere. "If you've heard him say nasty things to her, tell me what they were."

"I forgot," Snowdrop said. "Hattie asked me to talk

to the aunts for her and give them something. Of course I will. She's fond of them. And they've asked her to come and visit them again, so I think they're fond of her, too.''

Rather than seem pleased, Lord Granville stood up with his hands curled into fists at his sides. ''Thank you for that, Snowdrop. Did you hear Mr. Leggit being unkind to his wife?''

She blew at all the strands of hair that curled onto her face. ''Not exactly unkind. Unsuitable, I suppose. It was when Hattie took me to the conservatory. What a beautiful place. I never saw trees indoors like that.''

''Quite.''

Men always wanted to hurry you. ''She showed me the door she used when she has to get out without being seen. And I said of course I'd drive her in my coach if she ever wanted to go somewhere again.''

He considered, frowning, and never moving his eyes from her face. ''This is a request and I'll try to understand if you decide to refuse me, but I have been concerned for Mrs. Leggit, as I think you know. Will you tell me if she asks you to drive her?''

Oh dear, she'd said too much as usual. ''I wouldn't be at all surprised if I did. Tell you, that is. If there's time. And I can find you.'' She sucked in a quick breath and said, ''It was the way Mr. Leggit said it that didn't sound very nice. I made light of it because I didn't want Hattie getting upset once she was on her own.''

''Very good of you,'' his lordship said.

''I said she should find some special needs for this new servant to perform. After all, he's a lovely man.'' She winked, but Lord Granville's face grew paler once more. ''It wasn't nice of Mr. Leggit to talk about the man being a superior sort of servant Hattie could call on if she had

some special needs. Not appropriate unless he really meant what I thought he did. Still not right even then.''

Lord Granville put his fists on the desk and leaned on them. ''I'll just let you wander through your thoughts until you get to the point,'' he said.

No need to be like that. ''I thought I had got to the point, my lord. Mr. Leggit said what he said like he was suggesting something unsuitable. Something unsuitable for Walter Stack to do to—for her. He's the servant Mr. Leggit just retained. And take it from me, Walter Stack is too good-looking and too sure of himself for his own good. He looked like he could hardly wait for Hattie to send for him.''

Let the marquis make whatever he wanted to out of that.

Curl me liver, she thought, he looks as pleased as punch.

27

"Albert's keeping watch from there," John said, pointing out a copse of trees below. "Nevertheless we should waste no time getting away from this place."

Dominic and John sat down on a log in a hollow tucked into the rim of a forest above Leggit Hall. "A pretty mess you've got us into," Dominic said. "Three days I've been in Leggit's lair, watching his loathsome behavior, and listening to his disgusting plans for mine. Why do you continue to oppose dealing with the man? For good?"

John skirted that question. "How are you faring? Something must have changed or you wouldn't have sent for me."

The hollow was perfectly situated and John could not imagine how Albert had found it. The house was distant yet visible. Anyone setting out in this direction should be seen.

"I asked you a question, John."

"I have had my own doubts about the course I set. But not anymore and now it is too late anyway." If Leggit died suddenly and from an attack, Hattie would forever suspect he was behind it all. Knowing how gentle she was he doubted if she would approve—or forgive him. A fool he might be, but he didn't want Hattie to think poorly of him.

"I don't see—"

''Take my word for it.'' John cut his brother off. ''Let's get to it, man. Albert said you seemed desperate to meet with me today.''

''Did you think you could send me into that vulgar house and leave me alone to deal with the monster, Leggit? And he is a monster. Did you think I would sit in the room I've been given, also vulgar but exceedingly comfortable, and just wait until Leggit paraded me out to do his bidding? Do you know that after telling his wife he'd retained me, he's led the staff to believe I've been turned down for employment at the hall? He's put it about that we have acquaintances in common and for their sakes he's allowing me to remain until I find a place elsewhere?''

John looked into his youngest brother's eyes, eyes not blue, not green, but which the family all agreed could look into the head and heart of a person. Dominic had an uncanny gift for stating another's thoughts before they could be spoken aloud.

Dominic looked away. ''This is a hellhole, John.''

''That I know. You mean you haven't been pressed into service as an entertainer at Leggit's pool galas?'' He knew better than to chuckle.

''No. But I already know a good deal about those affairs. Leggit sent a woman to entertain me. She told me all about what you call galas, and showed me a sampling of the delights offered there.''

''You bedded her already?'' John grinned. ''I see little has changed about you.''

''A great deal has changed. It's time you stopped thinking of my behavior as similar to yours. It is not. If a woman with a beautiful body enjoys showing it to me, who am I to rebuff her? If she wants to dance naked for me, who am I—''

"To rebuff her?" John finished for him. "Your restraint impresses me."

"Leggit has asked me to force his wife. My gorge rises at the thought."

John bowed his head and shut his eyes. "Your gorge may rise, but I am mortally sick at the thought of him using her like this."

"You don't know the half of it." Even in his jacket of rough cloth and his cheap linen and waistcoat there could be no doubt about Dominic's strength. Muscles in his calves flexed stiff and hard below breeches made of the same stuff as his coat.

Assessing the brother he had barely seen for more than a year helped John to gather his thoughts without being overcome with fury. Vaguely he smelled the underbrush moldering in the damp shade of mature larch and fir trees.

"John, do you love Hattie Leggit?"

"Damn your impertinence."

Dominic half turned away and averted his eyes. "Forgive me. I wouldn't blame a man for loving her, though. She's beautiful and charming."

John churned inside. "Hattie's attributes are no affair of yours."

"They've become so," Dominic said.

"You always were one to press what seemed like an advantage," John said. "You think you have power over me because I've asked for your help."

"If I were a scoundrel, I would have power over you. I'm not a scoundrel."

John braced himself against a tree. "No, you're not. I apologize." If he didn't settle down, he could jeopardize his usefulness to Hattie. "Bloody hell, I'm beside myself. Leggit is responsible for the deaths of our cousin and his wife. My plan for dealing with the man is perfect as far

as making him suffer goes. But I wasn't prepared... I didn't think through all the possible eventualities.''

"It's easy to chastise yourself for that now," Dominic said, "but you did the best you could at a time when passion had you by the throat. You're not alone, John. Nathan and I are with you and, for whatever reason, I do believe that odd Albert would die for you."

John looked at Dominic, but didn't ask for an explanation of his remark about Albert.

They were avoiding whatever had caused Dominic to send an urgent note with Albert. "You have something to tell me. What has happened?"

"I have an assignation in a private room where the pools are."

Oh, my God. It was happening exactly as he'd hoped, yet as the horror of it all came nearer, disgust overwhelmed him. "Go on," he said.

"Tomorrow evening the house will be cleared of servants. I am to go down there and do exactly as I have been told. I will not, Leggit assures me, be interrupted and I may take as long as I need to complete—"

"Just spit it out," John said. "The fewer words, the better."

"At eight tomorrow evening I am to wait down there. The room will be dark and remain dark. Hattie Leggit will be sent to me. Leggit said I should seduce her gently if I could, or take her by force if I couldn't. When she is definitely increasing, after we've been together as often as necessary, I will be handsomely paid and sent on my way. Rather a delicate way of saying Leggit plans to have me killed. He thinks I'm the perfect candidate for his purposes because I supposedly have no family."

"I'm going to kill him now." John made to leave the

hollow but Dominic stopped him. ''You said you believed I should have dispatched him by now.''

''He is surrounded by his hired help. His personal guards. You should meet Smythe. He slithers rather than walks and holds his head on one side as if preparing to be struck. If you go in there after Leggit now, you are likely to be shot and there will be plenty of witnesses who will attest to your unprovoked attack. Nathan and I would finish him, but you would have died unnecessarily.''

Every word was the truth. John never recalled feeling so vengeful, or so desperate to protect someone. ''What do you intend to do? And how am I supposed to manage, waiting to hear how my Hattie has fared?''

''Your Hattie?''

''Don't push me,'' John said. ''You're correct in thinking that she means something to me.''

Dominic thumped his shoulder. ''Believe that I will do everything I can to help. We do have a complication, though. Leggit has his own tame sawbones. Today the fellow checked my eyes and teeth—and other parts—as if I were a horse Leggit might purchase.''

''And he found you sound?''

''Evidently.''

Whatever happened, Hattie would be frightened.

''John,'' Dominic said. ''I couldn't possibly do as Leggit wants, but the sawbones will examine Hattie after she leaves me.''

''Why?'' John said, and felt the fool. ''Why didn't I think of that? Of course they'll want proof. They'll humiliate her to get it. You know Leggit says it's all her fault she hasn't conceived?''

''That *could* well be, y'know.''

''Bosh. It could as well be that she is repulsed by him…

I don't want to discuss this any more than I have to. We must decide how to do what is necessary."

"John, you won't come to hate me for my part in all this, will you?"

"No." His heart beat like a drum. "What do you intend to do?"

"Make sure there is no question that Hattie has been with a man."

John dropped his head back and the distant specks of blue between the trees blurred. "No, no, no, no."

"What choice do we have?"

John swallowed a yell, but he beat his fists against the rough bark of a larch tree, beat them until Dominic threw his arms around him from behind and hauled him away.

"There are people who need you to be steady. If you go on as you are, you'll be useless. Look what you've done to yourself."

Dominic held John's hands up for him to see. Blood seeped from gouges on his knuckles, and the sides of his hands.

John shook Dominic off. "To hell with my hands. Let's discuss every move to be made. Start now."

28

Hattie yanked her arm free of Smythe's grasp. He shrugged his narrow shoulders and let his head sag even more than usual.

Nausea, and acid in her throat, drained her and she leaned against a wall at the entrance to the Pool Rooms. "I will not go," she said. "Leave me at once." Her head pounded, and her heart, and she was sure she would be sick.

"Such a fuss," Smythe said, looking at her sideways from his considerable height. His wispy gray hair sprayed out around his collar. "A wife does what her husband says. And no arguments. Just remember that and things will go better for you. The sooner you accomplish the necessary, the sooner there will be no more need for any of this. And you'll be happy enough. You'll have your babe to moon over."

"Stop. Be quiet at once." He knew it all. Mr. Leggit had told this horrid man everything and Hattie could not bear it.

Smythe caught her by the elbow and pulled her beside him. She dragged her feet until she almost fell on the marble stairs. Her *escort's* reaction was to jerk her upright again and hurry her along until they reached the bottom. He just about carried her. Her shoulder hurt because it had taken her weight.

Her *husband* had sent another man to do this to her.

"It's dark," she said. "Put on the lights."

"No," he said. "I know the way well enough and there's enough light from the moon to make our way. When I have delivered you, I shall go upstairs to wait in the foyer. Come straight to me when you're told to."

They carried onward beneath shafts of colored light shed by the moon through leaded glass. Hattie could see the big pool like polished ink and quite still. No steam. That surprised her.

Smythe took her to the door of the room where she'd been with John. Please grant her the strength to endure whatever was to come. If she'd had warning of Mr. Leggit's arrangement for tonight, she would have tried to reach John, but nothing had been said until Smythe knocked on the door to her boudoir. The horrid fellow had pushed her down before her mirror and pulled all the pins from her hair before handing her a brush.

She'd ordered her hair with shaking hands, and asked to be spared this indignity. Smythe had not answered her. At least he had not ordered her to wear some revealing garb.

But there would be no reprieve from this and when it was over, her shame would keep her from going to John again.

"You're to encourage this man, mind," Smythe said in his nasal voice. "But not with conversation. You have no need to know him. Mr. Leggit told me to say he's proud of you for being so brave. Now, in you go and there's nothing to be afraid of. Your husband wouldn't choose a man who couldn't be trusted to be good to you."

Hattie couldn't speak at all.

"All right, then. Get inside and no more making a fuss.

Best you try to enjoy yourself.'' He turned the door handle and gave her a little push at the same time. Then he shut her inside.

The only sounds were of water running from the pipe into the pool.

If she tried to leave and run away, she was bound to be caught and returned. Like an animal who must do as its master ordered. She had no more power than a pet dog. Her own master held all the authority and had the law on his side, the law that said a woman belonged to her husband. If she were to tell someone of influence what Mr. Leggit had done, she wouldn't be believed. Or she might be believed but nothing would be done about it since her husband was a wealthy man with contacts he could draw on to squelch anything she said.

Hattie crossed her arms tightly and pressed herself against the wall. Even if she screamed, no help would come.

Silly she might be, but she longed to be with John. Imagining the bed he'd made of silk, satin and velvet in the costume room turned the longing to an urgent plea from her heart that he take her away from this.

Faint, she sat on the hard floor so suddenly she jarred her back and head. Hattie rubbed her forehead. As her eyes became accustomed to the gloom, she made out the pool and the shape of the divan. She thought the table piled with food was where it had been before.

"Is there someone here?" she said, and her voice broke.

"It's me, Hattie. John. Come to me."

A trick. This man with the rasping voice was not John.

"Lie on the bed," he said. "Don't be frightened. You know I would never harm you." He spoke rapidly and sounded breathless.

Hattie got up and walked near the curved walls until she got close to the bed. She peered around but didn't make out a man's shape.

"Light a candle," she said. "Let me see your face."

"The orders are for the room to remain dark," he said. "Your husband's orders."

"I'm frightened," she said. She couldn't help it.

"I know. Will you take some wine?" he asked.

"No."

"This is a bad time for stubbornness. Take just a little."

Panic overtook her. She turned back and made a run for the door.

An arm, an arm like iron, closed around her waist. He lifted her from her feet and carried her to the divan. The moment he set her down, he pressed a wineglass into her hands.

"No!" Hattie said. She threw the glass and watched broken shards glitter when they flew up. "I take no willing part in this. And I will not have my senses softened by drink and lies just to make me more receptive to this, this, *rape*."

"You're not thinking, you can't be," he said. Now she saw him, not clearly but as a gathering of deeper, more ominous darkness. A large man standing very still and breathing hard.

"I will not pretend this is acceptable. It's *mad*. Unbelievable. Whatever you intend to do will not be easy if I have my way." She pulled pillows behind her back until she could almost sit up. "I will leave my mark on you."

The shape came toward her and she heard her own terrified sob before she could control it.

At the bottom of the divan and facing a wall, he sat,

and she imagined the only part of him that moved was his mind—planning how he would take her.

Hattie clamped her hands over her face and slammed it against her drawn-up knees. She sucked in pain at the force with which her forehead banged her knees.

"Hattie, Hattie, it *is* me, it's John." He stroked her hair. She couldn't move.

"Hattie?"

"You don't sound like John." She shook hard enough to make her teeth chatter.

"Yes, I do," he said. "I'm out of breath because I, too, fear for you and for how we will manage here."

There was no stopping the flow of her tears. It *was* him, she felt it now. "How did you come here? What of the other man, did…did my husband come to you direct? Were you his first choice?" She caught her breath. "Am I a prize for the pleasure you've brought him?"

He continued to run his fingers over her hair. "No. He didn't come to me and I am not his choice at all. We'll get to that soon enough. Why did you stay until things came to this pass?"

"I told you."

"You need money to pay off your parents' debts and money to live on once you leave Leggit. You don't tell me how much money you need, how much you already have, and how long you think it will take for you to be ready to leave."

"A long time."

"Then that is too long. I know you are proud and wish to do this yourself, but let me deal with the money, please."

She cried again, but very softly. John barely stopped himself from telling her to dry her eyes. "Dearest, if it

will make you feel better, you may pay me back when you can and there will be nothing official drawn up.''

"You'd like that," she said, her voice rising. "Another man prepared to use money to buy my body. And you know well that I would never be able to pay you back.''

Anger, like a red wash in his mind, tightened every muscle in his body. He had to take charge of what happened here and he had to do it now. "You know better than that.''

"Do I? What have you been trying to persuade me to do ever since we met?''

Swiftly he launched himself over her, took her head in his hands and brought his face close to hers. "Damn you," he said. "I admit I want you, but I would never have forced you.'' At this moment he wanted her more than ever.

Hattie felt him tremble. The trembling of anger scarcely controlled. "But you will force me now.'' She pressed her eyes. "My husband came to you with an offer. How could you be here otherwise? I cannot imagine how much he is giving you to do him this *favor*. Poor fool, he doesn't know you are smarting over my refusal to go to your bed. You would pay him for the pleasure of crushing him, wouldn't you? What I don't know is why. But there is a reason and I'd like you to tell me about it. And I want you to tell me how he approached you and what he told you would be your reward, because I had best tell you the truth about the nature of my husband.''

John continued to hold her down on the divan with the considerable weight of his body, and with his hands pushed into the hair on either side of her head.

"Think what you will about me," John said, tormented that she didn't trust him at least a little after the time they'd spent together. "And while you're about it, con-

sider how best to trick your husband into believing we have done as ordered.''

''He is a bad man. When you have had your way with me, I will be watched to see if I am increasing. If not, you will be allowed to live longer and repeat the acts of this evening, but I believe—and what I say is heartfelt because I cannot bear to think of you being hurt—but I think he will have you killed in the end. And when your brother and aunts look for you, there will be nothing to lead them here because you will not have shared all of this with them.''

He'd like to tell her the truth about his brothers' involvement, but it would be unwise.

Suddenly she grabbed at his wrists. ''Let me up. You must get away now, before there can be any risk to you. Oh, John, please save yourself. Don't let it be my fate to feel responsible for the loss of your dear life.''

An aching rush, as if of water and ice, flowed through John's limbs. Hattie did care for him, even though she thought him capable of taking her by force and accepting money from her husband for the deed. Frustration pounded him.

''There is a man here in the house,'' she said, ''a servant, and I honestly believed he was to be the one.''

She wasn't to know that Snowdrop had already told him the tale of Walter Stack.

''You came to a logical conclusion. I am not the man who is supposed to be here, but I found out who he was and struck my own deal with him. Disappointed as he was to be robbed of his chance with you, he was predictably greedy. He will slip in here the moment I dispatch you, and then I shall make it away. An easy enough task.''

''You asked how we could make Mr. Leggit think you

have done as he asked. I don't know about such things, John. Help me.''

What demons had he angered? ''Will you allow me to show you what seems the best way?''

She whispered, ''Yes,'' and turned her face from him.

If she cared nothing for him, she wouldn't concern herself with what Leggit might do if he found out the truth of what had happened tonight. ''Here,'' he said, unfolding a fur throw. ''Be warm. Believe I would never offend your sensibilities if there were any other way. Let me lie with you a little while. Remember that I am your friend and I care a great deal for you.''

He removed his jacket and waistcoat, his linens, and slid beneath the fur with her. He settled as he had that last time at Worth House, with one leg over hers and an arm beneath her shoulders. Holding her so made him strong. ''You let your hair down,'' he said.

John had stripped to the waist. His warm body struck heat through her dress. She touched his chest and her breath caught in her throat. Hard and hot. The sensations in her womanly places almost hurt.

''Smythe took it down. He also told me I was to encourage you.'' How ridiculous she sounded, repeating every detail of the shabby treatment she had received. John could not be expected to care.

''Hattie, Hattie,'' he said, his lips a breath away from her ear. ''I'm going to touch you.''

Hattie kept quiet and still.

''Please, I asked you to relax. I will be gentle.'' He would pay a ransom to put her on his horse and take her away from here forever. ''I'm going to kiss you because I can't wait any longer.''

Relax? She couldn't relax. He was big and muscular and she liked feeling just how powerful he was. Inside

she shivered. He could do whatever he pleased and she couldn't stop him—if she wanted him to stop.

He kissed her, but she did nothing to encourage him so he kissed her again, slowly, softly at first, then with lips that parted hers and his tongue probing her mouth. Her arms crept about his neck and she pushed her fingers into his hair. With his eyes squeezed shut, he molded his body to hers.

Hattie turned, inch by inch in his arms, her hands smoothing his bare back as if male skin was new to her. She slipped her hands between them to reach his chest with flattened palms and fingers set on running through the hair there.

Her light-colored dress had a low, square neck and short puffed sleeves. "I should like to see your breasts again," he said, squirming at the unfamiliarity of this approach. "I'd like to hold them in my hands and kiss them." He tucked his thumbs beneath her bodice and made small, hard circles over the tips of her nipples.

"It's all right to do that," she said, completely out of breath. "Oh yes, I like that."

John smiled in the darkness. The girl was a passionate one who had yet to come to terms with her own appetite for sex. He lowered his head and took a nipple in his teeth. Hattie whimpered, held his face against her. He didn't feel like smiling anymore. Opening his mouth wide, he suckled, drew hard on her flesh and felt himself harden to the point of pain. He played her with the tip of his tongue and she writhed.

Buttons on her bodice easily slid open. He bared her breasts completely and pushed them together, covered them with kisses. And he brushed his cheek back and forth over her, flattened each nipple, then watched when they sprang free and erect from beneath his face. Each

time he nibbled and sucked, and drove his thigh harder between her legs.

Hattie's arms fell away from him in a helpless spread. She arched her back to get closer to him. There was nothing she could do to intensify this, nothing necessary, and her heated mind gave up all control to John.

He left her once more to stand beside the divan, but within seconds drew her clothes off, leaving her naked, and lowered himself beside her again. His arm crossed her body, just beneath her breasts. She could see their fullness and her nipples grown large. John pressed his lips to her ear and ran his tongue inside.

He caused ecstatic sensations that shot downward and made her writhe.

"Listen carefully," he whispered. "I cannot do what Leggit wants me to do because it is wrong. And I must not do what I want to do because you will think it is only to fulfill my selfishness."

She turned her head, but he couldn't bear her looking at him, even in the dark, and nuzzled her ear once more to give him an excuse to nudge her face away. "You do know what must be done?" he said.

"No."

Damn it all. Never leave the initiation of a woman to a self-indulgent man who only cared for the ultimate goal.

"Hattie, you fascinated me the first time I saw you. Your face transfixed me and I admit that your body made certain my attention was shattered forever. That day my imagination fell well short of the truth. Holding you would drive any man mad. Knowing you and holding you fills me up."

Not once had anyone said such things to her. To hear them from the man she loved...she did love him even

though they had no chance to be together. "I don't think I can be your mistress," she told him.

"I should never have asked you, but who could blame me? Now, sweet, you must help me produce the evidence Leggit demands. You must touch me, excite me."

She said, "Yes," but her arms remained spread. John could imagine with horrible clarity how that man told her this was all he required of her while he heaved and sweated over her lovely body.

"Give me your hand," he told her, and when she tentatively did as he asked, he guided her fingers until he could close them around him. "Stroke me."

The size of him, the way his manhood stood up straight and hard from his body, the hair at its base, the round parts that made him moan afresh when she weighted them—all of it sent her blood to her feet. She didn't feel faint, but strangely cold and needy. She remembered to breathe, then forgot until she remembered again. And a heated flush replaced the cold. She closed her mind to thoughts of Mr. Leggit's fumblings, and how he'd felt in her hand.

Hattie sat up but pushed John with her free hand, indicating she wanted him to lie just as he was. With an arm wrapped around his thighs and her breasts prickling from contact with hair on his belly, she put out her tongue and touched it to the distended tip of him. He cried out and she shot away from him. Why had she done such a thing? John guided her back to where her face was only an inch or so from the spot she had touched so naturally.

Hattie couldn't laugh or cry but she knew the answer to her questions. Instinct had helped her do something that pleased John.

A droplet formed where her tongue had been and she licked it away. The salty taste surprised her.

"Hattie?" John's rough voice rang out and excited her more. He spread a hand on her back and urged her to continue what she was doing while he rubbed circles over her bottom and parted the cheeks.

A man who was really a man, John thought. That was all she needed to turn her into a passionate dream ready to respond with all the ripe mystery of her desire. Facing her away from him, he took Hattie by the waist to sit her on top of him. His slickness probed into the wet warmth between her legs.

Hattie felt beneath her and found the broad end she sought. Hot, pulsing, weeping the essence of his body. She settled her knees on either side of his hips, shifted backward until she sat on his middle. She bent over again and drew as much of him as she could into her mouth.

He cried out, then pushed up on his hands and kissed her back again and again. He liked what she did, Hattie thought. A thrilling sense of domination made her want to laugh.

When he pulled her away, she felt bereft and struggled against him. A futile effort. This time he pulled her down beside him, her face close to his. She felt right beneath his thigh and he tucked her into the curve of his long torso and legs. He kissed her mouth with restrained desperation.

"Now," he said in a whisper. "I think I can spill myself on you and give Leggit the proof he wants that we have lain together. Please, do not be disgusted by me. There is no other way."

Hattie had been told enough to understand what John meant. And she knew it had been Mr. Leggit's desire to grow hard like John—at least to grow hard—and put himself inside her where he could leave his seed to make her

with child. He liked to play with her body but lost interest when he couldn't accomplish his aim.

She had not given John the respect he deserved. He would not join with her as long as he was convinced she didn't want it.

John rubbed himself against the hair between her legs.

"John, I—"

"Just help me, Hattie. This is unbearable. The thought of it makes me sick."

"Come," she whispered, pushing her arms around him and urging him over her. "I think this will make everything easier." She held him and parted her legs.

John moaned, he couldn't help it. He had done many difficult things, but the cost of this might be higher than any of them. He pressed his fingers into the plump folds between her legs and found the hard little piece of flesh that dragged a cry from her. Her hips jerked rhythmically.

He pleasured her and covered her mouth at the same time. Hattie became a wild thing who reached and found what she wanted: his throbbing penis. He didn't want her to scream. Bending, his tongue took over his fingers' task, flipping back and forth, hard, but not for long. The dam burst and he surged up to take her scream into his mouth, sucking at the smooth insides of her cheeks and biting her tongue until, gradually, the spasms left her.

"My darling," he said, holding her as tight as he dared. "How could these dreadful circumstances have befallen you? You are so wonderful."

"You are so wonderful," Hattie told him while waves of intense feeling continued to make an uproar of her senses. And now there was only one thing to do. "Put yourself inside me, John."

His gut contracted as if she'd punched him there. "Don't make this harder. You are overcome by your re-

actions now. Later, if I did as you suggest, you would hate me.''

The man who had been desperate to cuckold Leggit held Leggit's wife in his arms while she begged him to make love to her. What could be more perfect?

If she had never married Leggit and had become John's instead.

Francis and Simonne had not been avenged. Nathan and Dominic would never stand for allowing Leggit to escape punishment.

''Please, John.''

He sat astride her hips and let his head bow.

''Don't you want to?'' She struggled beneath him. ''Let me up. I cannot bear the embarrassment I bring us both.''

''Stop it at once.'' John anchored her. ''You show your immaturity. It would be easy for me to accept what you offer. It would be wrong.''

Hattie breathed hard and he could see her chest rising and falling.

He kissed her white breasts, took one in each hand and shook them, loving how firm and heavy they were.

She had turned her face away again.

Blood, heat and deep, consuming need, ripped into John. He stretched himself on top of Hattie and placed himself at the opening to her body.

''Yes,'' she whispered, panting. ''Please, John, yes.''

He would not ask again if she was sure. With a single thrust, he entered her…and tried to stop. She was so small. How could this be? He couldn't hold back and Hattie gave no sign of distress.

John filled her up. And he broke through something inside her. She pulled air sharply past her teeth but swallowed a cry of protest. It was as if she was burned, or

wounded. She perspired and her eyes felt filmed. Why did he lie so still.

"What is it?" she asked. "Is that all?"

He tried not to continue, but each second he held back cost him too much. She had been a virgin. "I don't understand," he said, and his hips moved of their own volition. "Why didn't you tell me?" The pace set itself and his frenzied drive took over. As careful as he tried to be, he had to have release and he had to have Hattie. She wrapped her legs around his waist and offered herself, opened herself as wide as she could.

"You are a natural lover, Hattie."

Writhing on the divan, she incited him but didn't answer his questions.

"I've hurt you because I didn't know. I would never have been so rough if I had." Or would he? He might have had better luck restraining himself.

"Make love to me, John."

He did. And when he flowed into her, hot and insatiable, he wanted to scream himself. She drew on his life, sucked him dry, until they fell in a gasping heap, murmuring, kissing, touching, and finally gripped in each other's arms while they kept on fighting for breath.

"How much have I hurt you?" he said.

"Not much at all." Hattie lied. "I wouldn't change it. Can we do it again?" And she meant what she said.

The devil wanted his soul. "Not tonight, darling. You must use warm cloths and give yourself time to adjust." But he wanted her again now, how he wanted her. "You were still a virgin. Can you tell me why?" The tenderness he felt for her tightened his throat. He smoothed her hair and waited to see what she might say.

If she was increasing, Hattie thought, then her child

would be John's. She would have part of him forever. She was glad of the darkness that hid her burning eyes.

"Hattie, dear?"

"He cannot poke me."

"Hattie! What would make you use such words?"

She considered what words he could mean. "You mean I shouldn't say, 'poke.' Mr. Leggit calls it that and he cannot do it."

"Please don't call lovemaking by that term again. He cannot do it—why? Does he have some…illness?"

"If being unable to…if being unable to raise the pertinent part, to make it hard, is an illness, then yes. He spends hours soaking in the pools here and tells me his doctor thinks he is improving, but he isn't. It just—flops there and I don't see how making it hard would cause it to grow enough, not enough to be much of anything at all."

If he had the energy, and were a cruel man, he would laugh. John clutched Hattie against him. She had been with no man but him. He would have thought no less of her if she had, but to be the first only made him want to be the only one who ever made love to her.

"We must dress and make sure we get away from here quickly."

Hattie listened to his voice, the only voice she cared to hear, and wanted to make him stay with her. "Will I see you again?" she said.

He smiled in the darkness. "I don't have the willpower to stay away from you. We will continue as we did before. I will arrange more high-flown outings for Leggit and we will make sure our paths cross frequently. Let me help you dress."

John rolled away and stood up before Hattie could try to stop him again. He picked up her clothes, but she sur-

prised him by standing on the divan and bending over him. He felt her breasts on his face and closed his eyes.

"Hattie, Hattie," he said. "What have I created."

"A woman in…an awakened woman."

He helped her dress, suppressing laughter and the temptation to take her again each time she made another suggestive move.

Fully clothed at last, he lifted her from the divan and set her on her feet with the admonition, "Do not attempt to touch me again. We have been here much longer than you think. If they come looking for you, it could be bad. You don't look like a woman who has suffered a humiliating experience."

"Yes," she said, and turned her back. "That's because I haven't."

John pulled his shirt over his head and buttoned the front and the cuffs. His neckcloth he tied in a haphazard manner.

He reached for his trousers—only to yelp when Hattie swooped in to take hold of him again and to giggle madly.

"You will be the end of us," he said. She would certainly be the end of him. He struggled with her, in a manner he hoped she found convincing, and got his trousers on. His waistcoat and coat followed and, last of all, his boots.

Hattie felt light on her feet, and wicked. And she loved how she felt. John had said they would continue to see each other. He didn't want to cut her from his life any more than she could bear for him to do so.

"Now, my girl, settle down and think." His voice sounded steady, but the immediate kiss he gave her didn't help his case. He set her away from him. "The future depends on us. I will not give you up, but for us to be together as often as possible, our situation must remain

secret. Hattie, darling, when you go out of this place your demeanor will reflect how you have had a terrible experience. If nothing else, cry. Your hair will suggest you have—well, that you have, you know. And you will endure the sawbones without disguising your distress. Are you ready.''

''Yes,'' she said. If she begged him to take her with him he would have to refuse. As he'd already told her, their future depended on continuing to pretend with Mr. Leggit. But she had another thought. ''If I do conceive, I think I can trick them into thinking I haven't.''

To prolong their affair. ''You are brilliant,'' John said. ''Why stop a marvelous thing?''

''We won't stop it.'' Hattie leaned against his chest. The only polite thing to do was kiss and hold her. ''We shall do it more and more and more.''

He blinked. Just what had he created? The obvious answer tugged his mouth into a grin.

''John, did you want to make love to me because you have a reason to hate Mr. Leggit?''

He wanted to tell her the truth but if she knew, it could be a danger to her. ''I want you because you are irresistible. Now you must leave.''

John opened the door at the back of the room a crack, then led her around to the door she'd entered by. He kissed her cheek, turned the door handle and eased her outside without widening the gap more than necessary to allow her to slide out.

He closed that door and retraced his steps. Dominic stood against the wall.

''She will be all right,'' John said.

''Will you be all right, John?''

He frowned but said, ''Quite all right, thank you.''

Dominic gave a soft snort. ''I just bet you will.''

His brother, John thought, was jealous. ''You are doing me a great service in this house.'' He passed Dominic, left the room and darted into a passageway his brother had found. This led to a flight of stone steps and an exit at the top.

Using the key Dominic had also provided and which would be copied, John let himself out into the cool late-night air of a night bathed by the moon.

He prayed that Hattie would manage, that she would get through whatever examination was in store without crushing embarrassment.

And John prayed he would hold her in his arms again soon, naked and sweet, the lover of his dreams, an amazement. He started to harden again and stumbled at the same time.

He had said he would be all right and he would as long as he didn't lose Hattie.

His horse waited patiently in a lane beside the property and John swung himself into the saddle. Who could blame Dominic for being as jealous as hell?

29

"I am coddled today, Miss Prunella and Miss Enid," Hattie said, entering the salon at Worth House with Mrs. Dobbin and Bea. "Both of my helpers are with me."

Dobbin and Bea curtsied, coaxing smiles out of the aunts, whose faces had shown barely disguised irritation when Hattie arrived.

"Snowdrop expects us," Mrs. Dobbin said. To Hattie, she added, "You won't forget to send for us at once if you need us?"

"Of course not." She felt tetchy at the suffocating attention heaped upon her for several days, since the night she would remember as the most wonderful night of her life.

"Sit *down*, Hattie," Miss Prunella said.

Miss Enid called after Dobbin and Bea, "Kindly close the doors after you. *Thank* you." Her tone echoed the impatience Hattie had felt. "And please ask Boggs to bring tea and cakes."

The door shut quite firmly and Hattie sat in a red armchair at equal distance from either Miss Worth and facing them. That distance was hardly anything at all.

Miss Prunella raised her nose and examined Hattie through a pince-nez. "So, my dear, what is wrong with you?"

She blushed and was furious with herself. "Nothing at

all. I had a little cold and Mr. Leggit is overprotective.''
Why the words didn't stick in her throat—and choke
her—she had no idea. Just the thought of Mr. Leggit appearing in her bedchamber at least three times a day cast
her down. He appeared with expensive trinkets, and had
given her a small ransom in gold coin. She had put the
money in her reticule before leaving Leggit Hall that afternoon and the strings had made grooves in her wrist.

''When is the last time *I* took to my bed for the snif-
fles?'' Miss Enid asked Miss Prunella.

Miss Prunella forgot to turn her head to hide the huge
wink she aimed at Miss Enid. ''We're just glad you've
come today, aren't we, Enid.''

''Very glad. Do you have enough handkerchiefs or
would you like me to have Boggs ask Mrs. Gimblet to
bring you some of ours?'' Miss Enid planted her stick
solidly in front of her, leaned on the handle with both
hands and gave Hattie more close scrutiny.

''Why, you know I wouldn't come to you with a cold,''
Hattie said, deliberately turning the corners of her mouth
down when they wanted to go the other way. ''I have a
handkerchief which I shall not need, but thank you for
your kind offer.'' She wanted to laugh at the sisters' little
games. Perhaps a headache would have been a better excuse than a cold. Anything but the truth, that Mr. Leggit
had it in his head that if she were increasing, keeping off
her feet was a good idea. Such nonsense.

''I suppose you did get the invitation we sent with Mrs.
Dobbin?'' Miss Enid's dark eyes were sharp between their
wrinkly brown lids.

''Yes, I did. And you got my response, remember? I
told you I would come as soon as I could, then I made
sure you knew the actual day.'' Better to be polite than

show the temper that began to bubble. "And by now Snowdrop will have delivered the, er, second delivery."

"Don't mind Enid," Miss Prunella said. "She's been anxious to meet with you again, you see."

Miss Enid pointed at her sister. "And you, of course, have not been anxious. We are grateful to you for going to Porky on our behalf, Hattie."

Hattie didn't have a chance to speak again before Boggs, failing miserably to look disinterested, entered the salon. He stood before the sisters but averted his face to stare through the windows.

"Oh, *really*," Miss Prunella said. Her rouged cheeks became even redder.

Miss Enid nodded and said, "*Oh, really,* indeed. Such behavior."

"Tea and cakes will have to wait," Boggs said, tapping a foot. "How am I supposed to provide these little extras you demand when Cook is having her afternoon rest and Mrs. Leggit's servants have taken Dolly off to the nurseries with *two* pots of scandalbroth?"

"I'm glad they enjoy themselves so much," Hattie said.

"All very well for you to be glad, madam," Boggs said. "Some might pause at the thought of their visit becoming an opportunity for four, *four* servants to loll around."

Boggs had left the door open and Chloe peeked inside. "Chloe!" Hattie said, then remembered herself and looked to the Misses Worth. "Is it all right if I insist Chloe joins us?"

Both ladies looked anything but pleased. They cleared their throats and at last said, "Of course. Come along in, Chloe, darling." Miss Prunella made exaggerated welcoming motions.

Hattie managed not to announce that Chloe wasn't deaf.

"Run along, Boggsy," Miss Enid said, her mouth pinched so it appeared to have been whipped together with long white stitches.

"I should think so," Miss Prunella said. "Impertinent—and ungrateful, I should add." Miss Prunella's white skin seemed even more a contrast to her sister's today.

Hattie hurried to take Chloe by the hand and came perilously close to colliding with *Boggsy* as he left. The less said about the butler, the better, but she would so love to know how he came to be so at odds with the ladies.

"Chloe, you have the people from the dollhouse. How lovely." Hattie looked more closely at the wooden figures Chloe held clamped to her body with an elbow. "Four of them now," she said.

Chloe's small hand held on tightly and the child took command, led Hattie back to her red chair and leaned against it once Hattie sat down again.

"I should have brought a little something for our play," Hattie said. "I do believe I need my very own person."

At once, Chloe took one of the figures, the boy cousin, and thrust it on Hattie.

Not deaf at all. "Thank you," she said, turning the boy doll and walking him along her leg, then jumping him to the arm of the chair. She slipped into the voice she'd found for the boy. "There you are, Cousin Chloe. May we go to the park today?" Then she switched her tone and spoke for Chloe, "I'll have to ask Mama."

Hattie had forgotten about the fourth figure, but now Chloe held it up. This was a man in pantaloons and stockings who wore a bright yellow jacket with lace at the neck and sleeves. He also had a luxurious wig painted on. "Chloe's papa is here today. I'm sorry I didn't notice you

there, sir.'' Cousin spoke politely. ''Pah,'' the new fellow said. ''Disrespect from striplings.''

She looked into Chloe's eyes. The tears Hattie saw there silenced her.

''Well, what have we here?''

John's voice, and the sound of his boots as he walked into the salon, froze Hattie. She brought her lips together and looked at the rug beneath her feet.

''We have,'' Miss Enid said, ''a gathering of ladies for a pleasant afternoon visit.''

''I'm delighted,'' John said, and Hattie felt him only inches away from her shoulder. ''Could a man join in the festivities, d'you suppose?''

Hattie could not bring herself to look at him. Every bit of her face and neck flushed.

''No welcome?'' John said, chuckling at the same time. ''Chloe dear, what is it?''

Tears swam in Chloe's eyes.

''There, there.'' John strode behind Hattie and dropped to one knee beside his cousin. ''Are you having a bad day? Do you need a hug from your crusty old cousin?''

Crusty? Hattie smiled at the thought.

Chloe pushed herself against him and hid her face in his coat. John picked her up, pulled another chair into the group and sat down with the little girl in his embrace.

''Too many roses in that vase, even if they do smell good.'' He tugged four roses from a nearby vase and checked the stems for thorns. Leaning, he handed one to each of his aunts and gave one to Chloe.

The fourth rose, red, fragrant and barely opened, John placed across Hattie's folded hands. ''Beautiful roses are improved by beautiful ladies,'' he said.

Hattie didn't look at him, didn't move. She glanced at

his aunts and discovered them sending venomous glances in his direction.

"You look tired, aunts," John said. "You do too much. Let me call for Mrs. Gimblet and send you for a nap."

"Nothing of the kind," Miss Enid snapped at him. "We aren't tired a bit, of course, although Hattie may need a rest soon since she's been ill and in bed for several days."

If only she could disappear, Hattie thought. "Just a headache," she said, and raised the rose to her face.

"You mean a cold, don't you?" Miss Prunella said, her brows raised almost to her white hairline.

"Yes," Hattie said, and didn't doubt all present must think her a goosecap.

John stood up and narrowed his eyes on her. She was grateful Chloe continued to rest her face on his shoulder.

Dreadful, John's expression was dreadful, and questioning, and confused. Hattie feared he might demand answers from her at any moment.

Hattie scooted lower in her seat.

"Ladies," Miss Enid said. "We need that tea and if our servants can drink it in the nurseries, we can most certainly have some here. John! Ring for Boggs. He can make the tea himself and put cakes on a plate. He's watched it all done often enough."

Ignoring his relatives, John walked to block their view of Hattie, and to look down at her.

His black waistcoat fit without a wrinkle over an absolutely flat middle. Hattie looked there and saw it naked. She saw all of him naked and let out a little puff of air.

"I should like you to come with me," he said quietly.

The manner in which his body complemented his clothes must annoy so many gentlemen.

His voice rose when he said, "Did you hear what I said?"

"I didn't," Miss Prunella and Miss Enid said in unison. Miss Prunella continued, "But that may be just as well. You are a great glowering *lout,* nephew. How dare you address our guest like that."

"Mrs. Leggit," John said, "we have matters of mutual concern to discuss. I am a busy man, but I could spare you a few minutes now."

Hattie did look him in the face then. "How kind you are." She should be kind to him. Something had reduced his composure to shreds. Hattie tried a smile, but the straight-faced way he returned that smile didn't surprise her.

"John," Miss Prunella said, all sharpness and cross tone. "What are you doing? And what can you be thinking of? Hattie doesn't care how busy you are. And you are *not* busy since you took leave from serving the King to give your attention to your family. Whatever that means."

"Exactly what it says," John said, turning to look at his aunts. "Particularly Chloe needs my care. And, believe it or not, I'm glad to spend some time in this house. Even though it is a *disgrace,* run by the servants and completely out of hand. Why you don't tell Boggs off, I can't imagine. Why you beg me *not* to tell him off, I can't imagine."

Hattie could. Boggs knew too much about his mistresses and wouldn't hesitate to threaten them with exposure, she was certain.

The distraction didn't last long enough. John strode behind his relatives and stood there, patting Chloe's back and running his fingers through her curls—and sending

the most piercing looks at Hattie. He looked over every inch of her, again and again.

"You are good to be so concerned for your family, my lord," Hattie said in a shamefully small voice. "Most men are too impatient and think they are too important to look after those who need it."

"Too busy to meddle in the affairs of family members who are capable of tending their own affairs, you mean?" Miss Enid said.

Carrying Chloe as if she weighed nothing, John circled the group of chairs, casting looks at Hattie that changed from angry, to worried, to desperate, and back to worried again.

"John." Miss Prunella's voice rang out. "Please go away. Hattie is here to visit us. You are impolite."

He mumbled to himself, took a few steps, stopped to look at Hattie, beseechingly this time, and repeated the behavior until he finally turned on his heel and left the salon in a manner that reminded Hattie of a furious wind through supple trees.

"Thank goodness." Miss Prunella fell against the back of her chair. "That boy has been given too much responsibility by too many top-lofty fellows—and too early in life. He thinks he should control everyone. Now, Hattie, if you don't mind, we would like to discuss a few things with you."

Concentration wasn't easy. "I don't mind," Hattie said.

"Again, we must thank you for running our little errand."

A little errand that might well have left Hattie—and Snowdrop—seriously wounded. "I'm glad I could be of service."

"Tell us everything." Miss Prunella and Miss Enid leaned forward. "Don't miss a detail."

After taking a deep breath, Hattie said, "I expected Porky to be... I didn't expect him to be such a slender man."

"Oh, yes." A faraway expression slipped over Miss Prunella's features and she smiled a little. "Quite slender." Her eyes became sharp again and she frowned. "So Boggs has told us."

"A nice person. He insisted on serving me tea and I sat in a room behind the shop. Root tea, it was and I should like to buy more. Most invigorating."

"So you will need to return to the shop anyway," Miss Enid said quickly. "May we ask you to purchase some of this marvelous tea for us?"

Hattie smelled manipulation. "If I go I'll buy you some. I hadn't expected an apothecary shop."

"Did we forget to tell you that?" Miss Prunella slapped her hands on her knees and broke into her dry little laugh. "Enid, we must be getting old. Forgetting to tell Hattie she was going to an apothecary shop. Oh, my, yes. Did you enjoy it there?"

"It was interesting."

"And Porky is spry? And his eyes bright?" Miss Enid asked despite Miss Prunella's loud cough.

"Why, yes," Hattie said, thoroughly curious now. "And he asked how you were."

Both ladies twittered and giggled.

"And is Porky's brother well?" Miss Prunella asked, her giggle a memory already.

"That would be the other gentleman there? The one who called from another room? I didn't see him."

"Ah." Miss Prunella laced her fingers together in her lap. "So you didn't see his unusual eyes."

Miss Enid reached to place a hand on her sister's arm and they looked at each other.

"You sound as if you've seen them," Hattie said.

Miss Prunella looked at Miss Enid again. "Not at all. It was just that Boggs said something about one green eye and one dark gray. I thought that sounded absorbing."

"Well, we don't go out nearly enough," Miss Enid said. "I think we'll visit that shop ourselves, if you will come with us, Hattie. Our life is quite boring."

"I will be delighted to go," Hattie said, and caught sight of John on the path outside the windows. He stood where his aunts would only see him if they turned all the way around, and beckoned to Hattie with exaggerated motions. She returned her attention to the ladies.

"The ruby was very beautiful," she said.

John jumped up and down.

Hattie rested two fingers against her temple.

"There are plenty more lovely stones where that came from," Miss Enid said. "In fact, this is for you, to show our gratitude." She held the top of her stick in one hand and leaned forward, proffering a closed fist.

"I couldn't take anything," Hattie said.

Miss Prunella spoke up. "You can and you will—or you will make two old ladies sad."

Hattie put out her hand at once and Miss Enid placed a small, brown leather pouch in Hattie's palm. "Open it quickly," Miss Enid said. "Isn't this exciting, Prunella?"

"Very exciting." But the sisters exchanged glances more troubled than excited.

Inside the pouch rested an emerald the size of Hattie's thumbnail. She gasped and said, "This is fabulous, and it's much too much to give as a gift."

"Not at all. And here's a guinea. We said we would share what you got for the ruby."

"No—"

Miss Enid wagged a finger and said, "Not another word

on the subject. We are so grateful for your kindness to us.''

John's arms were crossed and his brows pulled low over his eyes.

Forcing herself to look away again, Hattie smiled at the aunts.

''Prunella,'' Miss Enid said, ''do you think we should tell Hattie our entire story?''

After mulling for some seconds, Miss Prunella said, ''If you think so, then yes, but I cannot do it.''

''You don't have to,'' Miss Enid said. ''When we were young we met two wonderful men. Charles and Philip. It's not very complicated, really. We fell in love but they were poor and our father wouldn't hear about it. We continued to see our beloveds, behind father's back, of course. Then they did something amazing.''

''At the Baths,'' Miss Prunella said.

''Quite.'' Miss Enid nodded, but even her brown face grew paler. ''They discovered that very often those who were placed in the waters lost rings and other jewelry. They just slipped off. Sometimes the whole piece of jewelry, sometimes the stones by themselves because they broke loose of their settings.''

Hattie didn't interrupt, but she did find herself moving toward the front of her seat.

''One of our friends got a job working on the drains. He knew about those things and the way they worked. Very educated he was. They both were. And I'm sure you can imagine what happened.''

She couldn't. ''No, I haven't any idea. Oh—'' she held up a hand ''—the jewelry and stones used to get caught in the drains, and—''

''Yes, yes, exactly,'' Miss Enid said. ''Our friends got together to gather what had been lost to others forever.

The original owners gave up on their trinkets, you see, because they had no idea how to look for them."

"And that's how they came to us," Miss Prunella said. "Hoards of them. Our dear ones brought them to us for safekeeping while they went to America on a business venture they thought would allow them to return and impress our papa with their ingenuity—and their considerable wealth."

Hattie sighed. "And when they returned, what happened then?"

"They never returned. After many years we followed their instructions and used the jewels as they had intended. In the event that they never came back, we were to sell their treasure to bring us a source of income. Income to spend on the extra things, our extra needs that we never want to grovel to our family for."

Prunella wiped away a tear. "Boggs, blast him, was taken into our confidence, too."

"*Sister,*" Miss Enid exclaimed.

"Yes, and I shall blast the man again. He served us well for some years, but recently he decided he should take a portion of the money and that was *not* on."

The sad tale of lost love cast Hattie down. But she did think Boggs deserved small gratuities for the service he'd performed. Also, the stones belonged to other people and the young men should have reported what they found.

Wilder motions from John could not be ignored. Silly thing. If he knew what he looked like leaping around like that, and…oh, dear, he gestured toward the back entrance to his rooms.

"Could we go with you to the apothecary shop tomorrow?" Miss Enid asked.

She would not look at John. Did he really think she could get up and run outside to join him?

"I have to think about it," Hattie told the ladies. "There is someone I must speak to first, someone we'd need to help us. And our journey would have to be after dark because I can't do these things just when I please."

John marched away, but Hattie felt more bereft than relieved.

"Whatever you say is what we'll do," Miss Enid said. "Just give us our instructions."

"I shall get a message to you later today."

A tall man wearing an old coat and a floppy hat arrived outside with a pair of shears. Promptly he set to work trimming the bushes.

Try as she might, Hattie could not stop herself from grinning.

"It is exciting, isn't it?" Miss Prunella said. "We could be wrong, but—well, we shall all see."

The *gardener* used his shears to indicate that Hattie should go from the salon and up the stairs and…yes, all the way to the top of the house and turn left. Hmm, could that mean she should go to John's rooms? Of course not. She was imagining things.

Hattie smiled at the sisters, then looked directly into John's face. More stabbing directions followed. His garb didn't make him less imposing or, in this case, more difficult to recognize.

Without warning, Miss Enid swiveled in her chair and saw her nephew prancing about, dressed like a tramp and brandishing shears.

"Sister," she whispered, "John may not be well. Perhaps he has worked too hard for too long."

Miss Prunella caught sight of John and didn't seem disposed to feel pity for him. She rose from her chair and stalked, a little stiffly, to the windows. Waving him away,

calling him not very nice names, she closed every window tight.

She turned back toward Miss Enid and Hattie. "Just like Papa," she said. "A joyless snoop intent on knowing everyone's secrets and not a bit slow to use them against you."

Miss Prunella continued, "That boy is just like his grandfather. Spying on us to find out our secrets and use them against us."

"He won't do any such thing," Miss Enid said. "I, um, mistakenly opened one of his letters today. Forwarded from his London office. From a French ladyfriend apparently."

"You shouldn't have done that," Miss Prunella said, clearly flustered and disapproving.

"Ha, I know how to unseal and reseal a letter without anyone being the wiser. He'll never know unless we need to mention the contents. *Ooh-la-la* and all that. That letter isn't suitable reading for ladies, I assure you. The woman was thoughtful enough to remind him, in detail, of their times together, *and,* to warn him that her husband is trying to hunt him down!"

30

Hattie's cheeks stung. The contents of the French-woman's letter consumed her. She wanted to read what had been written there but could never as much as mention that she knew of its existence. If she did, the Misses Worth would be in trouble, or at least Miss Enid, who had done a wrong thing. And John would never discuss such things with Hattie.

She had left the salon to go in search of Mrs. Dobbin and Bea. Slowly climbing the stairs, she wondered if John might have returned to his rooms, or left the house altogether because she had refused to go to him.

Miss Enid had said the letter described what had happened between the Frenchwoman and John. Ooh, Hattie couldn't bear it. She wanted to know, but she didn't want to know. Wait till she saw John, she'd find a way to punish him, and—

"Hello, Mrs. Leggit." Snowdrop came down the stairs toward Hattie. "Have the old ladies worn you out?"

When they drew level, Hattie put her silly jealousy aside and pulled Snowdrop to the banister. "Could you drive Miss Prunella and Miss Enid—and me—to the apothecary shop tonight?" She spoke softly.

Snowdrop's eyes sparkled and she sprang up and down on her toes. "I'll say I can. Someone has to be with Chloe, though."

"Mrs. Dobbin could remain here after I leave and we'll hope her failure to return with me won't be noticed. Once it's dark, get the aunts to your carriage and drive to Leggit Hall. From there, all will be as before."

The grin on Snowdrop's face cheered Hattie up.

A sound from above caught their attention and they both looked up. Bea hovered there, hands pressed into her skirts and her anxious eyes fixed on Hattie.

"I'll be off," Snowdrop said. She waved to Bea and to Hattie then dashed to the foyer and out of sight on her way below stairs.

Hattie climbed to meet Bea on the nursery floor and followed her around a corner where they were out of sight. At the end of the corridor blue drapes framed a tall window with a deep window seat. Hattie pointed at it and the two of them hurried to sit down, only Bea stopped them just in time. A layer of dust turned the blue cushions to light gray on top.

"Dear, dear," Bea said, "let's see how they are on the other side." Turning them over raised fusty smelling clouds into the air but the cushions were cleaner underneath.

They sat and faced directly forward where they would see and hear the moment someone approached.

Bea trembled. Hattie looked at the girl's clenched hands, then at her face. Pale and perspiring, she blinked tears away.

"Bea, dear, tell me why you're upset?"

"I...can't." She bowed her head and her fingers were so tightly laced they appeared bloodless.

Hattie put an arm around her shoulders. "There's something you want to say to me. Please trust me and speak up."

"I'm sorry, Mrs. Leggit. Please don't have me lose my

place—if you can see your way to forgiving me a little.''
She pulled a pocket from the inside of her waistband and
produced a sovereign. ''I took it, you see. I don't know
what came over me, but I thought to myself that you had
so many and you wouldn't notice one was missing. Then,
when I knew I couldn't keep it, I tried to put it back but
the box wasn't there anymore.'' The shaky breaths she
took sounded painful.

If Hattie had to guess, the first thought she'd have
would be that, like herself, Bea had a problem which
money could solve and she was trying to gather enough.
How very long it would take her to put aside even a little
from her meager wages.

''Put that back in your pocket,'' Hattie said. ''There is
nothing to feel badly about.'' Not when, although Hattie
had more or less extorted money rather than steal it, she
was nevertheless no better than Bea.

''Stealing's wrong,'' Bea said, pushing the sovereign
on Hattie. ''I have learned me lesson, honest I have.''

''Look at me,'' Hattie said. She settled her hands on
Bea's shoulders and looked closely into her eyes. ''There
was something you wanted this for, wasn't there?''

''I can't believe I've done this,'' Bea said. ''Me mum
and dad were strict about doing the right things, but never
cruel in the way they taught my sister and me.''

''Will you tell me why you took the coin? If it was
other than because you just wanted money for money's
sake?''

''Oh, Mrs. Leggit, never. I wouldn't want money for
itself. I've got a good position—even if it—'' She stopped
abruptly.

''Please finish, Bea.''

The girl's face shone damp, and she shook.

''Bea?''

"Well, I've already done it to meself so what do I have to lose? You're treated shamefully. That's all. A sweet person like you treated badly by your husband, and by that slippery Mr. Smythe. And there's plenty else going on in that house. Particularly in those so-called *Pool Rooms*. Dens of iniquity, they are."

Bea's florid term might have made Hattie smile if she weren't shocked that her own maid knew so much. She couldn't bring herself to probe for further explanations in that direction.

"You don't want the money just because you want it," she said. "So what was it for?"

Bea huddled into a corner of the window and rubbed her arms hard. "We were always poor. I'm not complaining, just saying the way it was and is. We had fun together. The worst part of being in service is having to be away from me family. You're not interested in all that. Mum and Dad come to visit about four weeks ago and Dad's shoes had holes in the bottom. That's nothing new, we've all been used to holes in our shoes when we couldn't afford to get them repaired. We lined them with thick bits of paper to keep our feet dry."

One day, sooner rather than later, Hattie hoped she could tell Bea how it was to grow up with scarcely enough in London.

"I wanted to buy me dad a new pair of shoes because he's never had new ones before." Bea's face turned scarlet. "I don't want pity. That's just the way life is for some and there are too many other things to think of to waste time feeling hard done by. I'm very sorry, Mrs. Leggit. I was wrong and I was stupid."

And I feel so guilty. Hattie was bound to save her parents from being Mr. Leggit's prisoners, but she felt dis-

honest, especially after hearing Bea so penitent for her small crime.

"Give me your hand," she said to Bea. "Don't hold back or I shall be cross with you." When Bea didn't offer her hand, Hattie took it, placed the coin in her palm and folded her fingers over it. "I am giving you this to buy your father a pair of new shoes. Now, not another word. Although I would like to know what he says when you give them to him."

Bea looked at the sovereign then dropped it back into her pocket. She cried quietly and brushed at her face with the back of a hand.

"Please don't—"

"You'll just have to let me cry," Bea said with unexpected determination. "You can't expect to show me so much kindness and for me not to cry. I've never heard you say an unkind thing. You've a heart of gold, you have. And you're abused."

Hattie turned cold but she couldn't bring herself to speak.

Tentatively Bea reached for Hattie's hand and held it tightly between both of hers. "The ones from the pools, they all gossip. They sit around being shameful and saying things they shouldn't. I'm scared for you."

Bea's eyes brimmed with tears and she sniffed. "There's people who don't care what happens to you, all sorts of people who only think about themselves and they laugh about you. They say you're like a babe. The way you hang on Mr. Leggit's arm and gaze at him as if you loved him when they know you couldn't. Some of them talk about you getting money just to pretend you adore Mr. Leggit, in public, that is. I don't think Mr. Leggit's good enough for you, but he only gives what he wants to give and other people shouldn't say anything about it."

Everything inside Hattie clenched and her heart thumped madly. "Some people love to gossip."

"Do you really mean you want me to have the money?"

"I do," Hattie assured her. "Please don't speak of that again."

"Someone's tellin' tales on you," Bea said.

Prickling climbed Hattie's spine.

"They tell them to the ones who like to say bad things about you to Mr. Leggit."

Hattie held her breath and barely managed to say, "What bad things?"

"They reckon you're…oh, I can't say it." Bea swallowed, pressed her lips together and then blurted out, "They say you've got a lover and you're making a fool of Mr. Leggit. They say that's the real reason he gives you so much, so you won't let the truth slip and humiliate him in front of all his friends. Especially now he's moving in such toffy circles."

"Bea." Hattie pulled her close and hugged her. "First I need you, and I love you. I always know I have a friend in you—and in Mrs. Dobbin. And you never have to worry about your position, because it is with me if you want it."

Rather than regain her composure, Bea broke down and sobbed on Hattie's shoulder. When she could catch her breath, she said, "You've got to look after yourself. If you think it's time for you to leave Leggit Hall, I'll come with you and help you. We'll manage all right."

Hattie fought against her own tears and they would be shed out of fear. "I'm looking after myself."

"I've got to tell it straight. It has to be Mr. Smythe what's talking about things he shouldn't, because I can't think who else it would be but him. And there is whis-

pering about it all. How there's a servant Mr. Leggit's being kind enough to give quarters to while he looks for another place. They say this man has got you on your own…to have his way with you.''

''That's not true.'' Hattie couldn't help being sharp.

''If Mr. Smythe insists it is, then Mr. Leggit will believe him.''

Since Mr. Leggit had arranged for Walter Stack to come to her, this made little sense.

''Apparently the man, Walter Stack his name is, disappears for hours and they've decided that's when the two of you are together. Oh, Mrs. Leggit, they say Mr. Leggit won't want to lose you, he'll just have you disappear.''

''Disappear? As in have me killed.''

''I won't talk about that. But some man come to visit Mr. Smythe. He wasn't very clean but his clothes was fancy. Big shiny boots that made a lot of noise on the stones below stairs. Lace hanging from his throat and cuffs and a black velvet coat embroidered with gold. He had curls to his shoulders, a big mustache and beard and one of them tricorn hats. And he had a pistol tucked into his trousers and a cutlass at his side. Loud, he was, and I didn't like the way he looked at a body.'' She shuddered.

''Took him off to see Mr. Leggit, Mr. Smythe did. I reckon the man was a pirate.''

''He could just have been a seafaring man,'' Hattie pointed out. ''Perhaps even a ship's captain.''

Bea didn't look convinced. ''There's rumors Mr. Leggit took him down the pools and shut them stone doors at the top of the stairs behind them. But you could still hear shouting, some said, bellowing and banging, and when the doors were open again and someone dared go down there, things was smashed and broken all over.''

"It's probably not good to listen to gossip," Hattie said, kindly enough.

"Mr. Leggit swore when he got back. He said something about he'd take a lot of convincing before he backed any windfall again. That was when he come back inside Leggit Hall. I saw that meself."

"You didn't mention he'd left," Hattie said. "Was the other man still with him?"

"They went down to the pools and not a soul saw them come up again. Later on Mr. Leggit come back from outside like he'd been walking. The other man didn't come back, but Mr. Leggit said there was to be a room made up for his friend."

Hattie turned over everything Bea had said. "Mr. Leggit does have a great many dealings with ships, so I suppose it makes sense he'd know a sea captain or two," she said.

"This one spat on Cook's floor and she gave him an earful, I can tell you. She called him a foul-mouthed pirate." Bea slapped her free hand over her mouth. "Pirates get rid of people, don't they? Take them out to sea and make sure they never come back."

31

After Bea had slipped away in the direction of the nurseries, Hattie waited a few moments before following her.

What if Smythe persuaded Mr. Leggit to do away with Walter Stack? No, she must save him.

John would know what to do. Better yet, with two of them it would be easier to find a solution. And it must be a rapid solution since Mr. Stack could be set upon at any time.

Hattie backed away from the nurseries, then retraced her steps to the stairs and ran upward.

Going to John wasn't so easy. She approached his door but changed her mind and stood with her back to the wall opposite. She loved him, really, really loved him.

Common sense assured her that if she were free the marquis would probably never have given her a second glance. For some men, or so she'd been told, the appeal and excitement lay in the danger of pursuing a married woman. The letter Miss Enid had been naughty enough to intercept suggested John made a habit of seducing unavailable women.

His door opened so abruptly she jumped.

"I thought it was you," he said. "About time."

"How did you know...of course, your sneaky bell warned you. I'm not here because of your embarrassing

behavior downstairs. And in the garden, for goodness' sake. It isn't for you to tell me—''

"Did you hear the bell, Hattie? No, you didn't because it isn't on." John took a single stride from his doorway, seized her by the waist and deposited her inside his room. "I *felt* you." He shut the door.

"What do you mean, you *felt* me?"

"Just what I said. I was aware of your presence, just as you were apparently aware of mine the evening you came to this house to hide your money."

"Yes…well." Men were not intuitive the way women were, but she would not play games with him. "It isn't for you to tell me what to do," Hattie said rapidly. "And civilized men are patient enough to allow a woman to use her own two feet rather than toss her around like you just did."

He scrubbed his face and she noted he did not appear to have shaved recently. "I was gentle with you," he said. "You started telling me what I do and don't have a right to tell you, or say to you. I have *every* right to say and do things for your own good. I am responsible for you now. It's my job to look after you."

"You—" Hattie stopped, her lips pushed out on the "ooh." She sniffed and watched him narrowly. "You amaze me. What can you mean? Of course you're not responsible for me." As nice as it might be if it were true.

John spread his arms wide. "You see, that's exactly what I mean. You cannot be left to make your own decisions because you don't understand the reality of a situation like ours." He paused with the back of one fist to his brow. "And I had to get you in here quickly because it wouldn't do to discuss our private business in a hallway."

"We don't have private business anymore. That is behind us."

"Behind us?" He laughed and walked toward her until she backed away. He walked her all the way to his grandfather's huge leather chair, made certain she sat in it and pulled up an ottoman for her feet. After consideration he raised her feet again, sat on the ottoman and lowered her ankles to rest on his thighs.

John's thighs felt quite nice beneath her ankles. They felt wonderful.

Hattie, John thought, had slim ankles and feet. He'd never been one to consider such parts of the female body as erotic, but his mind had changed that very moment. She wore the finest of silk stockings embroidered with a tiny red rose just where the instep of each foot began to disappear beneath the slipper.

"Thank you for deciding to come," he told her, fascinated by those roses. "I knew you would, but there is always that moment when one doubts."

She settled herself into the chair and closed her eyes. How perfect, John thought, just the two of them and he had made her his. He tried to concentrate on the embroidery again but failed. His plan had been to sleep with another man's wife, not to take her virginity. Leggit incapable? How could anyone be expected to consider such a thing?

"Since you're the masterful one, please lead the way into a useful conversation," Hattie said.

"You, Hattie, can be a madam. But I love the way you are." He had better consider the ramifications of anything he said while in his current state. "What happened between us will never be *behind* us, as you put it. I must make sure you are well cared for."

The way Hattie tightened her mouth didn't bode well.

Sometimes a man must stand fast against a lack of understanding or cooperation in the female. Eventually they often saw how unreasonable they were and in the case of an intelligent female like Hattie, he had no doubt she'd come to her senses.

"My dear." He patted her ankles. "I've been beside myself. The last thing I expected was…well, you know."

"That I would be a virgin."

"Quite."

"Well, I'm not anymore."

She might as well have hit him. "Hattie! Dear girl, don't make me feel worse than I already do."

"Why do you feel bad? You aren't the one with the sore…" Hattie turned her face from him. "You're embarrassing me. I'm not…sore, anymore. I'm just perfectly wonderful, thank you. And a woman who has managed to look after herself in a place like Leggit Hall doesn't need *anyone* to feel responsible for her."

"That would be because you've done such a sterling job of looking after yourself?" How could she even suggest she wasn't in dire straits? "How did you come to be pushed into a room with a man who was supposed to be a stranger and who had been paid to, to—"

"Rape me?" The worst happened. She pounded her fists on the arm of the chair and started to cry. "You have a horrid way of making terrible things sound absolutely, well…"

"Terrible," he finished for her. "Hattie, thank fortune you told me what Leggit intended to do and that Dominic was close enough at hand to step in and be my eyes inside that place."

"Dominic?"

How interesting to watch John behave like a cornered

animal. He appeared completely undone and looked into her eyes as if he could pluck back the name he'd used.

"Slip of the tongue," he told her at last. "Can't think why I said that."

"What you can't think," Hattie said, "is how to avoid explaining your reason for *Dominic*. And there is a reason you said the name."

"How are you feeling?" John said, his color high. "I have wanted to be with you. I've wanted to care for you and show you what you mean to me."

And he made her very cross. "How dare you say such things to me just because you don't want me to persist in asking who Dominic is." She didn't want to blubber, but too many emotions came too fast. "I'd advise you to respect my intelligence a little more."

"Hattie—"

"Don't. Stop it. Don't you think I want to hear you say those things to me—and do you believe I don't understand there could never be an opportunity for you to *take care of me?* I won't pretend I'm not hurt. It's because I can never have what I want. When you talk about things that would mean my life was changed and wonderful, talk about them lightly—not as if you mean them, I'm devastated."

This was even more than John had bargained for. His own feelings didn't simplify his predicament. He wanted to tell her he would take her away from Leggit and away from Leggit Hall. He couldn't do it.

"I will take care of you," he told her quietly. "No matter how poorly you think of me, I will never allow you to drive me away. Somehow I will make sure you are safe…always."

With the fingertips of one hand over her lips, she reached for him and gripped his wrist. "You are strange,

John. But you say things that make me so happy I can hardly take a breath. Please tell me who Dominic is?''

"My brother." Why try to avoid the truth. She wouldn't let him get away with it. "My brother Dominic is the man posing as a servant—as Walter Stack."

"Oh, my goodness, John. Oh, no! Heavens, how silly and selfish a little vexation can make a person. The servant. Walter Stack. Your brother?'' She shook her head. "He is a kind man who has been polite to me, but I've learned there are rumors about him. They're saying he takes me where the two of us can be alone."

John gave her a blank look and she didn't blame him. "I know it was Mr. Leggit himself who arranged for me to be with Stack—or Dominic—but it could never have been part of the plan for the household to find out *anything* about it, or for the story to be built up as it has been. If there's one thing Mr. Leggit can't bear, it's any suggestion of a stain on his reputation. He would kill to get rid of the problem. I'm worried about Walter Stack—Dominic."

"He's only been there—"

"I *know* that, John. Not much more than a week, but still there is the rumor."

"I thought you'd been in bed...alone."

She frowned at him. "On another occasion I might find that funny."

"Find it funny now." He was to meet Dominic in a couple of hours. They would assess the situation then. "How could you possibly be trotting off to be with Dominic when it must be known that you've been resting?"

"Only those closest to me know I've been in bed. Those were Mr. Leggit's orders. Dobbin and Bea know. Bea brought me food herself, but she told the kitchen staff

Mr. Leggit asked for the trays—that's because he told her to.''

"I had no idea you and Leggit had similar appetites and tastes.''

Hattie wrinkled her nose and sank a little deeper in the chair. "We don't. Dobbin and Bea had to help me do away with ham buns before the empty tray could be left in Mr. Leggit's rooms. We fed bread to the birds, too, and I gave Bea and Dobbin some things to have in their rooms.''

"I shall seek out my brother. He'll know how things are at Leggit Hall.''

"I fear for him. I know it was Mr. Smythe who spread the rumors and he will likely have told Mr. Leggit, who is so unpredictable.''

"Be calm,'' he told her. "This isn't a good time for you to get upset.''

Hattie stopped herself from telling him he was being silly. "You will see your brother soon?''

"Yes, it's arranged. Dominic is also very good at looking after himself.''

"Little wonder he looks so distinguished,'' Hattie said. "Or so handsome.''

John gave her a frown, but he grinned at the same time. The course she must take became clear. She would deal with the present, fulfill what obligations she must, and leave Bath. "I think it's safe enough for me to have my money back at Leggit Hall,'' she said. "That was something else I wanted to speak to you about. In my reticule I have more coins to add to the rest. I intended to leave them all here, but I think it would be best for me to take them back instead.''

He saw the moment when she made up her mind about a course she intended to take and he didn't like the way

it made him feel. "Well, if you think so, that's a good thing. But it would not be a good idea for you just to walk in with it, do you? Even if I could allow you to carry so much weight, which I can't."

"I'm not a ninny," she told him, all sharpness. "I should find a way to deal with it."

"In this I must stand firm. I will deliver the money myself. Leggit is holding a little gathering himself within the week. We'll work out the simplest way to return your money."

She wanted it now. Pushing John more wouldn't help. She still had a key to the house and she'd come alone to get what she needed.

"Will you be happy with that?" he asked.

"Oh, yes." His forefinger, tracing a rose on her stockings, diverted Hattie. He slid the finger beneath her instep and she shivered.

How easy it would be to get drawn into his arms again. This time they would see each other as they made love. She would like to watch his face.... "I must go," she said. "Please make sure Dominic is aware of the possible danger he's in."

She scrambled from the chair, but John was on his feet helping her before she could make it to the floor.

"When will I see you?" he said.

Hattie's mind skittered in different directions. "Well, I'm sure I shall probably visit Miss Prunella and Miss Enid again very soon."

"Come to me," he said, slipping an arm around her waist and pulling her against him. "Come tonight. I would meet you where Snowdrop waited with her carriage and we could spend time together."

How lovely it sounded. "Not tonight," she said, mostly because it didn't fit in with her new plans. "But soon."

She intended to take the aunts to Porky's tonight instead of tomorrow and carry with her some of the expensive pieces of jewelry Mr. Leggit had given her. Perhaps Porky and his friend would sell them for her.

Within two or three days she intended to be in London and persuading her parents to go away with her.

"There's something you aren't saying to me," John said. "You're not telling me everything."

Hattie started. "You have too much imagination. Oh, I meant to tell you something quite strange."

His mouth descending on hers put off anything she might have said. John held her face and kissed her, a long, probing kiss. He caught her to him and searched her face. "What do you feel for me? Is there anything—I mean *anything* deeper than simple attraction?"

She wouldn't lie to him. "Yes. Now don't ask me anything else." Her heart thumped and the beat echoed in her ears. "I really must go." She eased away from him.

His smile, a brilliant, happy smile made Hattie all the more muddled inside.

"I'll let you go," he said. "But finish what you were going to tell me."

"Bea told me about a man who came to Leggit Hall. Apparently he stirred up quite the fuss. Spitting and shouting and throwing his weight about. Bea said he came looking for Mr. Leggit and they had a terrible argument down by the Moon Pools. Nobody saw them come back up, but they did hear them shouting and breaking things. The marble doors at the top of the stairs were closed, but they could still be heard."

Hair rose on the back of John's neck. "The man is gone now, I take it?"

"Apparently, although Mr. Leggit has asked for rooms to be made ready for someone." She giggled. "The man

spat on Cook's clean floors and she told him off. Told him... I'm not sure what she told him, but Bea said he was dirty and looked like a pirate. All very flamboyant in a tricorn hat and black velvet jacket. A cutlass and a pistol, too. And big, black boots that flapped.''

John's blood stood still.

''I told Bea he sounds like a seafaring man to me but not a pirate, for goodness' sake. He could be a captain, couldn't he?''

''He could be,'' John said. This man didn't have to be anything to do with what had happened on the trip home from France, and John had assumed the story of the escape of two witnesses to murder would have reached Leggit some time ago. ''Don't worry your head about it.''

''I don't like the idea of him being in the house,'' she said. ''He scared Bea, too—and some other staff, from what she said.''

''There are occasions when these things happen,'' he said. Could it be the man who had ordered the killings of Francis and Simonne?

''Mr. Leggit told the pirate—or whatever he is—that he'd have to work hard to convince him to take any further interest in a windfall.''

"**I** want a word, please, Hattie," Snowdrop said into Hattie's ear.

Leaning forward and with a foot on the steps to leave Snowdrop's coach, Hattie whispered, "Then *have it*. The aunts will wonder what's happening if we keep them waiting." They were already irritated at traveling in so small and unconventional a conveyance.

"Keep your hair on," Snowdrop muttered. "I came like you asked me to. In your note you said you'd be waitin' in the usual place for me. How could I do anything else? But what's all the 'urry. Why tonight instead of tomorrow?"

The aunts grumbling grew louder. Over her shoulder Hattie said, "Just a minute please, Miss Prunella and Miss Enid. These are dangerous parts and we must make sure you'll be safe." She faced Snowdrop again. "And these are dangerous parts, we already know that. I'm fulfilling a promise while I still can—and dealing with a piece of personal business. Tomorrow may be too late. I'm getting out of this carriage before my back breaks."

The instant Hattie set foot on Farthing Lane Miss Enid's head popped from the door of the coach. She scrunched her nose and said, "It doesn't smell nice here."

"What do you mean, while you still can." Snowdrop

held Hattie's arm tightly enough to hurt. "Tell me now or we aren't going on."

Hattie swung around and caught Snowdrop's shoulders. She brought their faces nose-to-nose. "I'm in terrible trouble," she said. "I can't discuss it. I can only ask you to help me. If the day comes when I can let you know what this is all about, I will. And I pray I can."

"Ooh," Snowdrop moaned. "It sounds 'orrible. I'm frightened for you."

"But will you help me?"

"Yes." Snowdrop shrugged free. "Come along, Miss Enid, let's be careful getting you out."

Darkness hadn't completely fallen, but the moon—a shaving of white moon—reclined against a purple sky. Shadows began to cluster in the doorways and under the eves of the mean houses on Farthing Lane.

Hattie helped Snowdrop assist Miss Enid and then Miss Prunella to the pavement. For the first time this evening Hattie felt daunted by the task of getting the ladies up to Porky's shop.

"I hope he isn't drunk and…" Would she never manage to tame her tongue?

"What did you say?" Miss Prunella asked.

"Just a joke," Snowdrop said loudly. "The house is built like a bridge, see. Held up by the houses on either side. Mrs. Leggit and I thought it looked—like—it—"

"Could sink," Hattie finished for her. "We hope it isn't sunk, you see. Let's hurry. We don't want to be seen if we can avoid it." Grateful as she was for Snowdrop's effort to distract Miss Prunella, Hattie still felt ridiculous.

Once they were in the entryway below the shops, Miss Prunella stopped, with Miss Enid beside her. She clutched the folds of a lace fichu at her neck.

Miss Enid stood close to her sister with a hand at her own throat.

Alarmed, Hattie said, "Are you feeling ill?" After all, both ladies were elderly.

"Oh, Prunella," Miss Enid said. "Perhaps we shouldn't have come. Perhaps it was just a foolish whim to think of it."

"I might be given to foolish whims," Miss Prunella said. "You never are, Enid. We have to do this, just to be sure."

"But we've waited too long," Miss Enid said softly. "What can we accomplish now?"

"Lead on, Hattie," Miss Prunella said. "Come along, Enid. We can accomplish something important. We can try to put our minds at rest."

They left Snowdrop with the coach and made slow but determined progress up the stairs to the apothecary shop. In fact, the progress was so slow that they were indeed in darkness by the time they reached the top.

"Let me just be sure they're open," Hattie said, already worrying about how she would get the two ladies safely back down the steps in the dark.

Even as she approached the doorway in its recess with the square-paned window to the shop on one side, Hattie saw candlelight flicker on inside. No sign had been jammed under the doorbell and she felt weak with relief.

She knocked and tried the door. It opened and she popped her head inside.

"Oh, my, it's you," Porky said, his round hat purple this time. "Come along in, do. I so enjoyed your last visit."

"Thank you. I've brought two dear friends with me. Miss Enid and Miss Prunella Worth. Can you accommodate all of us?"

Porky looked at her with brilliant eyes. He said, "Of course," but Hattie wasn't certain he meant it.

She ushered the two ladies ahead of her, entered herself and closed the door again.

The glass bowl of pink liquid bubbled away on the counter and she smelled again the rich scent of cooking rhubarb.

"It's a lovely smell," Miss Prunella said breathlessly. "Isn't it, Enid."

Hattie couldn't take her attention away from Porky, who had swept off his purple hat and now held it scrunched against his chest. He stared at Miss Prunella and Miss Enid, who crowded silently closer to him.

"May I help you?" Porky asked. "A little something to help you sleep better, perhaps."

"We were hoping you'd invite us to take root tea," Miss Enid said, her voice shaking. "Hattie told us it made her feel strong."

Porky's hair shone white and thick. "Er, root tea? Yes, yes, of course. Please come and take a seat at once. This way, this way." He waved Miss Prunella and Miss Enid past him and into the room behind the screen and followed them as if he'd forgotten all about Hattie.

She went after them slowly, not that she need have hurried at all. The ladies and Porky stood, staring at each other with tears in their eyes.

Suddenly Porky said, "Sit, please. Hmm, hmm, hmm," and bobbed on his toes. "There and there. The two most comfortable chairs in the place." He put the kettle on to boil, took out the root tea and set out cups. One and two. He hesitated, noticed Hattie again and added another cup. "And me," he said, setting out a fourth. He straightened and looked toward the door leading deeper into the house.

Without a word he added a fifth cup and said, "Excuse me, please."

He left and the rumble of male voices could soon be heard.

Miss Enid and Miss Prunella reached silently for each other's hands. They appeared changed to Hattie. They both smiled and their faces softened almost girlishly. The lights in their eyes shone warm.

Porky returned and went about making the tea, glancing at Miss Enid every few seconds. His hands shook so that he kept setting down the kettle and wiping his palms on his jacket.

"Let me do that," Hattie said, and he didn't resist.

Another man, this one quite tall and still straight backed, came to them with a firm step. He also had white hair, but his face was narrow, a little sardonic perhaps. Many wrinkles about his mouth and eyes suggested he had laughed a lot.

The four old people looked at one another until the newcomer said, "Prunella, you shouldn't have come here, but I'm glad you did."

Prunella said, "So am I, Philip, so am I."

"You see," Miss Enid said to Hattie, "we have wondered for some time if it was Philip and Charles who lived here so quietly and made sure the nest egg they left us would bring a little regular money. They know all about our need for that." She giggled. "And they know better than to give us more money, even though we always ask for it. They know it won't bring us more pleasure than we already get."

"You must be Charles," Hattie said, blinking. "I wish I could explain how the four of you look together. If you and Philip knew your sweethearts were only a short distance away, why didn't you go to them? Why didn't you

come here?'' she added to the ladies. She would not say how she couldn't bear to think of them wasting what might have been a lifetime together.

All four poured out their stories. Philip and Charles had made money in America and returned to England with enough to buy the shop, but at that time the ladies' father had still been alive. If they had approached him with talk of a shop as a means to support his daughters, their father would have forbidden them to see Charles and Philip again.

''But when your father died,'' Hattie said to Miss Enid, ''why didn't you get together then?''

''We waited and hoped they would come to us,'' Miss Prunella said. She stood close to Philip and he eased her face against his shoulder. Patting her back, he said, ''We should never have kept the jewelry we found at the Baths, but it was too late to do anything about it. There had been arrests of people who had done the same thing, but as long as we lay low and didn't draw any attention to ourselves, we were all right.''

Charles, with Miss Prunella at his side, said to her, ''We kept expecting you to come to us. But you did exactly as we had instructed you, dear girl. We never felt we could use Boggs to make an approach to you so we made the best of knowing you were safe.''

Hattie felt like an intruder at a very private party. ''You're together now,'' she said. ''All any of us can do is to make the best of each day.'' She wanted to tell them they had been foolish, but would never have managed to say the words.

She finished making tea and they sat around the low table drinking quietly.

''We want you to visit Worth House,'' Miss Enid said. ''The past is gone now.''

Miss Prunella laughed. "What a hoot," she said, sounding very young. "Just think of it. After all these years. By the way, we did bring a little bauble for you to dispose of." Miss Prunella placed a gold bracelet made of coins on the table and they all laughed.

Charles said, "You don't change," and counted fifteen sovereigns onto the table. "Could we hope that you have found a way to make your little investments grow?"

"Sometimes they grow, sometimes they shrink," Miss Prunella said.

Miss Enid raised her shoulders like a girl and said, "Mostly they shrink." The ensuing chuckles appeared to delight her.

Hattie grew anxious. She must deal with her business and get everyone home. The rest of them could continue their reconciliation whenever they chose. She had to find her way to London.

She opened her bulging reticule. "Forgive me," she said, "but I need your help. Would you be able to find me a buyer for these?"

There was more than one gasp when she set out the diamond circlet, diamond necklace, an emerald parure, rings, at least ten pairs of ear bobs and, finally, the emerald the aunts had given her. She looked at them and said, "Will you be angry if I sell this? I can't explain everything now, only that I have a great need for money and I'll explain one day if I can."

She felt the other four staring at her and met each gaze directly. "Of course we don't mind," Miss Prunella said. "Philip, this young woman is special and if she says she needs to sell these things then we should help her. If that's possible."

"It's all worth so much," Miss Enid said. "Knowing

how highly John thinks of you, I shouldn't mind asking him for his—''

"No," Hattie said at once, and began picking the pieces up again. "Don't give it another thought."

Quickly Charles stopped her, gathered up the jewelry and slid it into a carved wooden box. "I shall put this in the other room," he said. "In a safe place. And we will help you, Hattie. When do you need the money?"

She drank from her cup of root tea as if her thirst would never be quenched.

"You need it quickly, don't you?" Miss Enid said, and put a hand on one of Hattie's.

"I need it by tomorrow," she said, shutting her eyes because she couldn't bear to see the reaction.

A draft swept over Hattie's cheeks and rattled the cups and saucers. Candles flickered and she looked around.

"Where are they?" What could only be John's voice boomed from the shop. "Touch a hair on one of their heads and you're dead men."

Hattie cowered a little and caught Charles's eye. He whispered, "You shall have the money, or as much as we can get of it by tomorrow. You'll have it all soon enough."

"Thank you," she whispered back, just in time for John to sweep past the screen, pause an instant to stop it from falling on her, and enter the room with his brother Nathan, and Albert at his back.

"What's going on here?" John demanded.

"We are having a civilized cup of tea," Miss Enid said.

John pointed a long, steady finger at her. "Don't give me stories of drinking tea. There is tea at Worth House and you can drink it without making clandestine arrangements to come to this unsuitable place."

Miss Prunella made to leap up, but Philip put a calming hand on her shoulder.

"Unhand my aunt, I say," John bellowed.

"Oh, John," Miss Enid said. "Stop making a cake of yourself. We are old enough to be great-grandmothers and we don't need your protection. These are our friends, Philip and Charles. We've known one another since, well, we met when Prunella and I were no more than eighteen and nineteen. Philip and Charles couldn't have been older than twenty or so. Hattie was kind enough to help us come to see them after so many years."

"Silly romantical poppycock," Nathan said. "You ought to be ashamed of yourselves."

Philip, already standing, approached Nathan and said, "I don't advise you to insult these ladies, not in front of my brother and myself."

"Oh Gawd," John said. "Enough of this prattle, although I shall want to know a great deal more about this mysterious rendezvous. Listen to me, all of you. We just came close to being knocked down those damnable stairs out there by some rogue who ran from this place." He indicated the shop. "He came from in there. We couldn't go after him in case he'd done some mischief here. Who was he?"

"There hasn't been anyone else here," Hattie told him, and she got up. "You need not have wasted your time following us since this is an ordinary social gathering."

"You, my girl," he said, placing a heavy hand on her shoulder, "are behaving strangely. A man came out of that shop, I tell you."

Philip and Charles stood, side by side, and placed the aunts behind them.

Hattie spoke quietly. "We saw no other man, John. If

he came here, it was to spy, unless he had even more sinister designs.''

''To spy?'' John's eyebrows were raised and his blue eyes became so dark they appeared black. ''Someone could be following you around.''

Hattie's spine prickled. ''Well, he's gone now. And I must go, too.''

''You will be leaving with me,'' John told her, and she knew better than to argue in front of the others. ''Albert, please see that my aunts get home safely, and Snowdrop, of course. We'll take our own coach.''

Albert nodded but didn't appear his usual taciturn self.

John addressed Philip and Charles. ''I think it's time we put an end to all this clandestine nonsense, don't you?'' He didn't wait for an answer. ''In future you should visit my aunts at Worth House—if they'd like that.''

Miss Enid said, ''Well, nephew, thank you so much for your permission. Very generous of you, I'm sure. In fact we have already invited our old friends to visit.'' She slipped out from behind Charles and began picking up the sovereigns she'd been given. These she put into her reticule.

''Damn and blast,'' John said.

''I say, brother,'' Nathan said, mildly enough. ''Go a little easy, would you?''

John gave him a withering stare and returned his attention to the older generation. ''You, sirs, must stop giving money to your *dear* friends. We've wondered where you came by it, aunts, and you certainly didn't use your allowances. Now we know the source. You're a little old to be scurrying around for money just so that you can lose it, aren't you?''

''We have no idea what you mean,'' Miss Prunella said.

"You certainly do," Nathan said. "Look, I understand the need for some excitement in one's life, but it isn't suitable for ladies such as yourselves to be sending Boggs off to place bets on horses."

"Exactly," John said. "Ladies like yourselves *don't* bet on the races."

"I see," Miss Enid said through white lips. "I suppose only Frenchwomen are allowed to be so flamboyant as to have fun. Frenchwomen, I take it, may do what they please and you don't care a jot about that. You rather like it, in fact. I'm sure you'd have no objection to a *Frenchwoman* betting on horses."

Hattie held her breath. Her head felt light and perspiration on her back turned instantly cold.

"What the devil are you talking about?" John asked. To Hattie he seemed to loom even larger than usual and the candlelight made stark shadows beneath the sharp angles of his face.

Miss Prunella stepped forward. "Enid is saying what she means. But no matter. You've got it all wrong as usual. We don't bet on horses—we take the tiniest fliers on pugilists. Enid and I are particularly partial to pugilism, although we have only seen a few fights in our entire lives."

"Unfortunately," Miss Enid said, "you haven't seen anything so stirring as two fine male specimens using their fists."

33

"Don't take another step," John ordered Hattie when she'd made a break for the outdoors and reached the top of the stairs. "Why are you leaving like this?"

"Have a care," Nathan said, catching up with John. "She doesn't look well. You don't want her falling down there."

Hattie stopped and leaned against the wall of number eleven.

"Hold on!" John lunged and caught her as she slid toward the ground.

She resisted his attempt to carry her. "Please, let me catch my breath. It got too hot in there, and emotional. I hate it when people shout."

"Let me help you."

"If I can hold your arm, I won't need any other help."

He took her right hand in his and put his left arm around her. "Come along then."

Hattie stood firm and said, "Thank you, I'm strong again now. I'll go alone. Good night."

Weak, simpering, whimpering women bored John, but Hattie's stubborn resistance began to grate. "Where will you go alone?" he said through his teeth. "Don't you see how pointless it is to even *pretend* you can be in control?"

"John," Nathan said. "D'you suppose you and the

lady could either get to the carriage or allow me to do so? A fellow might have other things to do."

"Damn it!" John lifted Hattie, carefully, not in any manner a lady could object to.

"Bully," Hattie said. "Big, mean tyrant."

John rolled his eyes and kept his mouth shut.

Nathan went ahead of him and they reached the coach quickly. "Put her inside," Nathan said. "We shouldn't loiter."

"I'm not getting into your carriage," Hattie said. "You will not understand that you have no right to toss me around, will you?"

"In," John told her, worried for her, and seething at the same time. "Do you mind driving, Nathan?"

"I don't mind anything as long we get away from here." He threw open the door and stood back. "Don't be silly, Hattie. Do you think we can drive off and leave you here?"

"Couldn't have said it better." John lifted her inside the coach and followed.

"Gad," Nathan said, putting his head inside. "I didn't notice that thing of Snowdrop's. Where would one get a coach like that? She's a maid, John—what is a maid doing with a coach?"

"Later," John told him.

"I want to get out." Hattie made to push past him. "Snowdrop will take me where I must go. You wait for your aunts."

"Snowdrop," John said, deliberately fierce, "will not be driving you anywhere. Albert is finally at the end of his patience." He placed Hattie firmly but gently back in her seat.

Nathan slammed the door and the coach sagged as he sprang up to the box. Off they went in a jangle and clatter.

"I must return to Leggit Hall," Hattie said.

"You're not going back there. Ever."

"I must. Sometimes we have more to think about than ourselves. I must get Bea and take her with me. Mrs. Dobbin is already at your house. She'll stay there because she thinks I'll come for her." She peered from the window and cried out, "I will have my way. Tell Nathan to go to Leggit Hall. Leave me where I can go in by the conservatory. *Tell* him, John."

One look at her horrified face and he did as she asked.

"Leggit Hall?" Nathan yelled back. "Why in the blazes would we go there?"

"Later," Hattie shouted, and reached past John to bang the trap shut.

He looked over his shoulder to find her already seated again, with her hands crossed over her reticule in her lap, and looking outside.

Nathan reversed directions.

"What was all that stuff Aunt Enid said about French-women?" John swung off his cloak, tossed it aside with his hat, and placed himself opposite Hattie. "I saw how you looked when she said it."

"Ask her."

"Aha, so you do know. Tell me now."

She deigned to look at him and he could tell she would never give him satisfaction on the subject. Fair enough, since some secrets were bound to come out, he would assume the wretched letter had been opened—in fact, he could tell it had—probably by the aunts who had shared the contents with Hattie.

"She told me she was unmarried," he said.

Hattie raised an eyebrow. "When did marriage become an issue to you?"

Some things couldn't be argued. "I got a letter from a

French lady and I can tell it was opened before it reached me. You may wonder what such a thing could have to do with you, particularly now. Everything, that's what. That woman, together with my bad judgment, brought you and me together and it is because of my misguided liaison with her that we're here now.''

"You don't have to explain these things to me," Hattie said, and she lowered her eyes. "They aren't my business." The corners of her mouth jerked down.

He wouldn't look at her. That way he could squelch some of the guilt. "It's all your business. Together with my cousin and his wife, and their daughter Chloe, I caught a ship bound from France to England a day earlier than planned—to get away before the unexpected husband of the Frenchwoman caught up with me. The name of that ship was *Windfall*."

Then he studied her face, watched her realize the connection to what she'd told him about her *pirate*. She looked at him and nodded. "A ship called *Windfall*," he said. "A greedy captain who took us aboard for a ransom, intending to kill us before we reached England. Only everything didn't go according to his plan. Francis and Simonne were murdered—Chloe's parents. Chloe and I managed to live, thanks first to Albert Parker and then to Snowdrop.''

Hattie said, "Poor little Chloe," and bent over so that John couldn't see her face.

"You won't find a public record, but Mr. Leggit owns the *Windfall*. She was headed for England crammed with contraband and the skipper—your pirate from the sound of it—couldn't have us around to tell the tale of his deeds, so he had to kill us, you see. He chose to do it when the smugglers rowed out to meet him.''

He told her all of it. She wouldn't allow him to skirt

details he thought she shouldn't hear and insisted he treat her as an equal. She listened to every word, eventually with her head against the squabs and her eyes squeezed shut.

When the tale was all but told and John paused to consider a way to tell her why it all involved her, Hattie said, "So in the end it was my husband's fault. Does he know you and Chloe escaped?"

"I'm sure he knows someone escaped. That would have been the reason for his fury with the ship's captain."

"If Mr. Leggit is aware of you, and Chloe—" she reached for his hands "—he will want to get rid of you. John, he is dangerous!"

"So am I. But he doesn't know my identity. I didn't use my full name."

"He will discover it, I tell you." Her fingers ground into his. "You must leave at once."

"I will never run from Bernard Leggit." But he would need a different plan for dealing with the man. "Stories about you and Leggit are repeated among the people who work for him in dangerous ventures. Those who fear him revel in gossip about how he is married to a beautiful girl who would only have had him for his money."

"Don't," Hattie said softly.

"Leggit's pride is legendary. His wife must show the world how she adores him. He is afraid of nothing but losing the so-called respect of his acquaintances. You are his Achilles' heel."

"Please don't say any more. Let me out here. It can't be far now and I know my way."

John's response was to reach back and hammer for Nathan's attention. "Pull over and wait," he said, when he got Nathan's attention.

"You're not going anywhere alone," he told Hattie,

blocking her from getting to either door. "We've stopped because I must make you understand what has happened before we go on."

"You think I don't know? You think me such a weak brain that I haven't worked it out. Cuckolding Mr. Leggit would pain him more than death, and for so much longer."

She stunned him for an instant.

"You've done what you set out to do."

"Just when I think you can't surprise me again, you surprise me again," John said. "I should not care to have you as an enemy." Now those were words that invited an unkind answer.

"We decided to use each other," she said.

"But you were honest with me, first. And the idea didn't come to you until after we'd met."

"We were both wrong. Now we are even. John, thank you for caring about me—and you have—otherwise, you would have rushed to shame Mr. Leggit by spreading the news that we had been together." She looked at him sideways. "Or do you still intend to do that?"

"Never. You shouldn't have to ask me such a question."

"You have already admitted how you set out to do it." Hattie took a deep breath and sat as tall as she could. "Please don't argue with me anymore. It's best for me to go now. I'm sure Mr. Leggit doesn't know who you are yet. If he did, I should have heard about it by now. And as long as he doesn't find out we've been together there's no risk to me. If he does eventually find out, I'll be long gone."

"Hattie—"

"I'm sure there is no baby, but if there is, I shall be

glad to have a part of you. Please don't detain me any longer.''

"You can't be serious. If you think I'll allow you to walk off into the night, you're definitely out of your mind. Let's stop this now. You are coming with me."

"No. John, what about Dominic? He is away from there now?"

She didn't miss a thing. "He soon will be."

"But he's still there. I might have known it. Why didn't he leave?"

He shifted and sat beside her. "He wanted to be there in case I didn't intercept you before you could return to the hall. Then he was going to help get you away."

"You shouldn't have allowed him to stay. You *shouldn't* have. But now you see I must return, don't you. Not just for Bea, but for Dominic."

John's muscles ached with his need to act. "He will take care of himself." By God, Dominic had to be safe.

So fast he almost failed to stop her, Hattie grabbed for the door handle.

He plunked her down again and said, "I'm sorry. I meant to be more gentle. I know what we shall do. I'll go to Leggit Hall myself and get Dominic. Nathan will wait with you."

"Nathan will turn about and race back toward Bath with me, you mean," Hattie told him. Tears pooled in her eyes. "And you will never manage to get Bea. While we sit here and argue, my hopes of getting Bea and Dominic away grow smaller. I am going back there. There will be no more discussion. And tomorrow, just as soon as I have—just as soon as I can, I will go to London and take my parents to a place where Mr. Leggit can't find us. I beg you, John, let me go now."

"I'll never let you go."

She angled herself to kiss his neck, and the underside of his jaw, and whispered, "There are things we can't control, things we want badly and can't have. You'll get over this, John."

"I won't." The pliant feel of her against him, her kisses, drove him mad. "And I won't do what you ask. Look, there must be a compromise. You owe it to me to allow me to help you."

"Do I?" Her sigh cut through him. "Perhaps I do. Before we met I had nothing, nothing to look forward to but my pitiful efforts to outwit my husband, and nothing to look back on with pleasure. You changed that."

"Then you'll come with me?"

"I'll let you help me. We'll get close to Leggit Hall and you'll allow me to make sure Dominic is safely out and that I have Bea with me. Mr. Leggit would kill her if he ever decided she knew about us."

He asked Nathan to continue on and they moved almost too quickly for John. "This is what I ask you to do," he said. "I think you will see Dominic on your way into the house although I'm not sure at what point. Ask him to stand by and wait for you. Go immediately to your rooms and light candles in each window, all three of them so I know you are there and still safe. Tell Bea to wait a few minutes while you return to Dominic. Then she should follow. The coach will be exactly where Snowdrop met you."

When she didn't argue, he felt lighter and stronger. He touched the pistol at his waist and the knife he carried at his ankle. Nathan was similarly armed, as was Dominic, and they had fought together against a dangerous enemy once before. They still lived. The enemy didn't.

The coach arrived beside the tall hedge, close by Leg-

git's ugly stone gateposts. John held Hattie tightly. "Do exactly as I've asked you, hmm?"

"Yes." Her voice sounded choked. "Thank you."

He got out and handed her down.

Hattie turned from him at once, but spun back and ran to hug him. Slowly she slipped from his arms and walked backward, away from him.

"Hattie, don't go."

"I must. I'll always love you, John."

34

Bernard sat on the only chair in the darkened room. Before him and atop a single step as wide as the room, an illuminated rice-paper screen separated him from the man and woman who moved as shadows on the other side.

His sawbones had described this "remedy" for Bernard's trouble. The trouble Hattie caused. This would, his man had told him, be what he should visualize in his mind when he confronted his stone of a wife. He hadn't expected the faceless charade to interest him. He had been wrong.

The players had been brought in for this purpose alone and Bernard thought he would make shadow shows a habit.

They had shed their clothes. Or rather the female had undressed the male, then stripped, sliding each revealed part over her partner's skin while he stood still and allowed her to pleasure him.

Just as it should be.

The brandy Bernard swallowed in gulps burned in his veins and turned his face hot. The heat between his legs came from another source.

"Make her please you," he whispered to the shadow man. "Make her try. Punish her when she falls short. She will always fall short. Yes."

The woman's breasts turned up at the tips. With her

back to the man she put her arms over her head, bent over backward, and walked her hands down his body far enough to let him tongue and suck her nipples. And she stayed there just long enough to bring his manhood to its full, thrusting, unlikely length.

Bernard squirmed and undid his trousers. This could well become his cure, his antidote to his wife's coldness.

Straight once more, the lady lover guided her master to the floor where he lay, his arms at his sides, passive in all but the one reaction he couldn't control. The woman stood astride his hips and bent double from her hips to prime him with her mouth. She did a handstand, still holding him between her teeth.

There was definitely a change, Bernard decided, spreading his legs and pushing inside his trousers to fondle himself. Some movement there, indeed, yes. But it wasn't enough yet.

A knock on the door flustered and infuriated him. "Go away," he called out, working harder on himself.

The knock came again, more insistent this time.

Bernard pulled his trousers into place and shouted, "Come in, damn you."

It was Smythe who slipped into the small room. He moved like a tall gray wraith, never as much as glancing toward the screen. Bloody eunuch, he had to be.

"Mrs. Leggit returned to the apothecary shop, sir," Smythe said. "I followed when she sneaked from the house and saw her drinking some sort of potion."

"Potion? Hell and damnation, is she trying to kill my son? If it's true, I'll wring out her life myself."

Smythe rested his weight on one leg. "That place is also a pawnshop. She took jewelry there. Jewelry you gave her and one of the fellows who runs the place put it in a box."

Bernard's head pounded. "But she would only do such a thing to get money. She doesn't need more money. I give her plenty."

"Perhaps she has a secret. She may be paying someone to be silent."

Forcing her to lie with a stranger had been a great risk. "Could what I...you know. Could what I made her do have impaired her mind?"

Smythe snorted. "I didn't intend to tell you, but now I will. I went down once while they were there, just to see if I could tell how things were progressing. She liked it. She begged for more, and she laughed. Laughed, mind you."

"Get out," Bernard told him. "Get out now and if you speak of this you will never speak again."

"Your pleasure is my reason for being," Smythe said, letting his head dangle forward and clasping his hands together. "I live to see you have everything you deserve."

Nothing would bring Bernard solace. So she had found it pleasurable to copulate with a stranger, had she? He might have had her taught to talk like a lady, but she would never overcome her lack of breeding. "Leave me, I tell you," he said, and Smythe drifted from the room as silently as he'd entered.

Lighting candles beside his chair, Bernard yelled for the couple to leave and when they were too slow in stopping their acrobatic coupling he threw his glass at the screen. "That's enough," he shouted. "Go. I'll send for you if I want you again."

They dashed about, gathering clothes and ran from the makeshift stage.

He breathed hard, spread his feet apart and drew in long, shuddering breaths. And once more there was a tap

at the door and this time it opened before he had time to respond.

The stupid bitch who walked in thought she could take Hattie's place with him. She grinned as if he should be glad to see her. He sat down again, with his back to her.

"Mr. Smythe said you were alone now."

Bernard ignored her.

"I told you I'd keep a close watch, didn't I. I've waited and gathered information. You won't believe what I'm going to tell you. It isn't hard to find things out, not with the way people talk over a cup of tea."

35

Before Hattie could shut the conservatory door behind her, a hand covered her mouth and a large person closed the door before walking her backward into deep shadows.

"It's Dominic." He removed his hand. "You knew me as—"

"I know. John told me your name. You shouldn't be here anymore."

"There's no time to talk," Dominic said, and swung her toward him. "Leggit's gone mad. He's in a room at the back of the house smashing things."

"He does that well," Hattie said.

"Follow my instructions. Here." He pressed a key into her hand. "He may already be rampaging through the place looking for you."

"Why?" What had happened? She trembled, but locked her knees to stand steady. "Tell me—"

"Did you return with Snowdrop?"

"No. John. He's waiting out there with Nathan."

"Thank God. Take that key and go down to the pools. Beyond the room where you were with John there's a passageway to some steps and a door at the top. You could pass it and never think it was more than a place to store things. It leads outside. Go now. Get out and find John."

She searched about, expecting Mr. Leggit to leap out

at her. "Bea. I must get her out with me. She'll be in her room, or in mine. I'll go quickly."

"I'll get her," Dominic said. "Leave this place at once."

To make sure she did as she was told, he hurried her to the foyer and behind the stairs. Without a word he waved her downward and she went, praying hard that they would all make it to a safe place.

When she glanced back, Dominic had already gone.

Even her soft slippers made an echo from the marble walls, a breathy little sound that scrunched up Hattie's muscles. Just as on the last occasion she'd been there, the sconces were not alight, but even the pale radiance of the moon caught the stained-glass disks in the ceiling and threw their bright colors across the pillars and stone sculptures, over the gaping black mouths of gargoyles.

She sped beside the pools. Those gaping mouths should be spewing water, but she realized the pools were empty. All that mattered was reaching John.

Following Dominic's instructions, she hurried behind the room—that room—and found the passageway. Her throat felt raw and ached with every breath. Thank goodness Mrs. Dobbin had remained at Worth House. One less person to worry about.

The passage rose upward, just as Dominic had described, and turned slightly when she reached a flight of stairs with a heavy door at the top. Her hands didn't want to work properly when she pushed the key into the lock.

At last it was in and she turned it. And turned the other way. Hattie pulled the key out again and examined it, then peered into the keyhole before trying again. The lock didn't budge. She sweated, tore off her bonnet and pushed hair out of her face.

It had to work.

But it wouldn't.

Once more she tried to force the lock to open and once more the key jammed in either direction. The only thing to do was return to the main floor and get out of the house as quickly as she could—as long as she didn't run into Mr. Leggit.

A thunderous bang rumbled toward her, then another. The doors to the pools. Hattie had never seen them closed, but there could be no other explanation for the noise.

"Hattie? Are you down here?"

Mr. Leggit's voice bounced about like a hard ball in a cavern. He had come looking for her, and he'd found it necessary to close them into this horrible place.

"Answer me," he cried.

Hattie looked at the door again, and at the key in her hands. So close, she'd come so close to getting out into the clean air and going to be with John.

If she tried the key again it probably still wouldn't work and the noise she made would guide Mr. Leggit to her. He would come up the passageway and stairs toward her, heavy step by heavy step until she felt his breath on her skin.

Cautiously, holding her skirts well above her ankles to be certain she wouldn't trip, Hattie retraced her steps until she stood in the corridor behind the private rooms.

"You go that way," she heard Mr. Leggit say. "I'll take the other direction."

"Of course." It was Smythe who answered.

She felt them circling the room, squeezing her between them, giving her no means of escape, except... She turned the handle on the nearest private room and almost cried with relief when it opened. Closed inside, she crept around to the other side and pressed an ear to the wall, listening for any movement. She heard nothing but that

didn't mean anything. This place had been built like a fortress. She recalled how she hadn't heard noises from outside when she'd been here on the two previous occasions.

Surely they would have entered the corridor behind the rooms by now.

This was her only chance. Hattie opened the door an inch or two and peered out.

"There you are!" Smythe slammed the door inward and it hit the wall. He grabbed Hattie by the arm and dragged her out. Looking at her down his long nose, he sneered but didn't speak again.

Mr. Leggit arrived beside Smythe and his face was a terrible thing to behold.

Using all the strength she had, Hattie jerked down suddenly and twisted her arm from Smythe's grip at the same time. She sped away, around the pool, gagging with fear and scarcely able to see through her blurred eyes.

"Little fool," Mr. Leggit said an instant before she ran headlong into his solid body.

Smythe arrived, panting. "How would you prefer to proceed?" he said to Mr. Leggit, who pulled out a pistol and waved it as if showing off a prize.

"I'd be glad—" Smythe didn't finish his sentence. The pistol roared and blood spread over the man's chest.

Smythe's mouth gaped open. He buckled forward, the light gradually fading from his amazed eyes. When he fell, he went slowly and toppled headfirst to the floor.

Noises she couldn't control scraped from Hattie's throat.

"I don't need him anymore," Mr. Leggit said, and took Smythe's pistol. "And he knows too much. Now, my girl, you'll go into that room where you had so much fun with

a servant, and you'll laugh with me as you laughed with him.''

''Please,'' she said.

''Don't beg me for anything. My patience is at an end.'' He caught her by the back of her neck and hustled her along. ''I understand you can be a very enthusiastic lover. I am your husband and it is with me you should be enthusiastic, and imaginative.''

No hope remained. ''Let me go.'' She ducked her head and turned on him. They struggled and Mr. Leggit lost all control. He hit her, first with an open hand, then with a fist. Her mouth swelled instantly, and her eye puffed even while she pummeled him as best she could.

He closed his hands around her neck and squeezed.

Hattie couldn't scream. His grip tightened and blackness edged the vision in her good eye.

My dad taught me how to… She brought a knee up between his legs. Her bone smashed into his soft parts and he fell back, moaning and gasping and supporting himself.

She'd made her chance. Hattie spun toward the way out, tripped, and fell. The ledge beneath the lip of the pool broke her fall, but she rolled off and landed with one leg twisted beneath her.

''Still no lights,'' John said, climbing down from the roof of the coach where he could see Hattie's windows. ''I shouldn't have let her go in there.''

''Trust in Dominic,'' Nathan said. ''She could have forgotten about the candles.''

''Not Hattie.'' Not Hattie, who had left him with her declaration of love squeezing his heart. ''I want to go after her.''

''And miss each other as you search blindly?''

John shook his head. "It's been much too long."

He heard footsteps too heavy to be Hattie's and pushed himself back into the hedge. "Get behind the coach," he whispered to Nathan.

"John? Nathan?" Dominic skidded to a halt. "Is Hattie with you?"

Both Nathan and John rushed to join their brother. "She's not here," John said. "When did she leave the house?"

"Preserve us," Dominic said. "I can only think she didn't leave, but she went down to the pools to use that passage I sent you out by. I went back for Bea, but one of the servants said she'd gone on an errand much earlier so I came out."

"We should go in by the door to Leggit's damnable pools," John said. "I still have the key on me."

The three of them ran as one, silent, tucked into the shadows of trees lining the driveway. They ducked and made it around the circle in front of the house, then broke for the hillock built to conceal the hidden door.

"The devil take it," Nathan said when he caught his toes a few feet from the door and fell, arms outstretched, to the ground.

"Hush," John told him. "Not a sound."

"I bloody well fell over…a body," Nathan said.

"There's no time," Dominic insisted, but John crouched beside the dark mass that had downed Nathan. He touched it and drew breath through his teeth. It was a body all right, and from the way its head didn't move with it, he assumed its former owner had been decapitated.

"Captain of the *Windfall*," he said slowly. "Killed with his own cutlass if I had to guess."

"Damn him," Nathan said. "He got off lightly."

"Leave him." John went to the door and slid his copy of the key into the lock.

Too many minutes later he threw it away. "It won't work."

"It's the same as the one I gave you," Dominic said. "It worked then."

"Is it the same as the one you gave Hattie?" He knew the answer. *If there's a baby, I shall be glad to have a part of you.* "I will get in here." *I'll always love you, John.*

"I'm going to see if those stained-glass plates come off," he said.

Dominic held his sleeve. "If they do, you won't just be able to lift them out. I say we go through the house."

"Yes," Nathan said. "Quickly, man."

If Hattie was down there, John wanted to know. He shook off Dominic and hurried, bent double, in the direction where he thought he'd find what he sought.

This way and that he searched, longing for a lantern.

Tonight the moon shone, but it was a weakling of a thing…and it shot a glancing glimmer off something shiny in the ground ahead.

He made a dash and landed on all fours over one of the plates. Looking straight down, he saw the flicker of candles, but the glass was too thick to make a window.

"We need our knives," John said. "The plates fit tightly into rims, that's all. I'm going to pry this one out, but I may break my blade."

The very tip of the blade did snap off, but the result made a better tool for the job. Slowly he raised one side of the plate and Nathan was quick to grasp it with both hands.

The opening was almost as wide as John's shoulders.

He put his mouth to Dominic's ear. "I can go down there. You and Nathan will have to help me."

A voice rose in an eerie wail. "Get up, Hattie. Get up, now."

John shoved his head into the marble room and blinked while his eyes adjusted to the poor light. He made out Hattie. The pools were empty and she lay at an odd angle on the dry bottom of the one immediately below.

Leggit was the one yelling for her to get up. On his knees, apparently nursing his privates, he rocked back and forth calling out her name. And every few seconds he took a watch from a pocket in his waistcoat and checked the time.

"I'll go feet first and drop until I'm hanging from my hands," John said to Nathan, noting that Dominic already had another plate off and must be seeing and hearing what went on below. "Lie on your stomach and get me as close to the floor inside as you can. Then pray I can land without breaking my legs."

Dominic joined them and gestured that he was going in. "I must be the one," John said. "You and Nathan will help me."

A breathless shriek froze them all. John threw off his coat and prepared to drop through the hole.

"Hattie? Oh, Mr. Leggit, tell her to get out of there."

John couldn't understand whatever Leggit mumbled.

The new arrival, Hattie's maid, Bea, said, "What time is it? It must be almost time. Hattie, come out."

"Almost time for what?" Nathan said hoarsely.

Leggit had his watch out again. "Hattie," he moaned.

"The pool was emptied for cleaning," Dominic said. "It's about time for it to be filled again."

"She'll drown." John sat on the edge of the hole with his feet and shins hanging inside.

"She'll scald first," Dominic said. "What Leggit says about the water coming from a lost Roman hot spring is a lie he tells to impress people. Water gets pumped through some steam contraption he's got in a tunnel and when it goes into the pool it's boiling. It doesn't stay that way because they add to—"

"Get ready to take my weight," John said. He breathed through his mouth and the thunder of his heart shook him.

"Hattie," Bea shouted. She went to Leggit and stroked his head. "It's probably best for all of us this way. An accident. She fell in and the water covered her. It's coming, you know. We'd only have to kill her in the end anyway."

"Shut up," Leggit said, struggling to his feet.

"It's nothing to do with you really," Bea said to Hattie. "I was in a position to help Mr. Leggit find out what you were up to so I did. Now he doesn't want you anymore, he wants me. You can't blame me for taking the opportunity."

"Down," John said, wriggling until he supported himself by the elbows.

Hattie rolled her head to one side and looked up at Bea. At least she was alive, but fear for her made John's hands clammy. He worked one elbow beneath a brass rim and held it with his fingers, then, too slowly, eased the other elbow through.

"Get that left shoulder down or you won't make it," Dominic whispered. "You're stuck until you do."

"Fool, fool, fool." Leggit's voice rose to a scream. "Why would I want a drab like you?"

Helpless to stop it, John saw Leggit take the maid by the throat and shake her until she dangled like a wet sheet. He threw her aside and turned back to Hattie. "You're

awake. Thank God for that. Come along, pull yourself this way and I'll help you out.''

''Why doesn't he go down there and get her?'' John said softly.

''He doesn't know when the water will come,'' Nathan said. ''He's afraid of being burned.''

''Aah.'' John couldn't pull his shoulder down. ''Push on it,'' he said. ''Give it everything you've got.''

''And break a bone?'' Nathan said. ''Then what good will you be?''

''Push it, I tell you. I can take him with one arm.''

Steam flowed from the open mouths of gargoyles in the wall beneath the grotesque statue at the center of the pools.

Leggit capered, yelling at Hattie to climb up to him. She watched the steam until, as if awaking from a dream, she struggled to sit up. John saw how she tried to stand and how she gave up and began to crawl, much too slowly, to the side of the pool.

His shoulder shot free of the hole and he gasped. His damp hand slid and he braced himself for a plunge to the stones.

Leggit screamed, and screamed again. With arms outstretched, he leaned toward Hattie as if he could will her to reach him.

Through thickening steam, John saw the first trickle of water from the stone mouths and, without waiting for his brothers' help, he let go and dropped.

He landed well enough, although the shock of impact blasted through his body.

Stopping after every move she made, Hattie struggled to escape the approaching water.

If Leggit shot him, so be it. He would die trying to save Hattie and that was all that mattered.

The water reached within inches of her feet. John sprinted past Leggit, leaped to the ledge, then into the bottom of the pool and snatched Hattie.

A roar burst forth. Fine hot spray speckled his face and pricked at him through his shirt. His one glance behind him revealed the water, gushing and tumbling like a great wave as it flowed free.

With Hattie all but unconscious in his arms, John escaped. He felt hot water seep through the seams of his boots as he vaulted clear.

"Unhand her!" Leggit held a pistol pointed at John and Hattie. "If you value her life, put my wife down."

John obeyed at once, set Hattie against a pillar and stroked her cheek.

"No, John, *no,*" she said, barely above a whisper.

"I love you, Hattie," he told her. "I did almost from the moment we met."

With a last look at her, he swiveled to confront Leggit.

The pistol barrel addressed his chest. Leggit took several steps closer and raised his weapon until John looked directly into the face of his death.

He dared not look at Dominic whom Nathan was lowering through the hole, headfirst. Dominic took aim at Leggit.

No shot sounded, but the man's mouth opened wide and his face became the color of cream run through with purplish streaks. His stretched lips turned purple and he retched.

The pistol fell from his fingers and he toppled silently sideways into the rising flood of boiling water.

36

Five Weeks Later

"Look on the bright side," John said. "I've got a fifty-fifty chance."

"Yes," Nathan said. "A fifty per cent chance of winning and a fifty per cent chance of putting an end to all your hopes for the rest of your life."

Dominic stood at John's other side and added, "Indeed, yes. Right here and now the Marquis of Granville's happiness hangs by a thread and he's most likely about to cut that thread."

"Dominic," Nathan said, "promise me you'll help me tie him down and transport him to an asylum afterward."

"I promise—"

"You two are every bit as foul, with just as much poor judgment as when you were boys. In fact, I think you may still be boys in everything but size. I need your support, and flapdoodle jokes will not help me at all."

They stood in a row behind the small maze in Hattie's garden at Riverview, the house she had secured for herself and her parents. Mrs. Dobbin also lived there, as did one maid and one handyman. Apparently Mrs. Alice Wall wouldn't hear of Hattie hiring a cook since she and her husband insisted on control of the kitchens.

"We joke because we're terrified," Nathan said, looking disgustingly dashing, if hot, beneath a sun already high in the sky and sharpening every brilliant color in the flower beds. Even the grass, dotted with clover, smelled warm and fragrant.

Nathan bumped John with a shoulder. "Are you sure there's no other way to accomplish your ends, John?"

"Like kidnapping her?" Dominic suggested. He'd pinched off a piece of sweet-smelling honeysuckle and stuck it behind an ear.

A pull on his hand reminded John that Chloe was with him. Snowdrop, now Mrs. Albert Parker, had made the child look like a pink confection and despite his argument that there would be a disaster and the animal would run away, Raven nestled comfortably in Chloe's arm. John smiled at Chloe and shook his head at the sight of a pink satin bow tied around the cat's neck.

Chloe pulled on his hand again and looked at him, he would swear, with a message in her eyes.

"I think Chloe wants us to get on with it," he said.

His brothers sighed and Nathan asked, "Are you sure everyone's in position?"

"Yes. They're sitting on chairs behind a hedge in the maze, the hedge closest to the lawn. They'll be able to come forward as soon as I signal."

"Are we sure they will be able to find their way out of that thing?"

"Yes, thank you, Nathan. It's a very small maze and Mr. Wall is organizing all that."

"By now they're melting," Dominic remarked.

John shifted a bouquet of yellow roses from his right arm to his left. These roses had no thorns. "What can I do about that? She was supposed to come into the gardens an hour ago."

"She could have taken a nap instead and now she's not coming at all."

This would not be the ideal moment to punch Nathan on the nose.

Chloe pulled once more.

Raven gave a ladylike meow.

John ground a first finger and thumb into the corners of his eyes.

"Duck, you lot," Dominic whispered, probably loud enough to be heard in the next county. "Here she comes."

They ducked. Nathan seated Chloe on the crackly grass and smiled at her. And John walked, doubled over, until he reached the path.

He stood tall and looked across flowering shrubs, across the maze, at Hattie armed with shears and a basket while she sized up which flowers might be ready for cutting.

Twitching his neckcloth didn't make it more comfortable and probably didn't improve its appearance.

They were right, by George, if all of this went badly, his reason to live ended today. *"Dramatic fool,"* he muttered. "It will, though."

With measured steps, John began the longest walk he ever remembered. Up the path toward the lawn in front of Hattie's house, the lawn where she stood with her back to him, engrossed in her flowers.

If she refused him, all the people he cared for most would hear her. They'd feel sorry for him and he hated pity.

Rats, she'd heard his approach. He would have preferred to just about reach her first. John was a great believer in the element of surprise.

"John, what are you doing here?" She wore an old straw hat with a ribbon threaded through two holes in its

brim and tied under the chin. The sun shone so strong she still shaded her eyes to peer at him.

"Good day, lovely lady," he said. "I'm saving money. It gets expensive, tipping delivery boys all the time so I decided to bring your flowers in person today." That had sounded so good when he'd rehearsed it in front of his shaving mirror.

"I sent a message telling you how much I love the flowers but that it's outrageous to send them every day," she said.

Her dress was of a yellow chintz and very pretty, too. Every other step she took reminded him of her injured ankle, but the damage to her face was much improved and hardly any bruising remained.

A loud meow froze him.

Hattie glanced around, then shrugged.

A subdued fuss broke out on the path behind and he looked over his shoulder in time to see Mrs. Wall, a sturdy woman with a sensible air, guiding the Reverend Lloyd-Jones, Vicar of St. Mary in the Field, toward them.

"What's he doing here?" Hattie said, frowning at the minister. "I'm in his parish but I'm not really a parishioner yet."

"Hello, John," Alice Wall said. "And Hattie. The Reverend's come to 'ave tea with me. Take no notice of us."

John did take notice of the uncomfortable way the minister shifted his shoulders, but Mrs. Wall moved him into the house so fast he had no time to say something inconvenient.

How much longer could he expect the gallery to remain still and quiet in this heat?

"I miss you, Hattie," he said. "Here. Yellow roses. You loved them."

She set her basket and scissors on the grass and took

the roses. "Thank you. I did love them. I still do, especially when you…" She raised her eyes to the sky. "It hasn't been easy to give some respect to the dead, but I've tried. I've needed to keep to myself for that."

"And that meant you must refuse to see me at all? Every time I called, you had Mrs. Dobbin tell me you were resting. But you were avoiding me."

He didn't worry about the audience keeping quiet now. They would be too busy hanging on every word to make a sound.

"I made terrible decisions," Hattie said. "I got myself into situations I shouldn't have. I should never have married Mr. Leggit, and if I'd been open with my parents instead of taking everything into my own hands, they'd have chosen for the three of us to get away even if we were left with nothing."

"You care so much for them," John told her. "You didn't want them to leave everything they knew when there was no definite place to go."

Birds with yellow beaks swooped to the grass at Hattie's feet, then hopped back and forth, pecking about among the flowers in her basket. She watched them quietly and John recognized how thin she was, and how pale, despite her daily ventures outside to be in her garden for a little while.

"I can't do this any longer," he said. He had promised himself there would be no outbursts. He couldn't help it. "You told me you'd always love me."

"I will," she said, leaving him with his mouth open.

"And I'll always love you," he told her when he'd recovered some of his composure. "I want you to be my wife. Marry me, Hattie, I beg of you." To hell with all the ears behind the hedge.

Hattie squinted up at him and her mouth trembled as if she might cry.

"Please," he said. "You and I love Bath. Apparently your parents like it. We have my family, too, and they already love you. We'd go to London from time to time. My mother is there and no longer cares to travel, and I have business there, but our home would be here. Hattie?"

If he didn't get his hands on her and very soon, he would just have to feign a collapse. She would tend to him then and any touches from her would be better than none at all.

Hattie crouched and picked several daisies. She made a slit in one stem with a shaky thumbnail and slipped another stem through, fashioning a daisy chain but, John thought, more as a diversion than for any other reason.

"This is because you think I'm increasing with your child, isn't it?"

The ladies and gentlemen of the gallery would be falling out of their seats to hear as clearly as possible.

"I don't know if you are," he said, feeling himself blush. He crouched on his haunches beside her. "A child would be wonderful, but if you aren't increasing now, we know how to make that happen in the future, don't we?"

"How blunt you are," she said, but with a smile. "There isn't a child, so you don't have to feel responsible for me."

"How do you know?" His face throbbed now.

Hattie said, "I can't talk about this. It shames me."

"Why should it? There's nothing shameful about normal behavior between men and women, and its results. Marry me. Just say you will and save me from fading away."

"Fading away," she muttered. "Very likely."

Chloe, still holding Raven to her chest, arrived between them in a rush. She kept checking behind her and John knew why. She had escaped Nathan and Dominic and feared they would come after her.

"Chloe," Hattie said, looking into the girl's face. "I'm so glad you're here. And you brought Raven, too. And you look beautiful."

She closed her eyes and cuddled Chloe. Even the cat seemed to enjoy it.

"When do I get cuddled?" John muttered. "Little girls and cats but not me."

Hattie smiled up at him. "You sound like a spoiled boy."

"My English is good now, I think," Chloe said.

John stared at her and didn't move a muscle. He couldn't believe she'd spoken.

Hattie kept her attention on the child. "So you do. And very pretty it sounds with your French accent."

A gasp came, much too clearly, from behind the nearest close-clipped hedge. John said, "This is wonderful, amazing," very loudly and behaved as if he hadn't heard a thing other than the conversation about Chloe.

"I caused it all," Hattie said, staring at the hedge. "Now I discover how Chloe suffered because of me."

"I did not," Chloe said, perfectly clear. "I should 'ave spoken to Uncle John. I was too silly and frightened so I didn't. That could not be your fault, 'attie."

John helped Hattie to her feet and said, "I can't live without you," while he made sure not to look at Chloe.

"So much has happened," Hattie said. She looked at Chloe. "I made things harder on a little child who had already suffered. She'll continue to suffer."

Scrabbling, rocking and shaking along the hedge paralyzed John. Before his eyes, Mrs. Dobbin gave up look-

ing for an exit from the maze and beat her way through, catching her lovely gray silk gown as she came.

"I couldn't help overhearing what you just said." She batted at her skirts. "Hattie, I should have guessed Bea was up to something from all the questions she asked and the comments she made. I didn't. So this is on my shoulders, not yours."

"Mrs. Dobbin?" Hattie looked from her companion to the wrecked hedge.

"I panicked," Mrs. Dobbin said. "I was, er, pulling weeds in there and couldn't seem to get out. Mr. Wall will help me repair the damage."

"Weeding." The glance Hattie gave Mrs. Dobbin's silk gown spoke volumes. "Yes, well, thank you."

Dobbin rushed away into the house.

"Marry me, Hattie."

"So much has happened," she said.

"To both of us," he told her. "We can stand together against the past. Marry me today."

"Say you will, please say you will," Chloe said, her bright blue eyes filled with pleading.

"I just don't know. I won't let you marry me out of duty. You have no duty toward me."

"Very well, one last question." A man who was really a man dared anything for what he wanted most. "Do you still love me?"

She buried her face in the yellow roses he'd given her.

"Do you?" Chloe said. "You could be my aunt."

Hattie shook her head and sniffed. She looked small and lost.

"Then tell me you don't love me," John insisted. His gut contracted painfully and he felt as if tears collected in his chest.

"But I do love you. How ridiculous of you to suggest I don't. I only want to do the right thing."

"The right thing is to marry me."

She sighed and, just as he began to feel destroyed, said, "All right. Yes, I'll marry you."

Chloe bounced around until Raven fought to be free and she had to settle the cat down.

"Everything's all right," John said, and moved to take hold of Hattie and kiss her. He stopped himself and backed off a few steps. "No, no, can't kiss the bride until after the ceremony. Bring on the Reverend. The banns have been called three times," he told Hattie earnestly.

"How could they be?" she asked.

"My aunts know the vicar well so there was no problem."

"And he's come here to marry us? With me looking like this? Look at you, you're dressed like a prince. What would your family say?"

"They say it's all wonderful, don't you?"

This time the sounds of scuffling and trotting back and forth were huge.

"Take your time, ladies and gents." Hattie's father spoke with authority. "It's taken long enough, why 'urry now? Follow me."

Hattie held her bottom lip in her teeth and smiled. "I don't have a wedding dress," she whispered.

"Whatever you wear looks like a wedding dress to me."

"You, m'lord, are a shocking flatterer."

"I mean every word."

Nathan and Dominic strode along the path in time for Hattie's new maid to come out of the house and all but faint at the sight of them.

Dobbin returned carrying a basket filled with rose pet-

als, which she strew over the lawn. Chloe immediately set about seeing how many she could collect.

Mr. Wall led a chattering parade out of the maze to line the other side of the hedge while the handyman scuttled to move the chairs for them.

"John," Hattie said, "what are we doing?"

"Getting married."

"Don't you be clever with me."

"Hmm." Keeping his mouth straight, he regarded her and knew his laughter was in his eyes. "Practicing shrew techniques already, are we?"

"I'll forgive you that piece of audacity just once. Tell me you don't intend to annoy me again."

"I don't intend to annoy you again, Hattie."

She poked him in the ribs and they both laughed.

Only then did he become aware of those who had gathered to help celebrate—or rather gathered hoping there would be something to help celebrate.

Hattie also looked at them now, and smiled, and waved, and blew kisses, at Boggs, Dolly, Cook, old Mrs. Gimblet and a collection of other servants from Worth House, at the aunts who positively fluttered, and their gentlemen friends, at Snowdrop, who cried and smiled at the same time, and Albert, who bent to kiss her cheek and wrap her close in his arms.

Mr. Wall went to stand beside Hattie. A lean, gray-haired man with a sprouting mustache and thoughtful eyes, the pleasure he showed had to be genuine.

Dobbin returned to the house but only for long enough to step inside and then come out immediately and join the others.

With the posture of the naturally dignified, Alice Wall walked across the lawn to stand at her husband's side.

She leaned around him and whispered to Hattie, "We're givin' you away, see. Here's the minister."

Hattie Wall Leggit became the Marchioness of Granville on that sunny morning in a blossom-filled garden near the River Avon in Bath.

37

John led Hattie through the musician's room, the prop room, where satin, silk, velvet and brocade remained heaped on the floor, through the opening covered by the mirror and eventually into the narrow space behind his ebony bed and the green-papered wall.

She stopped there and pulled him back.

"What is it?" he said, looking at her as he had since the wedding, like a man who had found his bliss.

"You're a romantic, you know," she told him. "Why else would you bring me here by this way?"

"No other reason and I'm not apologetic, sweet one. I hardly dared hope this day would come. Are you ready to move on?"

"Yes." Nothing had been mentioned, but she was still a little weak from her ordeal and walked slowly. Hattie had refused to allow John to carry her, so they had paused regularly on their way up the flights of stairs.

"I wanted us to spend our wedding night here," John said. "In a way it's where our story began. Now you have to let me pick you up, just for a moment."

She had little choice but to allow him to lift her off her feet, back through the heavy green curtains and swing into his bedchamber with her. "That's all part of it," he told her. "Carrying you across the threshold."

"Of your *bedroom?*" She chuckled.

"When our new home is built, I shall carry you across that threshold, too."

He didn't put her down at once and she looked aside at a white silk night rail, devoid of any decoration, that lay atop his bed with a matching robe.

Hattie's tummy rolled. How she wished they were coming together for the first time. Yet she trembled and felt every bit the new bride.

"A penny for your thoughts," John said, waiting for her to look at him again.

"Here we are again with you carrying me around like a child," she said, but smiled at him. "I have some things I wish to discuss with you."

He put her down with obvious reluctance. *"Now?"*

"It's daylight, John, and nowhere near time for bed." She paused with her lips parted, scarcely believing she'd said such a thing. "The first thing I want to talk to you about is Albert and Snowdrop."

"When our house is built, they will come with us. It's already been agreed upon."

Wine and two glasses stood on a chest beside the bed. Now what a strange place to put wine. She thought she could also see a silver plate piled with delicacies. Best not to mention she'd noticed any of it.

"Do you approve of retaining Albert and Snowdrop, my love, because, of course, your wishes will be my wishes."

"I approve, but what I'd like is to send them to Brighton to see the Pavilion. I've never forgotten how dreamy Snowdrop looked when she spoke of it."

John lit candles on the mantel.

"Such a waste," Hattie said. "It isn't dark."

Without a word, he went to close thick draperies over the windows, turning the room into a rich, shadowy place

where candlelight became magical. He looked into the fireplace with disappointment since there could be no excuse for lighting fires today.

"Albert and Snowdrop will leave for Brighton next Friday," he said. "Their trip is already arranged. They will also go to London and stay at my home there. My mother looks forward to it, just as she looks forward to meeting you."

"Oh. Already arranged." Hattie let her eyes wander over the graceful silk things awaiting her on the bed. "Um, Chloe will need time to accept me."

"She already has. You saw how badly she wanted you and I to look after her together."

"Her grief will take time to overcome."

"We'll help her," John said at once.

Hattie got up and walked slowly around the room, touching fine fabrics and wood worn to a soft patina. "You can't hurry these things."

He sat in his favorite Indian chair, steepled his fingers and expelled a satisfied sigh. "We have the rest of our lives to care for Chloe. Are you afraid of me, Hattie?"

"Of course not." She laughed, but the sound wasn't convincing.

"Shy, then?"

Tears she couldn't control rushed into her eyes. "That would be ridiculous given what has already happened between us."

"I disagree," he told her. "I think you are a shy woman and, given the unfortunate circumstances of our first time together, I'd be amazed if you weren't afraid, as well as shy."

"Being married to you is like a dream I never dared to have," she said. "Lying with you excited me, but I didn't

know enough and I fear I may have offended you with my forwardness. I didn't seem myself at all.''

His soft chuckle made her blush.

''Perhaps it would be best if we don't rush things,'' she said. ''We could get used to just living in the same place and hope the other comes naturally later.''

He got up and went to the marble-topped commode. A basin and tightly-sealed jug stood there. He touched the jug twice, very rapidly.

''You are wise,'' he said. ''We shall not rush a thing. Excuse me.'' He went into his dressing room and she heard the splash of water in there. John prepared for bed and so should she.

The jug and basin he'd checked must be for her.

She looked from the commode to the garments on the bed. John had said that her mother packed a bag for her, but Hattie didn't see it.

Trying to decide how to proceed was an agony. Summoning her courage, she went to pour water into the bowl...and couldn't lift the heavy jug.

''Let me,'' John said, coming into the bedchamber wearing a green silk dressing gown. ''Please don't overdo. Take your time and you'll recover to full strength and health.''

''I'm perfectly healthy,'' she said. ''The injuries have slowed me down for a while but that is all.''

''Hush,'' he said, putting his lips against her ear and nibbling the lobe. ''Let me care about you as you would care about me if the positions were reversed.''

She cocked her head at him. ''I may have been married before, but I am not practiced at this. My previous experiences were quite different, I assure you.''

''Put them behind you, then, and indulge me now.''

John undid the row of buttons that closed the front of

her modestly cut dress and slipped the sleeves from her shoulders. He let the dress fall and she stepped out of it. Before he turned back from putting it over a chair, she crossed her arms to cover her breasts beneath her thin chemise.

Splashing water into the bowl, John took a cloth and soaked it. The soap he used smelled of lavender, one of Hattie's favorite scents.

Carefully he washed her face and neck, then patted them dry with a large towel. He repeated the process with one of her arms and then the other.

The sensations she had didn't bode well for taking things slowly between them, but she was tired and her eyes began to droop with the languorous way he washed her.

There seemed no need for words.

John spread a white comforter on the carpet, concentrated intently while he removed the rest of her clothing and helped her stretch out.

Her limbs, her whole body felt heavy and sensitive to every touch of his fingers.

Next he carried the bowl of water and set it down beside her. He shrugged out of his robe and, naked, ministered to her until he'd left no part of her untouched. Hattie tried to hold still, but again and again, her body tightened and she pushed herself toward him.

Without a shred of awkwardness John walked to get the silken clothes. When he returned, he pulled her to her feet and prepared to pull on the night rail.

When Hattie's arms were raised above her head, she stood on tiptoe and fastened her mouth to his. She layered their bodies together and let her eyes close to concentrate on how he felt. He held both of her wrists in one hand and stroked the length of her back all the way until he

played his fingertips over her bottom and moaned when she brushed her breasts from side to side over the hair on his chest.

"I don't want to hurt you again," he said. He spread a hand on her belly and she saw him concentrate, and frown.

"I'm sure I'm not carrying your child," she told him.

"Absolutely sure?"

"Well, it's too early to know, really."

"I see." He didn't look convinced. "You do seem tired. I should let you sleep."

"Mmm."

"Shall I help you with the gown?"

"I have never slept naked. This seems a good time to start."

He blew a monotone whistle through pursed lips and stood aside to allow her to approach the bed. She needed every bit of assistance the steps offered, but she managed to push herself headlong onto the mattress and closed her mind to the picture she must make.

She had to kneel and pull down the covers and again felt him watching every move she made. Hattie aimed a glare in his direction but sat down abruptly on the sheets. Did men look at women in such a way? He didn't smile now. Instead he watched her with blue eyes turned black and veins raised in his temples. He braced his arms wide apart on the foot of the bed.

Hunger. That was what glimmered in the look he gave her, but if there were such a thing as wonder, he felt that, too. Hattie read his emotions.

He bowed his head and said, "Perhaps it would be better if I didn't join you tonight."

Her heart set up a frantic beat. Disappointment ban-

ished any sign of fatigue. "Please, do join me," she said. "I'll never sleep unless you're with me."

His back rose and fell and he gave her the most false smile she'd ever seen on his face. "Of course," he said, and got onto the bed at once. Leaving her sitting up beside him, he stretched out on his back without a stitch of anything covering him, put his hands behind his head and closed his eyes.

The covers were ruckled beneath him.

Pouting wasn't one of Hattie's habits, but she pouted at him and considered and discarded all manner of wicked things she might do to him.

Within moments he breathed regularly. He had gone to sleep, for goodness' sake. Well, that wouldn't wash.

Supporting her head on one hand, and very close to his face, she blew lightly on his lips. He passed his tongue over them and settled again.

She blew once more, this time into his ear. That got her an "Mmm."

It wasn't right to push herself on him. Hattie turned away from him, curled on her side and managed to heave a scrap of sheet over part of her.

They were married. She had a sudden desire to squeal with joy.

She turned toward him, scooted close to his side and placed her arm across his waist—which meant if she moved the arm a few inches lower it would collide with the base of the only part of him that hadn't gone to sleep.

"Wait a minute," she muttered. Her experience with male parts standing at attention was narrow—limited to seeing John, in fact—but it didn't make sense for him to be sleeping in such a condition.

She didn't believe he was asleep. In fact he was most

likely enjoying everything she did to him while he pretended to be restraining his urges in deference to her.

He wanted to play games!

She could wash him, only with cold water. No, that could cause a disaster. On the chest with the wine and goodies stood a pot containing some sort of potion. She turned hot. That was probably meant to make it easier for John. After all, he'd made a fuss about her being small.

We will see how long you lie there like a log.

She took the stopper from the decanter of red wine and sniffed the contents. Fruity and full. Probably quite nice. She poured a little into a glass, set down the decanter, then wiped a wetted finger over his lips.

Predictably, he licked them.

Reaching across him was a nuisance. She sat astride him, sat where she could force his shameless part to lie down even if it didn't go to sleep.

John shuddered and she smiled. There was nothing relaxed about his closed eyelids now.

Tipping the glass, she drizzled wine in a thin, thin line from his throat, down the center of his chest. Then, holding the glass steady against the bed, she lapped the wine up again, starting at his chest and finishing with a final lick beneath his chin.

A low grumbling sound came from his throat. Hattie wiggled, realized what she'd done and held still, but John's hands had closed into fists beside his head.

"A little more wine," she said softly. "It's so good."

And, slop! into his navel went the red wine that made her feel so nice. And drizzle, drizzle went the next few drops to wet the sprinkling of hair on his stomach all the way to the point where it spread wider and mingled with her own.

Moaning, she sucked his navel dry and proceeded on

until she had to shift down his thighs to keep finding more to lick. And more to lick.

She emptied what was left in the glass into her palm, took hold of him and massaged.

"That could sting," he said suddenly, jackknifing to a sitting position, but she was too busy removing the wine again, with her mouth, to give his comment serious consideration.

"You are insatiable," he said, his hips rising from the bed each time she withdrew her mouth. "Shy? Ha. You are carnal, my love, and it's my responsibility to make sure you're fulfilled."

While Hattie shrieked with nervous laughter, he reversed their positions and kissed her for a long time. He was careful not to go too hard on the bruised side of her mouth but managed to make her head swim with wanting him just the same.

He sat on his heels again and rubbed her body gently. He tweaked her nipples and checked the slippery, pulsing flesh between her legs. "I think you're ready," he said. "Are you hungry?"

She blinked to focus on him. "Hungry?"

"We shouldn't waste such lovely little cakes." With that he popped one into her mouth and while she chewed, he squashed two more, one on each of her breasts.

Hattie swallowed and squeaked. "Icky. Oh, John, I want you. Icky, that's disgusting."

"Is it?" Following her example, he licked the cake away until only a dollop of cream remained atop each nipple. He sucked the cream from one side, then the other, and made hard circles with his tongue, growing closer and closer but never quite doing what she longed for.

"Still icky?" he asked.

She stretched and whimpered. "Are there more of the cakes?"

He laughed while he took a nipple in his teeth and flicked the tip of his tongue over it.

Hattie struggled wildly. She reached for him and guided him to the entrance to her body.

John held her down, took the stopper out of the decanter with his teeth and pulled wine into his mouth. He swallowed and drank again. Then, with smiling eyes and hands that caressed, he rolled her to her side, kept her pressed against him as if their skin were one, and passed the wine from his mouth to hers. With their closed lips pressed together, they gradually swallowed.

For a moment they lay still, tasting the wine they'd shared, feeling their bodies meld.

John tensed. He gazed at her an instant then all but threw her onto her back and drove himself into her. She cried out and he held still. She didn't want him to stop and began the ebb and flow between them herself. Each thrust he made pushed her farther across the bed.

"John!" If he stopped she would die. She drove her fingers into his hard buttocks and fought back against him, twined her legs around his.

He reached a hand between them to touch her, but she wrenched him away. She cried out, "It's started," and the hot waves shuddered into her again and again.

John drove them together, used the tide of her release to push her to the edge of sanity, and then she felt the warm rush of fluid fill her.

"This can't be right," she said when they fell, still entwined, to the mattress. "You must tell me how to love you properly."

He arched his neck and let out a soft howl. "Hear that," he said, cuddling into her neck and playing with

her breasts. "That's ecstasy. Your love is right, your loving is incredible. Don't ever change."

It had taken so long to get dark, Chloe thought. Snowdrop still looked after her by day, but at night Albert came for her and they went away to be a husband and wife, so a nice maid came to sleep in the nanny's room.

Chloe gathered her pillow and a soft woolen blanket. She took a few precious possessions and crept from the nurseries. Clicking meant Raven was going with her and the cat's claws tapped the floors.

The climb upstairs with so much in her arms was difficult, but she got to the top and tiptoed down the passageway to Uncle John's rooms. Aunt Hattie's rooms as well now.

The house was very quiet.

Chloe spread out her blanket and put her pillow on half of it. Once she lay down with her back against the study door, she pulled the second half of the blanket over her and snuggled down in the warmth of the night.

Uncle John and Aunt Hattie would be excited to find her waiting for them there in the morning.

Raven poked her cold, wet nose beneath Chloe's chin and crawled inside the makeshift bed to curl up against her mistress.

Partly by feel, and partly by faint light from the single sconce alight outside Uncle John's rooms, Chloe piled her five wooden figures beside her pillow. "Uncle John," she said, putting a carved man beneath the blanket. "And Aunt 'attie.'' Hattie joined the figure of John to be closely followed by, "Chloe, your Uncle John and Aunt 'attie want you to go to sleep now. Your Mama and Papa will watch over us all from beside your pillow."

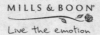

1105/059/MB146

Experience the magic of Christmas, past and present...

Christmas Brides

Don't miss this special holiday volume – two captivating love stories set in very different times.

THE GREEK'S CHRISTMAS BRIDE
by Lucy Monroe
Modern Romance

Aristide Kouros has no memory of life with his beautiful wife Eden. Though she's heartbroken he does not remember their passion for each other, Eden still loves her husband. But what secret is she hiding that might bind Aristide to her forever – whether he remembers her or not?

MOONLIGHT AND MISTLETOE
by Louise Allen
Historical Romance – Regency

From her first night in her new home in a charming English village, Hester is plagued by intrusive "hauntings." With the help of her handsome neighbour, the Earl of Buckland, she sets out to discover the mystery behind the frightful encounters – while fighting her own fear of falling in love with the earl.

On sale 4th November 2005

Stella Cameron was born in Weymouth, Dorset. She was editing medical text and working in London's Harley Street when she met her husband, an officer in the American Air Force, at a party. He asked her to dance, and they've been together ever since. They are now the proud parents of three grown children.

Stella Cameron writes both historical and contemporary women's fiction. She regularly hits the bestseller lists and has a strong international following.

Coming soon from
Stella Cameron
and Super Historical

TESTING MISS TOOGOOD

Hattie. An honest woman without pretensions. An intelligent woman who didn't doubt her own reasoning. A woman made for love, for passion of the wild kind, and of the sweet, subtle, languorous kind.

With each breath she expelled, he was sure he felt its warmth brush his mouth. Her breasts rose and fell softly, as if she'd slipped into a place where she felt quiet and safe.

He could stay there with her, and say nothing, forever.

He must, and he would, do what he had set out to do. A different kind of woman would make the seduction easy to justify. But with Hattie, the promise of ecstasy waited, and the whispered warning that even sweet revenge could leave a bitter taste.

"An enjoyable and often compelling read"
—Romantic Times